MW01195063

FLORIDA PALMS

A NOVEL

Joe Pan

Simon & Schuster

New York   Amsterdam/Antwerp   London   Toronto   Sydney/Melbourne   New Delhi

Simon & Schuster
1230 Avenue of the Americas
New York, NY 10020

For more than 100 years, Simon & Schuster has championed authors and the stories they create. By respecting the copyright of an author's intellectual property, you enable Simon & Schuster and the author to continue publishing exceptional books for years to come. We thank you for supporting the author's copyright by purchasing an authorized edition of this book.

No amount of this book may be reproduced or stored in any format, nor may it be uploaded to any website, database, language-learning model, or other repository, retrieval, or artificial intelligence system without express permission. All rights reserved. Inquiries may be directed to Simon & Schuster, 1230 Avenue of the Americas, New York, NY 10020 or permissions@simonandschuster.com.

This book is a work of fiction. Any references to historical events, real people, or real places are used fictitiously. Other names, characters, places, and events are products of the author's imagination, and any resemblance to actual events or places or persons, living or dead, is entirely coincidental.

Copyright © 2025 by Joe Pan

All rights reserved, including the right to reproduce this book or portions thereof in any form whatsoever. For information, address Simon & Schuster Subsidiary Rights Department, 1230 Avenue of the Americas, New York, NY 10020.

First Simon & Schuster hardcover edition July 2025

SIMON & SCHUSTER and colophon are registered trademarks of Simon & Schuster, LLC

Simon & Schuster strongly believes in freedom of expression and stands against censorship in all its forms. For more information, visit BooksBelong.com.

For information about special discounts for bulk purchases, please contact Simon & Schuster Special Sales at 1-866-506-1949 or business@simonandschuster.com.

The Simon & Schuster Speakers Bureau can bring authors to your live event. For more information or to book an event, contact the Simon & Schuster Speakers Bureau at 1-866-248-3049 or visit our website at www.simonspeakers.com.

Grateful acknowledgment is made to Puppety Frenchman Music, Joe Escalante, and The Vandals for permission to reprint lyrics from the song "And Now We Dance," written by Warren Fitzgerald, copyright © 1995. All rights reserved.

Interior design by Ruth Lee-Mui

Manufactured in the United States of America

3 5 7 9 10 8 6 4 2

Library of Congress Cataloging-in-Publication Data
Names: Pan, Joe, author.
Title: Florida palms : a novel / Joe Pan.
Description: First Simon & Schuster hardcover edition. | New York : Simon & Schuster, 2025.
Identifiers: LCCN 2024042025 (print) | LCCN 2024042026 (ebook) |
ISBN 9781668052181 (hardcover) | ISBN 9781668052198 (paperback) | ISBN 9781668052204 (ebook)
Subjects: LCGFT: Novels.
Classification: LCC PS3616.A3578 F56 2025 (print) | LCC PS3616.
A3578 (ebook) | DDC 811/.6–dc23/eng/20240906
LC record available at https://lccn.loc.gov/2024042025
LC ebook record available at https://lccn.loc.gov/2024042026

ISBN 978-1-6680-5218-1
ISBN 978-1-6680-5220-4 (ebook)

for those who met at the end
of the Black Road

PART I

VARIATIONS OF PALM

PART II

THE ARMSTRONG CREW

PART III

THE MISSION

PART IV

SEIZER REDUX

PART V

THE SKY THE LAND THE SEA

PART I

VARIATIONS OF PALM

In the blue dark of morning, Cueball arrived at Eddy's doorstep with a cube of hash seasoned with cherry tobacco and wrapped in aluminum. As Cueball drove, Eddy used a paper clip to jab holes into a Dr Pepper can, fashioning a makeshift pipe. Heading over the Melbourne Causeway en route to the beaches, Cueball pulled his red truck along a grassy shoulder, and taking up their fishing gear, the boys hiked the long catwalk under the bridge as a pale new light stripped the gunmetal sheen from the Indian River.

The catwalk ended at a boat channel mid-bridge amid tall pylons. After assembling their segmented poles and casting out, the two best friends huddled together on the cold concrete slab, taking hits from the can as a fussy wind teased their hair and unraveled their smoke rings. Along the eastern riverbank, porch lights winked off as kitchens brightened, people rising to coffee and dewy lawns. Barges fashioned entirely from rust forded the channel in dutiful solemnity as commuter cars bumped rhythmically over expansion joints overhead, encasing them in a muffled echo. Everything held a music, a tension.

Brackish smells soon mixed with the blood of the day's first catch—Cueball captured the slick dagger spine of a bullhead catfish between two fingers, tucking its fidgety body under his boot. Using a quick sawing motion, he decapitated the fish with a steak knife and tossed the body back—cats from the lagoon were considered inedible—then pinched the embedded hook from its open gullet for reuse. Eddy swam his hand through the catch bucket and rebaited the hook with the final shrimp as Cueball rummaged from his hoodie a baggie of pills pilfered from his mother's medicine cabinet, after she'd passed out between bottles of Smirnoff.

He set one pill on his tongue, motioning for Eddy to do the same, as together they watched a white sailboat glide out from the wood dock of a beachside mansion. Saw the wind catch low in the mainsail, muscling the billowy shape northward. Cueball handed Eddy his flask and together they swallowed their breakfasts.

An hour later they sat perched eighty feet up, shaggy hair alive and tanned legs swung over the wrong side of the causeway railing, shouting their hoarse demands at a sun turned carnivorous. People mistook the two young men for suicides, given the honks and near-collisions. Below them the tea-green river contracted in ripples like heated cellophane. A wooden wharf just right of the catwalk they'd fished earlier promised a gruesome death for any mistake made by a rookie jumper, but these boys were pros, and unafraid.

Cueball held out a fist, middle knuckle extended. Eddy leaned over and bumped the middle knuckle with his own. Sucking air, they disappeared together over the railing.

This time they wore shoes and remembered to fold their arms over their chests to avoid the painful fleshy arm smack and underwater howling. This time no one landed on a manatee.

The world transitioned to white-green foam and sun-spattered salt spray. Heavy with clothing, they swam awkwardly toward the barnacled wharf, the ladder there.

Time was slipping, and Eddy drifted through the haze to find himself back in Cueball's truck. Soon they were clopping down a flight of wooden stairs leading to a beach peppered with gulls, fishing poles in hand, the frothy Atlantic Ocean spread out wide before them.

Eddy's stomach churned; was he sick or having a good time?

The tinny, hollow ping an aluminum bat makes when shattering the carapace of a ghost crab is markedly different from the collapsing crunch erupting from a wood slugger, and the enthusiastic kid nearby took turns testing both, chasing in halting zigzags the nimble creatures scuttling for their holes, switching bats as his snoring father lay sunbathing in a rubber-slatted chair.

Cueball approached the child with a five spot as Eddy collected the crab pieces for bait.

The beach was otherwise isolated save for a few portly snowbirds whose gazes scissored between the child's disturbing hunt and a lone surfer of no real talent. As the day's heat sank into the sand, the vacationers soon packed up their towels. Cueball chuckled loudly as they passed, bodies tawny as the pits of white peaches.

Eddy snorted in agreement. These weren't folks visiting family, these were suits in shorts—predatory investors buying up cheap foreclosures with plans to sell them back to struggling residents after the economy recovered. *Carpetbaggers*, is what the old italian barbers called them, opportunists who wrote off vacations as business expenses.

As Cueball refreshed the catch bucket with seawater, Eddy forcibly twisted two slant-cut PVC pipes into the sand. They had clams and now crab, but if Eddy hoped to catch any pompano for the grill, he'd need sand fleas—hard-shelled creatures made discoverable by bubbling holes in the hard-packed sand. Cueball, however, was done fishing, swallowing another tiny pink pill, so Eddy opened the Igloo and took out the bag of clams. Using a construction hammer, he smashed the clams and shucked the meat with a pocketknife. Baiting one line with clam and the other crab, he cast them both into the ocean before dropping the poles upright in the piping.

The noon heat burned away all moisture and reflected off the sand bright and hot. Eddy didn't regret the hash but maybe the Ritalin, feeling equally wired and spent, wondering if dizziness was an early sign of heatstroke. In any case, he needed to sober up, as he was expected to begin chugging beers in a couple hours.

He peeked into the bucket housing the day's catch: three blues, two sheepshead, and a speckled trout. The fish flopped and barrel-rolled in the spare inches, fighting for oxygen.

Eddy empathized. The last few months of high school were a struggle, cramming for finals. A wholly uncertain future bore down on the Class of 2009, which led to crazy anxiety dreams, where he'd rush on his clothes and race to the bus stop, only to discover the bus had already left.

He took a water bottle from the cooler and joined Cueball sitting cross-legged on the sandy slope. Together they watched casino ships cling to the far reaches of the bay. Eddy imagined they carried all sorts of rich people: rocket scientists, moguls, rock stars—wishful thinkers riding out a good-luck streak. Types of people he would never be. People he'd probably end up working for.

"Those things sink sometimes," said Cueball, as if intuiting his thoughts.

"I've never heard of it."

"If I ever get just fifty grand," said Cueball, "I'm buying some land beachside and pitching a tent. We can hang out all day getting ripped. Sell driftwood shaped like alligators or some shit up at the Cocoa Arts Festival. Take summers off like basketball players."

"Dream on," said Eddy. "Beachside you're looking two-fifty, three hundred thousand, easy. Shit would have to be underwater before it dropped back to fifty."

"A tall, stilted house," said Cueball, clenching and unclenching his fist, bleeding into his new high. "All's you'd need is fishing gear, maybe a boat. Don't have to see anybody ever. Bathe in the ocean, grow your own weed. Like the apocalypse, but with internet."

"Please stop speaking," said Eddy. "Your level of dumb is giving me cancer."

What power responsible for this bright blue empty heaven required so much from them? The crazy-ass life they'd imagined for themselves post-graduation—epic parties and mailbox baseball and fumbling sex in the back rows of the dollar theater—had quickly buckled under the unforgiving gravity of food costs and bills, as they were now expected to pay their own way through life.

So they took jobs moving furniture. The area's go-to work—construction, masonry, roofing—dropped off a cliff after the housing crisis cold-cocked the building industry. Even skilled vocational work was hard to find. Young people moved back in with their parents as an infestation of FOR SALE signs plagued neighborhoods everywhere. It was like some biblical parable involving moneylenders and shame, a caravan of U-Hauls drifting up I-95 as the unemployment rate scraped upwards of ten percent.

The Space Coast was more susceptible than other regions to such debilitating trends, tied forever to its namesake aerospace industry. Whenever a new Congress played politics with the budget, contracts got slashed and engineers trickled out in a sad, slow exodus—taking their money with them. It was a game of neglect and economic vandalism in which the boys were well versed, thankful to have any work at all; but they also sensed a clear future being kept from them, promises unfulfilled, as the countrywide recession continued to flatten dreams like a demented steamroller.

"Did mine just twitch?" Finger on the taut line, Cueball squinted hard. "Do I got a fish?"

"Are your eyes closed?" asked Eddy.

"That's racist," whispered Cueball.

"No," Eddy said. "*That's* racist."

Mesmerized by drugs and the dancing point where the fishing line disappeared into the ocean, the pair turned inward and nostalgic, recalling the departures of former classmates and friends. There were the two scenesters who had OD'd—one off Oxy, the other heroin—and at least three killed by guns—accident, officer, suicide. The rest had simply moved on, shuttling off to other cities, prospects, lives. A few even inexplicably headed to college, an option Cueball never considered, not in any serious way, and for Eddy seemed a distant if unremarkable daydream. The public schools of Central Florida conferred upon the lowborn little beyond a direct, almost systematic transfer into manual labor and an aggressive, even performative brand of alcoholism. It was survival-living dressed up as culture, a Mad Max reboot stocked fresh with angry retirees, felonious transients, debt collectors, religious wackadoos, wastrels, legit killers, and the working poor.

Or so Eddy believed, naming off the various types like grievances as Cueball smiled knowingly, enjoying how weirdly heady his friend got when high.

"Oh shit, what time is it?" asked Eddy.

"Don't get your dangle in a tangle," said Cueball. "She'll be there. Besides, I came to hook a shark."

Eddy peered over to find that Cueball had, at some point, emptied the catch bucket, leaving the fish carcasses rotting in the sun.

"What the *actual* fuck! Why would you do that? We can't cook those!"

"I need my dad to smell them before he sees them," offered Cueball with a pout. "He don't believe a trout can live in salt water. He don't believe a fucking word I say. Well he can suck it: Cueball one, jackass zero."

"Goddamn waste," cursed Eddy, rising to sand himself off. "I need to rehydrate. We should go."

"I will stay, and you will go," said Cueball in an oddly stilted manner. "I will catch one dolphin, and one nurse shark. I will shove one foot into the blowhole of the dolphin, and one into the gills of the nurse shark, and I will ride them like skis into the horizon, where the ghost of Ponce de León will greet me with delicious puerto rican rum. And maybe a bagel. And together we shall conquer the cruise ships pronto and rob the snowbirds of their gold and spread the wealth among the suffering people of this sorry-ass land. And freaky, fat-assed women will throw themselves upon me and—"

"Did you take another pill?"

"I took a different one," Cueball replied. "For flying. For the fear of it."

"*Dude* . . . you're driving."

"For the funk of it." Cueball winked. "For the fans."

Eddy tilted Cueball's whole body to one side, scouring his pockets for the truck keys. "You think you can manage carrying the Igloo?"

Cueball tested the salty beach with the tip of his tongue and giggled stupidly.

Twenty minutes later they crossed the causeway west toward Downtown Melbourne and headed south along the mainland's Dixie Highway. Eddy flipped up the visor to find a group of thunderheads hugging the western pines as if jockeying for positions in a horse race. Spotting no dense purple clouds, he was confident the weather would hold up—confident, not cocky, as any passing subtropical storm could drop inches.

Upon reaching the scarcely populated township of Malabar, marked by a single blinking traffic light, Eddy hung a right, passing Ma Kettle's Saloon, the infamous biker bar, its sandlot packed with motorcycles.

Beyond plant nurseries and ramshackle houses, over train tracks with a busted signal, they continued into the palmetto-tufted pinewoods of Palm Bay, their home. Before an abandoned car dealership they swung south again. The city asphalt turned country macadam and snaked the interior before narrowing to a street encroached by forest on both sides, smelling of greeny sap and twittering with bug life.

Clusters of motorcycles flanked Cueball's squat yellow house like weights on a barbell—softails, panheads, road kings, with a slew of rusted-out pickups and junkards extending down the block, some of which Eddy didn't recognize. Laughter and music carried over from the backyard, where an enormous biker party was well underway.

Before Eddy could pull onto the front lawn, Cueball swung the passenger door wide and hopped out, landing funny but adjusting as he ran to chase down an armadillo he'd spotted wobbling into the road. Seizing upon the creature, he pumped it overhead like a trophy, the tiny claws pedaling air.

"Survival of the fittest, my ass!" yelped Cueball. "Millions of years, these suckers!"

Eddy killed the engine, shouting, "Those things have leprosy!"

Cueball scrunched his face horridly and walked the frightened animal to the woods. He always kept a lookout for potential roadkill, after his child-hood dog had its paw run over by the ice cream truck, chasing the jingle.

Eddy grabbed the two beer cases hidden behind the seat as Cueball popped the tailgate and lifted high a yellow stringer coiled through the death-shocked mouths of the fish, their once-bright colors bleached by thin layers of mucus.

Eddy retched. "Ugh! Smells like used Band-Aids."

"We'll grill 'em up with tangerines and onion salt," said Cueball. "Nobody'll know the difference."

"Except when they die of food poisoning."

Cueball flicked his tongue erotically under the catch. "If it's a girl, you can leave the resuscitation part to me."

Good-times paraphernalia littered the front lawn: crunched beer cans, discarded boxes of Camel Lights, a leopard-print thong. Someone had filled condoms with water and tossed them to the grass, where they lay exposed like beached man-o'-wars, filmy and translucent.

Cueball kicked one and it exploded over Eddy's jeans.

"Aww, come on!" Eddy whined.

Cueball ignored his friend and clicked the front door open, where a blast of voices escaped the house like pressurized gas.

Bikers clogged the hallway, beers at their chests. A woman pawed Cueball's straw hair teasingly in passing. Some were old friends of his parents, Bird and Charlotte, stretching back to when they roamed the western hinterlands as outlaws. Neighbors from down the block as well, and even a few Harris engineers, strip club investors who built satellites by day and who ultimately fell in with their patrons. Onetime rival gang members traded shots at the kitchen table as the stereo swam through ballads by Neil Young, Black Sabbath, AC/DC, the Eagles, with the occasional dip into Pearl Jam, the Stooges, Hank Williams III. The sliding glass doors televised a swarm of leather and denim out back, folks bedecked in peacocking hairdos and inventive beards and oily dungarees and wallet chains, spangling like shook foil. But no club patches or colors, as most were out of the game. Eddy recognized a number of faces, but there were new ones in the mix, which was intriguing.

He searched for a place to set down the beer, flinching when Cueball slung the dead fish over his shoulder. "Sheezus!"

"Wrap them in Saran Wrap for the fridge."

After Cueball left, Eddy quickly dumped them into a trash container under the sink. He wet a paper towel and wiped the gunk off his shirt, then headed out to join in the fun.

The backyard buzzed. Every direction offered shit-talking rowdiness and mild exhibitionism. Longbeards wolfed down oysters and deviled eggs at a picnic table on the porch, an estuarine bouquet mingling with the corpulent, gamy sweetness of wild boar rising from an unseen grill. Loudspeakers propped haphazardly on the slanted roof inspired free-form go-go dancing. A cellblock of old-timers shrewdly developed hands of prison pinochle, laugh wrinkles cinching their eyes, as a band of adventurous ladies nearby knocked back mescal shots over hands of euchre, V-necks pulled tautly over breasts, their bras abandoned early on in an act of solidarity. All manner of consent faltered before a level of flirtation that tolerated excess—tops were yanked down, skirts lifted, asses flashed and spanked, nipples pinched, cocks threatened and exposed, and hot dogs wiggled provocatively before noses. By the fence, a woman held her friend's hair aloft as she puked, the other hand ready with her next beer.

The party was living up to expectations, much to Eddy's delight. Gazing into the heart of the bustle, he surfed the faces for the real reason he'd persuaded Cueball to knock off fishing early—a girl with green eyes named Gin. Figuring she might be seated among the crowd, Eddy pushed into the melee.

As he navigated the foldout chairs, snippets of conversation reached out to him: lives punctuated by intense, inexplicable beauty. Long drives through grassy plains; afternoons spent lounging in canyon streams; the ear-clogging, lonesome beetle silence of scrub deserts. Eddy could only imagine these places, lacking the money to travel. And though he hadn't attended church since he was five, he recognized in their voices that easygoing, good-natured sense of belonging, an atmosphere of fellowship.

Once, for an essay in gifted class, Eddy tried articulating the reasons he admired this rambunctious crowd, while detailing their shortcomings. It wasn't just that some smoked weed in public or slugged Jack straight from the bottle, or recounted tales that should have ended in dismemberment or death, it was how they'd come to work chaos naturally, even fruitfully, into their lives—accepting what they could not change and bettering what they could. This roulette wheel spoked 'round just once. Jobs came and went. Money too. And love. Bird and Charlotte's merry troupe of reprobates weren't perfect, or even always well-intentioned—among them were honest larcenists, skippers of child support, casual bigots, hustlers, abusers of chemicals, and even a few killers—but as with any congregation, there existed space for mercy and forgiveness, opportunities for second chances and shoulders to cry on, a corner of the earth where beat-down dogs licked each other's wounds. All this was offered freely, so long as loyalty was sworn and respect given, though Eddy noted these "fair shakes" weren't necessarily afforded people outside the group. Self-examination was neither a vice nor virtue, and often avoided, keeping some from better jobs and more rewarding relationships, perhaps, and making the worst of them small-hearted, petty, and sad. But aggression came with the territory, and despite all the "personal liberties" talk, they often sought out rigid hierarchies, with punishing leadership.

That said, nobody here was out to try and dominate the world. Like other folks, they bitched and railed against the daily trivialities of which their lives seemed atomically comprised. And though participation in the dangerous and inadvisable was a source of pride, yes, and youthful deaths a common harsh reality, and though members of the tribe openly mocked Fate (be it forever out there, ear cocked), and hoped to dull with drink whatever fears kept them unpaired with larger freedoms, they prioritized friendships and family above all, courting a vision of the good life Eddy shared. Every living day was a blessing, a bonus, affording yet another karaoke binge or drag race scene or fireside political debate in the haunted woods of the Three Forks marshland. The fact was, they reveled in self-determination—bring it fame, ignominy, or total collapse—and Eddy found this brand of living intoxicating.

Where is she?

Among the partygoers only a handful of women carried straight black hair that wasn't dyed or graying—and none of them Gin. Casting about, he accidentally caught the upturned gaze of a cougar—pancaked makeup, big eyelashes—who openly leered as he passed. He felt so awkward under her animal tracking as to forget how to walk properly. He'd been warned against speaking to pretty older women he didn't know—for one, they rarely kept without a jealous boyfriend or hopeful counterpart close by, and two, "biker chicks are a particular kind of crazy" was a common enough mantra to be believed, despite the fellas being no less vindictive, combative, or nuts.

Striking out, Eddy put aside his search and headed for the kegs, stopping first to watch a small group of children splashing each other in a blow-up pool. Half of everything today reminded him of things he'd outgrown and the other half the uncertain future he was wading into.

The beer kegs resting in large tubs of ice were manned by a pair of twin brothers in their mid-twenties. The duo eyed the crowd with a practiced calm, cups of ginger ale at their chests, as the Twins didn't drink. Duke and Lisbon had arrived in Palm Bay from North Carolina only a month earlier to begin moving furniture part-time for Bird—alongside Eddy, Cueball, and their friend Jesse. Duke was the larger of the Twins, muscle to Lisbon's flab, and eldest by a minute.

Eddy requested a red Solo cup and watched Duke unsheathe one from the stack and flick it at his feet. Eddy smiled as he bent to retrieve it.

"I hear twins have lower IQs than normal people," he said, pulling the tap himself. "Like a brain meant for one person gets shared."

Duke pondered the matter. "Yeah, that feels right."

"It's science," said Eddy, blowing a cloud of foam off his beer. "Sharing makes everything smaller."

Duke grabbed his belt. "You asking to see?"

"Let's not upset the children," said Eddy, raising a hand and smirking.

"Well the truth is, *small*'s a matter of perspective," said Duke. "It all depends on the woman you're trying to satisfy. When we're sandwiching your mom, size isn't the issue. She's tighter than a scared pedo in prison. But your gramma . . . I have to keep banking the sides just to feel anything, she's so loose. Plus she keeps shouting your name, which kinda kills my whole confidence in the thing."

Eddy shied away. "Yeah, Granny's a talker."

Lisbon jerked in controlled laughter, but said nothing, as Lisbon was mute. Eddy pushed his middle finger into the young man's face until it was smacked away.

"Why they got two straight-edgers back here pouring the brewskies?" asked Eddy.

"Easy money," said Duke. "Fifty bucks each."

"*Each?* Shit, scoot over," said Eddy. Instead he leaned against skinny pine. "You get a lot of bikers in Carolina?"

"Sure. Bikers. Hippies. Our guardian's both."

"You say *guardian?*"

Some slight discomfort crossed Duke's face as he moved past the question, sipping his ginger ale.

"Anyhow," said Eddy, "I wanted to check with you guys and see if you thought we could knock out the widow's place in one day instead of two. Push hard, so we get a day off. That fucking La-Z-Boy, when the flippy part shot up? I think I tweaked my back. It felt like someone pulling tape off my spine."

Duke held out his busted knuckles. "I can barely make a fist. Lookit. Smashed it on a doorframe when monkeybitch here ran with a couch. Doesn't matter, though, we're not doing that job no more."

"No? Why's that?"

"Talk to the bossman. Said we're going national. *Expanding the possibilities.* Sounds like we'll be on the road, which is fine by me."

This was news to Eddy—and he wasn't excited about it.

"But I heard you've never even crossed the Georgia border," said Duke. "Is that true?"

"I went to Georgia once with my mom for a cheeseburger," said Eddy. "She heard the Burger Kings there made them better. With organic meat, instead of bean meat? Some kind of meat conspiracy. Where's Bird?"

Duke gestured with his plastic cup. Eddy tapped it with his own, raised a silent cheers to Lisbon, and marched back into the crowd.

Sliding between chairs, he again wondered what compelled the brothers to settle in Palm Bay, of all places. He'd been surprised when Cueball's father hired them, as Bird was notoriously picky about those he allowed within his circle. Yet Eddy also knew the elder biker held a soft spot for underdogs and misfits, being a collector of troubled but loyal individuals. So maybe this kid with a speaking disability and his stocky, stoic brother weren't such outliers. Maybe this was how the middle-aged biker sought to balance out his past sins and certain deplorable prejudices, believing like others that one good deed magically offsets another, when the truth was we're each of us paradoxes and canting hypocrites.

As a boss, though, Bird was fair, paying everyone equal salaries well above any other moving company, the downside being the job wasn't necessarily stable, as Bird wasn't particularly good with money or marketing. His earlier business attempts included a drywall team, a portable toilet company that catered to construction sites, and a small carpentry outfit. The last venture barely broke even, so for his fifty-fourth birthday, Bird bought a fifteen-foot parcel van from an Enterprise auction, slapped a coat of paint on the sides, replaced the brakes, and hired on his son and two fellow classmates as weekend movers. When Duke and Lisbon signed up, Bird completed a full crew that could empty out a two-bedroom home in less than three hours.

Presently the famed biker held court at yard's center, hands aloft and drawing in listeners like a Baptist preacher at a rededication service. With puffy gray-black hair, a scraggly handlebar moustache, and deeply opaque, predatory eyes, Bird was not a man easily ignored. Tattoos covered every square inch of his naked torso. A bulldoggish frame added to his toughness, as did the terseness with which he pounded out his words—a cold, calculated stripping down to facts.

This one was a prison tale: a young latino hit man who hid impossibly thin razors in the calloused soles of his feet, a regular Houdini caught skimming money from the Aryan Brotherhood. Having served time in San Quentin for dope running, Bird invoked a tantalizing autobiomythology with his storytelling, which in turn produced an aura of damaged light around the patriarch. He'd earned the nickname *Bird* after busting out of a juvenile treatment facility as a teenager. *Jailbird to freebird.* By twenty-five he'd buddied-up to three different drug kingpins, and was rumored to have helped the mob mend strained relations with Tijuana. There were assassination rumors linking him to Gumby, a pale and chiseled biker who now sat quietly among the listeners. *Freebird to bird of prey.* Borrowing the politician's waver, he neither admitted nor denied involvement. His detailed knowledge of events proved only that he was present, but as witness or provocateur, none were certain.

Bikers were prone to self-glorifying, Eddy knew, and so he took each tale with a grain of salt. Besides, in his usual relaxed state, the old leatherback seemed normal enough: barking swears over scratched DVDs, squirting too much ketchup on his eggs. Take away the wardrobe and the beard, throw on a long-sleeve shirt, and Bird could pass for someone's overweight grandpa.

Laughter brought the intrigue to a close.

"Whoever the guards could grab, they dragged off to the hole!" Bird hollered. "The nightsticks were flying and Ringo was up on a table yelling, *Extra! Extra! Houdini drowns in a toilet!*"

Eddy positioned a chair next to Gumby. "I miss a good one?"

The former hit man said nothing. Reached back and tightened the rubber band around his ponytail, then withdrew a pocketknife to pick leisurely at his dentures. There Eddy spied the famous single eyetooth, vampiric, filed to a point.

Eddy gave it another go. "How's the easy life?"

Gumby leaned forward to spit a black wad of chew into a soda can. "You so young you think this shit's easy?"

Eddy let it go. The man kept a septic tank full of baby gators behind his house, along with a collection of poisonous snakes and frogs in terrariums in his garage. He also fabricated a rather unique addition to his Harley's handlebars: a human kneecap, centered and framed in a welded casing. Eddy once scratched at the patella bone when no one was looking, wary of its authenticity.

Gumby craned his neck. "Bird! Your appointment's here."

With the audience departing for refills and the bathroom, Bird shifted to Eddy. "We need to talk."

"Not that one," Gumby interjected. "Over by the porch there."

Together they watched Cueball, who'd been milling about a food table, stop to admire the newly tattooed span of a biker's sunburned back. Eddy had inked the colorful Hydra earlier that week, and was agitated to catch the idiot disregarding his warning that direct sunlight caused premature fading. Cueball was so struck by the mythic beast that his attempt to eat a hush puppy went sideways, leaving him stooped over and hawking violently enough to garner the concerns of bystanders. When he finally forced the snack down, tears in his eyes, the audience applauded, and he gave them a thumbs-up.

"Boy's a prizefighter," said Gumby, offering a grin. "Reminds you of a Mayweather. Wed to his own thing, don't give a fuck."

Bird grumbled, "You should get your eyes checked."

"Naw," said Gumby. "Cueball might walk into a punch now and again, but he's quick on the upturn."

"He's got all the brains God gave a flea's ass," said Bird. "And his name's *Heath*."

For some reason, Bird refused to use the nickname he'd coined for his son some years back, and discouraged others from using it as well. It was always Heath, never Cueball.

Bird regarded Eddy strangely, as if faulting him for befriending this gangly, squalid creature that was his son. Eddy turned away. He was used to hearing Bird sound off with remarks that ranged from disparaging—*Did you hear Heath made goalie for the dart-throwing team?*—to the off-kilter and troubling—*That boy's a few clowns short of a gangbang*. There was a familiar tough-love element to his father's ribbing, and Cueball took his knocks in stride, but lately Eddy sensed a bit of resentment building in his friend.

Gumby wasn't letting his sentiment drop. "I'm serious. You harness a bit of that devil, throw a little soul-building work his way, watch out."

"I wouldn't trust him to hammer a nail," said Bird, growing agitated.

"Some folks sleep on nails," countered Gumby, darkly serious all of a sudden. "Tests the spine. Sorts out the weak."

The elder biker weighed these last remarks heavily for reasons Eddy couldn't fathom, the mouth working quietly under its thick moustache. "Maybe so. Tell him to wait for me in the parlor."

Gumby rose and left. Eddy turned to find Bird concentrating on his pupils as if attempting to pin down a certain frequency of thought.

"Congrats on your graduating, if I didn't say it," said Bird. "Diplomas are rarer than you'd think. Feel all growed up?"

"Ha, I don't know," said Eddy, tucking his legs back as a naked child twirling a diaper ran by.

"Still thinking about college?"

Eddy shrugged.

"You're smart. Smarter than most. Life's about options, Eddy. Keeping as many open for as long as you can. They disappear fast, if you don't watch it."

"I'm thinking of taking a year off, see what happens. Plus I'm broke. College is expensive."

"Look here," said Bird, "you want something in this world, you gotta chase it. You get my age, wait too long, everything gets sorted without you in mind. Stake a claim early and stand by it. You'll probably wanna get out of your mother's place."

"No reason to, really. She shacked up with a literal rocket scientist up in Port St John," said Eddy. "It's basically my house now. I pay the bills."

Which was true, and why Eddy felt compelled to confront Bird about taking the moving company national. Half of Eddy's income came from lugging sofas and vinyl records around Brevard County, but the other half came from tattooing, which would suffer greatly if he was traveling. He couldn't imagine Bird would let this happen, though, as Bird was his partner in the tattooing business, having converted his garage into a fairly decent underground parlor. Though notably less skilled, Bird proved a decent teacher to Eddy, sharing what he'd learned in prison. Eddy's apprenticeship began as a junior in high school, with drawings sketched in sociology class transferred to grapefruit rinds he'd ink for practice. By winter Eddy had secured a calendar of appointments, and Bird, mindful of losing his protégé to one of the hipper, legal tattoo shops in Downtown Melbourne, agreed to split the profits, minus expenses. It was the first spending money Eddy had ever earned, and he was proud of his work. But the celebration was short-lived: placed haphazardly on some back burner in his mother's mind were her utility and mortgage payments, and soon their mailbox was crammed full of threatening letters. Her phone calls—rare, short, often accompanied by club music pounding in the background—were always the same: her job search had failed to turn up any positions befitting her qualifications. *I've got irons in the fire, baby*, she assured him, *but it's tough out here*. And though the NASA engineer provided for her financially, his philanthropy stopped short of the mortgage, which constituted crossing into "serious relationship territory." But she had faith Eddy would do the responsible thing, which he took to mean paying the bills. In those words he also heard a damaged resolve: she could no longer be bothered with the tiresome aggravations of motherhood. Eddy would have to fend for himself.

The last time he'd spoken with his mother was nearly two months ago. She was vacationing in Hawaii. She may or may not have remarried.

Together, the moving and inking jobs were enough to stave off foreclo-sure . . . for now. But if Bird was going to cap his ability to earn, Eddy needed to ensure a hefty raise was involved.

"Duke said you might be expanding the moving business," he broached cautiously.

A stark displeasure crossed Bird's face. "Well, it wasn't his place to men-tion it. What else he say?"

"Just that. But I'm guessing this'll make us more money." The *us* here, Eddy hoped, implied himself.

"More than you think," said Bird, fastening his gaze to some internal vision. "It's steady work, but there's a bigger picture here. I consider all of Heath's friends my boys, you know that. Since you first showed up, I've given you my trust, which I don't hand out lightly. I've fed you, taught you a trade—"

"I appreciate everything you've done for me."

"All I'll say for now is I've landed a money backer. We'll share manage-ment responsibilities." He smiled. "This is it, Eddy: my retirement."

There it is, thought Eddy. The R-word. Bird's obsession. For some in Palm Bay, retirement meant living off the blessings of workers' comp, un-employment, or social security. Almost two decades ago Bird made the trek from Los Angeles to this swampy coastal region of Florida in an effort to start anew. He'd served his time in prison for a drug charge and scraped to-gether out of sheer will business after failed business in an effort to procure a comfortable decline into his golden years. Yet for all his hard work, Bird still lived paycheck to paycheck in a small house with well water on a plot of sugar sand and pine.

Beyond the crowd, Eddy watched Gumby usher Cueball indoors.

"I'm talking independence here," Bird fired home. "In the end, we have . . . what? Friends, family? The rest are strangers. This is the high seas. You're either with us, or sailing under some hostile flag." He slapped Eddy's knee. "We'll continue this later. Now go get you some of that boar meat. Fuck-ing behemoth. Took four men to load it on the truck and two to dress it out."

The gruff patriarch ambled away before Eddy could ask if he'd just been fired, which made his stomach sink. Racing back through the conversation, he decided to believe Bird was offering him inclusion in some larger project, details to be worked out. The mention of family felt hopeful.

The sweet aroma of greasy fat returned, accentuated by raw pine sap fogging up the tree boughs. Eddy wandered over to the back fence.

A group of drunken men loitered about the grill fashioned from a halved oil drum to gaze lovingly upon the smoking hulk of a wild boar poached from the marshy thickets of Malabar. Wiry hackles and blue-gray eyes bloated and warped repugnantly into a kind of false life by the heat; a feral creature completely undone—neutered, disemboweled, and stuffed with vegetables like some warning to shape-shifting gods or vegans. Life's dependency on life's sacrifice was a fact of the wilds, and Eddy studied the men focusing on the coal's glow and sizzle, brooding perhaps on their own mismanaged lives, and wondered if his own future involved inheriting a spot beside them.

Bird's weird bootstraps and pirate speech lingered. Lately it seemed every minor thing came saddled with some new responsibility.

"Think you could take down a beast like that?" rose a low, musical voice behind him.

Eddy stepped aside for Del Ray, a haggard but stately biker from the swamps, longish brown-blonde hair, and along with Bird and Gumby the third member of the once notorious California clan to have made a home for himself in Florida.

"Sure I could," said Eddy, raising an invisible rifle to his eye.

"Shit. You couldn't kill a turkey buzzard, much less empty the filth from a hog."

Eddy conceded. "I'd eat it, though."

A jack-of-all-trades, Del Ray's pursuits involved everything from deck carpentry to computer sales to evangelical preaching along the banks of the Suwannee in his youth. People said he was even a professor once. The way Del told it, though, one day he woke up, sold off his stake in a covey of rub & tug massage parlors, and began pursuing opportunities in the less respectable trades of photography and journalism, specifically for biker mags.

Widely regarded for his affluent tastes and circular reasoning, Del was a true arguer.

More to Eddy's concern, if Del was at the shindig, it meant Colt and Gin were likely close by.

"Where's Colt?" Eddy asked.

"That's not what you're after," said Del Ray. Though well along in his drunk, his posture remained aristocratically upright. "You got that daughter in mind, so why not ask about her? Besides, her mom and I aren't an item anymore, if you haven't heard."

Eddy hadn't heard.

"This is our world now," said Del Ray. "Men are dartboards, son. Common machines. Swappable carriers of genetic data. Look at our sorry-ass lot—there's nary a real man among us. We're stand-ins for a dying breed: emasculated turd dumplings, thirsting for reinvention."

That was the other thing about Del Ray: he talked like nobody Eddy had ever met.

"It aggravates my ulcer to think about the once-nuanced history of Last American Rebel boiled down to these beer-bellied burnouts. Some pretending they got native ancestry so's to adopt this bullshit notion of a *warrior culture* to wear as a false skin. Repugnant shit. Such delusions do not, however, pass muster with the female. Nawsir. The wretched stench of our idiocy and pride entices them, as they sense a slip in the fault lines of power. Men have failed them, failed the planet—our incompetence the single thread run through every plotline. To wrest power, the female must play to our damaged egos, luring us in with promises of ecstasy and re-creation. They will trap us in their lovely mitts, and we will praise them their charity and kindness, even as we are devoured."

Eddy measured the partygoers against these allegations, opting to keep his trap shut and steer clear of reinjuring the biker's hurt by playing into his bitterness.

"The camera lies too, but it lies better," Del Ray continued, tilting back his beer. "I prefer my place *behind* the lens. It's pure surface out here now. All these sad and mixed-up people, empty and exposed."

Eddy couldn't help himself. "Surface?"

"All what's meant for inside is out now. Nobody hides their prejudices anymore, because they're not ashamed. People just mean, hurtful, dumb as fuck, and proud of it. Inner turmoil is a precious thing, allowing one the opportunity for self-reflection, growth. Having all your knee-jerk reactions spilt out into the world gives them a different authority and weight. Understand? Our surfaces are indefensible! We should cherish our secrets and fears, our patient struggles. We've abandoned mystique."

Eddy had questions. "What's indefensible, exactly?"

"Us!" proclaimed Del Ray, drawing a wide arc over the crowd. "This lawn trash here. The truth is, we were elevated to a status we neither deserved nor could live up to. Bikers never had no real power! Movies and television endorsed our myth for decades, and we lost ourselves in that promotion. As the smoke clears, this idea of rugged individualism induces a soft nostalgia, but there's little truth to it. Our clannish tendencies have been baffled by technology, our rumored lives reduced by academics to the systemic effects of poverty, and so here we stand, forced to figure out, for the first time, truly, who we are exactly. Are we even a *we*? Are we a lawless band of misfits? Or the racist base of the conservative party, outted by Obama? Bigotry, rejuvenated as a voting bloc. What corner will they paint us into next? Will we *abide*? Are we the simple equation of what we do? Stonemasons, mechanics, a/c installers. White-knuckling it until we can hit the road forever, writing the grandkids postcards from the farthest expanse . . . We had something once, something that felt permanent. A code. A dream-cult of, what? Brotherhood? Blood? Maybe it was all patriarchal whitey horseshit, and here we are, the strawmen ghosts of necessary reparations. Poor and undereducated, bankrupt, vestigial. Is there no honor left undiminished? What's our goddamn *code*? Get me? And that loss, that realization, is felt, son! It's *felt*. And spurred a great deal of quiet contempt. But you're still young—" Del said, lighting a smoke and transfixing his gaze. "Whiskey and rough sex, there's our lasting heritage. A bathroom romp with the woman who earlier gnawed a hot dog dangled off a string while straddling the backside of a speeding Sportster," he scoffed. "But where's the code that legitimizes us? Where are the rituals that induce meaning and radicalize life? We're just praying nobody sees us for who we turned out to be: uncultured, frightened citizens. Shades of more sinful eras. Soy people, excons-found-gawd, and whatever else."

"Shit, man, that's some speech," Eddy hooted, genuinely delighted. A few people who'd stopped to listen exchanged condescending smiles before moving on. "You got that written down on your arm or something?"

"Next month's column," snorted Del Ray. "They won't print it, though, the fuckers. It attacks the readership, stirs up questions. Gotta keep that advertising money rolling in. I got a backup piece on exercises to avoid deep vein thrombosis, another on Sturgis and litter . . . that'll go through. But I gotta dumb it down a little," he clucked. "Gotta keep it real. 'Cause once we start acting outside our allotted roles, folks don't know what to do with us. *Lord a'mercy, son! T'aint no honest po' whites talk thatemaway!*"

Eddy drew his lips thin. The truth was, he'd remained listening for selfish reasons. "So hey, what happened between you and Colt?"

"Dammit, Ed, know your business!" But as Eddy balked, Del winked. "Concentrate on that daughter. She's got eyes for you, I've seen it. I'd advise against hanging your hopes on a single gal, but you wouldn't listen. Follow that pecker, son, it's the only thing you got that'll forever know what it wants." Turning to the crowd, Del Ray hollered, "All agree say *aye!*"

Most shied away, but a weasel of a man resting under a tree gave the thumbs-up. Del Ray squinted at him. "Say aye, motherfucker!"

"Aye!" yelped the weasel.

"There we go!" Del shouted. "Whoo-ee! Brotherhood!"

Eddy watched a biker by the grill unsheathe his blade and slip off the dead boar's ear. Whether as food, prize, or talisman, he couldn't hazard a guess. As a woman passed with a pail of boiled palmetto hearts, Del Ray followed her legs all the way up. "This land provides, but only if you know where to look. And only if you're willing to work for it," he said. "Sometimes an opportunity arises, that rare blessing, and we're asked to step up and receive it."

Eddy found Del Ray glaring at him, a hand over his heart.

"What'd I do?"

"Will you step up if you're called to, Edward? Will you receive the blessing?"

" . . . "

The biker exhaled wistfully. "Son, your lack of participation in this conversation has inspired me to get drunker."

The sound of a beer bottle exploding against the patio wall snatched their attention.

. . . you little wetback faggot!

Everyone turned to find Jim Barns, the neighborhood drunk, barking out expletives as he fell into a little anger dance.

"Finally!" barked Del Ray. "Some action!" And started off with Eddy in tow.

They found the slur-hurling bearish man hunched over and poised for attack. When people called for him to quiet down, Barns shot a black stream of tobacco their way. Meanwhile, the person for whom the insults were intended, a husky brown kid named Jesse, dutifully slurped down oysters and played it casual. Jesse was one of Eddy's best friends, and fellow coworker on the moving crew with Cueball and the Twins.

"I'm half filipino, you drunk fuck," said Jesse. "You think everyone not bird-shit white as you's a fucking mexican?"

Jim Barns walked in a small circle, stomach pushed out and slapping hands away from him. "Naw, I can say it! I can say whatever the fuck I want! This here's my *right*! This is the U-S-of-motherfuckin-A! You wanna see what I got waiting for you, boy? I live right up that street and I'm well stocked up for whatever, whenever when. You can bring your camel jockey, monkey-ass—"

Jesse had a right hook that could cure this mean drunk quick; instead, he held back and continued to employ the restraint and easygoing nature that granted him respect from even the more vocal bigots in the crowd. That, and he was one of Bird's boys, which for harassers carried a penalty as of yet untested.

With surprising verve, the drunken miscreant flew into a scrambled tirade that touched briefly on terrorism and jobs stolen from the "american workforce." As chuckles turned to whispers, Barns grew more upset. He tried yanking off the table cover, but lost his grip, succeeding only in displacing a few bowls.

"Sit down and have another beer, you old prick," Jesse said, shooting Eddy a *what's up?* nod, followed by an arched eyebrow. *This fucking douche-bag again.*

What happened next they would revisit in many future conversations.

Gumby rose quietly from behind Jim Barns like the shadow of the drunk's own malevolent spirit. The time to warn him, had anyone a desire to, passed without affair. Barns' right knee buckled under a swift kick as Gumby pulled his head back by the hair. A blade appeared, catching sunlight. Eddy felt the man's scream enter him, viscerally, as a shiver—pure and mortal and electric.

Once finished, Gumby hopped up and stood behind his victim, tugging crudely at his belt as he re-sheathed the razored belt buckle. A squealing Barns was hoisted to his feet by a couple of large bouncer types as onlookers shied away. His chin had been laid open straight down the middle, pulsing blood, and two thin slits wept under his open eyes, the strokes of some aboriginal mask. Barns whimpered and squalled as he was escorted through a side gate.

Spectators continued to confer in low tones. A woman bent to retrieve a child in orange arm floats from the pool, but seeing no one else leave, simply toweled him off. Someone laughed sharply in back. Then Duke triggered a bullhorn near the grill and everyone lined up for plates, the drone of conversation returning.

Jesse asked to see the belt knife. Gumby said no, he'd seen enough.

"Where'd you get it?"

"Frontenac Flea Market. $9.99."

Though Gumby was known to carry at least three knives on his person at all times, blowguns were his supposed weapons of choice. Eddy doubted the hype until he saw, firsthand, Gumby's extensive period-piece collection of antique darts, showcased alongside a series of mason jars, each with pink rubber stretched over the top like a bongo drum. He then watched in horrified amusement as Gumby gaffed a diamondback from its terrarium, pinched its jaws open, and stapled its fangs to a drum, juicing the venom.

"Man, that was brutal," said Jesse, who clearly felt this was an overreaction. "You have a history with that guy or what?"

Gumby kept his skinny frame shrink-wrapped in a black leather vest over a white T-shirt like some greaser refugee from the fifties. His undressing gave one the impression of peeling away a sausage casing. Still twitching with adrenaline, he strengthened his abdominals for show, lowering a shoulder. Some strong-arm had chiseled into his back an arabian warrior brandishing a scimitar. It wasn't a tattoo — it was done with a blade, looking much like a woodcut. Eddy traced the hit man's high, sharp cheekbones, the shallow cheeks and stony jaw. Gumby clapped his chest, arms out, spreading pecs. "Quarter camel jockey! Cracker-ass fay didn't expect that."

"We're all mutts," said Jesse.

"But no taco," Gumby said, twisting his pointy beard. "Least none I know of."

Riots begin with the first hurled rock; backyard brawls, a spilled beer or territorial glance. Eddy felt untouchable in the presence of men whose final word was violence, men who lashed out in passionate, irrevocable ways, rather than risk having meaning misinterpreted through language. Yet he also understood he was lucky to be on this side of things, and the casual slurs bandied about with frustrating regularity exposed him to feelings of cowardice and shame, his silence a rock in his stomach.

Jesse slapped his shoulder, startling him. "You seen Cueball?"

"Uh, yeah, he's inside. When'd you get here?"

"Fifteen minutes ago?" said Jesse. "How was fishing? Dude, you cannot call the house before eight a.m. If Mom hears me answer the phone, she'll have me doing laundry, mowing the lawn . . ."

"Duly noted, chubs."

"And if I get good at shitwork, well, that's just another job I'm stealing away from the white workingman."

Eddy sent a kick to Jesse's thigh, who returned the favor with more oomph. Rubbing his ass, Eddy scooted away with a promise to return with an extra beer as he moved indoors.

The overhead fan failed at cooling anything. People waiting out an extensive bathroom line howled David Allan Coe's "You Never Even Called Me by My Name" in broken unison as Eddy plucked two bottles from the fridge and lingered by the wood-shuttered butterfly doors separating the kitchen from the garage-turned-tattoo-parlor. He dropped an elbow to the counter and squinted to better hear Cueball's voice within, wondering what kind of trouble his friend had gotten himself into now.

"A little help!" sang a raspy voice, sending Eddy upright. A woman with fried wavy hair, sunken eyes, and a long sloped nose wobbled through the front door lugging four bags of ice. Eddy hurried to her side.

"Oh thank you, honey. Put them in the sink. We need to break it up."

Charlotte was, among other things, surrogate mother to the corruption of boys invariably yanked like weeds from her carpet each Sunday morning. In certain lighting she looked like a performer in drag, years of late nights and various addictions having taken their toll, with features so pronounced as to invoke caricature; yet she was, beyond dispute, the instant sweetheart of everyone she met. It was generally agreed that men admired her quick tongue and ability to hold her liquor, as women strained to imitate her casual, hardened style. In a previous life she'd dragged a mouthy shopper out of the Cerritos Mall by her hair, then ran over her legs with a Jeep. Shakes her head to heaven at the thought—heroin and coke at the wheel, a past life. Clean for eighteen years, including the three she served. "Where's my hubby?" she asked, emptying ice blocks into the sink.

"In there with Heath," said Eddy, motioning to the parlor.

Peeking over the butterfly doors, she whispered, "Sorry! Just wanted to check in." She blew a kiss over the top, then searched the kitchen drawers for an ice pick. "Business stuff. I live with a businessman now, only he don't wear a tie." She took a wine cooler from the fridge.

"Starting out simple?" said Eddy.

"I may have to go out again. We've been drinking since morning. Plus I'm expecting a call. We're doing the Toys for Tots drive and need to work out the routes. This year's going to be humongous. We'll clog every street in Daytona. I hate the traffic, and forget about eating, the lines are crazy. But it's for the kiddies, should be fun. Is Del Ray out there?"

"Last I saw. You know Colt dumped him?"

"Honey, I had to take the call at three a.m. That's why she's not here. I'll telephone when Ray leaves. Why's it smell like dead fish in here?"

Eddy searched for a distraction. "Gumby just split open your neighbor's face with a knife. Outside, a few minutes ago."

"What? Don't tell me that! Jim Barns? Jesus, the cops! Just what I need! Did anyone leave?"

"I don't think so. The food was ready."

"Figures," she announced, quirking her eyebrows as if mystified by the sum of it all. "Wife beater, that one. I told Hubby I don't want him over, but he just shows up, unannounced. Thinks he's one of the gang. But that's Hubby's fault—he hooked the old coot up with Rusty at the shop, got him a used Shovelhead at discount. So as he'd fix our bathtub? He's a plumber when he's sober. And an Angel when he's angry, but that don't mean shit to me."

Bird's voice issuing from the parlor grew momentarily louder.

"Listen, hon, do me a favor and finish busting this up into little chunks? Layer in some beers to keep 'em cold?" Charlotte finished off her wine cooler, dug into the fridge for another, then strolled off toward the sliding doors, taking slaps to the ass along the way in good humor.

Eddy glanced about. Nobody was paying attention. He'd think of what to say once he got inside, shuffling back through the butterfly doors.

A hatchet of lamplight split the parlor. He'd stumbled upon an interrogation scene. Bird crowding a metal chair, leaning in, as Cueball shied away. The biker's expression devoid of niceties as he turned, all fire and nails.

"Some people knock," Bird huffed over his shoulder in an attempt to assure Eddy the situation looked worse than it was. But Eddy wasn't buying it; the air hung stale with Cueball's sweat.

"Dude, did you throw out the fish?" Eddy asked, hoping to dilute the palpable anxiety. "Did he tell you about the trout?"

"I told you to put them in a cooler," Cueball said in a low voice.

Bird sighed. "Eddy, a minute?"

Eddy raised his hands and backed out.

What the fuck was that about?

He stayed in the kitchen, loudly shoving beer bottles under ice. When it was obvious they weren't coming out anytime soon, Eddy popped a beer and headed back outside.

On the porch he toed a fat spot of Jim Barns' blood into a red streak on the concrete. He'd forgotten Jesse's beer, but Jesse was somewhere off in the swarm. A few clouds moved in, ushering a cool breeze as Eddy watched the burnt leaves of barbecued corn brush the face of a young girl, as if insisting the world still contained a small measure of playfulness. Beyond her some movement near the fence disturbed his vision—a black banner of sorts, streaming before palmettos. Two women, replicas in stride, their long water-dark hair seemingly intermingled, caught the upturned eyes of partygoers as they passed.

For a moment Eddy simply watched. Then he pocketed his hands and shuffled their way, almost skipping.

Unfortunately, Del Ray beat him there.

Normally Del initiated conversation idly, building up momentum, but now he was absolutely vibrating. Colt steeled herself against the disparaging onslaught from her newest ex-beau, first by ignoring the biker's petty insults, expecting the crowd to bandy together against this collective buzzkill, but when that didn't happen, and Del really started carping, she threw back her hands and unloaded, cutting him down to size.

Charlotte intervened, nudging and guiding Del Ray toward the house with her fingertips as he protested loudly, giving everyone within earshot the facts. Colt, hands to her head and speaking rapidly, broke away from her daughter to join Charlotte along the fence and air her grievances.

This offered Eddy the opportunity he'd anticipated.

Gulping his beer, he made minor adjustments to his overall look: sweeping back his hair, palming his breath, pinkying his fly. Genevieve, or Gin, as she was known, had arrived in Palm Bay from a planet of loose exotic skirts about six months previous, a free spirit transported during the final semester to a school of woodland suburbanites, prep-school rejects, stoned alcoholics, addled immigrants, and texting addicts. Her natural beauty and peculiar style made her a public target, as one by one a slowly advancing army of knuckleheads descended with whatever pathetic lines their libidos devised in earnest haste. Secretly Eddy enjoyed these public humiliations, with each pursuer forced to endure a shocking throng of obscenities before being allowed to retreat. To the guys, Gin was the resident cocktease freak. The girls were much more calculating—every other week another rumor singled her out as the school's queen mother of slutdom, providing ever more fuel to the vicious cycle of curiosity, rejection, and disdain.

"Hey there," Eddy announced.

Gin turned to face him, all clover eyes and black eyelashes, stealing his heartbeat. Apparently she found him funny-looking.

"Did you just get here?" he asked, feeling much like a newspaper thrashed to a phone pole. "I didn't see you."

She tilted her head. "Were you looking for me?"

Goodbye charm.

"It's just that Charlotte said you weren't coming till Del Ray left."

"So you were asking about me?"

Done *and* done. Maybe he'd regroup and try again later. Gin had too much power in her, an overwhelming suggestiveness and calm that rendered him incapable of engaging in casual conversation. Fortunately for him, Cueball approached carrying an extra beer. Eddy instinctively reached for it.

"Whoa there, cowboy! You're a grabbin motherhumper, aren't'cha," said Cueball, pulling back. His face looked drained. "First you throw out my fish, which I was saving to prove him wrong, wrong, wrong . . . and now you're sharking drinks from beautiful women."

Handing the cup to Gin, Cueball nearly dropped it.

"You okay, man?" Eddy asked.

"This is a party, right? I'm partying. Hey there, sweetheart, welcome to the show. Can I get you anything else, or you just fine looking good?"

"Hey, Heath," Gin smiled. "Are there any more veggies left, with the dip? Seeing that pig like that . . . ugh."

"You want me to get you some?"

"If you get some for yourself, I might eat a little."

Cueball snapped his fingers and dropped into a martial arts stance. "Be back in a jiffy."

Eddy turned to apologize, but Gin's breath was in his ear. "You got a car?"

Embarrassed by the sudden proximity, he shook his head. "Not here."

"Heath does, though, right?"

"Yeah. But it's a truck."

"Um, it doesn't matter *what kind* of vehicle it is. Can you borrow it?"

"Worth a shot," said Eddy. "Where were you thinking of going?"

"Surprise me."

"You serious? Yeah? Now?"

Gin stepped back, puzzled. "Is that your thing? You ask questions?"

Eddy located Cueball mindfully spooning tzatziki onto a paper plate and laid out the details.

"You threw away my fish," said Cueball.

"Man, fuck those things . . . why do you keep bringing them up? They smelled like butt plugs."

"I don't get how you don't understand this," said Cueball. "My dad called me a liar. I got the proof. You threw out the proof."

"Listen," said Eddy, "we'll go back tomorrow and catch more trout. A *million* of them. But right now . . ."

"Alright, settle down, dickweasel. But you owe me. Bring me back her panties. *I'm just fucking with you!* Next time at Golden Cue, pool's on you."

"Abso-fucking-lutely!" Taking the keys and almost rushing away, Eddy quickly backtracked. "Hey, is everything cool? It looked like your dad was really tearing into you."

"Naw," said Cueball, closing an eyelid. "You know him. Always scheming. There's things we don't see eye to eye on. I just need to get wasted. Find a fat filipino to hang my arm around. You go on, get. Leaving a hottie right out in the open, with all these fucking buzzards circling? Sheeeeit."

"You're an ugly son of a bitch with a good heart," said Eddy, "and don't let nobody tell you different."

Cueball snorted and offered a raised middle knuckle, which Eddy bumped with his own.

At first Eddy considered taking Gin over to the Black Road, a popular drinking spot at the end of a deserted cul-de-sac nearby, but that wasn't going to cut it.

So he headed north to Eau Gallie, a tiny riverside hamlet engulfed by Melbourne proper, where they marveled at enormous moss-draped oaks and grabbed coffee in the diminutive downtown, chatting freely about whatever subjects came to mind, before heading over the causeway, one of three immense bridges in town linking the mainland to the barrier islands. Small boats set a northern course toward Merritt Island and Kennedy Space Center, where the Indian and Banana rivers, each a mile and a half across, sluiced in opposite directions. The causeway's incline always inspired in Eddy the feeling of having been launched by catapult across a great expanse, a medieval suicide astride some shuddering package of doom. He even lifted his arms at the top.

From on high, beachside seemed entirely composed of salmon-colored mansions and distant high-rises, but soon leveled out to strip malls that clung to the highway like sugar crystals. Dead-ending at the beach, Eddy steered them back south along A1A toward Indialantic.

Realizing neither of them had actually eaten at the party, they stopped over for comically large slices at Bizzarro's Pizza before Eddy brought them to a secluded beach where ocean access was limited to locals in the know. A narrow path cutting through sea grapes ended before a rickety staircase that split the dunes and opened upon a dramatic view of the Atlantic, waves tubing.

Gin walked on ahead, shoes slipped off and held, her body heat persisting long enough for Eddy to sense as he passed through. They skipped shells and kicked sand at each other's ankles, watching the waves obliterate and reform the dusky light, sharing opinions on fruity drinks and trash TV shows, agnosticism and the number of eggs a sea turtle could lay, what zombie rabbits might eat—humans or other rabbits. Trudging along the soft upper banks, they exchanged the sort of glances that remain forever fresh in the memory, micro-gestures of desire: the prized lower lip bite, syllables drawn out to a sexual purr. Evening arrived with yellow oxeye flowers glinting on the waves and shells spun upended in the surf. Lying back on a dune, Gin made the first move, capturing his tongue and sucking it until he chuckled. Her waist felt easy in his hands.

Suddenly she shot up, pointing.

Against the night sky a single stroke of white emerged, a long glowing thread, as if the earth were being unspooled.

"It's the shuttle," Eddy explained. "I heard it got delayed. They're headed up to fix the Hubble telescope."

"Oh my god! You mean they just blast those things up from here?"

"How long have you lived here and never seen a launch?"

"I mean, I knew it was a thing, in theory. How often does this happen?"

"Three or four times a year? It's pretty amazing," said Eddy, only then believing it.

He'd grown up with the launches. Most people he knew had witnessed the *Challenger* explosion firsthand, from underneath. Yet now, relishing in Gin's childlike surprise, the reality of the thing touched him unexpectedly. People could actually leave Earth—and here he was, some yokel who'd only been outside his home state once, for a cheeseburger.

What might trigger depression in some activated in Eddy a keen ambition. Yeah, he was a townie fuck. But he was thoroughly convinced he'd do great things one day, beyond any reason to believe it. Something special, something that would change the lives of everyone around him.

As Gin watched the shuttle vanish into the outer dark, Eddy felt the moment slipping—felt the real world, operating in real time, eke its way into their precious space. Pressing his knee inside her thigh, Gin pressed back. They moved purposefully, tugged close and spun into each other's gravity.

ueball's red pickup glided over the Melbourne Causeway beneath a sky the true colors of a marlin. Condos in the distance throbbed in and out of drifting sheets of rain. The beach was never really Cueball's scene—often overcrowded, and surfers were pricks—but he'd begun seeking out its breezy quietude a lot more lately, driving out to perch cross-legged on some boardwalk's weathered railing. Nighttime was best, alone with the salt spray and blue dunes, when all sorts of provocative thoughts sluiced through him.

It was now morning, though, and he was already agitated. Eddy sat slouched smoking beside him in the truck's passenger seat, a cupped hand grooving the wind like a canoe navigating river channels. The radio played back-to-back Bob Marley, revolution songs sung as love songs to poor people. Eddy sang along, transmuting the famous verse into a rendition Cueball very much enjoyed: *Emaciate yourself with menial slavery.*

Always the smart-ass. His friend was in a good place, had himself a new girl, and seemed generally optimistic. Cueball felt terrible for having to spoil the vibe. He'd picked Eddy up earlier that morning, saying he was itching for a drive, but that wasn't the truth.

Cueball's gaze kept frequenting the rearview, baseball cap pulled low. Occasionally he'd reach over and scratch the bandage on his right wrist, but stopped when Eddy caught him. It had been three weeks since the party, and a week since he'd received the tattoo.

"You should change that bandage," said Eddy. "Might get infected."

Cueball straightened up. "It's not infected."

"You said whenever you got a tat, you'd let me ink it."

Cueball's eyes shot back to the rearview. "How many times you want me to apologize? Dad wanted to do it himself. I couldn't say no."

"Why you being all secret agent about it?"

"I'm not."

Eddy made a face. "You won't show it to me and get antsy when I bring it up."

"Why you riding my ass?"

They drove Fifth Avenue past the surf joints and breakfast stands, then headed south along A1A. Pastel mansions, dolphin mailboxes carved from driftwood, BMWs in the driveways. They used to go egging back here. Out of boredom, they said, but neither ever suggested rolling into the dumpier neighborhoods with a full carton.

Soon they were coasting along the misty ocean, dune oats gripping each other for balance as the sand percolated under a harshening drizzle. The water was so monochromatic, so windswept and barren, it almost registered as sound.

"Things change," Cueball said.

"What's that?"

When Cueball didn't respond, Eddy huffed his annoyance. Then tried spitting through the cracked window, but failed.

"Dude! Don't be hawking loogies in my truck! Show a little fucking respect!"

"*Je*-sus! Sorry," said Eddy, rubbing the window with his shirt before falling back and lighting another cigarette. "What's all this talk of respect lately? Why does everyone feel suddenly disrespected?"

Cueball let it drop. Eddy didn't get it, but he would. That and a whole lot more.

"If you don't want to talk about it—fine," said Eddy. "But don't be a little bitch and grumble and moan and expect me not to ask why."

"Eddy, man, you see like two feet in front of your face sometimes."

"This is a good example," said Eddy, "of you acting like a little bitch. Just say what you gotta say, brah, I'm here for it."

Cueball snubbed the radio off. When Eddy clicked it back on, Cueball yanked the truck through oncoming traffic.

They spun into a beachside alcove, bouncing and churning up a funnel of sand before coming to a sudden halt.

Ignoring Eddy's shouts, Cueball killed the engine, got out, slammed his door shut, and slowly ventured up the narrow path breaching the wet vegetation.

On a raised wooden platform above stairs, Cueball waited for his friend to catch up, giving his tension over to the marbled ocean.

"It's cold out," said Eddy, hugging himself, looking worried. "Alright, hoss, spill it."

Cueball scanned the beach and tugged his ball cap low, then thrust his arm out to the mist. Carefully he unraveled the bandage with his fingertips. Mushy, gauzy, bloody layers gave way to a pictograph swelling at the base of the wrist: a Sabal palm tree, its green fronds like barbed hooks, with a jagged trunk where the vein's greenish color negated any need for ink. Poised as if its true aim was to flourish and expand into the hand.

Cueball watched his friend recognize the design—one of Eddy's own initial forays into tribal.

"Dude, you got that on your soul spot?"

Cueball squared his jaw, pointing. "This is the club symbol."

"What club?"

"You notice all the new people at our party? Guys you've never seen before?"

"Your folks have a lot of friends. But, yeah, okay."

Cueball flung the nasty bandage over the railing. "They're starting up a club, and Dad wants us in on it. Let's get further away from the truck."

"Why?"

"I don't know. It might be bugged."

"*Bugged?* No, c'mon," said Eddy, but chanced a furtive glance back. "So what, is this a motorcycle club? Shriners, Masons, Mickey Mouse, what are we talking about here?"

"They're gonna start shipping a new designer drug up and down the East Coast," Cueball explained. He caught Eddy's eyes. "And they need drivers."

"Whoawhoawhoa," crooned Eddy, eyebrows cocked, mouth awry. "You serious?"

Cueball sympathized. When his father first broke the news, back at the party, the information glanced off his brainpan like a ping-pong ball, unwilling to stick. It made no sense, and all the sense in the world. At first he was curious, then angry, then deeply embarrassed. Over the past week, these divergent emotions congealed into a single flutter of fear.

"Wait, have you already agreed to do it?" Eddy asked, stunned. "You're going to be a drug runner? For *real*? What about your mom?"

Cueball placed a hand on his friend's chest, bending him against the wood railing. "Listen, you can't say shit to anyone. This is people's lives. Drugs. Prison. No bullshit. This guy Seizer, he's the real deal."

"Who?"

"Some old guy Dad used to work for out in California. He's seriously bad news. I mean, you've heard Dad's stories! I go, *Why would you do this?* And he's like, *Money*. But we're not as bad off as he pretends. We're not on food stamps or anything."

"So your mom does know."

This possibility left Cueball speechless. He dropped his head and descended the stairs.

At the bottom they unlaced their shoes and plugged them with socks. An ear-stoppering gale nagged their hair and rushed over the crushed shells as waves crashed and glossed the sand with a lightly ruffled and reflective tapetum. They sat together on a low bank.

"What else?" asked Eddy, pinching the sand.

Cueball shook his head, eyes puffy, encumbered by dark thoughts.

"Tell me."

He didn't know where to begin. "It involves stuff that happened a long time ago. Back in the day, it was Dad, Gumby, and Del Ray—dumb kids Seizer got ahold of and trained up. They were deep into it with the mexicans, not even kidding, actual drug cartels. Seizer had a cover business called Marble & Tile Industries. Sold shit up and down the West Coast. One day a shipment got busted and Dad wound up taking the fall. Off he went to San Quentin."

"Damn, I always wondered. What were they shipping?"

"Easter egg baskets. No joke, plastic eggs full of coke, heroin, crank. They were a small operation, bought everything in bulk and broke it up themselves. Mom told me the deal once. She sounded worried to hear Seizer was in town, so I don't know what all she knows. Point is, Dad got busted for a major shipment, which was apparently his own fault, so he went to prison owing Seizer a shit ton of money. But Seizer owed Dad too, for not turning him in. You'd think that junk cancels each other out, but it don't—it just means each owes the other."

"So your dad's doing this to pay back a debt?"

"And land a monster payday. Seizer is looking to move quick. Del Ray said they got buyers lined up the coast. Yeah, *right?* Everyone's on board. New guys coming in. Dad said they already got a camp out in the woods making the stuff. A superlab."

"*Super*-lab? Is it meth?"

"Yeah, no, it's weird," said Cueball. "It's a mixture of things, like a speed-ball. A *designer* drug, mixing highs and lows. Make it so it pumps you up, like *arrrrrg*, meth bulldog, I'm-gonna-conquer-the-world, get your dance on, but then you slip into a real chill vibe, touchy-feely, like ecstasy. They've got actual chemists working on it."

Eddy puffed his cheeks. "But you're doing this. You've decided."

Cueball shrugged, glancing up the curved bay. He'd never felt more unsure of anything. He wouldn't be the first person to run drugs, or have a father doing something illegal. All those mob kids—or hell, those senators' kids, the Wall Street kids, the Big Pharma kids. People did all kinds of things for money. *Everyone cheats a little on their taxes*, his father said. *Nothing too big or too risky. Just enough to put us back over the top.* But watching the old dynamics play out between his father, the toughest guy in any room, and this Seizer character told a different story.

They were huddled around the dining room table, watching Seizer sort through tattoo designs in a folder. Impatient, the old boss kept dismissing Bird's attempts to be helpful, like one quieting an overactive child. Cueball had never before seen his father talked over, much less down to. The tats would be small, to make cover-ups easier, so that lower-tier club members could have their tats redesigned and expanded with promotions. Presently, the choice of image fell between a Royal and Sabal palm frond. The Royal seemed to Bird the more obvious pick, laying claim to a sense of divine power, or supreme force, but Seizer found it condescending, maybe even dangerous. *I don't want them thinking about who's on top. They need to see this as a family business, where everyone involved is family. We need to instill in them a sense of pride, place, history. A sense of themselves working toward a goal. You say Sabal, folks think sunshine and cocktails, bikinis — the good life. You say Royal, they think inbred weaklings and revolution. Make no mistake, this will be a revolution, but it will be one for the workingman, in brotherhood, against a state that suppresses ingenuity. Sabal says all that. It literally means "strength," I looked it up. Sabal's a New World palm, and this is a new world.*

"He stayed for three hours," Cueball said. "Talked like he'd been planning this shit for years."

"He a big guy?" asked Eddy.

"Not at all. Looks kinda like Robert Duvall, the actor? But short and thick, and squintier. Like a preacher, who was also a boxing coach, who maybe stabbed someone once. He can't stand cussing, and hates anything racially *insensitive*, from what I hear. He's relaxed, but there's something off—"

"What's the drug look like?" Eddy interrupted. "You smoke it?"

"They're testing kinds you can smoke, snort, whatever. He was talking about a fucking extended-release capsule, dude, to manage the highs and lows. It was like a marketing meeting or something. It might even come in different flavors."

"You're excited by this."

"No."

"Dead people stay that way," said Eddy.

"No shit. But they're keeping it simple," said Cueball, switching gears. "It'll be real low-key. You and me, we'd just be going for a long drive and dropping off some furniture. Up and down 95. Turns out Dad bought a parcel van instead of a big box moving truck because anything under five tons doesn't have to pull over at weigh stations. It's all been planned out."

"If I say no, am I fired?" asked Eddy.

"I don't know. They want you and Jesse to meet with Del Ray."

"Oh man, Jesse too?"

Cueball pushed the heels of his shoes into the sand.

"I honestly don't know what to say, bro," said Eddy. "I mean, we've seen all kinds of shit together, but this is . . . this is messed up. I still can't believe you got the tat."

"Man, they hung around to watch Dad do it! It was a trust thing—like I'd fucking tell anyone! That mute motherfucker Lisbon pulled out a pistol and cleaned it right there on the table, with Seizer going on about how he always dreamed of bringing our families together."

"Why was Lisbon there?"

"Because Seizer's his *uncle*! Duke and Lisbon are Seizer's *nephews*!"

"Fuck the *what*?" Eddy cawed. "Oh jeez. So much for two college kids looking for a summer job."

Cueball pushed up and walked a circle in the halting sand, looking every bit like someone who had discovered his girlfriend was pregnant. "Dad says he's doing what's best for us, but all he ever thinks about is himself."

Eddy looked distracted. "Would I still be able to tattoo at your house if I bail? I've got people lined up, man, but it's your dad's gear. I need that money."

"Maybe not, if you're not in the club," said Cueball. "Sorry, I don't have all the answers. You're my brother, so I thought you should hear it from me first. You gotta make your own decisions, figure your own shit out. And soon, 'cause there's definitely people ready to figure it out for you."

Cueball flopped down beside his best friend. He hated his father in that moment, feeling a growing pressure mounting within.

Eddy's hand found his shoulder.

"This has gotta be rough for you," said Eddy. "I can't imagine. I appreciate you telling me."

"Of course, bro," said Cueball, exhaling. "Shit's been weighing on me. I honestly have no idea how this shakes out."

That was the truth of it. There was more to say but Cueball was done.

Instead, the boys settled into a prolonged silence, watching the overcast afternoon roll out unscripted with the tides.

Gin was speechless.

"Are you kidding me?"

She didn't expect much from dates—ice cream sundaes at the Strawberry Mansion at best, or *maybe* cosmic bowling—but picnicking alongside a drainage canal beside an empty baseball field was surely the lowest of low bars.

The lone picnic table was decrepit and wonky and overlooked people's actual backyards. *Stellar*. But whatever—the birds were out and she was happy, cooled by an overcast sky and set to dine on what Eddy promised was the best sandwich on the planet: spicy Lebanon baloney and baby swiss on rye, with crushed salt & vinegar chips mashed into layers of german mustard.

Instead of stopping at the table, though, Eddy continued on toward the canal.

"C'mere."

She followed him, and there, floating just beneath the surface like drowned sofas, were more manatees than Gin could count, packed thick as bricks.

"Oh my god, this is amazing! Ohhhh, I wanna pet them!"

"It's a five-hundred-dollar fine, but be my guest," said Eddy. "They have more rights than felons. Whenever it gets even slightly chilly they swim inland to cuddle. I looked it up, and this is like three percent of all the manatees in Florida, all in one place."

Gin chirped excitedly and tugged his hand along the canal, searching for babies and ones with deep grooves in their backs, victims of boat propellers.

The sandwiches were also surprisingly top-notch, smoky and flavorful. Gin appreciated Eddy introducing her to his favorite things. He also made sure to include her opinions and approval, a sadly uncommon trait in young men. Asking where to next, her choice, Gin pursed her lips and picked the 905 Café, a hole-in-the-wall bakery with fancy teas and muffins.

They set off in his VW Bug—which was perfectly adorbs—a powder-blue bubble with beaded bucket seats that cupped her body snugly. He looked so cute driving, elbow jutted out, head bobbing to the music, wind spinning curls from his hair. Sometimes life could feel so carefree, which of course raised her suspicion—often whatever gave something away for free cost *two* somethings later on.

"You have no tattoos, but you're a tattoo artist," she said. "Why no ink?"

"My body is a temple," said Eddy, ". . . of Doom."

"Ha, cute, *Doktor Jones.*"

"It used to be nobody had tats," he explained. "Now everybody does. No tats is the new tats."

A few minutes later, Eddy turned down a random street, slowing mid-block.

"What's this?" she asked.

Eddy leaned over and pointed out a petite and unassuming house. "That's where Jim Morrison was born."

"Na-ah!" cried Gin. "Really?"

It felt exactly right: a tiny white bungalow sporting a thin chimney and clamshell awnings. She loved when famous people came from nowhere—it gave her hope. Nostalgia for history predating her birth was a major weakness, and Eddy had paid close attention to her musical tastes, derived in part from spending time in LA.

"One day I'll own a place in Laurel Canyon," mused Gin.

"Groovy," said Eddy. "*Flowa powa.*"

"It's mostly all gone now, sadly. I just always wanted to *be* Joni Mitchell. Hang out and smoke weed with Mama Cass and David Crosby. Catch Linda at the Troubadour, Jim at the Whisky. Sleep with the Byrds."

"I'm sorry, *slut* did you say?"

She slapped his stomach. "All of them, together! With Joan Jett! Free love and communal living, baby. I'm built for a cult."

She checked to see if Eddy was smiling. After telling him she'd made out with a girl in middle school, he hummed "I Kissed a Girl" and said: "We have so much in common!" But guys often hid their actual feelings about things, especially at the beginning.

"I miss a good road trip," she said. "There's more desert than you'd think. The Pacific is freezing."

"Let's go now," said Eddy. "Seriously, I can do tats wherever. California here we come."

Gin sighed. "This is the best part isn't it, the dreaming?"

"Maybe I'm not joking," said Eddy. "Life is what you make of it."

"Money helps," said Gin.

"Yes it do, girl, yes it do."

She smirked. "If things went sideways on the road, we could always pimp you out. You're shaggy, but baby-faced. Mama's little lot lizard."

"Awww. Well I do keep a rubber Elmo suit under the seat, in case I need gas money."

"A *what?*" Gin snorted. "A rubber what?"

"And a Pikachu too, if they like me fluffy and yellow? Red cheeks, tight little mouth . . ."

She giggled as he pursed his lips to make a weird squirrel sound.

The patisserie was located in Downtown Melbourne, the oldest part of the city, lined with open-air bars and antique shops. Crossing the railroad tracks, they passed a woman painting a watercolor of a large clock. At a stop sign, a homeless man blew her a kiss.

For once the 905 wasn't packed, and lit by lamps, with no interior windows. They found a table in back under shelves of porcelain teakettles. "I know some secret spots too," said Gin. "I'm officially a local."

She opened her purse lined with jangling soda tabs and placed a twenty on the table. Eddy grumbled at the bill, waiting behind his chair, as orders were taken up front. "When's my turn to pay?"

"When I run out of savings," she said. "Till then it's dutch."

Eddy scrunched the bill and raised an eyebrow: "Latte for the hot-*tay?*"

Gin quirked her entire face into a horrible frown as Eddy scowled comically and left.

Alone, Gin found the café quiet as a storage room and weekday sad, the wallpaper overly ornate, garish even. She was again confronted by the pressing knowledge of needing a job, which was just . . . ugh. *Yay, I have no skills! Dog-sitting, house-sitting, waitressing—take your pick!* She scrunched her long hair in a fist and fanned her sweaty neck, wishing for a dress instead of shorts, as the space wasn't well ventilated. But she still had a little money socked away from waitressing in St Augustine—money purposely set aside as a nest egg of last resort—and she hadn't decided if "last resort" meant community college or *escape*.

She was deep into a book of poetry when Eddy returned, balancing an italian soda, her latte, and a key lime tart in his arms, setting each gingerly between them. Then flopped down in his seat, sighing, his mood having shifted along some axis Gin couldn't name.

"You okay?" she asked.

"Yeah, I'm good. Just a lot going on." Eddy rubbed his face. "Things change so quickly sometimes."

Gin asked with her eyebrows.

"I might be out of a job soon," he said.

This was news. "Oh, why?"

"Long story. Bird sold the moving company, and this new guy has big ideas. It's got me stressing out, with the mortgage and everything. I should probably call my mom."

There was still a lot Gin didn't know about Eddy, but he rarely mentioned his parents—like, ever—which made this all the more concerning. She didn't know if he wanted her to pry.

"Okay, well, so let's brainstorm," she said. "Worst outcome, you need a new job. What're you good at? Your tattoos are *amazing*, so that's a possibility . . . But what else? Don't be bashful. *My name is Eddy and I'm good at . . .*"

"Avoiding responsibility," he said. "Saying the wrong thing at the right time. Ducking hard truths."

Gin squinted. "Are you *me*?"

"Uh, no . . . I have standards."

"Nice. Says a lot that I'm here with you, huh?"

"Bingo."

"Maybe we can take some classes together at BCC!" she offered, perhaps too earnestly.

Eddy swam the idea around. "I've thought about it. You got something specific in mind for yourself?"

"Psychology?" said Gin. "I'm fascinated by human behavior, but maybe I'm too judgmental to be a therapist? I'm not *not* empathetic, but I get upset when people hurt other people and then just rationalize away their own culpability."

"Cul-pa-bility," said Eddy, tasting the word. He peered over at her book. *The Incognito Lounge*, by Denis Johnson. "That something I should read?"

She lifted her arm off it: "If you like sad poems about sad people in sad situations. Bus stops and dingy motels, but yeah, they're . . . incredible. The writing's really lovely. He doesn't discount anyone. Everybody's human and worthy of love. Or maybe just appreciation?"

"Why not take a writing class?" he asked.

"Why would Bird sell the moving business?" she countered. "Isn't that how he makes money?"

Eddy rubbed an eye. "I feel like you always get me talking about me so we don't have to talk about you."

Gin stuck out her tongue. "You like me mysterious."

"I don't know if that's true," he said.

Gin forked a piece of tart. A week before, she'd let him read a short story of hers, along with a few poems. Surprisingly he wasn't quick to dismiss them. Most poetry was overwrought with emotions or flowery as hell, he said, but she employed pond loons and desert mice to raise feelings lingering just beneath the surface, where they could expand. And did so without manipulation or outright direction, which he admired.

Eddy's words made her feel seen. Which she had imagined wanting, but the sudden exposure left her feeling weirdly embarrassed and protective.

"Maybe a writing class might help you hone—"

"I write for me," she said, ending the subject. "Besides, writers don't make money, it's a fact. And I *cannot* end up like my mom. Being broke means ending up someone else's consort."

"What's this, *consort?*"

"Beholden to other people," she said. "People who expect something in return for 'helping you out.'"

Gin was reluctant to get into all this. Opening up felt good, but divulging personal details introduced more opportunities to hurt her, and she equated vulnerability with target practice.

Still, she hadn't made a real friend since moving to Palm Bay, and missed having a confidant. So she decided, okay, he's gonna keep asking anyway, and gave Eddy a breakdown of her itinerant childhood.

How to begin? Maybe with some of her mother's more questionable choices, which included hooking up with her father, whom Gin never knew—some alcoholic Deadhead who hiked seventeen-year-old runaways into the mountains for drug-fueled music gatherings. Hence Colt's pregnancy. Gin's earliest memories were of a commune in Maine, a farmhouse in Nebraska, a single-wide trailer perched beside a blue lake in the Black Hills of South Dakota. It was a merry-go-round of bus passes and secondhand stores, campsites and natural springs. God in the roar of machines; heaven in the misty, stone-tumbled rivers. Her mother's lovers were kept on a three-month rollover plan—after three months, if things were working out, you got dealt another three. Or you lost your wallet. She was a child forced into training, developing a deep disdain for social institutions and the claustrophobia of suburbs. To symbolically declare her own independence, her mother adopted a new name—Colt—and had her daughter pick one for herself too.

Enter Genevieve: patron saint of derelict playgrounds, stray dogs, and board games with missing pieces. Gin didn't remember why she'd chosen Genevieve, only that once her mother learned it was germanic for "woman of the people," the deal was sealed.

"Intriguing," said Eddy, chin on his fists, watching her like some rare specimen in a zoo, she felt. "So what's your real name?"

"Gin *is* my real name," she bit teasingly. "The other's a secret."

"You're not gonna tell me?"

She shook her head no. "There's a little girl, way back . . . and she gets to stay who she is . . . forever."

Gin continued: they were a family on the move, encountering new groups in random places, outlier cultures ignored by broader society. By age twelve she had visited all but eight states, sidekick to Colt's wanderlust, and though she never considered her mother an outlaw, she recognized a profound sense of struggle shared by these new acquaintances, many hiding out from their pasts. When a DEA sting operation uprooted a tribe of squatters occupying the huts of a closed summer camp in the Florida Panhandle, Gin found herself whisked through the morning woods and tucked under blankets in the back cargo of a station wagon. Duct-taped around her waist were twenty sheets of acid in plastic baggies, courtesy of Colt's newest beau, a college dropout who'd go on to win a state Senate seat. But after Colt discovered the drugs during a restroom break, the boyfriend, two coffees in hand, stepped out from the convenience store and into the Pensacola night to discover his car missing, as the duo sped deep into the state's interior.

"We ditched the car and bused it to St Augustine," Gin recalled. "Rented out a weekly room by the ocean, had me enrolled in junior high halfway through the semester. Then one rainy night Del Ray happened into the bar my mom was working at, and the rest is history."

"Incredible," said Eddy. "Sounds fun, honestly."

"Nothing romantic about being homeless," quipped Gin. "Gallivanting around with stolen money. Whenever she'd shake me awake and throw my teddy bear in a pillowcase, I knew we were leaving. I never had close friends, except in LA, where we stayed put for *a whole year* before she got the bug again. I did get to see the country, it's true, and I read a lot. Am I better or worse for it? Who knows. But I make the decisions now, I'm responsible for me."

Eddy leaned back. "You're the most interesting person I've ever met."

She pushed a fork toward him. "Please don't make me eat this alone."

"Question: a colt is a boy horse, is that right? Why'd your mom choose a masculine name?"

"Colt is a type of gun too."

"Fair enough," said Eddy. "She saw herself as your protector."

Gin pulled a napkin across her mouth. "Actually, with regards to all things masculine, she used to say, *It's not the penis that's envied, but the power.*"

"That sounds smart as hell," said Eddy. "But I have no fucking clue what it means."

"Which is why you should be in school!" she countered playfully. "You took AP classes, right? Well don't you ever wonder, sunshine, if those books you've read didn't help prepare you for a larger world? Maybe don't waste your time hanging around with a bunch of rednecks."

Eddy's guffaw was real. "Okay, *sunshine*. Not a fan of bikers, is it? Or just white trash."

Gin didn't wish to exacerbate his mood, but he'd asked, and she sensed this was a threshold they'd have to cross sooner or later.

"Bad luck has a way of rubbing off on people," she said. "They're just not who I'd choose to spend my time with."

"Because . . ."

"Because they treat women horribly, for one," said Gin. "Like we're doormats. Worse than dogs. Plus they're drunks. Racist. Homophobic. They don't wash," she said, lifting her coffee. "Act like babies, always angry for no reason. Full of conspiracy theories, thinking the government's always out to get them."

Eddy seemed poised to mount a defense; instead, he cut into the tart. "People aren't one thing," he said. "Or all the things. They try . . . I see it. Maybe your mom sees it too."

Gin rolled her eyes—no no no, all that woman saw was opportunity. "She's almost worse in the bad decisions department. Jumps on whoever has whatever she needs: money, a place to crash, a ride to the post office. Before Del Ray, it was a long line of useful idiots. Richard—*Dick*—the senator, who was already rich but sold drugs anyway. Before that was Donald, who ran a farm up in New Hampshire, and who hit her. Steve, who owned a lumberyard . . . and also hit her. Lance, who didn't hit her but screwed her only friend in town. And sold my grandmother's wedding ring for coke . . .

yeah! Karl, who was actually kind of a mellow dude. Wood sculptor, had a place near Mount Rainier with these big carved statues out front. But when Karl got drunk, he changed. He propositioned me . . . twice."

"Eek," said Eddy.

"Yeah, eek."

"Were they all bikers?"

"No, but they shared the same mentality: get yours and screw everyone else," said Gin. "I mean, don't get me wrong, Cueball seems nice, and I really like Charlotte, but Bird and his friends . . . I really don't understand how Jesse puts up with any of it, it's gotta be tough. They don't see him as equal."

"Most do, actually," said Eddy. "I do."

"But you're not one of them."

"No?"

"Can I ask, do you actually enjoy being around these people? Or is it just that you're friends with Cueball?"

Eddy grunted.

"Sorry," she said. "I was born this way."

Eddy had a nice laugh, a deep inviting chuckle. "There's a lot to say on the subject, I guess. Difficult to put into words."

"It's none of my business, really."

"There's goodness in their hearts," he began, as if struggling with opposing thoughts. "I think if you give folks space, while encouraging new outlooks, they'll eventually find their way. People are softened by time, proximity. If you push too hard too quick, you become the outsider, and they won't listen to a word you say. But I'm optimistic."

"That makes sense," said Gin, thinking they'd found a happy medium.

Instead, Eddy set down his fork, moving past her resistance, or perhaps further into his conviction. Cueball's family was his family, he explained—brought together by certain social realities and bound by locale, yes, but chosen still, and loved. Bird had been like a father to him, at times, and Charlotte a doting mother, concerned when his own was not. And you don't just toss that away and pretend it doesn't mean anything just because your thoughts or values don't one hundred percent align.

"Hate the sin, not the sinner," Gin piped in her best church-lady voice.

His eyes looped. "I just mean we've all done things we're not proud of. You *are* as much as what others think you *can be,* and it's hard to act outside of upbringing, or education. I got lucky with a few good teachers who hounded me. Most people . . . nobody's looking out for them. They feel trapped and dismissed. Don't know where to look for help, or even what's missing. It's a whole complex system of inequities and resignation."

Gin put a fist to her head. This all felt very adult; they were adulting. Here was a smart boy, forced to grow up quickly. His tenderness felt somehow earned. She wanted to pull him close, but that desire threatened to breach some well-established boundaries.

"I mean, these people in your book," he said, pointing. "Sad people in tough situations, but everyone's worthy of love."

Gin felt herself getting prickly. "There's a difference between understanding why people do things and letting them ruin your life."

He shrugged. "I guess I feel responsible for them. That's the deal—they got my back, I got theirs."

And here it was again: that stubborn brand of loyalty they taught in small towns everywhere, alongside kickball and active shooter drills.

Certain things were indefensible—this was something Gin wouldn't budge on—and despite his claims, she sensed a bit of ambivalence in Eddy's devotion, some internal friction. Yet she couldn't help admiring his idealism, believing errant humans and even legit scumbags might eventually find their way to common decency. In her opinion, people never changed.

"Dear Diary," said Eddy. "Today I flustered a girl to death."

Gin laughed loudly. "No no! I like this! A guy who actually communicates what he's feeling."

As Eddy raised his soda, a robotic mutter escaped: "*Sexist girl is sexy . . . must resist.*"

Gin frowned, then kicked him under the table. Eddy barked and hugged his shin, making a big show of it. Then settled back and raised his eyes dreamily.

"I'm a terrible human," Gin pouted. "Adios California?"

"Honey, you say go, I'm with you."

She couldn't stifle the smile. Eddy was sweet, he was—she wouldn't commit to *heartbreakingly sensitive*, as her corniness alarm forbade it. And though she felt the familiar tug of falling for someone, she needed to keep this easy, playful—uncomplicated. Which meant pivoting.

"Do you think popsicles were ever made of pop?" Gin asked. "I know Coke had cocaine in it. Also, how does a manatee even get that big? I thought they were vegetarians."

She knew boys thought *being random* was being flirtatious, which it could be, for sure—but it could also be deflection, a way to stifle momentum, as love was risky business.

The night sky ruptured with a forking pulse of blue light, detailing in full the reticulate inner architecture of a cluster of storm clouds.

Cueball sat up blinking, his dreams scattered like bats before the wide-flaring lamps of spelunkers. He waited patiently to reinhabit the space, or for the space to somehow reinhabit him. The living room's sliding glass doors held the fractured, ghostly image of a calm interior set against a violent and wet otherworld, as the thin buzz of a tattoo machine issued from beyond the parlor doors.

There'd been a pinochle game. Someone brought weed and he'd smoked most of it. The TV was dark but played a low, indiscernible music. His mother snored on the couch. How could she sleep? Gin lay bundled in an afghan on the floor, her pinched shirt revealing a hint of lacy bra. Cueball raised his nose but couldn't see more. The cable box clock showed he was already late in meeting Jesse down at the Golden Cue for buffalo wings and pool.

Stumbling to rise, his knee caught the edge of the coffee table, tripping him up. The struggle turned vaudevillian, arms and legs flailing. When it was over, he flung the emptied ashtray from his face and returned the table upright. The women slept on, unaware.

What the fuck's going on out there? Bird yelled from the parlor.

I'm tearing the place apart, Cueball thought. *Beating you to the punch.*

He unpocketed his new iPhone and texted Jesse to say he'd be late. The phone was his last purchase with legitimate funds, he thought. The business phone his dad bought him looked cheap, with a prepaid SIM card to help evade authorities.

The a/c chilled the room to an insular, atrium feel. Cueball yanked down a thin comforter from the side closet, wrapped it over his shoulders, and trudged through the kitchen toward the butterfly doors.

Goddamn, is that like fifty needles or what?

Shading takes more needles.

Can't you just do it with less, more times?

So we can listen to you whine all night? I'd rather pass out naked in a ditch full of chiggers.

In the parlor a shirtless biker named Mickey sat hunched forward on a green vinyl masseuse table, a halo lamp craned overhead. Eddy hovered behind, a white surgeon's glove at Mickey's shoulder, tracing the tattoo machine over purple lines used to predefine the image on his skin. Bird nursed a Jack & Coke in a tattered leather recliner, watching Cueball enter.

Mickey rolled a shot glass under his palm. "Nurse, dear, your patient's out of meds."

"No luck," said Eddy, stepping off the pedal and lifting a towel, his gloves filthy with bloody ink. "Whiskey thins the blood. Makes the ink fade."

"Makes it feel better," said Mickey.

Cueball lifted a razor full of back hair, turning it over in disgust.

"What's that shit all over your face?" asked Eddy.

Cueball withdrew a smudged hand from his eye. "Fucking ashtray."

"You look like a dog I once knew," said Mickey.

"Marked man," Bird offered, his sneer comical.

Cueball shifted his gaze to his father's heavily tattooed naked torso, which he'd grown up admiring—a virtual atlas of imagined cities, crouching animals, posturing pinups, spiderwebs, and in memoriam arrangements for lost friends. Across his chest, twin bald eagles clenched between their talons a breezy, torn american flag. A banner beneath it read: *The Meek Will Rise Again*, and in smaller lettering, *& Hell Follow*. Bird joked that when he died they should skin him and drape his flesh over the coffin.

"You sick or something?" asked Eddy.

"Stoned. And maybe sick," said Cueball. "I'm heading out to meet Jesse at the pool hall. You comin?"

"You go on," said Eddy. "I gotta clean up. Plus I promised Gin we'd watch a movie."

The whipping sound Cueball made drew a snort from Mickey, who tucked his curls under his bandana and said, "You girls don't get into it while he's working on me."

"It's sad, really," said Cueball, the humor drawing him out of his funk. "Get a little action and your friends just fade away. Next thing you know, you're getting couples pedicures and shaving each other's armpits."

"Fuck off," said Eddy, trying to concentrate.

"Shopping for dental floss and bath bombs."

"Least my girlfriend aint some pregnant camwhore dancing on my laptop."

"Then one day she dumps your ass for some frat-boy linebacker," Cueball continued, goaded on by Mickey's contained snickering. "*Oh god, you guys, it's terrible! She said he's got a cock big as a baby's arm. Gets so deep, she hiccups.*"

Mickey snorted and Eddy buzzed the air near Cueball's face. "Who's got the gun, fuckboi?"

"Only a shitcan amateur calls it a gun," said Cueball, who was being an asshole partly for his own amusement, partly to convince Mickey he was a fun-times guy, keeping it all good-natured till he figured out just why the hell Mickey was hanging around so often.

The thirty-something biker had appeared out of the blue to request a cover-up tattoo, but stuck around after the sessions to hang with Bird in private. In a previous life, Mickey had worked as a stagehand for big rock bands—stadiums set aglow with lasers, pyrotechnics, fog machines—and could spout off 7-inch european B-sides for hours. People called him "the Connection" because he passed along valuable information in person, from Portland, Oregon, to Portland, Maine. *Memos eventually surface. Thirteen-year-old hackers download the contents of your hard drive.* Mickey owned a shiny Sportster with leather saddlebags and ate just once a day, what he called "din-din." The man spent more time staring down the mouths of lost highways than his own face in the mirror. *I don't get involved*, Mickey told him. *Just memorize and recall messages. I use the cover art from albums. Mnemonic devices, memory palaces. Google it.*

"Remember, no Neosporin, it'll suck the colors out," warned Eddy. "And no Saran Wrap until after you wash it. Wraps are greenhouses for bacteria." He wiped away the blood and leaned back. "Okay, we're done."

Mickey rolled off the table. Bird twisted around in his chair and slung forward, grabbing a mirror. The group stood admiring the moss-laden gargoyle, ugly and sullen, brought to life through Eddy's meticulous needlework.

"Good god," said Mickey, "that's a beaut. I'm glad to be rid of that damn mouse. Chicks thought I was a joke."

"Impressive," said Cueball.

"Hands of a dentist," added Bird, gripping Eddy's shoulder.

Three quick raps at the front door snatched everyone's attention. They listened for the screen door's click and swoosh.

"Hey! I still gotta bandage that!" Eddy pleaded to no avail as Mickey pulled on a shirt and scrunched the far end of the window blinds. He backed away, hissing, "Is there another way out?" His movements turned darty—a gazelle fired by the scent of a lion. "Hey man, you got a back fucking door?"

Bird's eyes went dark and calm, as if logging a mental inventory of weapons hidden around the house. "Living room. Is it the cops?"

Mickey bolted from the room, with Cueball close behind.

But Charlotte, sleepy and ambivalent, had already crossed the foyer. "Oh, hello you guys. Get in here, it's wet."

Duke and Lisbon pushed inside, followed by a wet black umbrella collapsed by an older gentleman with an owl's squint and a balding, freckled top. Short, powerful Popeye forearms ballooned from his weather-slick poncho. "Thank you kindly," he said, flashing a smile as he perked his lapels. When his eyes fell upon Mickey, they held there, purposefully, before returning to Charlotte. "I tell you what, this Florida rain comes outta nowhere and chills you right to the bone! Long time no see!"

"Lord, forever," said Charlotte, bending to his hug. "Few weeks ago a hurricane passed off the coast, you'd think the world was ending."

"Sorry I missed you the other day," said the old man. "But I had to run and watch the ink dry on some signatures."

Rocking, Mickey flexed his knuckles, which triggered an exchange of looks between Eddy and Cueball.

"There he is!" the elder crooned. "Old Ironsides!"

Bird gripped his arm near the elbow. "What's the good word, Seizer? Thought you were in Orlando till tomorrow."

"Well, you know me," said Seizer. "Sleeping in a motel feels like wearing someone else's boxer shorts. And Orlando doesn't have much in the good-eats department. What they got, they call *southern-inspired cuisine*," he joked, letting his jaw hang open. "Hey there, Heath, how you holding up?"

"I'm good," said Cueball, though the shadow over his demeanor spoke different.

Seizer complimented Charlotte on treating Bird so well, patting the biker's round belly and threatening to auction him off to SeaWorld. Then tried stoking her nostalgia with memories of her son at about yea high. His mannerisms theatrical, pulling his nose and clapping his hands. Everyone chuckled obligingly as an unspoken tension constricted the room like a boa. When Seizer's gaze again found Mickey, it was the snake's tongue, flickering.

"Mick-boy. Seems everywhere I think to look I can't find you, and now you're everywhere at once."

Mickey snapped to attention, a delinquent before the principal. "Oh, I just got busy today . . . turned my phone off. I figured since I was in town, might as well get Eddy here to work on a tat for me."

"You Eddy?" asked Seizer, cocking his head. "I heard a you. You work the moving van with my nephews," he said, jerking a thumb toward Duke and Lisbon. "They say you're a real hard worker. Eddy WIL-DE-BOAR . . . that's quite a name. Looks good in big letters, I bet. Bright marquee. Bird here mentioned your work. Artist, is what he called you. Well heck, son, let's see some of that craftsmanship!"

Mickey slouched his shoulders and tugged off his disgusting, blood-soaked shirt as Eddy returned with wipes to clear up the image.

"Oh, that's an ugly critter," said Seizer, leaning in to view the gargoyle. "A real beastie. Even the skin looks repulsed by it. You know you got this for life, don't you, Mick?" Seizer licked his lips, winking at everyone. "No, it's amazing. There's something of the spirit to this work. Always inspiring to see someone *walking in the manner of the vocation for which they've been called.* That's Ephesians. I'm no Bible-thumper, but sometimes the old lines sure do strike me as appropriate."

"Seizer," Mickey began, letting his shirt fall, "I swear I didn't know Del Ray from Adam."

"Let's discuss this—"

"He's the one started swinging. I honestly had no clue he's the guy I'd be working with. And I was hoping to straighten it all out before you and me met back up—"

"I understand," said Seizer, obviously annoyed Mickey lacked sense enough to swallow his grievances before a mixed audience.

"Is Del Ray okay?" asked Eddy, misreading the room.

"Oh, he's fine," said Seizer, clearly not enjoying this turn in conversation. "You see, Ray works for me. I own some magazines and he shoots pictures for them sometimes. Writes a little column. Seems Mick here didn't know that, got into a little scrap at a bar." Seizer raised his hands. "I'd just soon as forget the whole thing. Put a little alcohol in these boys and all they think with is their fists. But hey, Charlotte, I got a little something for you here . . ."

Lisbon produced a package laced with ribbon, which Charlotte opened to discover individually wrapped portions of saltwater taffy from Savannah. As Seizer drew parallels between the taffy makers and some korean chefs he'd once watched stretch noodles, Bird ushered him through the kitchen and into the parlor, offering tea.

Eddy and Lisbon followed, but Duke hung back with Cueball. They waited in silence for Charlotte to close the bathroom door before speaking.

Duke started. "Okay, just so you know—"

"You wanna bring your brother back in here, with his gun," asked Cueball bluntly, "make sure I pay attention?"

Duke seemed perplexed by this. "I just wanted to apologize, for not telling you about my uncle sooner. They had everything on lockdown. Personally I found it unnecessary, but I'm not in charge."

"Sounds like your uncle works every angle."

Duke smirked. "Even a swampbilly like you knows a man's gotta protect his investments."

Cueball scoffed, jangling his keys.

Heath, get in here! Bird yelled from the parlor.

"Tell him I left already," said Cueball.

Duke understood, offering a head-dip promise.

Inside the parlor, Eddy took his time sterilizing the doctor's table with antibacterial wipes and dismantling the gear. Normally he'd harass Lisbon for dipping a finger into the expensive inks, but found himself preoccupied with the elders' private conference in the corner, which consisted of a series of rapid apologies by Mickey and Seizer's inspired but muted retorts.

Bird disengaged to pull Eddy aside. "Don't worry about them, it's fine. Follow me."

They passed Duke pulling a soda from the fridge and Bird sighed to learn Cueball had already left. Eddy avoided Duke's eyes, suspicious of the liar.

Out front, Bird sipped his whiskey in the night air, his wild, wiry hair fraught with embers in the porch light. "Remind me to pay you for the appointments we had to cancel. But more importantly: Del Ray's going to contact you soon, fill you in on some new routes. It's time to step up, Eddy. Make this happen."

Absent was any consideration that Eddy might not stay on as a mover, nor any mention of a change in cargo. It took Eddy a moment to realize the recruiting part would be done by Del Ray, as Bird distanced himself from certain obligations. It was also possible that Bird suspected Cueball had already spilled the beans, and this private chat was a way to suss out that likelihood, gauging his son's ability to keep his trap shut. In that brief span, Eddy's understanding of Bird changed. Some past severity lived in his boss' countenance, sparking a discomfort Eddy hadn't felt since he was much younger.

"So who is that guy again?"

"Seizer's an old friend," Bird said, lost in the dark woods. "Keep him out of conversation. He's got a checkered past, and there's no use in us advertising he's here. We clear?"

"No sweat. But—"

"There's gonna be a lot of talk happening, Eddy. Don't believe anything you don't hear directly from me or Del Ray."

Bird slapped his shoulder and left him to finish his smoke alone.

Moths beat themselves against the bulb overhead. A car passed by, perhaps too slowly, and Eddy wondered if such trivial events would ever again feel random or arbitrary.

Back inside, he found Charlotte foraging the kitchen cabinet for pistachios.

"So that's Duke and Lisbon's uncle?" he whispered.

Charlotte made a face and motioned for him to join her on the couch. They stepped around Gin, still asleep on the floor. His heart sank a little, feeling protective.

Charlotte kept her voice low. "He's from Carolina, but did a lot of business back home."

"Who is he exactly?" Eddy prodded, hoping Charlotte's penchant for gossip would win out.

"An old friend. Why?"

Eddy was afraid to say anything. "I don't know. Everyone's acting weird around him, like he's important."

"He was a big player, once," she said, munching her pistachios, watching the butterfly doors. "He's supposed to be down here buying land, but I call bullshit. He's sneaky. Those nephews needed work, so Hubby gave them a job. They're good kids, but I'd just as soon send them back where they came from."

"You don't trust the guy."

"About as far as I can throw him. Hubby says he wants to invest in the moving business, but I say get a loan, that's what banks are for. But he says banks don't do that no more. Still, he's not a guy you want to owe anything."

"Why do you guys call him Caesar?"

"Back home, the old clubs had ranks. Lieutenants and Captains and all that. Well Seizer saw it for horseshit, you know, making it sound all military and war and glory. Vietnam was everywhere. Some of his best workers were getting shipped overseas. Contacts killed or lost in the jungle. Guys coming home with no arms and legs—you see? Weren't much use then. So instead of military names, they got tagged for what they did. He seized things, he seized people. The Seizer."

"Oh. Not like what's-his-face . . . Julius."

Charlotte mashed her lips together. "A little like that. The connection's there, for sure. He worked his way to the top. It was a business after all. Stepped over the right bodies. Even after the Feds lit a fire under his ass and he changed his name, the nickname stuck. I mean, just look at him: stocky, grabby. He's the Seizer."

"He's a bit short."

"Stalin was short. Napoleon wasn't, turns out. We watched a whole episode on dictators," she said, pointing at the TV. "He's lucky to be alive."

She shook her head and swept a handful of discarded shells into her palm as Eddy switched his focus to Gin, long black hair fanned over a throw pillow. "Lookit you!" Charlotte jeered, bumping his shoulder with hers. "I heard you guys took Heath's truck to the beach the other night."

"C'mon," said Eddy, intimating a good ribbing was on its way.

Some younger person in Charlotte smiled knowingly and pulled loosely at his arm. "She's a good girl. Smart. Got some bite. You gotta be good to her. Respectful. I'm serious, don't go getting her pregnant or anything stupid, or Colt will cut your little balls off."

"Jesus, Charlotte, thanks for the vote of confidence."

"You're men now, you got to think like men." She tugged his arm once more to make the point and let it drop. Eddy smiled, but the kitchen light burning over the sink left him feeling weirdly insignificant.

"You eat yet? I've got some leftover crab cakes and some sausages I can heat up."

"Thanks, *Mom*, but I need to get going."

"Hey, now," said Charlotte, slapping his head. "Don't give me that shit. You gotta look after the ones you love. It's in the contract."

Eddy smirked. "Should I wake her up?"

"I'm awake," Gin said, rubbing her knees.

"You little eavesdropper!" Charlotte whisper-shouted.

Gin squinted, toeing Eddy's shoe. "What time is it? Can someone take me home?"

"Waiting on you, sleepyhead."

Charlotte gave Eddy a *watch your ass* look as he helped Gin search out her things.

As they packed up, Eddy lingered near the kitchen, listening. Whatever was being discussed in the parlor would involve him later, he was sure of it. But then Gin knocked on the wall and he waved goodbye to Charlotte and followed her out.

Back in the cool safety of bed, Eddy found it difficult to sleep, his dreams haunted by an unnameable presence and clashing geometric shapes.

Lying awake at this hour usually prompted in him a dreamy sort of clarity, one that helped unscramble whatever complex messages the day had thrust upon him. That clarity was now missing, as questions he launched into the dark returned only as echoes.

He moved a finger over Gin's areola, felt the heft of her breast, nosing the sweaty crease of her neck. An uncanny nostalgia lingered, heartsick for the current moment already slipping away. He enjoyed their coupledom, the raw desirous new energy. Their commonalities (fatherless kids with crazy mothers) he interpreted as synchronicity, though Gin was clearly against moving too fast. Yet already she was proving to be a buoy for the slight depressions in which he swam. She did this funny trick in the bathtub, steadying her fingers atop the wavy surface until the water calmed. It was like that with everything she touched.

His mind drifted back to Charlotte—if she knew anything, she had one heckuva poker face.

He needed to hash out a plan before meeting with Del Ray. What were the actual responsibilities of a drug runner? Maybe he could find specific details online, average salaries and weekly hours. Even in reverie, his attempt to haggle earnings with Bird proved unsuccessful.

Outside, bullfrogs volleyed their impassioned cries back and forth. Perhaps if he turned on the fan, the whirring would help. The look in Mickey's eyes—that dude was flat-out terrified.

Maybe he'd just work a few months, bank the money, and quit. His thoughts turned to college—nothing specific, just an image of a large, manicured green lawn surrounded by brick buildings.

He flipped to his stomach, eyes closed, but again Seizer appeared like some goalie of sleep. Who was this squat patriarch? Was he a killer? Eddy's mind leapt to visions of conquistadors, charting backwards some unbroken history of hostile land grabs and deadly treasure hunts. He didn't know if a drug cartel of backwoods nobodies was closer in kind to the aggressors or the aggrieved, the bloody continuity of raider culture or the natural tendencies of victims fighting for survival. To be fair, havoc-wreaking was more or less a daily sport in Palm Bay, like football was for small Texas towns. And even if you chose not to participate, you at least knew some of the players, and everyone understood the game.

Seizer's words appeared to carry the weight of law; even Bird acted deferentially. The unglamorous garb and self-deprecating attitude failed to mask a truly authoritative presence. And even though Eddy knew bikers were prone to melodrama and sentimentality—Del Ray once said no story deserved recounting unless it included one of the Five G's: *glory, gold, God, guns,* or *gettin it on*—there was something peculiar about this guy.

By acknowledging his fear of Seizer, Eddy was able to relax a little, because it gave him an out—he hadn't said yes to anything. The old czar could remain everyone else's problem.

He wrapped a leg over Gin's. In the distance a motorcycle grunted to life. Eddy breathed deeply and felt himself getting lighter, first in his fingertips, then midsection, chest, until he felt his whole body floating above the bed. He sped up a little passing through the attic, out over his backyard, where he spotted the fire and police stations nearby, the Winn-Dixie off

Minton Road, up to where he could see the blue band of horizon set against a nascent black void, and higher still, into that deafening vacant potential. Twisting back around, he gazed upon the earth, accepted its smallness, happy to feel in control again, master of his own destiny.

Sleep snatched him just as he touched down on the surface of the moon.

For Duke, the heat of early summer invoked in large measure the noble beauty of North Carolina—from the high fruity sweetness of gardenias, to the piercing yet delicate calls of nested hatchlings, to the fresh, dappled grandeur of its forested foothills. A season of raw light and transient shadow, the tensile salvo of cicadas, when he would count the cricket chirps in the walls to guess the changing temperature.

A far fricking cry from this horseshit.

Florida heat clouded the lungs like pneumonia, threatening to murder you as you lugged around your body, sopping wet and unable to keep hydrated. At night you pounded cold beers to shake the feeling, then woke gasping with thirst. Even after months hauling furniture up and down stairs, he still wasn't used to it. His brother now slept with a dehumidifier, a droning machine Duke was convinced would one day mask Lisbon's gurgling death from sleep apnea.

Thankfully, the labor-intensive part of the job was coming to an end—he looked forward to driving with the truck's a/c on full blast.

Duke stood on the white beach of a small island, glancing out over a lake that was also a river. Lake Hell 'n Blazes—no bullshit, he'd looked it up online. Water the color of Lipton iced tea and the shorelines densely forested, with grassy archipelagos poking up here and there. No boats had passed by all morning, motor or otherwise. This was off-grid—wild with overgrowth and infested with gators and marine birds nesting inland. He'd spent the morning listening to a botanist run through what native species might best shroud the entrance from the views of local fishermen and water sports enthusiasts, as the main objective of constructing a secret lab out in the boonies was keeping it secret.

Behind Duke a project manager was trying to convince Seizer a custom-made ghillie tarp could easily camouflage a medium-sized structure or series of huts almost as well as a natural woodland canopy. Nearer the shore, spread out in a small clearing, a construction crew gathered around a city official wearing a hard hat. Duke recognized Jim Barns among the workers, the angry drunk that Gumby had cut up at Bird's party. The slashes under his eyes and up the chin were stitched, shiny, and bulging purple. Apparently Bird had promised the shriveled old avocado a job just to keep him quiet about the assault, which signaled Bird wasn't pulling bodies from his best lot.

The hard-hat official was currently crouched over a hole. Hunched about him, a circle of workers stared down in quiet contemplation, including Lisbon, hovering over his shoulder.

"Sad to say, but you got gopher tortoises," the official explained. "God knows how they ended up here. They don't swim."

"A gopher?" asked a mason in dirty jeans, some local dipshit.

"A tortoise!" barked Jim Barns. "Aint no fucking gopher."

"But he just said . . ."

"A gopher tortoise is a type of turtle," explained the official, experiencing the pangs of having bit off more than he could chew. "And these things, they're state protected. You can't just pick 'em up and move 'em when you want to build. There's a relocation program in place, with permits. You gotta pay a farmer to let you relocate the tortoise to their land. And once that land is claimed, it can't be used for anything else. At least until the tortoise moves on."

All the faces returned to the hole.

"How many holes, you figure?" asked Duke, walking back.

The official itched under his helmet. "Twenty-two, by my count. You could get lucky, there's sometimes just one tortoise, digging several holes. But then, you know, there could be babies."

"Babies?" asked the mason.

Jim Barns stared down the dipshit, ready to slug him.

Duke watched Lisbon suddenly rush toward a stand of palmettos. His brother was a curious chap, always scrounging around the dirt and underbrush, hopelessly awed by nature, and now he approached the group carrying a real whopper of a gopher tortoise, held out like some prized goose.

The crew gathered around to admire the creature. It resembled an unearthed stone, baked in mud and plated with pentagons on top and hexagons around. A stubby, cracked neck carried the ancient head slowly from one side to the other.

"What's the relocation fee?" asked Duke.

"Per animal?"

"Yessir."

The official creased his brow. "Eight hundred dollars each."

A shared gasp escaped the audience, punctuated by a whistle.

"Bullpucky," spit Barns.

"True as I'm standing here," said the official.

Duke turned back to the lake. The whole thing just deepened his mood. They were behind schedule on production, and every day brought new concessions: the state official was present because Seizer had promised Del Ray he'd do right by the island wildlife. To make matters worse, Bird hadn't even bothered to show up, because why fight a hangover? Half-wits and alcoholics and honestly, there already were too many bodies around—but somehow Seizer wasn't concerned. Yes, they'd all be blindfolded on the airboats, Duke understood, but still—the fewer outsiders who knew anything, the better. And this state official . . . this was maybe a guy who could be leaned on by the cops.

Whatever—it was his uncle's operation, and Duke's trust in Seizer's ability to make problems disappear was unimpeachable. Despite the setbacks, he had every faith they'd have Camp Sticks up and running by month's end.

Just then someone passed Duke on the right, and he glanced up to watch Jim Barns hobble by. In his grubby hands the brute carried the tortoise, stepping right off the beach and into the brown water, up to his knees, jeans and all, before dropping the creature *plop* with a splash. Then waded back, wholly unconcerned. "Aint worth a nickel now."

And there you have it, thought Duke. *This is the kind of people we're dealing with.*

And dammit, now he had to go calm down Lisbon, whose eyes were pearling with tears, having witnessed a murder. And someone — *by god jesus, was it true?* — someone had stolen his water bottle, which he'd left resting atop a very specific tree stump.

Just what the hell kind of place was this, exactly?

The phone stopped ringing in the kitchen and switched to the machine. Eddy quietly clicked the bedroom door closed as Del Ray's electrified voice crackled through the air.

Hey, it's me. Munching on something, agitated. *Listen, I know we were supposed to meet up all clandestine like, but seriously, that shit frustrates me. It keeps me sober, and I need a drink. I got a neighbor boy was supposed to come by and check in on things while I was away, but it don't look like he did, and now I have a skinny dog taken to eating rats and a paper clip of a bird here pissing bird blood. I'm liable to whip that bastard in this frame of mind, so I gotta get out of the house. I'm headed over to the Tit, so meet me there. Hope little miss jailbait is making you as happy as her mom made me.*

Eddy dressed quickly, careful not to wake Gin. The Tit was a bar off Sarno Road, a real dive. He hurried on his shoes, kissed Gin's forehead, and scribbled out a note on a coffee filter.

The drive took half an hour. Each parking slot out front was filled with a pickup truck save one, like a tooth knocked from a smile. Eddy was underage, but this place had a reputation for not carding. Still, it took a moment to build up the courage to walk in.

The bar was utterly dark, the windows blacked out. His eyes found a smoggy pair of Tiffany lamps hovering the pool tables in back, where jobless young men chalked sticks in silence. Those sidling the bar raised their heads to follow Eddy with the grave interest of fugitives or buzzards before relaxing back into their scheming and sports highlights. Eddy lured the barkeep over with a creased ten spot.

"You got any coffee?"

The barkeep considered this, throwing his ponytail over a shoulder. "We got beer that *looks* like coffee."

"Does it taste like coffee?"

"Nope. Tastes like beer."

Eddy took his pint to a far booth by the jukebox, crossing his arms to make his muscles look bigger. He didn't like day drinking, as it made him sleepy; beyond that, he worried about getting busted in some imaginary raid. As his eyes further adjusted, Eddy chanced furtive glances about the bar, but saw no one he knew and no Del Ray.

The front door swung open and two bikers fell through the boxed light, laughing and pushing each other into tables before settling at the bar.

Eddy pretended to be absorbed in the muted TV. Sordid lives of the wealthy, tales of wild abandon and botched celebrity. Next up, a correspondent standing outside a firebombed embassy; images of beheaded bodies dumped along the roadside of a mexican border town; a commercial where a donut mourned the absence of its center. Sometime over the previous year, public discourse had imploded into a vortex of desperation and fear not seen since 9/11. The economy had tanked and house values were plummeting — people were hurting. Confronted with myriad tribulations well beyond their control, some responded by erecting internal walls and going tribal, wedding their opinions to news sources pushing partisan agendas. Folks living month-to-month or completely underwater were fed the idea that someone, somewhere, was coming to steal their stuff, because in just under a year, a lot had gone missing. Outside their individual walls, prowling at all hours, came the whoops and hollers of tenacious enemies shouting that the villagers hadn't saved enough, hadn't read the fine print, had failed to protect their children. Some of the menacing voices even sounded like their own, full of loathing. For blame, the town preacher invoked godlessness, immigrants, racial strife, even the government itself, which was busy bailing out financial institutions by the billions. By day these villagers skulked in private, but by night they congregated and drank themselves into a frenzy, devising get-rich schemes and plotting paybacks, the threat of violence on their lips. Eventually they'd go home alone, nothing doing, each to pace their innermost cage like a tiger in a bombed-out zoo.

For example, Eddy's own mother, whose already fragile hopes were obliterated by the recession. Run down by the humiliation of unsuccessful job hunts and desperate to discover ways to feel important, she often threw herself at anything promising a quick door into something new. Eddy didn't blame her, but it was hard to watch—the drugs unearthed weaknesses he could not unsee.

He turned from the TV's negative energy and brought out a drawing pen, pulling over a napkin. He felt a nice buzz coming on and gave himself over to it.

As a boy, Eddy could draw anything he saw—it was his one true talent, aside from replicating machine-gun fire with his tongue. He'd filled shoeboxes with sketches of dragons and mutant dolphins and armored vehicles parachuting into trippy, alien landscapes. Bird saw promise in his portfolio, consisting of one such shoebox, but Eddy still had a lot to learn, like basic shading techniques. So Bird laid out the iconographic fundamentals— fonts, skulls, webs, roses, breasts, butterflies, geckos, tribals—which Eddy first studied in secret, hiding it from his mother, and later openly, when Bird insisted she know about his plans. *If it keeps him from selling crack like the kid down the block, I'm fine with whatever*, she said. After his mother was hospitalized for depression and substance abuse, Bird let Eddy lug a sleeping bag into the parlor and stay on rent-free. Eddy took the bus to school with Cueball and helped Charlotte with dinners. His mother was discharged, but almost immediately rehospitalized, and upon her second release, hooked up with her NASA-daddy and moved out, abandoning her clothes and everything else from her past, it seemed. Eddy moved back home, but never forgot the charity of his host family.

The boar he'd drawn on the napkin was similar to the one from the party, save for its eyes, which were human. Faceless men stood over the beast, plunging sharp sticks into its open belly. His former art teacher would have been pleased, a man who praised his work in class, and for graduation, presented him with a box full of graphic novels. The box still rested on a high shelf in Eddy's closet. It wasn't that he wasn't interested in such stories, but here again was someone else's idea of his own potentiality—an unwelcome burden teeming with expectations and the possibility of failure.

In the restroom, Eddy read a newspaper tacked to the wall. His country seemed to be falling apart. Patriots and terrorists, at times indistinguishable. Why did politics always read like gang warfare?

From outside came the sounds of a scuffle, which Eddy figured to be a gentlemanly bet gone sour at the tables. He took his time and washed his hands.

Stepping out, he found Del Ray pinned to the ground, a heavyset biker choking him from behind with a pool stick.

The pool sharks had emptied out the back and the barkeep held up a phone but hadn't dialed. Eddy kept to the stools, certain he wanted no part in this, but lacking options. The scrawnier biker noticed him approaching and moved to intercept, so Eddy swept a mug from the bar, aiming for skull. A clean miss, and his lip ruptured with an uppercut, sending him feeble-legged into a table. A second tag to the jaw dropped him, and there Eddy lay, grains from the unswept floor embedded in his cheek. The biker's hands fumbled over his body, positioning the softest parts. A boot caught his stomach and Eddy retched. Balled up, he turned over, hoping the pressure in his chest was only air looking to escape. When his head snapped back, he was sure he was dead.

"Mind your fucking business!"

Which he did from then on. The men took turns pulping Del Ray, ceasing only to bark out ready-made lines about owing and collecting. When their boots finally squeaked out the entrance, the door extinguishing the liquid light, Eddy rolled back around to watch Del Ray elbow himself up to a chair, cupping his ribs.

The pool players returned to gawk. One stepped over to help, but Del Ray spit blood on his shirt. The barkeep asked if he should call the cops.

"Why bother now, Jeff?" shot Del Ray. "I know you got a fuckin pistol back there!"

Del Ray looked ragged and whiskey-worn, but his eyes were quick. A stroke of blood stained his smile. "One peckerwood to another," he said, bending over Eddy, "you don't make much of a fighter."

"I can't breathe," whispered Eddy.

Del Ray pushed on different body parts. "You'll be okay. Sit up now. There you go. You've earned some bruises, is all. If it's any consolation, you may have won that one. Way he was limping, that's a broken toe."

The barkeep snapped at them to leave and Del Ray responded by whipping a chair toward the pool tables. He stirred Eddy to his feet and hugged him under an arm and walked him out.

The day's brightness stole the world from sight as the gravel crinkled nauseatingly underfoot. They climbed into Del Ray's dilapidated pickup and Del got a cigarette going and slid back painfully against the door for a better view.

"My god, Wildeboar. People all over trying to teach me the same lesson."

Eddy's busted lip was swelling to a ripe cherry. He tingled bone-wise and his jaw felt out of joint. "Were those friends of Mickey's?"

"Mickey?"

"I heard you two got into it."

"Shit. A flea's got balls enough to make that half-wit jealous. I had to swing first just to keep myself interested. Naw, they were just a couple friends of mine."

"Didn't seem too friendly."

"To let me live this long, they might just be family. It's a misunderstanding, really. They misunderstood I had their money, and I misunderstood its slipperiness. In the meantime we negotiate blood. But no worries, I'm set to pay off all my debts soon enough." His face wrenched in pain as he adjusted in his seat. "Fucking pongos."

"What?"

"Pongos," said Del Ray. "Apes. Orangutans. Sometimes when I look around I don't see people anymore, I see apes. Walking and talking, getting their hair trimmed at the barber's . . . kicking my ass. That's when I get my pongo-vision." He pointed two fingers at his eyes, then away. "When I see mankind for what it truly is . . . beasts set loose in the garden."

"I hear you," said Eddy. "I get that too, kinda."

"You do, huh?" said Del Ray. "Well then, it's official. I'm no longer ahead of my time."

After discussing plans, Eddy gingerly crept back into his blue VW Bug. He followed Del Ray down Apollo Boulevard, then Babcock, cradling his injuries, the humidity turning his car into a Crock-Pot of stale cigarettes and human grease. After Malabar they entered a lush stretch of forested ranch-land, dirt roads festering with dead cars and collapsing trailers, many of which quit inhabitants altogether. Soon they were crossing a rickety iron and wood bridge over sulfur water, where they were greeted by a thin-featured Doberman that trotted up alongside Eddy's car, leaping at the window.

"Down, Zippo!" Del Ray hollered back.

They jumbled along a mud trail past a tiny country pond as birds flashed and skittered over a yard of weed flowers and wild mushrooms. A laundry line strung between oaks hid the face of a greeny clapboard shack collapsing in on itself. Zippo bounded over as the truck rattled to a halt. Del and Eddy got out and ducked under the clothesline to reach an uneven, moldy porch gnarled by vegetation. A sleek black Harley rested under a tarp lean-to at-tached to the structure's side.

"Doesn't drain so well these parts," said Del Ray, explaining the cinder-block stilts at the house's corners. "Family of squatters lived here until I tracked down the owner in Apalachicola and bought it out from under them."

The interior, though, occupied an altogether different era, furnished ceiling to floor with antiques: an unmarked cherrywood desk, fading gilded mirrors, bejeweled lamps, a rug of turkish labor, smaller items of stained wood with beveled glass and pearling. Del Ray made particular mention of a Louis XV walnut nightstand with a marble top, saying, "That's one of two pieces I'm keeping. Got all of it from an estate sale."

The small room smelled of wet earth and dog. The windows were caulked shut against bugs, save for one befit with an a/c unit and another with blue-tinted jalousies. A typewriter Del Ray used for articles rested atop an ancient steamer chest that doubled as a coffee table. Eddy collapsed onto a musty couch of indeterminable fabric, holding his pummeled jaw. Zippo, he was glad to discover, wasn't a lapdog.

Del Ray returned from the kitchen with bags of frozen peas. "Put that against your face," he said, pressing one to his ribs. "How you like my setup? Got two bedrooms in back, despite the size."

Eddy nodded. "You collect this stuff to sell?"

"Nope. Objects aren't ethical in nature, but their commodification is, the buying and selling, and frankly I'm already struggling enough to justify some, shall we say, *contradictory* principles. Better I stick with redistribution, storing these items until such time they need to be relocated," Del Ray grinned, "by you, perhaps."

"Is this about the moving business?"

Del Ray raised his hands. "Don't play dumb, Ed. It's the mark of an amateur to lie at inappropriate times. I already know Cueball blabbed about the shipments."

Eddy reined in his surprise. "You bugged his truck."

"What, bugged his . . . ? This aint Homeland Security, son, we aint that sophisticated. No, Cueball had a row with his old man. Words were said. I can't say I blame the kid, it's a lot to get thrown at you all at once. In any case, here's the deal: to understand this new enterprise, you gotta think long-term. Any ditch-digging fucknugget can haul furniture, but not everybody can be trusted with a grandfather clock full of our new mojo medicine."

Here Del Ray noted a tall brass and mahogany-hooded specimen standing stalwart in the corner.

"Long and short of it, bud, is that your group of friends constitutes a close-knit society, built on loyalty and trust. Or better put, imagine you're a minor start-up being contracted to provide a highly secretive, highly lucrative service for a major firm. Yeah? This make sense? Okay, say you're playing *World of Warcraft*, right, and you've got your jolly old gang of lunatics—"

"You want us because we're less likely to turn on each other. Or you."

Del Ray snapped his fingers. "Exactly. And that's the kind of no-bullshit attitude I'll expect from you working under me. I need to know you're a safe bet, Ed, so I don't wake up one morning with my white ass in handcuffs or my throat cut."

"I get it," said Eddy. "Can I think it over? I would never say anything to anyone, anyway . . . you know that, right? But I might need some time to think about it."

"Absolutely," said Del Ray, and Eddy found in his expression what he hoped was true understanding. "Two weeks work?"

"Sure, yeah. I appreciate it."

"I'm hungry, you hungry?"

"I could eat."

Del Ray disappeared into the bedroom and returned with two bamboo cane poles.

"Until we sell our first batch of goodies, we still po' folks 'roun he-ya."

They used long-fingered branches to drag the algae off the pond and sat together baiting their hooks with refrigerated shrimp parts. The pair fished without talking, occasionally skipping small bream like river stones across the pond's black surface, where they erupted on the bank in a vitus dance. Del Ray gutted and filleted their catch and threw the innards to his dog.

"Faithful companion in misery," he said, petting Zippo. "Runt I saved from a neighbor, used to whip them as pups. One of the meaner bastards got loose from its cage, ripped a hole in the bastard's throat. Cops were taking the whole litter up to the injections, but they let me keep her on account of her size. She gets a little gitchy from time to time, but she'd take a bullet for me in a heartbeat." Zippo nosed his hand. "Back atcha, girl," he said, pulling her scruff.

Del Ray carried the fish fillets inside as Eddy wandered the tufted grasses, contemplating his options. The possibility of jail time worried him, as did letting Bird down. Nor was he comfortable with Cueball driving alone. If he declined, the loss of pay would be devastating. No moving job, no tattooing. Poverty, he knew, was an all-consuming disease, a withering ailment; in its grips, it was hard to think of anything else. He wished things could go back to normal, and imagined approaching Bird with less dangerous money-making schemes, like a phone app for a bikers-only dating site. But Bird was neither tech savvy nor particularly hip to social trends, and drugs never went out of style.

You still have a choice, he told himself. *You can find another job.*

There was always roofing. Knuckle-scraping, bust-ass work, and deeply mind-numbing. Rise to coffee at 4 a.m., arrive on-site by 5:30 alongside a band of shirtless men—yellow-eyed black dudes, mexican cousins, long-haired white guys red as lobsters. Climb the ladder in the cool of dawn and by noon you're broiling beneath the glare of an unforgiving star. He'd roofed the previous summer, but vowed never again, after a meth head shit himself and climbed into a wheelbarrow, weeping openly before a chorus of jeering coworkers.

There was a reason why, at eighteen, his mailbox choked with offers of high-yield credit cards, and why the military recruiters called out to him from across the mall. Here was another young body, a bounty of cheap labor, to be bundled and swapped like a bond. Able to fight a war but not sip whiskey.

Skipping town was still an option; Palm Bay really was a joke. But even leaving required money. It also occurred to him that if he didn't join up, Jesse and Cueball would make new friends inside the organization, pushing him to the fringe, a weekend acquaintance who smiled idiotically at their in-jokes. Boredom, that generous negation, would wear down his future self like a tooth drill.

The portentous sound of wind chimes brought him back. He found Del Ray on the porch, two plates of food by his side, keeping Zippo at bay with a licked hand.

They drank sun tea from a milk jug and peeled the fragile bones from fillets breaded and fried with slices of nectarine. Del Ray's willingness to accept all manner of inquiry made the awkward situation palatable—though Eddy sensed that once among the ranks, he'd be afforded less patience. Truth be told, the dangerous tint of their conversation was even a little fun.

"So where's the drugs come from?" Eddy asked.

"Can you be trusted?" asked Del Ray, sliding a bone from between his teeth.

"I'm here. I don't know how else to prove I won't talk."

This seemed to satisfy the biker. "We make it ourselves. Fairly complex process, but we got the right people and primo ingredients. Designer drugs are the future. Brew it in the swamps, ship it up the highways and byways."

"What's in it?"

"Fairy dust and swamp magic."

"You ever try it? Any weird side effects?"

"Hm, well. It's like slamming Red Bulls and vodka while on MDMA. You sorta tilt in and out of different experiences. Makes you feel like you can just party forever. The crash, is, uh, something fierce, but not a deal-breaker. It carries a little soft-dick blues, from what I hear, but that's maybe rare. I was fine."

"Can other people make it?"

Del smiled. "Right on. Well, folks could brew it at home, I guess, with the right ingredients, but nobody's making it in bulk. And we're way ahead of the game. What's on the market is ours. Swear to god the production labs are like walking into an open-air factory. Deep woods, super-isolated. We have a storage unit in town, but the chemicals are highly volatile, and the labs stink to high heaven of ammonia. Unmistakable odor, too risky."

To dissipate the gravity of the subject matter, or engage with it a different way, Del Ray began naming off the varieties of palm trees in his yard — some native, some from a previous owner's shoddy attempt at landscaping. He began with a high-necked species with fanning fronds and a barbed trunk; moved on to a drooping lion's mane, which he called a *petticoat*; then to a towering brown rocket with a slick green capsule; another with fronds as luxuriant as infant's hair; and finally one that could pass as the world's largest pineapple.

"Sabal, Washingtonia, Cuban Royal, Foxtail, Bottle, respectively," said Del Ray.

"Yep," said Eddy.

"Don't fucking yep me. Experience the world! Smell it, let it sit on your tongue! By learning the names, you give them meaning. The palm is not inherently purposeful, or beautiful. It is made beautiful and purposeful by you, the viewer, and in viewing, makes you purposeful and beautiful to yourself. Experiencing nature is a way to make meaning, and will lead to a more fulfilling life. My question for you is, are you experiencing the world in a way that is fulfilling?"

Eddy couldn't say. Del was always digging little pits in his mind and filling them with nuggets of hippie wisdom.

"Which one you like best?"

Eddy considered it. "The Bottle."

"Why?"

"It has a . . . it feels complete. It has a sort of squat symmetry."

"Goddamn," chortled Del Ray, regarding the plant. "I totally feel that. You think you know a person. You're a poet."

Eddy smiled, despite himself.

"Now, if you sign on, you gotta get the tattoo, like Cueball."

"I designed it, you know."

"I do know. Bet you feel like a rock star." Del Ray opened his arms to the woodland amphitheater. "The palm tree is a symbol of your relevance, reminding you of who you are and where you're from. This will be a tribe of blood brothers. And I'll say this once, Ed, with zero levity—nobody can know who we are. If anything gets discussed outside the group, the repercussions will be . . . substantial. Not to scare you, but you understand. We're all in this together. Along with my other duties as Fixer, I'll assume command of the drivers. But I don't get the tat. That's you boys' special something."

"What about Bird and everyone?"

"Well, that's privileged information."

But Eddy needed more. "I mean this with all due respect, Del. I trust you and Bird, obviously, but I don't know, for example, Mickey. I just gave the dude a tat. How am I supposed to make an informed decision—"

"I get it," said Del Ray, licking a joint he was rolling. "You have your mom to think about."

The context of their conversation suddenly expanded into an uncomfortable space; the mention of his mother didn't feel like a threat, exactly, but rocked Eddy back a little.

"I appreciate you needing to make a fair assessment. And nobody's trying to bust up any friendships," Del promised, handing the joint for Eddy to light. "Mickey'll be on the road, drumming up distributors. Solid worker, even if he is a prick. Bird will be the Interlocutor, which is just a fancy word for 'underboss'—the second-to-final judgment, where all conversations end. Seizer will only be available to the big boys. Even in that future I believe we'll make possible together, with each of the core members controlling their own franchise, Bird and Seizer will not be spoken of. For all intents and purposes, they do not exist."

"And Gumby?"

"Gumby's never existed. I don't even think he was born. He was engineered."

"But he's part of it, right?" asked Eddy, recalling the jubilance expressed by the hit man after slicing open Jim Barns. "What'll he be doing?"

"Unspeakables. And we'll honor that by not speaking of them. He's a freelance hire, his own animal. No tying that one down."

"A palm tree," said Eddy. "Isn't that a bit cheesy?"

"What's more Florida than a palm tree?"

"I don't know. Citrus?"

That killed Del Ray. "You want a fucking kumquat on your arm forever?"

Eddy glanced at the blue veins of his wrist, the soul spot. To some old-timers, this area was considered sacred, a place reserved for one's most intimate expressions. Eddy looked into the future and saw an army of kids marked with his design. A wincing pain in his jaw reminded him violence had found him already. "You got any more whiskey?"

They drank and watched the July sun chalk bands of color over the tree line as Del Ray spoke of sacrifice. His new position had forced him to quit writing magazine articles and snapping photos as he worked to help get their start-up off the ground.

"Some odd years of this and we're free to do whatever, become full-time beach bums, rappers, directors of short films, anything. Being a details-oriented kind of guy, just know that money-wise it'll be a windfall for all involved. Bird mentioned you're worried about your mom's mortgage? Well that worry disappears. And hey, if this don't fit into your moral framework, we shake hands and that's that. Truly, no hard feelings."

But then Del added that if Eddy refused the job, he'd lose the use of Bird's parlor, and the tattooing equipment.

"We'll have too many club people around," he said. "I know it stings, but understand, the rest of us are in this thing whole hog. Everything needs to be kept in-house, for security purposes. If you say no, Bird can't rightfully keep you in a position that amounts to you saying yes, as you'd be aware of goings-on. I mean, you could be arrested as an accessory. Nor could he ask those who've signed on to trust someone who hadn't. *Whole hog.*"

Eddy's stomach lurched; Del Ray had just effectively rendered him unemployed. He quickly calculated how long his savings could last, arriving at three months.

"Do you trust Seizer?" he spoke to the ground.

"It's not a matter of trust: I'm confident he can't *not* do this, and neither can I. We both need this to work. So yes, absolutely." Del Ray stretched out and stole the roach back. "I'm no Army recruiter, Ed. I won't lie and say it's for everyone. But if you want a solid income that's not laying drywall or fitting tresses, well. This is a onetime offer. Regardless, I'll be pulling Jesse aside, giving him the same pitch. You'd be doing me a favor if you didn't mention any of this to him."

"Of course," Eddy said. "Can I ask one more thing?"

"Shoot."

"If so many people are involved, how can you trust nobody will talk?"

"Only the top brass knows who's in my crew. We'll remain somewhat decentralized and anonymous. We hire people to hire people until no one knows who they're working for. You have my word your name will never appear in any ledger."

He punched Eddy's knee.

"Now, c'mon, let's jet. I've been busting my ass on this project and lost my best girl in the process. Need to do a little poking around in someone's no-no joint, if you get me. Hop on my bike, do a little zoom-zoom. A little sniff-da-dee-doo-dah. How's that wild child treating you?"

"Gin? I really like her."

"Well," said Del Ray, "we all got our weaknesses."

Cueball's estimation of the club skyrocketed after he was gifted a black '72 Chevy Nova pumped full of muscle, its 350 block engine bored to a 383 stroker—bad on gas, but undeniably badass. All white leather and a pair of fuzzy dice strung from the rearview. The plan was to coast behind the Twins' moving van, and if there was any trouble, Cueball would red-herring the cops by swerving between lanes or gunning it past a hundred, forcing a chase. The Nova was his to keep, company perk, but Cueball soon had the car outfitted with subwoofers and painted a shiny Hazzard orange, lighting the underside with purple fluorescent tubes. Eddy wondered if it wasn't some last gasp, a final retaliation against his father and the inevitable, but that didn't matter, as a few nights later Seizer had two men yank off the tubes and bash out the front window, clipping the dangling dice from their strings, a metaphorical neutering lost on no one. Only then did Cueball realize what Seizer meant when he'd said: *Your job's to remain inconspicuous until need be.*

"They made me pay for the glass," Cueball complained as he steered. "Wiped out my savings."

"You're just lucky it was the car that took the beating," Eddy replied.

"Dad said Seizer wasn't mad, just making a point," pouted Cueball. He pet the dashboard. "Who's my baby girl? Creepy old man hurt you? Shit, I'm tapped till that first paycheck. Now I *need* to work. At least they didn't make me repaint it."

"So now you're all gung ho?" asked Eddy. "They give you a shiny new toy and you do your little monkey dance?"

"Dude," said Cueball. "I didn't fucking ask for this. But like it or not, I'm in it up to here. It's my family, man. Maybe things'll change, but till then, what . . . I should just stay pissed off all the time? It's pointless." He smacked the dice restrung to the rearview. "Sometimes you gotta run with the bulls."

After stopping for breakfast tacos, Cueball coasted to an abandoned library sporting a rickety wood wharf and an unbeatable view of the sil-ver river and alabaster causeway. As Eddy finished his breakfast, Cueball skipped clamshells at a rotting houseboat delivered by storms onto the mossy shoals. As tranquil as it was—cool breeze and wavelets batwinging against the rocks—Eddy still felt restless. The movers had been informed their old jobs were ending the following week.

"Your dad say how much you'd be making?"

"It's all up to the marketplace," said Cueball. The words foreign, some-one else's words. "But maybe enough for me to put a down payment on a house before the year's out."

"Really? A *house?*" Eddy tried imagining what sort of house Cueball was talking about—a twenty-thousand-dollar Sherwood Park foreclosure or a three-hundred-grand Melbourne Beach deal, front yard painted with exotic plants.

"Jesse's on board, by the way," said Cueball. "Took him all of five min-utes to decide. Apparently his mom's car died again, and he'd just applied to the Publix off Babcock."

Eddy wasn't surprised. "If you get caught, they'll try you as adults."

"Can't jail what you can't catch," quipped Cueball, massaging his chest.

"I don't get how you're excited about this."

Cueball pointed. "Did you see my new ride? Listen, man, if I'm stuck doing this, I'm gonna try to enjoy it. Dad laid out the details, and the truth is, it's a fucking cakewalk. Almost no furniture lifting—it's ninety-nine percent driving. I know there's risks. And I'll be honest, I'd feel a helluva lot better with you riding shotgun."

Eddy imagined Bird selling the job to his son, adding a glossy shine to the whole affair. "Where's the drop-offs?"

"Different places up the coast, small towns outside larger cities. Orlando, Jacksonville, Savannah, Winston-Salem, Richmond, to start with. But only one stop per trip, and we keep changing routes. With legit paperwork—invoices, contracts. We'll have a meeting."

Eddy made a jerk-off motion. Cueball smiled and skipped a shell off the river's surface.

"So how do we feel about the Twins?" asked Eddy, who despite reservations still liked the brothers. "Maybe we let it go? Invite them out to Jesse's for some *Assassin's Creed?*"

"Fuck them basic-ass bitches," said Cueball. "They lied to my face, multiple times. I'll work with them, but we're not hanging out."

"Sounds like they didn't have much of a choice, either."

Cueball let both eyes go lazy. "I 'on't fucking care."

They were driving. Eddy toked a joint as Cueball drummed the steering wheel, scanning the crumbling houses and forest acres for anomalies and signs of bucolic horror. Jesse lived in the southernmost part of Palm Bay—podunk in the harshest sense. The pinewoods suffered a plague of lunatic children, reared on listless aggression and apt to wreak havoc on their families, each other, and the earth's more innocent creatures, as illustrated by the squirrel carcass nailed to a telephone pole as the asphalt dipped to muddy potholes.

They found Jesse working on his motorcycle in his mother's garage, surrounded by empty beer bottles. His greasy shirt off and over his shoulder, the glasses he wore on occasion smudged at the edges. He greeted them by patting his big brown belly. "You guys are *not* gonna believe this. Dude. Walk with me out back."

Rounding the garage, they followed a perforated garden hose fanning rust-colored water over the stucco.

In back they found Draco, Jesse's enormously muscular and mustachioed younger brother, relaxing in a lawn chair, hose in hand, casually squirting down a man lying unconscious in a seeping crater of mud. The kitchen refrigerator, powered by extension cord, had been dragged outside and its contents emptied to the back lawn. Eddy recognized the mud kid, a giant italian with a lightning stroke of cleft palate, from the pizza parlor where Draco worked.

"These animals came home absolutely obliterated this morning, stomping through the house," Jesse explained, "then dragged the fridge out back. Then this savage started pissing himself and just *collapsed*. Draco's been trying to clean him up since."

At his name's mention, Draco looked up, delighted to find an audience. His pupils were cartoonishly tragic balloons. "Bless my stars," cooed Draco, his hands suddenly alive in the air. "To what do I owe this fantabulous honor?"

It was either shrooms or LSD. Eddy approached, but stopped short at the sight of groin hair.

"Holy hell! Where's your clothes, you fucking scuzz?"

Draco's hands flew to his face. "Oh my goodness!" he cried. "What has happened to my clothes?"

Nobody could ever quite discern if Draco was trolling or participating in an altogether different reality. He used to be a polymath and a history buff until the day he stuffed two sheets of acid into his mouth on a dare, thereby mutating his brain and shifting his personality into one that vacillated between uncomfortable giggling and uttered lines of hypnotic spoken-word poetry.

Jesse's eyebrows did all the work. "Get this," he said in hushed tones. "These guys went shrooming yesterday, filled a bucket, I'm not kidding a pickle bucket full of shrooms, boiled them up, and were drinking like gallons of the tea last night. Then they drive over to this dude's uncle's bar at like four in the morning, broke in with crowbars, and stole . . . just a shitload. Here, check it out."

Jesse yanked open the refrigerator door. Inside were beer bottles stacked floor to ceiling, two feet deep. Cueball cursed in disbelief. Then, as the kicker, Jesse swung open the top freezer. Inside was a hairy black mass Eddy's mind refused to address.

"It's his uncle's guard dog!" said Jesse, hopping with excitement. "Draco whacked it with the crowbar . . . and DROVE HOME WITH IT!"

Another thing about Draco: he once used a pair of pliers to yank out a thumbnail he'd squashed with a hammer. For this and other reasons, nobody hung out with him alone, as only Jesse could defuse, with a brother's knowing care, whatever appalling notions Draco hoped to carve into reality.

Back in the garage, Jesse drew an elaborate picture of his motorcycle's combustion process.

"Dope ride," said Eddy.

"Rebuilt the engine from scratch," said Jesse. "It's crazy how these little parts have to work perfectly together for it to run smooth. Like eyeballs, or something."

"Like the club," said Cueball.

"*Like the club*," Eddy mocked, lightly kissing his own tattoo-less wrist. "I'm so special. Poppa Bird just loves his special little boys."

Cueball sprayed a mouthload of beer over Eddy's shirt and soon they were wrestling. It ended with Cueball in a half nelson. "Get off!" he shouted, hopping away and rubbing his neck. "My mole's bleeding. What if I can't work now? I aint got insurance."

"Aww, my little angel," said Jesse, rubbing a nipple. "Mama make it better."

"Eat shit."

"They say what you'll be doing?" huffed Eddy, out of breath.

Jesse closed the door to the kitchen, in case his mother woke from her nap. "Del Ray thinks I'll be at the camps. Not mixing chemicals, but like, keeping track of inventory."

"Sounds like glorified stock boy to me," said Cueball.

"Don't be a prick. They gave me a small advance so I could buy a new bike, but I'm just gonna fix this puppy up and buy Mom a new car. What about you fools?"

"Shipping. I'll be driving," said Cueball. "This here's my sidekick, maybe."

"Don't make it sound like you'd be in charge," said Eddy. "I haven't made up my mind yet."

Jesse turned over Cueball's wrist. "That's a mondo slick fucking design, my man. I can't wait to get mine. Del helped me come up with some shit to tell my mom, if she asks. It's fucking lit, get this: the palm tree represents an assertion of my filipino heritage, while also signaling my respect for the culture in which I've been raised. How awesome is that?"

"Sheesh," said Eddy. "What happens when she sees it on us?"

"No sweat. I'll say you're a couple rednecks that saw a brown man doing something cool and copied it."

The boys helped bag the spoiled food in the yard and drag the refrigerator back inside while Jesse woke up the italian, who abruptly and without speaking disappeared into the woods, the frozen dog tucked under an arm. In an effort to preserve his mother's sanity, Jesse convinced Draco to leave the house and take them hood-surfing.

Until a week ago, Draco had owned a long, black Cadillac Eldorado—his sixth. That car was now toast. Once a month, he'd hunt down a cheap, busted Caddy to fix up: new belts, new starter, whatever it took to run. But selling wasn't his ambition. Instead, he'd drive the cars out to the woods and slam them into trees, or float them into lakes—abandoning them, often in flames. The Caddy hoods, however, were saved for a sport, one that required use of the only ride he never demolished, an old Chevy truck.

The "back forty" began at the end of Garvey Road, a hundred square miles of nowhere. A long, well-traveled trail ending at a wide clearing.

With the truck still doing 10 mph, Draco leapt from the driver's seat, abandoning his crew. Jesse cursed loudly and stabbed his foot at the brake, sending Eddy and Cueball, resting in back, into the cab wall.

Draco seemed oblivious, watching the truck slide to a stop, then popped the gate to retrieve the Cadillac hood. Flipped smooth-side down, he'd welded bicycle handlebars to its front, leaving enough space for sitting. He began tying the bike handlebars to the truck's hitch ball with nylon rope until his fingers became entangled and left him mesmerized, forcing Jesse to intervene.

A round of rock-paper-scissors won Eddy the first ride. He positioned himself cross-legged on the Cadillac hood, gripping the handlebars as the truck's exhaust sputtered in his face.

Jesse and Cueball piled in back to watch.

Death metal exploded from the speakers, rattling the truck and pumping into the countryside. Draco's face appeared in the side mirror, eyebrows raised. *Ready?*

"Go! Go! Go!" Eddy shouted.

The engine roared, tires spun up sand, and the makeshift sled leapt instantly beyond Eddy's control. He was swung once around the clearing before the truck lurched right and darted into the woods.

Riding the bare back of adrenaline, Eddy tightened his grip and leaned into the curves as Draco switched trails without braking, slapping him through palmettos and over dusty banks. Whenever the curved hood kicked a tree root and caught air, the butterflies arrived. Only then to be slammed back to earth and jerked across a waxy slippage of pine needles.

Eddy felt a transformation occurring within—a freeing of his nature—and gave over to it. He felt wholly alive, wholly himself, the blood pounding in his ears. It was exhilarating. In the monastery of his heart, he was purified, or why else would this wind embrace him? Why else would the sugar sand spit, or the wiregrass catch at his arms, but in envy? He was a simple being, good-hearted and easy-natured, dangled too long at the end of some unseen rope. What were these voices shouting his holy name? Could they see his true self? Could they tell he was capable of anything?

The truck flew from the woods onto a forgotten street of macadam, sparks fanning in wake. If Eddy slipped off, the road would skin him alive. A few overgrown lots sported paved foundations without houses, properties of a boondoggle scheme that duped investors out of their down payments. Here was life's analog, this incomplete city of ruins.

Faster!

He was already out there, coursing the nation's highways. The morning sun rose over green mountains and collapsed into a cool night smelling of diesel fuel and skunk, red lights wavering on a wet, wide road. The camaraderie and laughter—all very present, a world Eddy eagerly wished to consume. Not just another body sent up a ladder, days measured out in burger wrappers and beer caps. As the sentiment swelled, the wind pulled tears from his eyes.

Approaching a small pond, the truck suddenly cut hard at the bank, whipping Eddy out over the water, where he fanned up a high spray and screamed in delight. Shouts told him to hold on as the truck bounded across the road again and raced him up and over and back into the woods.

Drug running wasn't anything special. He'd bank the money and quit after a year. Take art classes and finally read all those graphic novels. The future immediately clarified by these simple decisions.

When the truck hit a hard patch of sand, Eddy felt the earth vibrate up through his knuckles. Skidding out, a decision had to be made: jump or hold on. Brave the razorgrass in a controlled tumble or hang on and hope things steadied.

Do it!

Choose!

But Eddy waited too long, and the choice was made for him. The sled caught a divot and suddenly he was airborne. Then sliding, skin burning off, a wet wound slickened by weeds and dirt.

He was tumbling.

The truck careened to a stop and everyone leapt out. Cueball ran back and gently raised his best friend to sitting. Jesse was shouting, elated, as Draco giggled far beyond what was reasonable. Dazed, Eddy eased himself to standing, wiping blood on his grass-stained pants.

"That must've hurt like a motherfucker," said Cueball.

"Batter's up, assholes," said Eddy, toking the joint Jesse handed him.

Everyone but Draco rode the hood, and everyone was tossed. Later they took turns elaborating upon the depth of their experience—that one curve, the tree that might have killed them, how everything pulsed in slow motion. Eddy couldn't describe his own ordeal, and maybe it wasn't meant to be shared. Uttering the word *spiritual* wasn't something they'd ever let him live down.

The crew was hungry, so they dropped off a tired Draco and took the Nova up to the Crab Shack in Eau Gallie, where a woman Jesse was sleeping with shared her worker discount. Under an outdoor umbrella, Eddy dipped his crabmeat in butter and watched a group of young boys in trunks leap into an inlet's brackish-brown water from an old train trestle. The trains, he knew, used to transport sugarcane rum up from the Keys during Prohibition, giving the moving business some historical perspective.

Still, he was afraid to take the leap himself. That gusto he'd felt riding the hood had all but vanished. God, it was like he had no faith in himself.

Next up was a coffee run in Downtown Melbourne, where the tourists were out in full force. Khakis and stretched polos clogged the cigar shop, while a gentry of unbalanced women in wide-based espadrilles perused various shops of an arcade where Al Capone once shot a game of pool, with a gold plaque that said so. It felt awful, having the fancy french café packed with snowbirds voicing their petty culinary frustrations with the staff, while across the street at Meg O'Malley's local patrons spent their unemployment checks on eighteen-cent Parliament bean soup and two-for-one beers, searching for a bottom. Had any of the vacationers marched through the arcade's rear exit, they'd find day laborers and busboys hurling dice for food stamps—for beneath the urbane lure of riverside shopping was the unmitigated reality of people struggling. It was as if the world was patterned for loss. No, not everyone could afford taking off a day to bring the kids to Kennedy Space Center, or blow a small fortune at Disney or Universal Studios, enjoying Orlando's monopoly on escapism. Eddy didn't know what he wanted from these people, exactly, but it had something to do with paying attention, with *respect*. An acknowledgment of what they were ignoring. Above all, he believed that if he had their kind of money, he'd do things differently. Tip big. Help the homeless. Not just be some giant oxygen-sucking fuckwad.

Heading out, they passed Big Mike's tattoo shop. If Eddy didn't sign up for the club, he'd scope out Big Mike's for a job, even though he feared they'd start him off as an assistant or some bullshit, lacking "legit" experience. Gannett was also hiring, he'd heard, but for the graveyard shift, and who wanted to stack USA *Today* newspapers till sunrise?

In the 7-Eleven parking lot Eddy answered a text from Gin asking if he'd eaten. He was still out with the guys, but maybe tomorrow they could stay in and make spaghetti and watch a movie. He could still afford that much, at least.

"What kinda pay you looking at?" he asked Jesse, who was scrolling through his phone in the back seat.

"Uh, they told me not to say. Think maybe I'm getting paid a little more for having, like, *experience*. I think they respect the time I spent in juvie. I'm a professional."

"Professional fuckup," said Eddy, popping another ibuprofen from a bottle in the glove box and blowing on his sticky elbow wound. His jaw still ached from the bar fight, but the bruising was almost gone. "I wonder if the Twins will make more than everyone else. I bet Cueball will."

"Totes," said Jesse. "You and me, brother, we're gonna have to prove ourselves if we wanna climb that ladder. We gotta hit the street hard. Put in the time, make Seizer that cash. Show we can be trusted with more responsibility."

Clearly this was what Seizer was after: young men with nerve and foggy futures. They were easy to spot: just head to whatever part of town was glutted with pawnshops and Mormon missionaries scouting the neighborhood in monochromatic pairs. Yet understanding how the world operated didn't necessarily make one immune to its influences, Eddy knew. Beyond being reliable, Jesse was also aspirational, had that drive and confidence. He'd go in *whole hog*, like Del Ray wanted.

Cueball hopped back in the Nova, throwing a can of chew at Jesse and a pack of Camels at Eddy. He paused at Eddy's smirk. "What's that look?"

"I'm in," said Eddy.

"Yeah?" asked Cueball, hopping to his knees.

Jesse was already crawling over the back seat.

"You sure?"

"Fuck yeah."

"Oh shit!" Cueball yelled, absolutely ecstatic.

"Hells fucking yeah!" chimed Jesse, extending his midsection between the seats. "Rub my belly! Rub the Buddha for good luck!"

Eddy rubbed his belly, laughing.

"Ohhh, you got me excited, Wildeboar!" Cueball yelped. "You done opened the cage! Watch out, bitches!"

Lifting a leg, Cueball fake-humped the steering wheel.

"Maintain, sir!" yelped Eddy, but he too felt the surge grip him.

Cueball brought out a baggie of tablets and they each took one, bumping them together in a toast. The radio soon hit decibels the speakers could barely contain.

They spent the early evening chatting excitedly and digging through vinyl at a surf shop in Satellite Beach, and once their buzzes kicked in, moved on to the ocean boardwalk in Indialantic, scoping out young women who amassed alongside muscle cars in the Wendy's parking lot as fire spinners performed spellbinding dances, amplifying the night's charged sense of inevitability.

The boys had no hard love for religion, but they did have ritual. Nor a discernible god, but there was a temple, a sanctuary of sorts, which exacted a charitable mood upon entry. Pushing through the doors of the Perkins diner, they were immediately thankful. They chanted a time-honored request. Eddy withdrew a palmful of crumpled dollars, his tithing. He was serviced. He drank from a bottomless cup.

The lighting was as stark as a morgue, but the atmosphere was somehow pleasant. The waitress, pumpkin hair and pushing forty, handed out menus like playbills to a show they'd seen a thousand times before. Eddy scanned the room. Two third-shift UPS workers crowded a booth under fake plants and frosted glass. The Wiccans were there, dressed for plague or colonial reenactment, hunched over their Magic cards, weighing counterspells. Plus some guy covered in drywall chalk, fingers laced over his face, nodding off. Everything imbued with the glamour of insomnia. Drifters and castabouts and night owls, this was their congregation.

Eddy wondered what his life might look like in a month. Should he open a savings account?

"Now that you're in, I got something to show you," said Cueball. He made Eddy extend his arm, then grabbed it, halfway to the elbow. "This is how we greet each other. See how the tattoos touch?"

"Wow, we even get a handshake?" laughed Jesse. "How fucking lame is that?"

"Seizer's big on ritual," said Cueball. "He might even be Catholic."

"He's Baptist if he's anything," Eddy said. "Or Methodist. Presbyterian? God, will we need guns?"

"Dad's gonna hook us up," said Cueball.

"Really? I'm not sure how I feel about that."

"So when's your first run?" asked Jesse.

Cueball shrugged. "When everything's ready."

"Man, I want my tat," said Jesse. "I'm excited."

"*You're* excited?" Cueball said, whispering. "I might just try to fuck Marilyn."

Marilyn, a local sex worker, had slipped into a nearby booth, crisscrossing her legs slowly but not importantly. None of them had ever taken her home and she'd never asked. She'd occasionally chat them up, jolting off one-liners from movies, made funnier by her thick eastern european accent. When Eddy's food arrived, she curled into the chair next to him, poking fries with a toothpick. Eddy offered to pay for her coffee, letting on he had a new job. Instead, Marilyn laid down a single bill for the fries she'd eaten and kissed his cheek. "Save your money. Good jobs are hard to find, harder to keep," she said. "Moji otroci. Who is a better mother than me to you?"

Marilyn returned to her booth and was soon joined by a thin, anxious man in a suit.

Cueball used his fork to puncture holes in three half-and-half creamers and set them out, raising his own up for a toast. "After our first paycheck, I say we all do Marilyn at the same time."

"I call purple starfish," said Jesse.

"Mouth," said Cueball.

"You're both disgusting," said Eddy. "C'mon, we need a real toast."

"To the Armstrong Crew," said Jesse.

Cueball cringed. "What the fuck does that even mean?"

"Like we're the first ones out there, you know? Exploring uncharted territory, like Neil Armstrong walking on the moon. It was Del Ray's idea, I'm not taking credit for it."

"Del's a fucking muppet," said Cueball, but crinkled his small cup against theirs.

Each squirted down his creamer.

"Space Coast represent!" squawked Jesse. "You feel me? We've rocketed a spaceship to the moon and put a goddamn vacuum cleaner on Mars!"

"Rockets blow up all the time," said Cueball, forking another creamer. "You guys went and jinxed us. Might as well call ourselves the Challengers."

On-screen, a busty young coed fled a psychopath in a ski mask chasing her through the woods, albeit at an unusually slow pace. The undead villain was already responsible for the murders of several camp counselors using whatever farm implements he'd found readily available during the orchestral climaxes—all in all, worth the buck admission for an eighties classic. What kept Eddy out of the action, however, wasn't the dated, bankrupt trope of murderer-takes-revenge-on-the-promiscuous, it was the killer's glaring resignation. That slow walk and vacant stare—hack 'em up, punch the clock—a total waste of an afterlife!

"You think he had a choice?" Eddy whispered in Gin's ear. "Like, you can either go straight to Hell, or stay trapped at the lake forever, doing the same shit over and over."

The screen absorbed a tumultuous spray of blood.

"Interesting," said Gin. "But he died of negligence, right? I read this as misplaced anger."

"Or existential sadness. Even evil gets the blues."

"It's more like a fairy tale," she added, "where nobody gets exactly what they deserve. Random stuff happens and you go with it. Animals talk and bad guys win, and look, here's another tragic old woman pushed to the outskirts of society. She's baking a pie, la la la. Oh no, the pie has a child in it—The End."

Eddy chuckled, pulling her shirt. "Let's bounce, I wanna take you somewhere."

A little ways north of Melbourne, near Rockledge, they pulled down a long drive of gravel and mud, parking behind a scrapyard. Eddy slunk between the chained gates, holding them apart for Gin.

Together they wandered into a treasury of junked vehicles, the lot portly with mangled wrecks and rusted machinery.

"This used to be my dad's place," said Eddy. He ripped off a high piece of grass, pinned it between thumbs, and blew until it whistled. "I come out here sometimes to think."

Under the only surviving mulberry tree, Eddy slid into the driver's seat of his favorite car, a broke-down Coupe DeVille—a real *hoopty*, his father called it—a gangbanger's ride, perched among the bones and sinew of a fallen century.

"How cool is owning a junkyard?" Gin exclaimed, thunking the hood. "All these former lives stacked on top of each other. Why'd he sell it?"

"His partner bought us out after he died. For way less than you'd expect."

Recently, Eddy had begun sharing more mundane and intimate stories with Gin, hoping to counterbalance the wild, hyperbolic tales he'd regaled her with early on. (If he seemed larger-than-life, he'd be harder to leave.) But some episodes involving his parents cut too close to the bone—they weren't just embarrassing, they were paralyzing, infantilizing. For this and other reasons he decided Gin would never meet his mother.

Together they watched a cardinal spirit through the crushed windows of a Dodge Dart. "What's that sound? Are those cicadas? God, it's so peaceful here."

Over breakfast that morning Eddy had raised the subject of his father. As he explained it, his dad woke up one day and quit fifteen years of marriage without citing a cause. Then rented an apartment in Cocoa and promptly died in his sleep from an undetected heart arrhythmia, which sent his mother into a tailspin. What followed were months of violent mood swings and hideous nights filled with his mother's relentless wailing, fought off with pillows over his head and hummed Nirvana songs.

Then one morning, when he was thirteen, his mother walked into his bedroom and announced she was no longer his mother. Eddy should instead consider her a friend—a roommate, even. Thus began the drug years, a nasty coke habit attenuated by nightly barhopping. Enter too the carousel of part-time jobs and hospitalizations, until she finally left for good, moving in with her boyfriend, who plied her with medications. Eddy kept going to school because that's where his friends were. Occasionally she might stop by with groceries—canned tuna, white bread, block cheese—but their relationship now felt amorphous, ill-defined. Somehow her weaknesses felt like his own.

"Yeah, no it's fine, whatever," said Eddy as Gin captured his pinky, keeping him from spreading jam on their english muffins.

"No, it's completely messed up," she said, determined to inject a proper perspective. "We all have histories, sure, and we deal with our shit differently, but we need to call this what this is—trauma. It's bullshit, and not our fault. And if we don't deal with it, process it, it'll keep coming back. Worst case, we perpetuate it—extending the history."

Eddy broke her grip and picked up his coffee but didn't drink, rankled slightly by her analysis, but also stiffened by two memories she'd stoked in him.

The first was of his mother's former friend, a redheaded gay man who cashiered with her down at the Krystal Burger. One day he brought over a Nintendo and taught Eddy to play *Mario Kart*. But the very first time Eddy got smashed off course by a projectile turtle shell, he yelled, *Ah, you faggot!* and instantly felt the heat rush up his neck, even as the dude laughed it off. In that moment, he promised himself never to utter that word again, and never did. A week later, his mother was fired for stealing a sleeve of packaged hamburger meat. Her friend never returned.

Losing her job was the thunder calling down an avalanche. Silently they agreed to forget breakfast was a meal. His second memory was of helping his mother sort change a few months later. She'd dumped a big yellow Charles Chips tin full of coins onto the coffee table, and they were stacking pyramids of multicolored sleeves, when she began crying—spookily remaining stone-faced. Without inflection, she explained how screwed she was, blaming the "History People"—as in, certain people had *history money*, or *history skin*, or *history families*, or attended *history schools*. Some still lived in the big old haunted mansions of their grandparents—shuttered things transformed by ivy, Eddy imagined—and refused to share their fortunes because it was easier to feel wronged and forsaken than responsible and generous. Dropping the bong from her chin, she blew the smoke out and said: *They think the only way to keep living like they do is to hold you down. Don't let 'em do it. Listen to me! When they try to push you down, you bite their little dicks off!*

Instead of poisoning Eddy against certain types, though, her words got him thinking twice about judging people straightaway. If he disagreed with someone, he tried imagining a whole past rising up behind their teeth, a whole language even, riddled with faulty information and weird beliefs that informed their every action and thought. It wasn't always easy, but if *he* was doing it, maybe they were too. Which meant perhaps they'd overlook his faults as well.

As Gin sprang the Coupe DeVille's windshield wipers into insect arms, Eddy silently prayed she'd forgive him when the time came. Every imagined iteration of him admitting to running drugs ended in a verbal bloodbath, and Gin leaving. All she knew about his job now was that he'd be crossing state lines.

"I'll be gone four to five days out of every seven," said Eddy, placing his hand over the gearshift.

"I miss those long drives," said Gin. "The newness of each small town. All the house parties, seeing how strangers live."

"We won't be hanging around at all. Just straight-up-and-back deliveries."

Gin nodded. "You, uh, looking forward to hooking up with some skanky motel cleaning ladies?"

"What?"

"Beat their pudgy cheeks with little Eduardo?"

"Wow," said Eddy.

"*I'm just fucking with you! Gosh!*" she mooned. "I think it'll be good to carve out some space for ourselves again, right? Enjoy some downtime, focus on work."

The previous week Gin had landed a job transcribing medical tapes for a group of dentists in Vero Beach. Apart from the job, she also enrolled in a Pilates class and talked about joining a poetry workshop. She enjoyed being self-sufficient and kept busy, which Eddy admired; less clear were her long-term plans, or where he fit into them. They were still in the testing and evaluating phase of their relationship. Most of their spare time was either spent on the couch or in bed.

"You ever think about moving out of your mom's place?" Eddy asked.

"Soon as I can afford it," said Gin. "I hear her having sex. *Yes!* Like all the time! Ahh! The walls are paper-thin. Plus she leaves dishes in the sink, and the lid off the salsa in the fridge. I love her but she's ridiculous. My mom's lost without a guy by her side. It's pathetic."

"Hmm," said Eddy. "Some people are weird like that."

Gin raised an eyebrow. "No comparisons, please."

Eddy patted the passenger's seat. "What would you say . . . hear me out . . . what would you say if I asked you to move in with me?"

Gin scoffed. "I'd say you were nuts."

"Keep an eye on things while I'm gone."

"You looking for a security guard? 'Cause I'm unlicensed, sweetheart. Nor do I aspire to be a live-in maid slash girlfriend."

Eddy cracked his knuckles, tongue-fishing a popcorn kernel husk jammed between molars. "You wouldn't have to pay rent."

"Eddyyyy," she deadpanned. "It's only been a couple months! We have tiiiime. Let's not do this now—"

"What's wrong with knowing what you want? We can turn Mom's old room into an office. A writing room. You can set up your machine in there—"

"I need to walk," said Gin, sliding off the hood. "No, you stay here. I'm not mad or anything, I just need to walk."

Eddy's failed protests seemed to only solidify Gin's resolve as she marched across the weeded flats filled with bent axles and abandoned carburetors. She wouldn't be enticed into feeling something she didn't feel, Eddy knew, nor forced into a situation she might later regret. Despite respecting her conviction, though, he felt deflated.

He caught his new Sabal palm tat glinting fresh in the daylight. He'd told Gin it was a stupid boy thing, a drunk decision. She didn't even give him a hard time about it. He felt like a scumbag for undermining the faith of a person who'd endured so much already, and whom he loved. If there was one thing she demanded above all else, it was honesty.

He watched her cup her hands to a car window. Graphite hair with shades of blue, a dream woke to flesh. If nothing went awry, he could quit the job early and she'd be none the wiser. Jump ship with a hefty sum and open his own tattoo parlor. The world wouldn't shed its need for artists in the meantime. And maybe Gin could work the front desk, answering the phone and scheduling appointments. It was a future imagined with such sudden intensity that it seemed almost fated. And just like that, Eddy had a new plan. Much better than college. One he knew he could make work.

Gin returned to find him sitting on the seat's headrest.

"You can put that look away," she said, folding her arms. "I just needed a breather."

"Listen, I'm sorry if I was pushy, or overstepping some bounds," he said. "I just don't want to lose you. And you're totally right, it's best we take our time. There's things I might take my time saying, mostly out of fear . . . but I want to be able to share everything with you."

Gin took his hand and led him hopping over the car door to stand together in the sun, gauging each other's expressions.

"You take whatever time you need to tell me whatever you need to," she said. "Just don't lie to me. And don't push, I make boundaries for a reason."

"I understand. I'm an idiot. I'm sorry."

"How about this," said Gin. "I bring over some clothes, just a few things, and put them in a few drawers—"

"Really truly? You sure?"

"Slowww! From now on, slow," she said. "I need to know we're on the same page. Not some dreamy page, but the same page. Wedding bells sound like fire alarms to me."

"No, absolutely," said Eddy, trying to keep his cool. "Let's celebrate! Anywhere you want to go, you name it. Bird gave me some bonus cash for starters."

"Yeah? How much?"

"Six hundred."

"Dollars? Wow. That's a mortgage payment. Shouldn't you—"

"He specifically told me to show you a good time," Eddy lied.

"How very thoughtful," Gin mocked coquettishly. She glanced about the junkyard. "And this was where you thought to take me? I must be the cheapest goddamn date around."

"Cheap *and* easy," Eddy said.

As Eddy inched a finger down her belly, Gin squirmed at the tickle. He undid the top button of her jeans as she watched, biting her bottom lip and surveying the lot for movement.

uke kept wiping his mouth and breathing heavily between bites. He peeked around at other patrons, relieved to see they were doing the same.

The food was gobsmacking good—crispy chunks of chicharrones de pollo set beside a perfectly bland mound of homemade mofongo, ladled over with a tart lime sauce. Jeezus H. Christmas, and this stewed pork: juicy as an overripe plum. He glanced up at his brother, but Lisbon's eyes weren't leaving his plate, scraping bits of food onto his fork with a finger and shoveling it straight back.

A solid tip from a cohort led them to this unassuming puerto rican joint named El Bajareque on the outskirts of Wynwood in Miami, just north of the artsy mural region that belied the carnivorous creep of gentrification. The city had its sites to check out, but this wasn't a vacation day—it was brunch, business, and beat it.

Lisbon swirled the last bit of his pork and tostones in a pool of sauce and stopped, making some silent bargain with his stomach—then finished the bite. He fell back in his chair, staring at the ceiling, then shot forward, pulling out his pad. Duke watched him write.

"Parrots," Duke read. "If we're lucky, bud, but I can't justify, you know, going on some expedition. We'll be out in the woods, so maybe we'll get lucky. Remember, though . . . we're not actually here."

Earlier they'd spotted a few ibis needling for earthworms in a regular old front yard, and Lisbon said he'd seen a roseate spoonbill under a channel bridge. But who knows, his brother sometimes got overly excited—it could have just been a pelican from a weird angle.

Lisbon checked his watch as Duke raised his hand for the check. Then Duke leaned over to read Lisbon's scribbling. "Kaos noon? Sounds like a band. I caught Kaos Noon opening for Chicken Incredible and the Dumpster Pastries back in '04." Which tickled Lisbon. Duke paid the bill, tipping enough to snatch a performed fainting spell from the matronly waitress.

"This is the kind of place you tell everyone about, or no one."

What if they try something?

Duke understood his brother's concern—the people they were meeting had frightful reputations. Leaning across the table, he whispered: "Then we murder the bastards."

Lisbon retracted, unsure if Duke was messing around.

"C'mon, man," said Duke, flicking a piece of dried rice at his brother. "They're expecting us. We've been vouched for. Stop looking for things to worry about."

Outside was warm and getting warmer, sunlight in every windshield. Duke wondered if today would be a migraine day for Lisbon. Hopefully the drive would cool things down. Yes, he was a little nervous himself, but his uncle had set up the meeting personally, with Del Ray's help.

They headed west from the city, past the neighborhoods and dwindling commerce. Beyond their destination lay wetlands and prairies, straight to the horizon.

The narrow cattle road branched off the Tamiami Trail, a hard sandy floor stabilized with gravel. This led to a country trail that entered the woods. About a quarter mile back, a Jeep pulled out from behind some palmettos and screeched to a halt before them.

When Duke braked hard, another Jeep boxed them in from behind.

Lisbon caught his eyes as the driver in front of them slid out and approached. A face like cracked mud, unlike the boyish countenance of the kid approaching on Lisbon's side with a raised shotgun. Both were latino.

Duke kept his elbow out the window—no sudden moves. The older man stopped at his door, hands on hips. His smile legitimized how dangerous he seemed.

"Road closed."

"We're expected," said Duke. "Check the plates."

The man didn't move. The boy on the passenger side shifted into a wider stance.

"Road closed," shrugged the man.

Duke softened his stare but kept his eyes.

A walkie-talkie slung from the man's belt went off. He remained smiling as he listened. After the static voice quit, he glanced over at the shotgun holder and nodded him away.

"Welcome to the Mission," said the man, rubbing his chest. "Today we learn things. You will see what I mean, and we will see what that means."

Duke had no idea what that meant, but nodded.

As the curious soldier ambled back to his Jeep, Duke calmed his brother. The Jeep found its gear and spun out, lunging up the trail.

They followed it deeper into the woods.

A little ways off, Duke spotted another soldier in a deer blind, a pair of binoculars strung about his neck. Not too shabby. It reinforced his feeling that the club should have broken ground with this Miami outfit before moving up to the Space Coast. Maybe even kept production and distribution separate. But that wasn't his uncle's way: vertical integration in close quarters—make it, house it, ship it up the coast.

Off to one side they passed the ruins of a small homestead. It wasn't old enough to be a spanish mission, in Duke's estimation, but it could have been a church at some point.

Minutes later they arrived at the warehouse, approaching from the rear. The structure was well hidden among tall pines and melaleuca. The exit had a rolling door and a cement loading dock, where two guards with automatics observed them with seemingly mild interest, but Duke knew what good training looked like—already in firing stances, fingers off triggers, a voice in their ear.

The two Jeeps pulled up to flank them, motors running.

"This is what a professional operation looks like," Duke told his brother. "It's supposed to scare you, unless you're on the inside . . . and even when you're on the inside. And we're about to be on the inside."

A well-dressed man appeared on the loading dock. Black hair, smart slacks: a businessman. But on the back of each hand, a bull head tattoo, black as charred bone. This was Alex, chapter head of Los Toros, a notorious street gang.

A young man sauntered up to his side, dressed in flashy urbanwear. This was for sure the guy they called Kaos. Smoking a rolled cigarette or joint, Duke couldn't tell.

Alex broke into a welcoming grin, motioning them from the car.

Duke put up a hand and killed the engine. Did he feel some trepidation? Hell yes, he did—but just like his college acting teacher used to say, it's always good to be a little nervous before a performance.

PART II

THE ARMSTRONG CREW

Eddy rose half-dreaming in the coolness of a trashed living room, the world softly intimate in the morning light. He lit a cigarette and came to. He'd lain awake till 3 a.m., chasing off nerves with beer, and passed out before the TV.

This was it, the big day. Put up or shut up. He lit a second Camel to get the blood pumping and stripped down, plugged his new iPod Nano into a speaker by the sink, and let the steam work its magic, coughing up phlegm as he sang into the showerhead.

He wasn't going to lie to himself, he felt ill-prepared. No school counselor ever extolled the virtues of drug trafficking. There were no manuals to follow, just movie plots and tales from the old-timers. And these stories were never drama-free.

As he dressed he watched Gin sleep, hoping he wasn't making the worst decision of his life.

The VW Bug's interior was a furnace, sweat prickling his neck, the steering wheel hot and sticky. The radio bellowed a Pantera classic: *Re-spect, walk.* The summer world lacked tone, shiny as an afterthought, a river of humidity hovering the asphalt. A week before, Cueball had moved out of his parents' place and into a red octagonal house on stilts. Bird co-signed on the property, but Cueball came up with the down payment, which confirmed Eddy's suspicion that Cueball was making more money than him. He didn't mind, but Jesse seemed to take it as a call to arms.

The tall red oddity sat on an acre of ranchland a mile away. Eddy parked beneath the wraparound porch, next to a battered rack of free weights, and took the stairs spiraling up.

"Knock knock!" he shouted at the top, hands cupped to the glass door.

Cueball appeared in a T-shirt and boxers, pulling up his jeans. Unlatched the door and returned to the couch, lighting up a bong and holding in the smoke. On TV, two women with enormous fake breasts swapped turns giving a football trophy a blowjob. Seconds later, a broad-shouldered man in a cheap suit strolled into the office and gasped, appalled by this discovery.

"You ever seen this one?" Cueball said. "He ties them up with a whip he got taming lions. They fucking love it. Man, these old ones are the best. Except nobody shaved."

"Didn't that dude die of AIDS?"

"What? Don't tell me that! I can't be watching dead people fuck."

Unwashed dishes rested in the sink, barnacled with half-eaten bits of dried sausage and tater tots. Eddy found the coffee pot going and poured two cups. Cueball excused himself to take a leak as Eddy brought the coffees to the table by the couch.

Not wanting to watch porn at 8:30 a.m., Eddy leaned over to close the laptop browser, which was streaming to the TV. As he closed the tab, another opened. This new video was muted, and showed a well-hung trans woman fucking a skinny soldier boy over a balcony. The backdrop was downtown Miami, aquamarine bay and high-rises. The progress bar showed twenty-three minutes completed.

"You ready, bro?"

Eddy furiously clicked the X in the corner of the browser and everything collapsed. He lifted the extra coffee over his head, which Cueball accepted as he entered the room.

"Thanks, bud."

"Yeah, man!" said Eddy, maybe too boisterously. "All set."

"Smokey and the Bandit!" barked Cueball. "Wait . . . was Smokey the cop? Who's the other guy, Bandit's partner?"

"Cledus," said Eddy.

"Who names their kid Cledus? That's some fantasy football shit."

Eddy chuckled thoughtlessly, his insides gnawed by anxiety. Not because of the video—that wasn't without precedent—but because of his unmitigated belief that everything he knew and loved was caving in, and by day's end he'd be in jail.

Or dead.

"We can't fuck this up," he said.

Cueball rested at the edge of a chair, putting on his shoes. "It's pretty hard to mess up driving a car, man."

Eddy shook his head no, then yes. "Listen, if anything bad happens, I want you to take the money I'm owed and give half to Gin. You can keep a quarter, and give the rest to my mom."

It was hard to guess what Cueball was thinking as he stared off. "Alright, bro. And if anything happens to me, promise you'll scatter my ashes at Turkey Creek Sanctuary."

"Turkey Creek?"

"You remember Suzie Fuentes?"

"That chick that dances online? The camgirl?"

"Yeah," said Cueball soberly. "She gave me my first handjob out there one night, off the trail, out by the water. We talked for hours, watched the sun come up. It might be my best memory."

Eddy thought that was the saddest thing he'd ever heard.

"Didn't she tell people your appendix scar looked like something from a horror movie?"

"Yeah, but she wasn't being mean about it," said Cueball. "You keep half my share, but maybe split the rest between Suzie and her brother, Jamie. You remember him? He was always a good guy. They lost their mom to cancer."

Eddy extended his arm and Cueball gripped it, tattoo to tattoo. "You got it, brother," said Eddy, who forced himself to think, *This is a day like any other.*

Soon Cueball was banging out rhythms on the Nova's chain steering wheel, challenging the guy in the Saab next to them with a racing nod, a rev. But the guy wasn't biting.

Traffic was thinner than expected, and they were set to arrive at the meetup site way too early.

"We'll just wait for them," said Cueball.

"No!" barked Eddy. "That's not the plan!"

"Whoa, amigo!" howled Cueball. "Pump the brakes."

Eddy reminded him that Del Ray told them to remain apart from the Twins until absolutely necessary—then never leave their side. Hoping to settle his friend down, Cueball suggested they stop off at Sebastian Inlet to kill some time. Maybe check out the tidal pool, see if anyone snagged a barracuda.

What they discovered instead was a parking lot jam-packed with surfers and news crews setting up for an ESPN surf contest.

At the toll booth, a crew-cut ranger asked for Cueball's license as Eddy slid his tattooed wrist under his ass—shades on, head tilted askance. The circular pool appeared on their right, dammed by a rock barrier, beyond which the colder oceanic waters rushed in to join the Indian River. Overhead, the sun slipped pebble-like into a huge basin of morning sky.

They parked outside a restaurant advertising grouper sandwiches and Vanilla Coke floats. The Sebastian jetty curved like a chewed fingernail into the widening Atlantic, where large-bellied retirees relaxed in aluminum chairs as waves smashed the mortar barricade, the water a vibrant blue garnished with golden sargassum.

"My dad used to take me fishing out here!" Eddy shouted over water rushing beneath the floor grates. "I can't imagine what he'd say about me taking this job!"

"He'd say, *Fuck me, when did I start giving a shit?*"

The jetty's farthest reaches erupted with battles over great fish—snook, red snapper, whiting—long poles dipping in measured sequence like fingers at the clarinet. Fishermen who'd graced the glossy pages of sports magazines flocked here to fight alongside the locals, hoping to catch some snippet of glory lurking deep in the sea. A toothless man with a squashed jaw and a hat rigged with hooks noticed Cueball eyeing his empty bucket.

"Got two nibbles. Big ones, no doubt."

"What'chou using for bait?"

"Mullet. I'll take blacktip or hammerhead, whichever. Both would eat their own cousins."

"Sounds like some folks I know," said Cueball.

The fisherman nodded wistfully. "Best watch yourself 'round people like that."

Nearby, a child with chubby hands groveled through a mushpile of pink-blue innards, smearing them on his shirt.

"I feel sick," said Eddy. "What if something goes wrong?"

"Like if they find our bodies dumped in a ditch?" asked Cueball. "Then we're dead, I guess."

"Listen, maybe you do this without me."

Cueball stopped in his tracks. "What the fuck are you talking about? No, man, absolutely not. We signed up for this."

Eddy watched some pelicans scoop up a mound of discarded fish parts. "Yeah, but maybe it's not too late to back out."

"It's definitely too late."

"Yeah, I know, I know."

"You got this," said Cueball. "Just pretend we've been doing it forever. You'll feel better once we're on the road."

Cueball raised his middle knuckle; Eddy bumped it, trying not to hyperventilate.

Leaving the jetty, they wandered onto a beach populated by adonis types in trunks and bikinied aphrodites spread out on blankets. A biplane dragged a banner across the great empty sky: *Enjoy the Luxury of Convenience.* Then a bullhorn ripped through the air, sending four surfers sprinting toward the water.

Eddy was having an out-of-body experience. Though above-average in the looks department, these people were just ordinary folks living ordinary lives. He and Cueball were the true misfits, their blue jeans and black shirts like neon signs flashing *bad guys.*

He froze as his work phone vibrated in his pocket.

It was Duke. Eddy's exhaustion spilled out. "Y-y-you boys ready to roll?"

"Tank's full," said Duke. "You close?"

A surfboard shot pale and manless over a wave.

"We're maybe ten minutes out. Is anyone else around?"

There was a pause. "You expecting someone?"

"No, just making sure you guys double-checked everything and made sure things were . . . double-checked."

"We're solid," said Duke. "Just get here."

They located the defunct supermarket south on A1A, perched along an unusually thin strip of land separating ocean and river, a flood-insurance nightmare. Heading around back, the moving van came into view. Resting on the bumper, Lisbon waved.

"Why doesn't he talk again?" whispered Cueball, parking.

"I don't know," said Eddy. "Just wave back."

Cueball waved, watching Duke slide out from the van's cab.

"Sorry you had to come all the way down here," yelled Duke. "Del said from now on we'll meet closer to I-95, so we can head right up the highway."

"Why? Is this place not safe?" asked Eddy.

Duke ignored this. "You boys ready?"

"Ready as ever," said Cueball.

"You got the address mapped on your phone?"

Eddy nodded.

"Roger that," said Cueball. "But hey, first . . . can we see it?"

"See what?" asked Duke.

"You know. The stash."

Duke turned to his brother, who shrugged.

"No."

"Alright, then."

Duke and Lisbon climbed back into the van. As Cueball pulled the Nova up beside them, Duke slapped his door loudly. "Just remember, you get pulled over, we don't know you. And if you see any flashing lights on my backside, you swerve like you dropped a smoke in your crotch. Break the speed limit twice over, make 'em chase you."

Cueball responded by revving his engine.

They drove four and a half hours straight before stopping.

At first, Eddy kept it together, lulled by the image of the moving van wobbling six car lengths before them endlessly. But after an hour on the road, reality crept in, and he began stealing peeks at passing cars, certain each contained an undercover cop. To calm down he flipped the station between music and talk radio. The political diatribes unsettled him, though, nearly as much as Cueball's irritating nonchalance. Wasn't he afraid the moving van might swerve into the median? Or suddenly tip over and explode?

"How's your stomach?"

Eddy couldn't describe it.

"Text Duke I need to piss," said Cueball. "Gas is getting low."

Both vehicles pulled into a truck stop at the next exit as Cueball waddled inside, followed a minute later by a trudging Lisbon. Eddy distracted himself by playing a game on his phone. When Lisbon returned with an arm full of pretzels and chips, Eddy watched his eyes—the younger twin disregarded him completely.

"I should invest in some long johns," said Cueball as they pulled away from the station. "You ever see snow before?"

"No. I've never been this far north before. I don't even know where we're at."

"You're kidding, right? You have the map."

"I accidentally closed it and the address disappeared, but I can—"

"Shit, Eddy! You're in charge of this stuff!"

"We're in South Carolina, okay?! I just don't know what town, exactly. 95 takes us to 26, which takes us to 77, which is most of the way there. Don't make it sound like I'm fucking up! Follow the van! I just need to re-input the address."

Shortly thereafter, the strong odor of Cueball's beef jerky became so nauseating that Eddy grabbed the package and tossed it out the window. When Cueball glared at him, Eddy said, "I know it! I'm being irrational! Do me a favor and don't give me any shit. I feel sick."

"Please god don't puke in my baby," Cueball prayed. "Do it down your shirt or something."

It was dark when they left the highway for the gloomy backroads of central North Carolina just shy of Winston-Salem, in a town of rolling farmland called North Wilkesboro. Driving a two-laner they passed a deserted filling station and no houses to speak of. Eddy lowered the window, airing out his shirt, pungent with stale sweat. Just then the van's red blinker shot on and Eddy fell back into his seat.

Duke turned up the dirt driveway of an isolated farmhouse. A single bulb burned over the porch. Cueball rolled in behind the van and killed the engine. The music of crickets filled the air. Duke hopped out and approached the house. A floodlight shot on. The front door opened and Duke was met, to everyone's surprise, by a kindly looking elderly woman, holding her hips.

"What the hell?" said Cueball. "It's Betty White."

"This is the wrong place. Let's bolt," said Eddy. Then, when Cueball didn't move fast enough: "Back up! Seriously!"

But Duke was already motioning for them to get out and help. Cueball clicked the headlights off before Duke told him to turn them back on. Eddy chanced another look at the old woman while Lisbon lifted the van's roll-up door. The grandfather clock full of drugs was hidden way in the back, with smaller items of furniture stacked along a side aisle for easy access.

"What's with granny?" whispered Cueball.

Duke shrugged. "She knew my name, so I guess my uncle knows her. Probably an old girlfriend."

"Is she an addict?"

"What? No. This is just a drop-off."

Eddy gingerly set down the back legs of the clock lowered to him, holding it at a diagonal as Lisbon jumped down to help.

"Does she know what's in this?" Eddy asked Duke. "I mean, she's not gonna try to wind it up and out pops the stash, right?"

Duke stripped off his gloves in the headlights. "Guys? We're movers. This clock here? It needs moving. Now carry this inside while I get the paperwork."

It was no use arguing: if the elderly woman was going to do anything, she'd have done it by now. Dressed in a white nightgown, she held the door open as they lugged the grandfather clock into the kitchen.

"Where would you like this, ma'am?" asked Eddy.

"Oh, right down the hallway and into the study," she said. "Set it between the sofa and the curio. Just try not to bust up the curio, it's family. Let me fix you boys some coffee."

They huffed the clock away and returned to find Duke sipping from a mug as the elderly woman signed all the phony paperwork.

"All set," she said, clicking the pen.

"I can personally assure you . . . Mrs. Lamb," Duke said, finding her name on the pages, "that your furniture will arrive without a scratch."

"Aw, hon, I could care less if it gets there in splinters. Boys set down, now, you're making me nervous! Here, get yourself a mug, I got coffee on the stove."

"Thank you, I'm good," said Eddy. "We should probably be heading out."

"Ab-so-lutely not. You've been driving all day and I got four made beds upstairs."

"Thanks kindly, ma'am," said Duke with a sudden accent. "But we got orders to stay in a hotel tonight. We sure do appreciate it, though. I bet you make a mean breakfast, am I right?"

"Only if you like farm-fresh eggs and country ham," she beamed, a tugged ear the only sign of any offense taken. "But before you go, at least take this." Lifting the cork top from a blue-gray earthenware jar, she retrieved a folded bank envelope, pushing it toward Duke. "You boys split that up between you."

Duke pursed the envelope to look inside. "Hm, well, we've already been paid, actually." He flipped over his hand, flashing the palm tree tattoo. "But it's a generous thought. Much obliged."

"Oh, no, that's a little something extra. They said give it to the drivers. Matter of appreciation."

Back outside, the young men reloaded the dummy furniture. Duke took Eddy aside to coordinate directions to the motel; then he handed him three thousand dollars. "That's for you two, to split."

"For real?" said Eddy, fanning out the hundreds. He glanced back as the porch light winked off, confused by the lack of calamity. "Is that it? We done?"

Duke pocketed the rest of the cash. "Beats the heck out of hustling sofas for milk money, don't it?"

• • •

Eddy stepped wet from the bathroom, a towel around his waist. The motel room was ugly and cramped, with two spring beds and an old TV.

On Cueball's bed sat fifteen origami swans fashioned from hundred-dollar bills, swimming in a circle.

"Where'd you learn to do that?"

"I told you," said Cueball, resting on the floor, "I'm gifted."

As Cueball knelt over to reposition the birds just so, Eddy found his jeans and rifled through a pocket. The crisp bills were so new they stuck together, chalky under his pruned fingertips. He carefully separated each, mentally ticking off the various debts to be paid off. When he ran out of payments, he lit a cigarette and thought about what else he might want to buy. Definitely some new shoes. Clothes. A fancy dinner with Gin, maybe. A stereo. A flat-screen TV and a PlayStation 3. He recalculated the figure, adding in another month's mortgage payment—but there was still money left. How could there be money left?

"Hey, man," said Eddy. "Thanks for talking me down earlier. Sorry I freaked out. I owe you . . . big-time. For everything."

When Cueball didn't respond, Eddy approached the wonderfully fashioned animals, admiring the clean lines of the folds. He picked up one of the birds.

Cueball shot him a glare and raised his palm, meaning, *Return the bird, please.*

"Hold on, I'm looking," said Eddy. "What's gotten into you?"

Cueball pinched the swan from Eddy's hand and placed it back in the circle. In a low voice he said, "Whatever happens from here on out, I got no excuses. I'm part of it now."

"It's not as bad as all that," said Eddy.

Pulling on some boxers, he sat in bed and flipped through channels on the TV. Six grand as a tip. What kind of money was involved where six G's was pocket change? What kind of security detail, kept unseen, might be protecting an old country gal seemingly unworried about four Florida toughs returning to her farmhouse to steal back the drugs? Had his head been an apple in some gunman's crosshairs? Or could he believe that someone actually trusted him with a major assignment, with real consequences?

But the larger issue—which Cueball probably realized—was that if it really *was* this easy, there'd be no reason for Bird to ever quit. This wasn't really about retirement, not with Del Ray talking about future franchises. The sheer complexity of a system of such magnitude would never be developed, Eddy reasoned, if the end goal was simply a few years' profits.

Eddy knew then that he would never see the big picture, never be told the whole truth. And maybe that was for the best.

The nature program on TV explained how certain bumblebees pilfered flowers of their nectar without actually pollinating them—robber bees, they were called—and that this brand of thievery was actually a learned behavior. Once they got what they were after . . . sayonara.

"I'm gonna give it a year," said Eddy. "After that, I'm done. No matter what."

Cueball made a throaty sound, indicating either disbelief or a present reluctance to discuss the issue.

Eddy's phone buzzed on the dresser. It was likely Gin texting. Leaning back, he pulled a pillow under his head. He didn't have the energy to lie to her just now.

No outdoor signage advertised the private club from the side street. The whole Miami block sat bare and desolate, lined with decrepit warehouses and a lone body shop. The wire-mesh windows were blacked out and graffitied, with a solitary door embedded in the wall. A rumbling, insistent pulse rose from the ground. No velvet ropes because there was no waiting: RSVPs only.

Two figures skulked behind a tall, lanky third, their hands pocketed under a steady drizzle. The bouncer shook his head, knowing full well two of them weren't old enough. As he checked his list, Del Ray argued his case jovially before pulling out his phone and soon the bouncer had orders, just as Del grew dead set on flattening his nose.

Inside, thick curtains gave way to a foyer lit purple with black lights and glow-in-the-dark tape where people lingered at the box office. A second bouncer approached them, more congenial than the first.

The next pair of curtains opened upon the fiery genesis of a glamorous universe, where new stars flourished in a dense fog overhead and colorful fractals splashed across a humid dance floor swarming with sweaty bodies directed in motion by a hard, electric beat. Del Ray took the first stairs up, finding a booth overlooking everything. He ordered drinks before venturing off to the restroom.

Eddy and Cueball kept their heads low, feeling ratty in jeans and hoodies, so white among the latino crowd as to be transparent. But they were not transparent, watched by some with a sideways intensity. When their drinks came, they finished them in gulps.

Without warning, a well-dressed man slid into the opposite side of their booth. Late twenties perhaps, he wore a white jacket over a black button-up with a simple gold necklace. He had no drink. A hard stare had been forced upon his youthful features by some drama of which the two boys were glad to be ignorant.

"You lost?" the man spoke over the music.

Cueball shook his head no. Eddy waited.

"You look lost."

"We're waiting for someone," Eddy ventured.

"Oh. Waiting for someone," said the man, straightening his jacket. "So am I. We can wait together."

The trio watched the dancers below in silence. A black tattoo of a bull skull decorated the back of each of the man's hands.

"Drinks?" asked a waitress.

Cueball glanced furtively about for Del Ray as Eddy retrieved his wallet. "Two Jack & Cokes."

"Bring the drinks, they don't pay," said the young man, caressing the waitress' leg. She flashed a practiced smile and left. The boys nodded their thanks. "What do you think of this place?" he asked.

"Pretty cool," said Cueball. "I mean, you know. Dope."

"Yes, I think so," said the young man. "This is my club. I sit up here so I can watch everything. There's people come in, dance a little, drink a little. Rub up against each other. Maybe they get lucky." He made a gesture indicating this was how it should be. "Then there's the other types. They come in looking to move junk in my place. In the bathrooms, on the floor, up here. You gotta have a good eye to spot them. I have a *very* good eye."

"Don't you have other guys to help with that?" asked Eddy cautiously.

"*Many* other guys," the man smiled. He shrugged his shoulders high. "*Big* guys. But if you had your own place, you would understand. Only when you personally look these pendejos in the eye, you can rest assured they won't come back."

"Makes sense," said Eddy.

"Crack is whack, yo," said Cueball.

The man's smile hardened, a finger to his lip. "*Whack*. Yes, I remember this word. From a movie, maybe."

When Del Ray returned, he found Eddy and Cueball absolutely despondent, fingering their glasses, eyes averted and hopeless.

"Hey hey!" the club owner shouted, rising to embrace Del Ray, who chortled as the boys collapsed inward like men pardoned.

"Hoo boy, Alex! You got these two pinned down like exhibits at a butterfly convention. They say anything regretful?"

"Not at all," said Alex. "They were . . . professional."

"Glad to hear it. This here's Cueball and Eddy, if they didn't say."

Alex slightly dipped his head. "You have a good friend here in the Devil Ray. Now if you would, please follow me. There's someone you two should meet."

Alex led them down an eerily luminous hallway lined with red-cushioned walls and purple doors. At the far end they entered a room where three guys watching baseball on a plasma TV shouted encouragements from a couch. One of them sported a clean-cut fade and the mere wisp of a thinly edged beard above a parabola of gold chains. Alex flipped off the TV, and without being told, two of the men disappeared. But before Alex could introduce his cousin, Cueball stepped forward. "Dude . . . Antonio!"

"Oh shit! Heath!" The young man with the fade sauntered over and slammed his shoulder into Cueball's, hugging him and fisting his back. "Damn, bro, where you been hiding?"

"How do you two know each other?" asked Alex, a man unaccustomed to surprises.

"We went to high school together," Cueball explained. "You remember Eddy?"

Eddy raised his hand to Antonio.

"I don't know, maybe. Wassup?"

The cousins exchanged a look.

"Alex, go on, take care your business, I got this. Trust me, I know this motherfucker!" said Antonio. "We had english class with, uh, what's her name, that iranian bitch with the hairy arms that hated me? My boy Heath here, he stepped on a joint I dropped right in front of her, so's I wouldn't get caught. Yo, we got so bored, we used rubber bands to slingshot paper clips into the ceiling, remember that?"

Alex casually relented and excused himself, along with Del Ray, letting his guests know the bar in the corner was at their disposal.

Antonio poured a round of tequila shots and the old classmates rapped nostalgic, trading stories of schoolyard brawls. They shared a love for the loser Dolphins and curvy girls with hair wrapped tightly in buns. Outside of class was a different story: everything fell back into the usual cliquishness and a certain racial intractability. Antonio's group of puerto rican friends kept lockers along the school's C-Wing, over by the gym, while Cueball spent his lunches huddled between the annexed portable double-wides, smoking and tipping flasks with Jesse, Eddy, and the other so-called *trash*. There was also a black wing, a science wing, and a theater wing, illustrative of an ugly truth that without the forced structure of the classroom, the school would have remained as segregated as the outside world.

One day Antonio didn't show up for class, and never returned. Cueball heard there'd been a death in the family.

"Bullshit, nah. After my cuz joined Los Toros, my moms sent me to mi abuela's in Poinciana. Kissimmee? They didn't want us too close, thought he was a bad influence and shit. I said *fuck that*, right? Aint her life. I been here in Miami for like, two years? Oh, and Antonio Pérez . . . forget it . . . that aint me no more."

Antonio was now Kid Kaos, head of the Puerto Rican Posse, or PRP, a small outfit of townie dealers who fell under the command of Alex, *don't nobody call him Alejandro*, who oversaw the South Florida chapter of Los Toros, a street gang with national presence. The Posse was a kind of internal experiment Kaos likened to the National Guard, operating more or less as a localized troop of reinforcements.

"We'll be working together, bro! I mean, I won't be at the warehouse all the time, but sometimes."

Antonio said the warehouse—a holding facility he called the Mission— was stationed out in the wilderness off the Tamiami Trail. It was a drop-off point for all shipments serving West Palm to Miami-Dade to Naples, and would soon be the newest stop for the Armstrong Crew.

"How many runs you do already?" asked Kaos.

"Eight or so," said Cueball. "Mostly small towns. We were just in Virginia—"

"Dude, we shouldn't—" said Eddy, which elicited an irritated look from Cueball.

Kaos waved a hand. "No, he's right. Not my business. But hey, you see where they make the shit?"

"I wish," Eddy replied. "We just haul it."

"I hear it's fucking swamp-ass nasty," said Kaos. "People always asking where the shank come from."

"Shank?" asked Eddy, realizing he was hearing for the first time the street name of the drug they were shipping.

"Shank, big yea, shawt stuff, twix," said Kaos, clapping his hands. "Shank, like *crank* with sugar on top. Club honeys think it de-*lish*. Gotta be careful, though, that shit rides up on you *real* quick. You hit too much too fast? *La*-ter. You canceled, lights out."

"You ever try it?" asked Cueball.

"I tell you, bro, makes you wanna suck your own dick," he laughed. "Powerful stuff. I don't fuck with it so much, honestly."

"So your cousin, he only deals shank or what?" asked Cueball.

Kaos shrugged, pulled out a baggie of coke and cut it up. "Nah, we do it all, whatever. But Miami definitely gots the *need* for *speed*. Alex says heroin, coke—too much competition now. If you push that, you gotta be in with the cubans. We cool and all, but you don't wanna owe them niggas shit. Plus it's got to be imported, and sometimes it's just low-grade shit. People always looking for pills, but they hard to stock consistently. Weed sells always, but everyone's selling weed. My neighbor kid sells weed. You got weed on you?"

"Back home," said Cueball.

"'Xactly. Weed's a motherfuckin weed, yo! With shank it's like, we got exclusivity. Bam! People want that designer shit. No one else got the recipe, and we in with the only supplier. We charge forty-five, fifty an ounce, no one blinks. Sells more than coke in some places. It aint like meth, where niggas can whip up a batch over the weekend, watchin the game. You wanna party, you gotta come to us."

Cueball's expression shifted. "How long you been pushing it?"

"Three, four months?" mused Kaos. "Devil Ray would bring us small batches, got these white boys dropping off a few orders at the Mission. These twins."

Cueball shot Eddy a look. The club had been active longer than imagined, feeding a test supply through at least one network in a major city. Eddy felt no animosity toward the Twins for withholding this information—they only answered to their uncle—but Cueball looked incensed. Eddy made himself another drink as Kaos rocked a few lines and fired up the console, embarking on a game where the object was to steal cars, shoot cops, proposition sex workers, and run down pedestrians.

"Why he's calling you Cueball?" asked Kaos, eyes on the screen. "You lose a nut or something?"

"Badass Kid Chaos," smirked Cueball. "People call you KC?"

"Not if they wanna live, they don't."

"No Sunshine Band?"

"Yo, man, people respect my shit. I got people working under me, look up to me. 'Sides, it's Kaos with a *K*."

"Oh, how charming! Kaos with a *K*!" Cueball preened with a mild lisp, garnering an inward chuckle from Kaos. "Well I think that's absolutely lovely. It suits this whole, flashy Jonas Brothers look you've got going on. Kaos with a *K*."

"Goddamn. You still all loud mouth and butter brains."

"Your cousin seems like a pretty intelligent guy," injected Eddy.

Kaos tensed as his avatar took a gunshot to the chest. "Yeah, he's smart at some things, but he can kid too much sometimes. He says stuff to undercut you, like, to show you who's boss. But you won't have to deal with that shit, he's hardly down at the Mission, with the workers. That shit's just for jokers like us."

The boys got blitzed and played video games long into the night.

Strangers wandered in and out, mostly to do lines. Cueball brought up the possibility of getting laid and Kaos pointed at the door, so Cueball left for the dance floor.

The novelty of the scene had a substantial effect on his daring. Eddy hung back as his friend entered into the mix, exhibiting the solipsistic madness of a champion executing his first real gambit by sliding intrusively against the leg of a woman twice his age. Del Ray appeared just as the woman's date, who found the prospect laughable, began to deepen into his annoyance. When Cueball turned his hips upon the man, people backed away, making room for a fight. Instead, Cueball received a shoulder pat from Del Ray and was amusedly escorted outside. Yet it worried Eddy how quickly his friend had shifted from unease to involved to invincible.

Back in the Nova, Cueball slept sprawled across the back seat as Del Ray drove.

"You boys have fun?" asked Del, searching for a late-night Denny's sign along the highway.

Eddy yawned. "That was some pretty heavy shit. I felt . . . I don't know. I'm not used to so much attention. Random people talked to me and I talked back. But it was like, they were trying to figure out how important I was."

"You like that? It can be a little strange when you crawl out of your hole for the first time, catch sight of the bigger picture."

"Fuck your holes," joked Eddy tiredly.

"Goddamn," Del Ray snorted, "someone must have fed you boys some chest-thumping shit. Naw, but you did good. Color me pleased. Every town's got its perks, Ed. And its players. Alex is solid, a real force to be reckoned with. We should discuss that cousin, though, that was unexpected." Del lowered his voice. "Did our boy happen to mention his father to anyone?"

"You said not to, so he didn't. Is everything gonna be a test?"

Del Ray assured him it wouldn't.

"Alex is sharp." Eddy almost said *intimidating*. "How old is he?"

"Twenty-seven, but he's a commander of men," said Del Ray. "Maybe one day, keep your head down, learn the game—you might be too."

Eddy thought maybe that wasn't so outlandish an idea.

It was a sports bar in West Melbourne called the 13th Step, and they sat together in a screened-in porch, Duke on one side and the cowboy on the other.

Duke had heard the name Corey Buffalo in conversation, but they'd never met. It was morning, so the bar wasn't open to the public yet, and the parking lot was empty save for Buffalo's Harley Cross Bones—everyone else knew to park in back. Buffalo wore brand-new blue jeans and a button-up shirt, tucked in. His belt buckle was fashioned into a ranked Marines insignia that if representative made no real sense for him to be here, but here he was—handsome, rugged, straight out of central casting. Duke didn't like how Buffalo sat, either—too straight—like a dancer, or a choirboy.

"You're Del Ray's friend," said Duke.

Buffalo nodded. "We go back a ways."

"Where'd you meet?"

He shrugged. "Somewhere."

Duke snorted. "Del's a popular guy, got all kinds of friends. You've been here, what, couple weeks? Seems Bird's real anxious to get you set up. Pretty quick timeline."

"If you say so," said Buffalo.

"Head of Camp Security. Big job. Whatever story you gave them must have checked out."

Buffalo broke into a half-grin, studying his boots.

"What'd they say you did before this?"

"You tell me," said Buffalo.

"Bounty hunter. Well, private investigator, but then you did some time," said Duke. "For uh . . . civil abuse? License revoked in the state of Texas."

"You're the nephew," said Corey Buffalo. "Or one of them."

"Observant too."

"Pleasure to meet you," said Corey. "I respect the hell out of your uncle."

Duke nodded. "Two weeks in and eager to please."

Buffalo actually chuckled at this, watching his boot click back and forth like a metronome. Duke wouldn't say it, but he liked what he saw. Guy was well-mannered and didn't overshare.

"Catch a lot of bad guys in your day?" asked Duke.

Buffalo grinned. "I've already been interviewed."

"Oh, I'm just making conversation," said Duke.

The handsome biker kept grinning, then stood up. He walked right over to Duke and extended a hand. Duke took it and was surprised by the skin's coarseness—goddamn rock lifter or something, callused and firm. But they did say he'd been working as a farmhand. Probably scoffed at the idea of carrying a weapon around; liked to strangle people right where they stood.

"It's a privilege," said Corey.

The door opened and Bird peered out. He caught their eyes, then shot to their handshake, which dropped. As Bird motioned them inside, Duke rose and opened an arm: *After you.*

Normally he could get a bead on people pretty quick, but this guy was unreadable. Not your average shitkicker. Might even be a decent guy. But decent guys Duke distrusted most, as decent guys did admirable things, and nothing about running security for a dope camp was admirable.

Seizer sat at a table with his pen and a journal; he always carried around a blue journal, and kept it close. Bird sat across from him, outsizing his chair, reading glasses perched on his nose. Two old men going over figures, Bird with a pint and Seizer lemonade, quietly shifting receipts.

Duke sat at the bar, scrolling through his phone and sipping a Big Gulp. Lisbon still wasn't back with the atomic wings from Frankie's Wings & Things, though the bar staff wouldn't arrive for another hour. Lisbon was clearly ignoring his brother's barrage of teasing texts, admonishing him for having supposedly stopped off at a massage parlor, the creep. It was a joke that always riled Lisbon up, but the truth was, Duke liked to keep him feeling missed and considered.

"Okay . . . drumroll," said Seizer. "Miami, Melbourne, Orlando, Jacksonville, Savannah, Winston and Durham, Richmond." He peered up at Bird. "And the nation's capital, DC."

Bird shook his head. "Unbelievable. I didn't think we'd hit these numbers this fast. We land one reliable distributor in whatever city, we're off to the races. We should talk about a raise for Mickey. He scouted most of these contacts and they move product, simple as that."

"But still no Atlanta," said Seizer.

The two bosses inspected the air between them. Dust motes drifted in the bulb light, and Duke watched them watch each other.

Bird snorted, lightly rapping the table with his knuckles. "We'll have Atlanta soon," he said, draining his beer.

"How soon is soon?" asked Seizer. "I keep hearing this *soon* like it's tomorrow, but every tomorrow brings me another soon."

Bird pushed his fist into the table's side. "Mick's close to locking down a guy in the suburbs. It'll happen."

"*It'll happen* is not a time, nor is it a date," mirrored Seizer. "C'mon, give me something."

"Early next month," said Bird. "We've done a street check. These people move fast and the product keeps a decent purity. We'll see how fast the rest sells. If he's slow, or skims, we find someone else."

Seizer returned to his paperwork. "I want Atlanta by the end of the month. Then Baltimore. Philly." He slapped the table. "Bring me New York! A proper corridor!"

"You'll get it," Bird replied, smirking, unfazed. "Might actually land Chicago first. The stuff we got is wildfire, and we're well ahead of schedule. Maybe take some time to enjoy it—you may not get the opportunity to be this poor again."

Seizer smiled broadly, squinting at Duke. Suddenly his voice was in the air: "*The Lord will open heaven, storehouse of his bounty, and send rain upon your land, and bless your working hands. And you will lend to many nations, and borrow from none."*

"Amen," said Bird.

Duke shook the ice from his Big Gulp into his mouth.

Bird turned fully to acknowledge Duke, his sleeve-tatted arm bulky on the chairback: "Sounds like you and your brother will get to visit home more often."

"This is our home," said Duke.

"Of course it is," said Bird. "Okay," he said and stood up, pushing in his chair. "See you in a few days. You'll know first thing when I hear back from Mick."

Seizer stopped him with a raised hand, eyes softer now. "We've accomplished a lot, son, and nothing without you. This is *good* work you've done. Old Ironsides. I'm thanking you, here! I'm proud of you! You came through."

Bird tugged his leather jacket, then ambled over. The two men exchanged a hard, slapping hug.

"Man with a plan," said Bird, piling his paperwork.

Duke watched behind his giant plastic cup. After Bird left, he wandered over to the table. His uncle was already back to scribbling notes in his journal.

"I spoke with Buffalo. Before we came in."

His uncle didn't look up. "Oh yeah?"

"I like him. Still feels too fast."

Seizer set down his pen. "I ran the names myself. He's armed forces, a hired tracker. Got a little boy back home in a wheelchair, needs a full-time nurse, got a muscle disease they don't have a cure for. Buffalo's here for the money, which is fine by me. We don't want romantics." Tapped his pen on the table. "Forward progress."

"Maybe that's what it was," said Duke. "Something felt off."

His uncle pulled an ear: "I need you to hear something . . . that edge needs to leave your voice when speaking to Bird. I keep him in line—you do not. You work under him. He is your boss."

"You're the boss," said Duke, playing with the double meaning.

"Any lack of respect you show him reflects poorly on me," Seizer explained. "Insolence breeds insolence, that understood?"

Duke thinned his lips. "I'll be more . . . conscientious."

Seizer checked his watch. "Where's your brother? Is he still not back with the chicken?"

"Stopped off at a massage parlor."

Seizer chuckled, but caught himself. "Don't I wish," he said, slapping his nephew's hand. "But seriously, don't tease, you'll give him a complex. Best to keep girls off his mind."

It fell upon Del Ray to introduce the new Head of Camp Security to his work environs.

They biked in tandem up a long vacant road on the west side of town where broad and imposing moss-webbed oaks barricaded the front lawns of private estates. Crossing a grassy isthmus over a ditch they swerved around a padlocked gate and onto the hard-packed shoulder of a circuitous trail that ended at a canal a few miles away. Tucked back into these northern woods of Lake Washington was the club's second production lab — Camp Crawdad — newly up and running.

At the canal they walked their bikes toward an expansive camphor tree under which rested three pickups and two motorcycles.

It was Corey Buffalo's first visit to camp, and he was anxious — fidgety and flexing, like someone about to enter the ring. And wearing more leather than was perhaps necessary, with zippered pockets that Del assumed hid specialty items related to bounty hunting. Another explanation was that the trade, recently popularized by reality TV, required such preposterous getups should a camera crew or teenage paparazzi leap out from the bushes to record a bust.

Del Ray plucked some leaves from a low-slung branch of the camphor and rubbed them together, holding them under Corey's suspicious nose.

"Strong! What is that, vapor rub?"

"It's a reminder," said Del Ray, "that like this fella, we're an invasive species. I'll spare you the song and dance, but I let everyone know we cannot . . . *cannot* . . . allow any chemicals from back there find their way to this canal. It feeds straight into Melbourne's main source of drinking water."

"I hear that, partner," said Corey.

"You ever operate an airboat?" asked Del Ray.

Corey grinned, spitting. "Manual or automatic?"

"It's not so hard, once you get the hang of it," said Del Ray, glancing at the two airboats drifting in the amber canal. "If one were so inclined, one could ride out to Lake Washington and jet straight down the St Johns to Lake Hell 'n Blazes, and just under an hour arrive at the island paradise of Camp Sticks."

"Paradise, huh?" beamed Corey. "I hear it's been trashed to hell already."

Del Ray closed an eye. "The cleanup etiquette amongst overnighters hasn't yet reached a degree of respect to shame the japanese, for sure, but I'm optimistic we'll get there. Now c'mon, let me introduce you to your constituency."

An autumnal path of golden pine needles led the way. While approaching Camp Crawdad, a sallow-faced young man stepped out from behind a palmetto, an M4 strapped to his shoulder. Del Ray uttered his name and introduced Corey as his new boss. The sentinel looked Corey up and down and nodded and shook his hand and disappeared back into the brush.

Several camp workers soon came into view. Dressed like back-alley surgeons, in black smocks and masks and neoprene gloves, they trundled between two camouflaged aluminum structures—one square, one rectangle—carrying covered trays and brown growlers. They did not look well—morose and haggard barflies at the closing hour of life—and kept their eyes to task, ignoring the visitors.

"Halloween came right on time," clucked Buffalo. "Let me guess, you searched a database of rap sheets for 'all-around dirtbag' and just started cold-calling folks."

One thing Del Ray enjoyed about Corey was his prismatic sense of humor. "We chose to start with warm bodies and optimize later. There were outstanding orders and eager clientele. These humans here are known quantities, and'll keep their traps shut."

Buffalo was unprepared for the sleeping quarters: an old school bus painted green and dappled black with a sponge. With a generator-fed stove and a short refrigerator welded to its side. Strips of camouflage ghillie dangled like a moppish hairpiece over the sides, shading windows where he could make out bunked mattresses.

"They don't leave," guessed Buffalo, pointing out the beds. "I suspect that'd be suspicious, a bunch of sweaty jacklegs wandering out of the woods together."

"Lake's full of bass," countered Del Ray. "They leave each Friday with camping gear and tackle. No law against fishing."

"Weekends off?"

"It is a business."

"That's wild," said Buffalo. "Why not just hire some homeless guys to live out here?"

"For the camps, we want people with families."

"Why's that?" asked Buffalo.

Del Ray picked a fingernail. "Well . . . it's good they have skin in the game."

Buffalo understood. "Familes are insurance if something goes sideways." Nodded to dispel the awkwardness. "Well-oiled machine, looks like. But hey, Del, I might sound like a broken record, but thanks again for helping an old man out."

"Thirty-seven old now?"

"My knees say so."

"I like to keep good workers in mind for future projects," said Del Ray. "Your past skill set perfectly aligns with this job."

Corey wanted a better look at the corrugated buildings. Thatched roofs with hidden ventilation ducts and plastic-slatted doorways. Underneath it all a persistent hum. From the diagrams he'd seen, the rectangular structure housed chemical tanks, a processing lab. The smaller square structure a refrigerated supply house. Beyond them, shirtless men sat around a picnic table under a live oak, breaking up and collecting the shank in its crystalline, smokable form.

"You know, I met one of them twins," said Corey. "Duke. Not a *subtle* person, exactly."

"Oh yeah?" Del Ray grinned, intrigued. "What'd you make of him?"

"He basically said: *Del Ray sure does got a lot of randos hanging around him . . . you think that makes him more of an asset or a security risk?*"

Del bleated. "I mean, he's got a point."

"He knew my license was revoked. Sounds like maybe he's got his uncle's ear."

"Don't you worry, you're our guy," Del Ray assured him. "Seizer wasn't bothered by how you lost the job. Sometimes rough jobs get rough."

"People fight back," said Corey. "Arms break. If the courts don't wanna assume some risk, make bail enforcement illegal. But you can't tell a soldier to walk into combat with rubber bullets."

Across the way, another young man with a rifle pushed through the lab's plastic slats and pulled a Gatorade from the outdoor fridge. Del Ray motioned him over and introduced him to Corey, after which he returned to his post indoors.

"Correct me if I'm wrong, but some of these boys saw combat."

"It lives in the eyes," said Del. "Happy to provide vets with stable work."

The smaller structure's door opened this time and Jesse emerged, a clipboard under one arm and a chocolate ice cream cone in the other.

Corey's head shook in disbelief. "Please tell me you got an ice cream machine in there."

"Creature comforts," said Del Ray. "One of our first amenities. The bus is full of all kinds of screens and gadgets. But wait, you gotta meet Jesse, he's a bright spot."

Del Ray whistled and Jesse hooked around. Raised his cone, sliding his headphones off an ear with a shoulder.

"Come here a sec!"

As Jesse meandered over, Corey said under his breath: "Why's everyone so young?"

"What up, Del?" said Jesse.

"How you holding up, brother?"

Jesse pushed his lips out. "Always fine in the sunshine."

"Tell this man how you come to have sex the first time."

"Jesus," said Buffalo. "Hey, kid, you don't need to—"

"Shit, man, I don't care. I skated over to this girl's house one day after school. When I get there, she's got her cousin and best friend on a fold-up couch. Get this, they're babysitting—there's three little kids sitting on the floor, watching Snoopy on TV. The couch is already unfolded, and when I walk over, I see this chick lying there in her underwear. She pulls me on top of her and her best friend folds the bottom half of the mattress over me, and sits on it. I get my pants down, but when I look up, sitting right there in a chair across from me is her cousin. She's all leaned back, watching, like it's a movie. Whatever, I don't care. I get going, and the best friend above starts scratching my back with her nails, and all I hear in the background is Charlie fucking Brown."

"Tell him how old you were," said Del Ray.

"Twelve."

"Jesus," said Buffalo.

"They just grow up faster here," said Del, answering Corey's initial question.

"I reckon so."

"I went home and immediately confessed the whole thing to my mom. Cried in her lap. So pathetic," Jesse laughed. "But hey, at least I never jerked off a horse."

He shot Del Ray a weird expression and Del held up his hands. "This is blending two ideas in a way that lends itself to false speculation."

"Do tell," said Corey.

"It was a paying gig," said Del Ray. "You've worked a farm! Legit breeding practice."

"I'm sure it was consensual," ribbed Jesse.

Del Ray introduced Jesse to the man who would be making sure he got in and out of the camps okay from now on.

"Where's our goodly friend Jim Barns?"

Jesse's face soured. "Other side. Nice meeting you," he told Buffalo. "Good luck on the new job. The freaks will glitch out every now and again, but it's mostly quiet."

As Jesse walked the trail out, Del walked Buffalo around the lab, which was clearly some repurposed wildlife station or water-testing site. Corey wanted to see inside, but there'd be time.

Rounding the corner, they spotted a man asleep on a picnic table, sunglassed under a paleontologist's hat, with a pack of cigarettes resting on his stomach. The remnants of a half-chewed ice cream cone bled into a sticky puddle on the bench.

Del Ray milled about the snoring disappointment.

"Nice work if you can get it," smirked Corey.

Del Ray rubbed his neck, determining the least brutal but punishingly effective way to wake him.

"What happened to his face?" asked Corey, noting the scabbed wounds put there by Gumby's belt buckle knife. "Looks like a rodeo clown."

"Ask him. Or maybe don't, to keep the peace."

"That's what you're paying me to do, right?"

Del Ray curled two fingers away and the pair strolled back the way they came. "Name's Jim Barns. He had your job till just now. We'll assume he's on break."

"Are you fucking joking?"

"He'll be the new camp Foreman, making sure everyone stays on task. He's responsible for everything inside, you're responsible for everything outside. Unless the inside tries to get outside, under the wrong supervision."

"Is he trustworthy? He looks like a loafer."

Del Ray nodded. "Beastly little bugger, but he won't get in your way. And if he does, you give me a holler. But you focus on security, get to know the area, run through escape drills. We'll get you whatever you deem necessary . . . more cameras, lasers, drones. We have a small arsenal in the bus. I've been told spare no expense."

Corey kicked the dirt. "I'd love to get some dogs out here."

"Dogs bark," said Del Ray, leaving it at that. "Let's go meet the cooks."

Rounding the corner of the windowless lab, they came upon two men with gloved hands picking up glass shards. A puddle of chemicals pooled in the dirt.

"Congrats on your superfund site," said Corey, and Del Ray chuckled somberly. "Shit, man, are any of these guys using?"

Del Ray shrugged. "You're head of security. You tell me."

"Goddamn, Del, this isn't some shitty three-month gig, is it?" asked Corey. "We're not headed straight down the toilet, right? 'Cause I got a special-needs kid I pulled out of school to bring down here, and he gets a little weaker with each move."

Del Ray placed a hand over his heart. "Your itinerant days are over, my friend. Hire your boy a nurse. This is what we call growing pains. Everything's gonna work out golden."

Buffalo hugged his large biceps. "You got me wondering who's doing who a favor."

Draco rocketed down the hallway with a milk jug of shroom tea tucked in against his chest like a football.

"The spirit subdues the brain, confusing the body!" he called out, his raised fist inadvertently knocking a jade tiger off a bookshelf. He replaced the knickknack just as a scant, middle-aged filipino woman in a floral dress, his mother, shut the laundry room door. She quietly resumed her station at the stove, eyes dragged down, dutifully tending to her fish head miso soup, the pot lid trembling with steam. Draco leaned into her ear: "We must find the devil within and eat his lousy demon heart!"

"Mom, we're going camping," said Jesse, kissing her hair poof, which sent the woman's arms up and batting wildly. She escaped to strip off and refold a couch afghan, then broke away to rub lovingly the dusty corners of a picture frame: an image of her sons as toddlers. The woman was so possessed by her preoccupations that Eddy wondered if she suffered from an actual disease, like early-onset Alzheimer's—a personality in its final act, a ghost with visitation rights. Yet her handling of the framed picture offered an equally sad possibility, that this static memento brought greater joy than her living children.

This incident played to Eddy's mood. It summoned visions of his own mother, and the only baby photo of him in existence, a Polaroid kept face down in her bedroom dresser. There, a man in a pale shirt and slacks held a diapered baby aloft, standing within the open jaws of a red-eyed, teal alligator—the lurid entranceway to Gatorland. Over the years, the photo came to unnerve Eddy, who felt the baby's arms extended not toward the huge, pointy tooth, but someone or something just out of frame, some mysterious other, while the father's expression registered not as discomfort or boredom but something more profound—resignation—the look of a person saddled with poor life choices.

Jesse drove the new minivan he'd purchased for his mother beyond the farthest townhouses on Emerson, where pineland morphed into densely clustered tufts of palmetto and stately oaks lowered their vine dreadlocks to the ground. Parking along an empty cul-de-sac, they got out and stretched, then marched together into the loam-pungent woods.

Birds skittered by as the group trampled past marshland hammocks raised like volcanoes from black and orange claybeds. In a small clearing, Jesse sat down and twisted off the milk jug cap and chugged the shroom tea before passing it around. Not long after his first sip, Eddy began sensing the opening illusory effects of the bedevilment conjured by the hallucinogenic.

"I'm freaking out," he murmured, possibly aloud.

Jesse, at home in wavering realities, again pushed the jug toward Eddy, who motioned he'd had enough.

"I need whatever's the opposite of that."

"You ever think a bunch of losers like us would get our day in the sun?" Jesse asked, resting in his own little patch of daylight, the corona of a lesser god. "Did I tell you this already?"

Mickey had apparently brought him out to Tampa the previous weekend for a belated welcome-to-the-club adventure. They'd caught a Rays game, then hit up a famous spanish restaurant before landing at a high-end stripper joint, where Mickey hooked him up with a busty date ten years his senior with salacious lips and a bubble ass. The bartenders all treated Mickey like a well-regarded concierge, a minor celebrity they hoped to impress.

"He said Seizer knows it pays to keep the talent entertained," Jesse grinned. "This is just the beginning."

A howl split the air and Eddy shivered. Cueball and Draco were gone, missing, but Jesse's voice reeled him back. "Mickey's a salty dog," he said. "We'll all hang the next time he's in town. But how about you? Any fun stories with the drop-offs?"

The question allowed Eddy to enter reportage mode, calming him greatly. "Nothing too crazy. Duke and Lisbon are cool, maybe a little conservative. Don't drink, don't smoke. Cueball says Duke acts like he's in charge, but he's the boss' nephew, so what'd you expect? But yeah, I dig the traveling. There's a DC restaurant we drop at, I can order anything I want. Club sandwich, omelet. It's all free and paid for."

"Smooth," said Jesse. "I'm jealous you get to travel. Tell me about the cities."

"They're all different," said Eddy, drawing in the dirt with a stick. "Savannah's gorgeous. Giant mossy trees, slow-ass river, gothic haunted-as-fuck Civil War homes. DC is shit neighborhoods and then suddenly it's ancient Greece. Full of tourists and yuppies, but everyone looks burnt out. Racially, people don't mix, looks like. In Baltimore there's this warehouse full of stereos and computers, every kind of electronic device. And we get freebies, like I got a laptop for Gin. In Philly the murals on the buildings feel holy, somehow. But the city feels run-down, in its soul—"

"Wait," said Jesse, perking up. "You're driving that far north? When did that happen?"

Eddy squinted. When *did* that happen? But more importantly, how long had they been in the woods?

The howling started in again and Eddy sat up, spooked. Bushes looked positively alive now, suffering endless growth. Did adults take shrooms? Eddy wondered if they were adults now, and supposed they were. Most days he still felt like a kid adrift. But people's forebrains didn't mature until age twenty-five, he'd heard, so maybe the intangibility of reality and feelings of aimlessness were due in part to this solidification process. Or maybe it was the shaping forces of hardscrabble breeding, his mother's distaste for normies, with their office jobs and babies, readying him for an edgier fate, like those enjoyed by spies or circus folk. Fringe people, like those unmentionables who worked the camps.

"Hey, man!" Eddy spoke urgently. "Can you get me in to see the camps?"

Whatever hideous snapshot was thrust upon Jesse's inner screen dragged him back through the drug's immolating fog, charged with the intensity of a prognosticator. "No. No way, dude. It's *batshit* out there. Chemical burns, masked dudes with automatics. It got filthy quick. Workers shitting in the woods, not showering. Like a concentration camp, straight outta Hollywood."

Eddy lowered his voice. "Cueball does a little shank to stay awake for the drives," he said, failing to admit his own experimentation.

"That's seriously dumb," breathed Jesse. "Some of these people, their brains are like deserts. And their faces are like scabs."

"Ewww. Why?"

"The shit is toxic, man. We got tubs full of nasty-ass chemicals. Smells like rank armpit and cat piss, which you can't wash out. Workers that use turn worthless and get shipped out. Disappear, who fucking knows. I'm just glad I'm not there all the time. I ride in, check the inventory, make sure everything's kosher, and split."

"Well, shit, at least it's interesting," said Eddy. "My job's boring as all get-out. Lift furniture, drive, watch a map, unload. I'm on my phone so much, I'm the number two *Angry Birds* player in the US. God's honest truth."

Jesse shrugged. "I told you, bro, gotta step up your game. Ask for more work, or a different job. You can either run alongside that river of money or grow some balls and dive in."

The mushrooms finally won out, as Jesse plucked a scraggly hair from his arm. "You think it hurts when porcupines release their quills?"

Soon the land's hidden textures revealed themselves, the violent colors popping. Every peppertree berry and beetle carapace distinct, endowed with conscious thingness. The forest loomed, impenetrable. The stiffness in Eddy's knuckles ached. His eyeballs swam like anemones in their sockets, and soon he had a new mission in life, to categorize the different types of fungi: noxious wafers with roulette underbellies; hatchet heads broke off in a tree; gazebos under duress; frozen balloons of blown glass. *Pay attention,* said Del Ray. Packed with reservoirs of nutrients, the forest floor was like a world salad. You could feed a billion people off these things, and why didn't people see that?

The howls, the howls!

It was too much, and Eddy finally leapt up to confront them.

Draco was naked again, crouched between flaming palmettos, ears perked like a wolf's. Tilting his head skyward, he opened the heavens with a peal.

The sun flashed and scattered through the canopy. From some intimate distance rose the drumbeats of the native ais, upon whose consecrated ground they dared trespass. Eddy surrendered when he felt the drumbeats match his pulse. The tattoo on his wrist flickered to life. An inchworm sexed a leaf. Mosquitoes drilled his pores. *My question for you is, are you experiencing the world in a way that is fulfilling?* The world seemed infinitely fragile, crushable. What a horrible privilege, to take life or let it be. What idiot god had made him responsible for anything? Was shank actually killing people? He spied Cueball squatting behind a floppy elephant ear, a grunt peering over the blasted sandbags of a trench. Eddy failed to recognize Cueball's enemy. Unless, of course, *he* was the enemy.

Trees. Are just hairs. On the planet.

O how the pebbles giggled.

Overhead, a green-tailed mortar ripped through the black bottomless stronghold of night, its rippling wake disturbing the constellations as Eddy struggled to breathe, drowning in air.

How did he get home?

A memory: Draco hanging halfway out the minivan's sliding door, hands flung away and clawing the outer dark as Jesse struggled to wrestle him back inside.

Standing in the darkness of his mother's bedroom, Eddy swore he sensed her presence, that human frequency. He located his baby photo in the dresser drawer. There was his father, and there he was, the sacrifice. God's little joke, offered up to a world clearly meant to savage him.

The garage was inundated with moonlight, the fiberglass door glowing like a paper lantern. He located the clothes dryer. Looky here, a wishing well. Dropping in the picture frame, he turned the dial several clicks and punched the button. After a few rotations, the glass shattered and opened a gateway to a parallel universe where a loud and persistent gong accompanied the perilous war song of a city of mice.

He groped his way toward the kitchen door, a child again, everything made anew. He imagined his mother overdosing. Gin hugged his arm at the funeral. Thank you. Around the grave, bikers rode Lipizzaner stallions in a circle. There was a salad bar. He handed out lotto tickets. The sun exploded into a million tiny droplets and rained down upon them, yet the attendees continued to sing, even as they caught fire.

"What the hell are you doing?!"

A figure stood in the kitchen, backlit by some faint light.

"Go back to sleep."

"What the hell's wrong with you?"

Gin bypassed him and soon the grinding stuttered to a halt. She reappeared, somehow angrier.

"I'm on shrooms."

"So you decided to wreck the place?"

Shamed but feeling blameless, Eddy fought to quell the acid rising in his chest. Slipping away, he left the kitchen and flopped down on the living room couch, patting the space beside him. "Family meeting, family meeting!" he bellowed.

Gin refused to sit. He stroked her arm, striking a melancholy face. "Come on, sit down. Please? I have to tell you something, but you can't freak out."

"If you're about to say you fucked some random girl, let me go get a knife."

"I hardly have the time to fuck you," he said, embarrassed by its truth. "Okay, here it goes. Gin, baby . . . I'm gay."

"What? You are not!"

Eddy cracked up and rolled over. Red in the face, he put a hand to Gin's belly, forcing himself to get serious. "Okay, wait, no. But Cueball . . . wait, no. Listen. I'm sorry I didn't tell you this before. But the furniture job . . . it's not just furniture. This is so weird. Okay. The furniture isn't furniture. It's drugs."

"Eddyyy," she complained, taking a seat by his legs. It was truly, blearily late, and he was being uber-annoying.

"Me and Cueball, we help deliver drugs. With the Twins. Jesse is a Camper, which means he oversees produce. Hold up . . . *production!* Ha! From Publix to production! Anyway . . . we work for Del Ray and Bird. And this old dude Seizer. Not the salad. We are the spacemen of the animal kingdom."

Eddy belched loud and territorially, and for a dramatic finish, popped a cigarette in his mouth.

Gin's expression was flat. "Wait, are you being serious right now?"

A weak smile confirmed he was. Nothing he could say would yield anything worthy of approval. Apparently Gin's world sought to encompass an ever-expanding acreage of fools and sons-of-bitches. "Are you honestly sitting here with that face telling me you're a drug dealer?"

"That's the thing, Lana Lang!" Eddy said excitedly. "I don't *deal* shit, I just ship stuff. I don't even see it!"

Her eyes found the front door, but any distance placed between them now would signify an irrevocable rift. A finality. "What drugs?"

"Just one drug. A new one. Called shank."

"Isn't that . . . meth? Eddy, do you know what meth does to people? Where's my laptop? Have you given this *any* thought whatsoever?!"

"People are people, babe," he argued, lying back, arm over his eyes. "If they want drugs, they'll get drugs. If they want sushi rolls, they'll get that too."

"You're a child," she said blankly. Here was yet another dawn rising behind filthy curtains, her mother shaking her awake, asking her to keep quiet. "They don't make freaking docudramas about gangs killing each other over sushi!"

"Gin, you're making a molehill out . . . what the fuck is a docudrama? No, would you rather I get some crappy burger job? Or stack newspapers in the wee hours? Look at what we have!"

"And Del Ray? *Really?*" Gin exclaimed. "I mean, I can see how Bird can get people to believe his bullshit, being everybody's daddy . . . but Del, and Cueball? *Cueball?*"

The red slits of Eddy's eyes opened. He had to hurry up—the room's ceiling was threatening to unhinge and collapse upon them. "He's my best friend. I owe him."

"You don't owe anyone your life," said Gin pointedly.

"Ah, okay, let's do this," Eddy began, shifting around. "My mom . . . she has problems. You know this. Of the mental variety. One night, a couple years back, Cueball stopped by looking for me, but I was staying the night over at Jesse's. We were out at Snake Lake shooting his dad's . . . something . . . shotgun. The door was open. So Cueball walked in and found her right here, right there, *there*, on the floor. She'd OD'd. Naked. Puked blood. No, just listen. He went into her room for clothes and found two random fuckheads in her bed. Asleep. He took a knife from the kitchen and chased them out. He did that. For me. Understand? He wrapped her in a blanket and took her to the hospital. And she *lived*."

"That's . . . truly horrible," said Gin. "It is. And we can discuss this when you're sober, but I can only focus on us right now, and I need you to tell me the truth: are you using this drug?"

"I did once to stay awake on the drive. It upset my stomach. I got nervous all over my body. I didn't like it."

"You're an idiot. No, stop, I'm NOT doing this! I'm not going to be some junkie's good time before the shit hits the fan. My mom had boyfriends!"

"I don't understand why you're blowing this out of proportion!" he yelled, refusing to sit up. "I'm not some raving lunatic *tweaker*. I tried it *once*."

Gin told herself she was being fair. They lived together now, and Eddy's decisions affected her life as well. "You lied to my face."

"I know, and I'm sorry. Truly. But I made a promise. He's my brother. Baby, you know me," Eddy said, flipping around to lay his head in her lap. "I'd never do anything to hurt us. We need the money, and it's just for a little bit. I've got a plan. I'll do the tats and you'll work the counter. But I'll teach you to ink too, if you want."

"What are you even talking about?" Gin pleaded nasally. "Eddy? It's not money I'm worried about."

"I've got a plan, hon. I promise. I swear."

"But plans don't always work out. There are so many factors you can't even imagine—"

But he'd already passed out. She watched him, refusing to palm back his crooked hair. This was *deception*. No other word for it.

Her purse was in the other room. Clothes in drawers. She was yawning, but her mind went to the Buick parked beside the house. Which he'd bought for her. She blinked hard to keep her mind present, but she was tired. She had work tomorrow. She stared at the blank TV as the room filled with the sound of his breathing.

The information was arriving late, yes, but he'd told her the truth, was entrusting her with a secret linked to both his finances and physical well-being, and that spoke to something, even if it technically counted as a betrayal. *Technically counted?* What the fuck. Already she was making excuses for him. It was all so confusing. What kind of selfish . . . ? And what kind of person was she, if she went along with it?

He wasn't *entrusting*, he was *confessing*!

But didn't she say, out at his father's junkyard, that he could take his time sharing his secrets?

Was this a secret or a lie?

She tilted Eddy's head, needing to see his face. A furrowed brow, even in sleep. This boy who'd lost his mother to drugs and bad decisions. So why take a job like this? Misplaced loyalty? She imagined him in handcuffs. Had he changed and she missed it? Shaggy brown hair bleached by the sun. A bony-kneed goofball, with a cute, crooked smile. Teller of filthy jokes. Patient, generous, but also a poor sport, a getter-on of nerves. But extremely receptive to loss in others. Protective. To a fault, perhaps. What else might he be hiding? He'd fixed the air conditioner before she'd moved in, surprised her with a new laptop, and even dropped seven hundred bucks on a Buick so she could pick up the transcription tapes from her doctors' offices. She would pay him back. Every penny. She was doing her share. *She* was the one who shopped for groceries, and *she* was the one who'd hung a dream catcher and silver-green ferns around the house, and *she* was the one who'd scraped together a garden plot near where his childhood tree fort once stood, which was felled to a stump by his mother and made into a pseudo-Druidic sundial — Jesus flipping Christ.

She just wanted to live like normal people, was that so bad? Oh god — but not really, right? But normal people made sacrifices too, doing whatever was necessary to keep food on the table.

But this? *This?*

Your boyfriend's a drug runner.

Gin didn't want to admit how deep this cut, how desperate her love felt at times. It was unsettling. And so unlike who she thought she was. He was changing her, which was doubly worrisome. She fingered the curls of his forgiving hair, toying with the urge to pack up and leave. She exhaled and closed her eyes.

For fuck's sake. You could plan your whole life out and have it messed up by Wednesday.

As Christmas neared, the Armstrong Crew grew more vocal about needing a break, citing long hours.

There'd been a close call in Virginia. Lisbon caught the attention of highway patrol after nicking an exit-ramp guardrail at the end of a long shift. Though Cueball tested the speed of his Nova in full view of the officers, nearly five tons of unbalanced metal outweighed the aggravation of chasing down a couple of hicks dead set on blowing an engine gasket. Luckily, the stop only earned the Twins a citation, along with the stern suggestion they switch drivers en route to a hotel.

Despite them being on the road nonstop since summer, and Jesse pulling ten-hour shifts since a third camp broke ground, Bird still denied the Crew their vacations. Yes, their boss understood the bleary-eyed boredom and low-level stress that accompanied such work, but the club had entered an integral stage in its development, growing exponentially, and he couldn't just yank the conveyor belt off the production line.

Still, Bird wasn't heartless, so to quell his workers' grumbling, each were gifted an elite waterproof backpack—stuffed with twenty thousand dollars in small bills.

It was more cash than the Florida boys had ever seen in one place. Eddy was pretty sure it eclipsed his mother's take-home salary most years.

Wealth brings fresh options, new avenues of entertainment and consumption, and the Crew reacted in kind. Their weekend trips became more extravagant: box seats at Bucs games, shopping jaunts along the Gulf Coast, snorkeling at Ichetucknee Springs, where they'd ride the lazy river aboard an inflatable raft that supported five or six drunken fools and an Igloo of beer. Even Duke and Lisbon were invited, dodging everything but deep-sea fishing. When New Year's swept in with its colorful brushstrokes—an expansive sunset and fireworks viewed from the Key West pier, followed by rooftop grilling at La Concha Hotel—Jesse raised a toast with half-and-half creamers, much to Eddy and Cueball's amusement. Instead of resolutions, they celebrated new achievements.

And despite the direct hit their relationship took in terms of trust, Gin participated in these festivities as well. In fact, she planned most of the excursions.

After Eddy came clean, Gin had a clear choice—leave or stay—and she chose to stay. It was a leap of faith, for sure, evidenced by anxiety dreams she'd rather not discuss, but the morning following Eddy's confession, she'd secured two very important promises from him. One, no more lying—which included never hiding matters of real importance. And two, Eddy would quit his job after a year. Or she would leave him—no ifs, ands, or buts.

Eddy was contrite, and heartily agreed to the terms, swearing off shrooms forever—something she hadn't even asked of him. He promised to update her on any potential risks, realizing his decisions affected her as well. Speaking of which, she should probably know about the bonus . . .

Eddy emptied the backpack on the kitchen table. They stared at the pile of cash, neither speaking.

"It's a ridiculous job," Eddy finally said. "But maybe not entirely stupid."

Gin closed her eyes. "I understand why this makes sense to you, I do, but it's not worth risking your life over. Rich people spend this in an afternoon."

"That sounds like a challenge," he joked, but failing to elicit a smile, added, "I'll be real careful. And I'll quit in a year, or sooner, I promise."

Encouraged by Gin's willingness to listen, Eddy felt compelled to share more: a creeping depression had followed him home. The tedious midnight drives left him feeling tanked—wallowing, sifting. Wanting to help, Gin suggested they take a weekend trip to St Pete and visit the Dalí Museum. Break up the monotony, get their minds off the heavy stuff. This wasn't "leaning in," though—she was searching for a new foundation. And they actually had a lovely time, holding hands on their museum stroll, marveling before the *Millet's Angelus*. Eddy's mood slowly began to pick up, so Gin planned more outings, eventually inviting others along at his request. Cueball and Jesse could actually be fun too, in small doses, and the Twins seemed odd but harmless. This was Gin reclaiming her agency, rather than devolving into what her mother called a "worrywort." She would manage what could be managed, executor of her own decisions.

On the money front, they kept their accounts separate—Eddy, along with the rest of the Armstrong Crew, was suddenly flush, and wealth management for them was an entirely foreign concept for which Gin wanted to play no part, in accounting or administrating.

Del Ray had offered only one piece of advice for the workers, which was to avoid triggering a federal report by depositing more than ten grand in any bank account at once.

As home foreclosures rocketed toward an unknown apex, Jesse began investing in real estate—his deceased father's game—snatching up contemporary coastals for fifteen grand a piece at auction. Knowing no better, and without seeking advice, Eddy pridefully halved the balance of his mother's remaining mortgage, while the Twins went dutch on a bass boat and pumped the rest into an Indian Harbour Beach villa they shared as roommates.

Cueball fared less well. Every dollar he earned was spent without much consideration on alcohol, fast food, gadgets, pharmaceuticals, a .22 rifle, porn subscriptions, or frittered away mindlessly on phone apps. This went unchecked until his father received a delinquency notice for the red octagonal house, only the fifth such required mortgage payment. Bird knew his son was irresponsible, but this was outrageous, and so began deducting the expense immediately from his salary, sitting him down for a talk. Yet come payday, Cueball could be found dropping fifties again at the Golden Cue, just to get served.

During one particularly grueling bout of self-loathing, Cueball bought a blue-eyed Husky pup from a family of breeders, but the dog escaped. So he bought a siamese fighting fish, which for all intents and purposes committed suicide: high jump, wood floor. He told no one. Welled up as he gorged its lifeless body with marijuana seeds and buried it in the yard. And sometimes—just to stay awake on the road, he assured himself—he and Eddy would split a nugget of shank Kid Kaos slipped them at a Mission drop-off.

"Gotta test each batch, right?" said Cueball.

Eddy hit the pipe. "This is nowhere near as crazy as people say it is. I feel it, but I'm not, like, losing my mind."

Only to be kept awake for thirty-two hours.

This wasn't anything serious. Nothing that would upset Gin or, say, trigger a discussion. One hit at a gas station, waiting for the Twins to fill up. Never to get fucked-up, no, this was about staying focused, entering the zone, letting the night wind pass through your fingers as you pounded root beer after fizzy root beer and sang your way through an entire NOFX album. *You* try riding shotgun for thirteen hours and not dozing, Eddy argued with his imaginary accuser. Plus it helped him vibe with the universe for a bit, and what's so wrong with wanting a little extra love in your life?

An hour before drop-off, they'd mellow out with a pinner, so that Duke and Lisbon, who would absolutely narc, wouldn't catch on.

Around the beginning of February, though, something in Eddy shifted, and he felt it. There's standing on one leg, and standing on one leg with your eyes closed—without a bead on the horizon, you wobble.

Gin noticed the change too. Was it anxiety? If a traffic light didn't change promptly or a food delivery order arrived late, Eddy might blow a fuse. Accompanying this impatience was a brooding cynicism, appropriate when unleashed on some corporate malfeasance in the news, perhaps, but weird when judging a stranger's clothes, or sharp laughter. To avoid alienating him, Gin picked her moments, touching his arm to ask what was wrong. But things were always *fine*. Still, he'd recently begun screaming himself awake from nightmares, speaking groggily of vacant roads distended to some restless, dark infinity.

Gin kept herself busy, taking on extra tapes to transcribe, her evenings alone spent reading true-crime blogs or watching DVDs. She couldn't write. There were no high school friends to reach out to, or an office environment to help foster new friendships. Nobody with whom to share her fear that her relationship with Eddy might be heading downhill. She used to meet her mom for lunch on Thursdays, but Colt was now in Memphis, apparently, following a southern rock band on tour. Not a groupie, per se, but not *not* a groupie.

The fights began to worsen.

In the past, they'd hide their disagreements in teasing winces or voice concerns in loving, agreeable tones, but lately their spats took on an edgier, biting quality. Petty disputes rapidly escalated into entrenched battles that Eddy obnoxiously referred to as *rematches*, after which one of them would retreat to the bedroom as the other escaped by car. And wasn't he tired of it too? Worse still, these arguments began to reference money, which was never an issue when they had less of it. Had the electric been paid? *Yes, remember? I helped you set up e-withdrawal.* Why're we always running out of groceries? *You just mean there's no more frozen mini-pizzas, is that right? Because I went shopping three days ago, and that's all you're eating.* Even though Gin always covered her share of the bills, he'd often bring up their finances, but the truth was, despite dumping most of his bonus into the mortgage, Eddy was still fairly well-off. Or at least they weren't destitute, not like other folks. Weren't on SNAP, didn't have an EBT account. If the septic tank overflowed or a car battery died, they had credit cards, and the means to pay them off. And if the Democrats got their way, they might even get healthcare soon. She must have emailed Eddy four different links to online budget programs, which went ignored, so far as she knew.

But then suddenly the clouds would part—and his anger disperse. Eddy would apologize and ask to sit down to discuss it all, like adults. No, of course she wasn't his shrink, she was his girlfriend. Yes, he'd been an ass-hole, absolutely, sorry, but maybe she could stop rolling her eyes whenever he mentioned "the Crew"? Asking if they were a cult, or a rowing team? And if he occasionally cursed over some small frustration, could she not make such a big deal out of it? His outbursts affected her, sure—but maybe allow a little space for his emotional venting?

Gin had originally balked at the idea of professional help—why pay good money when you had friends—but after a client's nurse shared how a psychiatrist had helped her quit smoking, Gin began researching couples therapy.

Instead, work got busier, and they went on less excursions. She'd get back to filling up the calendar as soon as she finished this next batch of tapes. Occasionally, though, for no reason she could name, the old Eddy made an appearance, rejuvenated, gregarious and witty, taking her hand to slow dance to the department store muzak as they tried on funny hats. They would embrace the ahistorical present and pretend not to know where the money came from, and if Jesse and Cueball led him off to a corner of the bar to confer in whispers, Gin would occupy herself with her phone.

They were young and in love. They were busy. They were still figuring stuff out.

Show me a couple without issues.

Eddy saw she was trying. This couldn't be easy for Gin, he knew, and wrestled with that guilt every day—tiny needles of regret reminding him he wasn't perfect.

To compensate, he made sure to voice his appreciation for her, like when she did the laundry when it was his turn. But which also bugged him a little, honestly, because he was going to do it eventually, and now did he owe her something? Was she secretly keeping track?

He felt permanently exhausted. The drives were soul-sucking. Mountain passes and silver lakes are pretty, sure, but mostly it was one long inexorable tunnel of trees. The mind nibbling itself for hours. Not all good thoughts. Irrational thoughts. Wondering where Gin was, what she was doing. And come night, the woods cloaked in ambiguity, who she was doing it with.

He was protecting her from a part of himself he felt collapsing. The fatigue had caulked up his joints and spurred all kinds of gastrointestinal issues, with shank cravings fueling his paranoia. The petty arguments with her were often his fault, he knew. Problems not resolved by the deadening charms of television were leveled by sex, or pocketed away in a quest for food—temporary fixes the couple used to banish symptoms of a growing unhappiness.

Yes, he'd scrolled through her browser history—he wasn't proud of it. She spent a lot of time in forums, lashing out at anonymous posters over politics, or watching gifs of animals being cute. She pursued new interests with an erratic, short-lived passion. For instance, she developed a weird exuberance for the plight of mollusks after hearing a lecture by marine biologists at FIT. Or this sudden urge to start a podcast. She didn't seem much interested in writing anymore, and said she missed having other voices in her head. She claimed to lack *direction*. She was fighting *stasis*.

"Why's it matter what she does with her downtime?" Cueball spoke into the phone, pausing a video where a grizzly bear rushed an amateur photographer recording his own death.

"She keeps mentioning her own independence," said Eddy. "Which is fine, but . . . is that, like, independent of me?"

"Are you guys still having sex?"

When Eddy grunted Cueball thought he'd hit upon the real issue. "Is she working tonight?"

"Yeah. They dropped like fifty hours of recordings in her lap. I might just crash."

"Wanna come over?"

"And what, circle jerk to your fucked-up hentai? No thanks."

Cueball was caught off guard—was this a knock against him, or hentai? Sure, he liked the big cartoon eyes and little mouths and squirting tits, but who didn't? And yeah, like with everyone, the algorithm would occasionally land on some gay stuff, and though he didn't much care for the overly muscular forearms, the blowjobs were interesting.

"No, if I spank it any more today I'll need surgery. Goddamn. I'm fucking antsy but I'm broke till the end of the month."

Eddy felt the bug too. The Crew's plans to jet ski had been sidelined by an arctic cold front chilling the lakes. He'd actually tried sketching some tattoos earlier, which resulted in a wastebasket of crumpled pages. Most nights that Gin thought he was sleeping, he was actually on his laptop, hunting little hits of dopamine. It all felt like killing time, the weekend jaunts a flagging entertainment, watching underpaid workers cater to monied people trying on different lifestyles.

"There's a party down at the Compound," offered Eddy.

"I don't wanna suck cans with no inbred trash," said Cueball.

"Wanna weasel our way onto a poker ship?"

"I need something more intense. Remember all the fun we had jumping off causeways? Getting chased by the cops? Just come over, I'll think of something."

That first night all they did was get drunk together and watch *South Park* and *Family Guy* episodes deep into the early hours.

The following Saturday, however, they binged on caffeine pills and snuck onto a hotel balcony, leaping into the shallow end of the pool, which got them chased onto the beach by a night manager. They threw knives at each other's feet by firelight and saluted the blue dawn with a bottle of Jack waist-high in the freezing ocean, the shadow of a great sea turtle passing between them. Eddy later stumbled through the front door to find Gin curled up on the couch. Instead of rousing her, he pulled over a chair and smoked, watching her sleep.

He woke the next afternoon to the sounds of keyboard clicks in the office. The door was closed, and he saw no reason to bother her.

So he rolled over to Cueball's with hot wings, planning to watch some football. He found his friend resting in a chair on the elevated porch, pecking banana spiders from their webs with a rifle, a skill at which Cueball was incredibly adept.

"Damn, you been practicing?"

"Life of a single man."

"Lemme see that."

Eddy would never shoot a living creature, but he could tear the heck out of some tree bark. Cueball took back his rifle and grouped five shots at the heart of Eddy's target.

As the weeks passed, their rivalry flourished. When the typical forms of childish grotesquerie failed to alleviate their restlessness, they upped the ante with theatrics fueled by narcotics and a craving for adrenaline highs. Gin soon fell behind on booking trips, seated before her transcribing machine like some fairytale maiden at the loom. So off to Cueball's Eddy went, popping beers until one of them, struck by some ridiculous notion, snatched the car keys off the coffee table.

Their games had one rule: any new suggestion had to one-up the previous—either in risk, complexity, or sheer stupidity. Draco was called, and instead of trying to hang on to the Cadillac hood, they'd hurl themselves overboard on purpose. After huffing Freon from a neighbor's a/c unit one night, they scaled the incredibly tall radio tower behind the Palm Bay Police Department, dangling from the highest beams. Pretty soon Cueball had them breaking into cars off University Blvd and ripping out stereos. Whenever Gin texted, they were out bowling or playing eight ball. They were in a meeting. You should see the size of this grouper Cueball hooked. In reality, they were smoking weed dipped in embalming fluid, driving golf balls off the community center rooftop into traffic. Or tossing live rounds into a bonfire as they drunkenly circled the perimeter, waiting for the popcorn explosions that sent them diving for sand.

These games were never spoken of beyond themselves, save once, when Cueball arrived prior to a club meeting at Bird's to pull Eddy into the parlor. Off in a leather chair sat Jesse, listening to music on his phone with his eyes closed. Cueball produced a plastic sandwich bag from his jeans. Swimming inside like a drowned thumb was a used condom.

"I fucked Marilyn," Cueball gloated.

"What? Perkins Marilyn?"

It was the first time Eddy had not witnessed a challenge firsthand, and even though he would have refused to participate if asked, he couldn't help but take it personally.

"Pink and stink, bitch. *Coolbol, Coolbol, I vant chew in my icehole.*"

After gingerly carrying the funky condom to the garbage, Cueball said the only way Eddy could beat him was if he fucked a donkey. Or some chick with AIDS.

Jesse awoke to sitting. "Dude, that's not funny." Then grunted his way to standing and stumbled outside as Cueball peeled the paper from his beer bottle. They knew Jesse's favorite aunt had contracted HIV a decade ago, and that he sometimes went over to cook her meals, after his mother refused to visit.

"Not like he's never made a joke before," Cueball muttered.

"He's under a lot of stress," said Eddy. "Camp's got him working over-time. You should go apologize."

"Fuck that, I didn't give his aunt AIDS."

"C'mon, man. Dude's your brother."

"My little brown teddy bitch, is what he is," said Cueball. "Shit, okay. I'll give him a smooch for you," and left to track down Jesse.

Eddy wondered if his friend would ever accept what he was clearly de-flecting with these jokes. It was tiresome to watch him smuggle it around like a flame in the wind.

His phone vibrated. It was Gin. "Hey."

"Where are you?"

"Bird's. We're having a meeting. What up?"

"*What up?* Orlando? Indigo Girls tickets? Ring a bell?"

"*Shit.*" He'd forgotten about her Christmas present. "I'm sorry, baby, I completely spaced. Listen, I can't get out of this. Why don't you go on ahead and I'll catch up with you."

"You mean drive out to Orlando alone and just *wait?*"

"Fuck, hon, I'm sorry, but this is important!" Eddy covered the phone with a hand, checking under the butterfly doors for movement. "Bird al-ready chewed my ass for being late. Can you take someone else?"

"Like who?"

"I don't know, an old friend or someone? For real, I'll make it up to you. We'll go to Disney or somewhere, you pick."

"Whatever," she said. "Call me when you're done."

"Are you gonna go?" he asked, but she'd already hung up.

Continuing the argument with himself, Eddy pursed open a small bag-gie of powder and helped himself.

"Hey there, kiddo," Del Ray spoke over the parlor doors.

Eddy thrust the baggie into his jeans. "W-w-wassup, Del?"

"Just wanted to check in, see if you boys got everything set up for tomor-row night." Del Ray ambled in and swung a leg over a foldout chair. He pointed at Eddy's pocket. "Friendly reminder, that stuff stays out the house."

"Naw, you're right, sorry, just needed a little jolt."

"Here's the thing—I'm thinking maybe you and Cubes are bringing along pick-me-ups for the drives, yeah? That ends now. If you get searched, that's legit jail time. We clear?"

"Crystal," said Eddy.

Del nodded. "I'll hold you to it. But hey, let's you and I discuss this upcoming shindig. Derrik is an asset, and our best bet on staking a claim in Jesutopia."

Jesutopia was Del Ray's nickname for the lower-central region of the southern states, the buckle of the Bible Belt. A week prior, over a steak dinner at the Gristle & Grease, Del informed the Crew of a side job coming their way. An old biker friend of his named Derrik was riding into town. This Derrik owned a chain of weapon and apparel stores, alongside a few brothels—*pleasure palaces*, Del called them—stretching from Knoxville to San Diego. *This here's highly privileged information, so keep it under your hat.* Turns out Derrik was also a semi-retired arms dealer with ties to major borderland traders, having been one of the first smugglers to railroad mass quantities of meth up through Nogales into Tucson. Seizer, ever the opportunist, saw the biker's collection of firearm and adult-oriented businesses as the perfect corridor for telegraphing shank out West.

What kept the boys' attention was Del Ray implying that the upcoming recruitment party would also function as an appraisal of the Crew's managerial skills, should any of them hope to eventually elevate themselves within the club. It was a clear opportunity for Eddy to prove his worth—if not to his bosses, then to himself.

"We're all set," Eddy assured him. "Duke's got the kegs lined up, and Cueball scored a little weed and some blow."

"Well, that's going beyond the call of duty, but probably not a bad idea," Del Ray said. "Know that Seizer's taking a big risk by having you boys serve as the welcoming committee. But I say, you set the bar high, people rise to meet it. All you gotta do is show the man a good time."

"Your will be done," said Eddy. "Anything for the club. Go team."

Eddy started off, but Del Ray eased him back with a brush of his fingers. "You know, Eddy," he said, squaring his eye, "I'm a man of few real talents, but one is the ability to recognize naked sarcasm. So let's have it, what's the problem?"

The problem was, a month of sleepless nights had left Eddy feeling sapped. His nerves got so bad sometimes, the wind felt like rug burn. The drug use no longer felt recreational, nor requirements of a job demanding long hours, morphing somehow into an honest habit. The pills and powders, the innocent-looking tabs of acid, were little more than veils he dropped over a very real sense of desperation, treading water. He felt little desire to do much of anything, the once-colorful world having congealed into a washed-out, lusterless gray. Sex with Gin felt more like forgiveness than fornication, and his penchant for mindless internet memes and trash TV, especially programs documenting lives destroyed by drug abuse or gangs, proved unquenchable. He could sense Jesse drifting away, maturing, while Cueball's everything was being extinguished at the altar of his father's choices, which Eddy could not—would not—let him suffer alone.

"I'm just tired," he said, rubbing his knuckles. "I blew this thing with Gin today."

"We're all a little beat," said Del Ray. "With a start-up, they say you don't sleep a full night for a whole year." He pointed down. "But maybe we cap the medicine bottle for a while. When I was young I sometimes nipped a bit too much and it cost me. Whad'ya say?"

"Sure."

"Everything kosher between you and Cueball? I sense friction."

"He can be a handful sometimes," replied Eddy.

Del Ray hung his forearm around Eddy's neck. "You two remind me of Bird and me when we was dumb shits. Guess which of you is me."

The sound of chairs being dragged together pulled Del back through the butterfly doors just as Bird shouted that someone had failed to order enough brisket with the takeout.

Sniffing, Eddy touched his nose. His fingerprint came back bloody.

Eddy returned from Winn-Dixie to discover his front door wide open. Jesse and the Twins were on his couch, hunched forward like downtrodden groundhogs. On his new flat-screen TV an enormous pair of breasts flopped in perfect synchronicity as a phantom voice moaned operatically in surround sound; it was like his entire house was vigorously, almost contemptuously, indulging in the orgasms he'd been unable to give Gin.

"This was already on," said Jesse.

Duke pointed at the shopping bags. "Got any Dr Peppers in there?"

"Cups and snacks for tonight," said Eddy.

Cueball was the only other person with a house key. Lisbon pointed to the backyard.

Eddy found Cueball on his knees, combing the grass for four-leaf clovers he might ingest for even greater luck. His eyes were wet, red welts. Eddy yanked him up by the arm and carted him inside, shoving him into a chair.

"Why'd you guys let him do this? They're counting on us!"

"We found him this way," said Duke.

Apparently Cueball had admitted to chasing lorazepam with a half-bottle of Robitussin. He swiveled from the armchair to kneel before the cable box, manually punching through stations until Donald Duck appeared on-screen, spinning in circles, a mousetrap clamped to his tail feathers. A slew of garbled curses hovered overhead as lightning bolts.

"I think," said Cueball, head slowly lowering to the cool floor, "that I am having a drug thing happening."

The situation was beyond discussion. Eddy calmed himself enough to ask Lisbon to make coffee.

"When are you picking up the kegs?" he asked Duke.

"Jesse's on it. We have to run to Orlando. There's a boat motor I won on eBay and the dude won't drive it over, so we'll be a little late."

"Can't that wait?"

"Relax." Peeling five hundreds from his wallet, Duke wadded them up and tossed the ball in Jesse's lap. "Robbie at Discount Joe's put aside two kegs for us. Bud Light and Blue Moon. Think you putzes can manage to hold down the fort till nine?"

Jesse tucked the bills away. "More beer for me."

Cueball groaned as he raised his head, surveying the room from the threshold of some ghastly dream.

"Should probably keep any weapons away from him tonight," said Duke.

Cueball's face went angry. A spasm jerked an eyelid. "I don't really think you motherfuckers know who you're dealing with — "

Then he arched his back and vomited over his arms.

The condemned, two-story spanish tenement hidden from the Dixie High-way by half an acre of woods was proof that Jesse could outright buy a house these days for what others paid in rent for a year. He took the top floor as his own and allowed the Vietnam vet squatting downstairs to stay on as security. The property lacked neighbors for a quarter mile and was run-down in a cozy sort of way that made it perfect for rambunctious get-togethers.

A grunting motorcycle slowed at the driveway, its headlight illuminating an early-century signpost: *De Frehn Tourist Rooms*. Gathered around a large bonfire in back, twenty tipsy partygoers listened in rapt attention as the Vietnam vet, perched high in a tree forked by lightning, warmed the older crowd to combat stories delivered in hushed and reverent tones.

Upstairs, however, Cueball had surprised everyone by packing Jesse's apartment with strippers from Bare Assets and freshmen from a nearby community college, lured here online by the promise of free alcohol, in case Derrik favored disillusioned young women who flashed for selfies and could swallow their weight in cheap liquor.

So far Derrik remained downstairs. A burly, scar-pocked wrangler, he'd arrived with a gentle dog named Missy. For some reason, Derrik kept an antique black satchel by his side, reminiscent of an old-timey house doctor's.

Gin didn't care for him. Watched in disgust as the loathsome figure, splayed across the ground, squeezed her mother's nipples unapologetically for the howling benefit of others, with Colt slapping his paws in modest scolding. The pair were introduced the night before at Ma Kettle's, the very day her mother returned from tour, and disappeared together before the third pitcher hit the table.

Gin leaned back into Eddy, who sat slumped on the broken jaw of a picnic bench. Cast in darkness and light, the fire sculpted from his face myriad expressions, as if he were not a being of sole stock but the sum of deeper, fractured selves, each struggling for possession.

"You look so old right now."

Touching his knee scattered the ghosts. He handed over his beer to sip, rubbing her ear.

"You see Duke or Lisbon upstairs?"

Having recently returned from the bathroom, Gin shook her head. "Just Cueball and his chlamydia squad." She tugged at his jeans. "Hey, babe? Can we go?"

"Mm."

"Anywhere. Right now, tonight, just you and me. Hop in a car, zip down to the Keys. Go snorkeling. Pet porpoises."

He exhaled and checked his phone. "I can't, hon. We'll take a trip soon, I promise. I'm working on getting some time away from you."

"*Hm?* What?"

"Once I get some vacation days. We'll rent a boat, go swordfishing."

Eddy's concentration was elsewhere, but she'd heard the slip—away *with* you, is likely what he'd meant. What she didn't hear, and hadn't for a while, was an answer not colored by ambivalence, using that certain irritated tone.

Another car puttered up the drive, parking in front.

The idea of stoned coeds and sex workers running amok did not sit particularly well with Eddy. It was especially grating whenever the top door swung open to rain shrill voices and laughter down upon the mellow group below. It felt like two parties, and Derrik obviously preferred this one.

Even though Derrik didn't seem like he'd be a problem, Eddy decided to remain stone-cold sober. It was high-end babysitting, but sometimes that's the job. Besides, the onus was on Derrik to prove his compatibility with the club—he was a Prospect, entering into a probationary period. Just because they were interviewing new players didn't mean he'd be granted immediate access to the Inner Circle. This wasn't a biker club, it was a business, and nobody sat down with the big dogs until they'd endured the probing banter of the firm's recruiters and low-level executives.

Eddy called Duke again but got no answer. He texted Lisbon.

Jesse picked up right away.

"Where are you?" Eddy demanded, moving away from the fire.

"Dude, this Robbie guy called in sick and now this needledick at the liquor store won't sell to me, so I called Draco. He's fifteen minutes away. How's our guy doing?"

"I mean . . . fine? Your neighbor's entertaining us with murder stories, but this half-keg of Michelob won't last."

The upstairs door opened for a brief, jarringly loud moment before two smokers slammed it shut.

Passing the fire as he hung up, Eddy met Gin's inquisitive eyes. "I gotta check on Cueball."

The exterior stairs had no railing and were dangerously warped, with rusty nails mushrooming from the planks. As he ascended, turning at the first platform, Eddy struggled to come up with a pitch that might convince his friend to shut down the party upstairs.

Unseen speakers blared the White Stripes into a living room overflowing with strangers—drunken young women in short shorts being hit on by callow men in skinny jeans whose coarse invitations lacked any real suavity or charm.

He found Cueball lying on the couch, straddled by a doe-eyed, sharply featured girl of questionable age with a gold-red weave spooling from her head. As she coyly tickled Cueball with a feather duster, he fired off a toy gun, blanks erupting in sparks of sulfur. *"You're* the monkey turd!" she shrieked, to which he replied, "Better a monkey's throw-thing than a no-tits lesbo fag hag!" Falling into laughter, Cueball then bent the duster into a shape she called more proof of his obsession with his *thingee.*

"Sir Edward!" Cueball proffered in mock civility, surprised to see him standing there. "So glad you could join us."

"What the fuck are you doing?" Eddy asked evenly. "Who are these people?"

Cueball smacked the girl's ass as she left for a drink. "Shit, I don't know. Those two there are . . . obviously strippers. These guys . . . the community college? Same with the girls by the fridge, I think. This chick here I met online—"

"You should get them out of here."

Cueball raised the cap gun to his temple. "Chillax, my dudester. It's a party."

"You're making me do everything alone!" whispered Eddy.

"Man, there's nothing to fucking do."

"Who is this guy, Golfball?" asked the girl, returning with a tumbler of straight gin.

"This is my brother, baby," Cueball replied. "Shannon Elizabeth, I'd like you to meet Eddy Wildeboar, who you will probably never experience biblically—" Which awarded him a slapped arm. "Whoa, hey! I said *probably*! Eddy, this here's my long-lost sister."

"I aint your sister, mister," she shot back. "If I was, you think I'd be this pretty? I'd be uglier than a wart on a flea's cock."

This got Cueball laughing so hard he turned red and hugged a throw pillow to his face. Calming down, he sighed at Eddy's rigidity. "What's your problem? You're like a bump on a log." Which of course started it all back up again.

"We're on duty!" seethed Eddy, mad at Cueball for forcing these ridiculous words from his mouth.

"Dude, seriously," said Cueball, picking through an ashtray of crushed joints. Instead, he snorted a bump off Shannon Elizabeth's tiny fist. "Hey, we got boiled crab legs in the kitchen, why don't you go grab some?"

"Or maybe you sit up," said Eddy, "lose the trailer trash, and do your fucking job."

Shannon Elizabeth responded by hooking her jaw, a look of defiance and incredulity surfacing in her eyes.

"Jesus, man, there's no need to—"

"You sonofabitch! Who the fuck you think you are?" she shouted, rising sprightly on the sinking cushions.

"Sit down, hot stuff. Eddy's just . . . culture shock. He gets nervous around sexy-as-hell, independent redheads."

"That still don't make it right!" she yelled. "I don't need this mess from some limp-dick little shit like this!"

"That's true, sweetheart, you don't. Now do me a favor and put that finger back in its holster before someone gets hurt."

This was a losing battle—one Del Ray could handle when he arrived. The best Eddy could do was make sure the two crowds remained separated.

"Keep everyone inside and upstairs!" Eddy barked, shouldering people out of his way.

"Wait, don't leave angry!" shouted Cueball. "We promised never to go to bed angry!"

The crisp night air was a welcomed relief. Beyond him faces flashed the glowing dark periphery like carp in a pond.

The vet clung to his tree perch, a leper at the castle walls, relating his grandest tale yet, one involving a venereal disease, a denigrated nurse who could double for Princess Di, a firefight in the paddies, and an asylum in Saigon—proving once again to Gin that men lived to tell tales emblematic of their own idiocy and pain, as if a sufficient lack of either threatened their very relevance.

She watched Eddy take the stairs down.

Sliding back onto the broken picnic bench, he took her shoulders in his hands.

"Everything okay?" she asked.

He grunted.

"Maybe I shouldn't have come."

"You're not getting in the way or anything."

"That's not what I meant."

Together they watched Derrik's hand move up Colt's inner thigh, his bare teeth finding her neck . . . and that was enough for Gin.

"Disgusting," she huffed, rising to pat away the sand. "You wanna walk me down to the river?"

Eddy rubbed his forehead. "I should stay here."

"Fine," she said, and set off alone.

She braved the unlit driveway and crossed a nearly vacant Dixie Highway to find a seat on a flat limestone shelf resting atop a steep embankment overlooking the Indian River. Barges slid quietly over the murky waters, lit up like a carnival. The river was something of a refuge for Gin these days, a place she could go unwind and read fantasy novels. She liked watching the red-faced joggers dig deep down when pushing themselves, enjoyed chitchatting the dog walkers at Ryckman Park, where families on the wharf scanned the water for stingrays. But it was entirely magical at night, the oil-black waves lapping the banks.

It took all of two minutes to wish she'd brought a cigarette. She rarely smoked, though the cravings were announcing themselves more often, along with a fear that Eddy and her were slowly becoming different people—not lovers, but others.

On her way back, she spotted a few figures drinking on the front stairs. As she approached, one clicked his tongue meaningfully, so she changed direction, heading toward the backyard fire, where she was greeted unexpectedly by a bounding, excitable dog greased in claydirt.

Gin offered her scent, watching the dog's head dart back and forth like a chicken's, one dead eye frozen in the moonlight. It gave a single yap, warning its owner of her presence, before licking its nose and allowing Gin to knead the loose scruff of its neck, tail wagging.

"Who's a muddy buddy? You's a muddy buddy! Aww, sweetie—"

Suddenly from behind Gin arose the rushing sound of swishing jeans and what sounded like snapping gunfire. The mutt bayed in blind confusion, spinning in circles until it fell sprawling to the dirt. As it struggled to regain its footing, Cueball pressed its rump with a shoe, forcing it crabbing sideways into a ditch, where it hobbled and bayed.

"You okay?" Cueball wheezed, his cap gun still pointed at the dog. "Wait . . . stand back. You can't tell which have rabies and which don't."

"What the fuck! Are you insane?" Gin yelled, fists balled at her sides. "Are you high?"

Cueball was confused. He *was* high, but that wasn't her point, apparently. "It yapped, and you jumped back—"

Derrik, impressively bulky by firelight, was now hustling toward them, whistling and calling out: "Missy? Missy? Here girl!"

With the foreign chemicals in his body positively boiling, Cueball retreated into the shadows.

The forlorn mutt howled again and Derrik leapt in its direction, taking up the animal in his arms. He turned to Gin for answers.

Gin shook her head no, and together they watched Cueball skirt the bonfire and ascend the stairs.

"Hey! Hey, you!" Derrik yelled, the ropes of his neck engaged. "I'm talking to you, motherfucker!"

"What's happening over there?" shouted Colt.

"Shut your piehole, you fucking cunt!" Cueball squawked from above.

A rush of party noises flared from above, then hushed.

The biker carefully traipsed back to the fire, laying Missy down at Colt's feet. Colt raised a hand against his intentions, but Derrik ignored this, stripping off his jacket. He swept up the antique doctor's bag and lunged toward the house.

Onlookers retreated into the darkness or crouched together, conferring in whispers.

"You have to stop him!" Colt begged Eddy from across the fire. "Something bad's going to happen to him!"

Eddy shot her a glare. "I think we're worried about different people."

They watched Derrik haphazardly bound up the creaky stairs, taking two steps at a time. The very second he yanked open the door to Jesse's apartment, Eddy charged the house, dipping under the platform.

The music above died abruptly.

There was shouting. Muffled voices issued from the other side of the building. A sudden thunder arose, rubber shoes on wood, as the inside crowd scrambled down the front staircase. Gin watched a young redheaded girl scurry across the vacant highway and slip down the river embankment. Car doors squeaked and engines sputtered to life with a cranky impatience, followed by billowing clouds of rocks and dust.

Derrik's silhouette reappeared in the doorway above.

Plodding down the stairs, he nearly veered over the edge of the platform under which Eddy waited, afraid to move, then ambled toward the bonfire.

Colt released a short cry as the firelight caught Derrik's face, a glowing phantasmagoric mask, red as engine fluid, the wetness soaking his curls. He stumbled, unwilling to relinquish his willpower, the black bag clapping at his side emptied of whatever required this ritual of blood.

The biker fell beside his dog, one eye puffing shut. "Is she okay?"

"Oh, honeybear . . . your face."

"I can't drive," he said. "Need to walk some. That boy—" And here the biker reenacted briefly with his hands a brutal exchange. Cueball had stolen the handgun taken from the bag and pistol-whipped him with it. "I's only gonna scare him. I swear to god I wasn't aimin at nothin real."

Ego maligned and skull throbbing, Derrik kneed himself to standing, and with the last of his energy, kicked over the beer keg. Then hobbled over to his motorcycle and unsnapped a leather saddlebag, rummaging inside. The vet in the oak tree, surmising what Derrik was after, fell from his perch and hobbled off toward his barracks, motioning for everyone to scat.

Jacket pulled across whatever he was hiding, Derrik careened toward the woods as Missy snaked his strides. Colt, following, swept her gaze over the crowd, as if implicating each in the night's misdoings.

Some folks around the fire bid the biker good riddance. Apparently he'd talked some game down at Ma Kettle's the night before, and all the bravado-engorging stories touting his personal heroics now seemed the cheap talk of a broken liar who'd just got his ass whooped by a teenager.

Unless, of course, Cueball was lying dead upstairs.

Eddy circled the stairs and raced up, chiding himself for leaving his gun in the car, alongside Cueball's, which he'd taken from his friend out of caution earlier that afternoon.

He paused at the open door, the living room cast in the ephemeral light of a destroyed lamp. No noise. His heart pleaded as he searched for legs, shoes. He stepped inside. Beer bottles stood at attention on the coffee table. A red purse yawned on the couch. Only then did he notice the black, bloody splotch muddying the carpet. A shiny cap gun lay beside it.

A latch came undone from down the hall and the bathroom door eased open. Cueball stepped out, shutting off the light. He dried his hands with a washcloth, the butt of a handgun snug at his waist. Seeing Eddy, he straightened his posture.

"You know what this means," he said calmly, moving to drop the washcloth over the discolored puddle and tamping it down with a foot. "We may have lost Jesutopia."

Eddy charged, head ducked, and slammed into his friend, forming a hip-shaped crater in the drywall behind him. They wrestled like ants, headlocks and awkward holds. Eddy unsheathed the gun and flipped it away. Cueball was easily manageable, his gaunt arms relaxing as he lay defeated, red-faced and pinned.

"This isn't just about you!" Eddy wheezed, breathless and desperate. "Over a fucking dog!"

Fiercely proud, Cueball focused on the ceiling, a luminescent streak of blood sliding from an ear. "He's the one pulled a gun. He was gonna kill me."

"You lost Seizer money," Eddy gasped. "You think your dad can fix this?"

Cueball stared straight ahead. "I saved people's lives."

From beyond the open door came the rumblings of an argument. Cueball used the distraction to dig a palm under Eddy's chin, forcing him aside and rolling away. Rising, Cueball discovered a mousetrap clipped to the back of his shirt. At first he swiveled around, trying to grab the trap—only to give up and begin hopping about erratically, arms flailing, quacking like a duck.

Eddy watched him, baffled, understanding now that Cueball's actions were a shared responsibility, and likely his misfortune.

"*Quack quack quack!*"

"Shut up!" Eddy scolded, unable to hear. "Something's happening!"

But Cueball wasn't listening. "Come bring it, you psycho cousin-fucking cocksuckers! I'm the *cueball*, motherfuckers. *Quack, quack!* You fetched some lousy-ass eight ball to mess with me?"

The voices outside intensified. Cueball paced in circles but stopped quacking. Eddy recognized Colt's imploring tone; Derrik spat a few harsh words back at her; but it was the third voice that made him perk up—Del Ray, thank fucking god.

Del's voice was cautious, reassuring, as if talking someone off a ledge.

Then the voices vanished altogether, and the apartment grew quiet. Instinctively, Cueball went to his knees. The two friends watched each other from sphinx positions.

The next shout they heard was the kitchen window exploding.

They didn't understand what it was saying until another round split the doorframe.

Cueball slumped tiredly into his parents' home, dropping his keys in the foyer tray, an old habit, and opened the fridge for a beer. He was tired and wanted to get home and crash, but he'd been summoned. The microwave clock read a little past midnight.

A side lamp by the couch clicked on.

His father had been waiting in the dark. Two tumblers rested on the coffee table.

"Come sit down."

Cueball twisted off the bottle cap, walked over, and flopped down in a rocking chair. "Mom's car's gone."

"She's out."

"Out where?"

"Charity fundraiser."

"The battered women's thing?" Cueball asked, flashing a smile. "Well, at least one of us is doing some good in the world. Balancing out the sins of the family."

Bird was up and on him.

Cueball was lifted in passing and dragged kicking to the wall and stapled there by a forearm. A gut punch crumpled him to the floor. His father's whiskey breath was everywhere, along with the word *faggot*, and then it wasn't. Cueball lay there a moment, watching his beer empty to the carpet.

"Get up and come here," Bird ordered.

Cueball pushed up, his fingers arthritic. The voice in his head, so often an ambient sound, dispensed instructions he could not misinterpret or ignore. He loped back over, gripping his stomach, and lifted the bottle from the floor, then uprighted the chair.

Bird filled the tumblers with Beam and placed one glass before Cueball. Then folded his fingers together over his large belly.

"Two things. One: you are my son, and under my protection. As a favor to God and your mother, I stood up to a man who could have you killed."

"Fuck him."

"You will FUCKING RESPECT ME!" Bird roared, rising and glaring, indomitable.

If Cueball was afraid, something else won out. "I didn't ask for this," he wept.

"Your thoughts on this matter mean shit to me," said his father, taking his seat. "I gave you a choice and you made it. Now shit's gonna get real heavy, real quick. If you're not with me, if you don't abide, you are my weakness. Understand? LOOK at me! If there's an ounce of blood in the water, there's men who can smell it." Bird paused to take stock. "You've put us all at risk."

Cueball wanted to hide his face, but the shame was too much even for that. "That guy was trying to kill me, Dad! Do you even care?"

"He wasn't going to shoot you, dumbass." Bird picked up the glass of Beam and held it dangling in his hands. "Christ, he came here *alone*. You made it look like we ambush our partners! That's twenty years of friendship for Ray flushed right down the toilet!"

"You weren't there," said Cueball. "The way he looked at me—"

"You lost your car."

"What?"

"You still got your truck, you can drive that," said his father. "But the Nova is for Runners, and you're not running anymore."

Cueball raised his hands off his knees. "Fine. Take it."

Bird slugged the brown in his glass and watched his son.

"You start your new job next week, and I don't want to hear a fucking word. I gotta say, Seizer didn't think it was demotion enough, or far enough away. After what you did tonight, I wouldn't trust you around my family, either. This is a shit ton of bad luck you brought down on us. All you seem to care about is yourself."

Cueball's expression hardened. "Then I guess we have something in common after all. 'Cause I know for a fact Mom thinks the same thing about you."

This time Cueball did not get off the floor for a very long time.

While scrambling up some eggs for Eddy, Del Ray broke the news that Cueball was off the Runner job, and barred from fraternizing with the other members of the Armstrong Crew for the foreseeable future. Del also sought to temper rumors that Bird had beaten his son within an inch of his life, downplaying the event as a family squabble with unfortunate rough patches.

Eddy couldn't argue a case — it was settled. Seizer was furious, wouldn't even schedule a meeting to discuss it, directing Del Ray to inform each worker that Derrik's humiliation and the loss of company business fell upon the shoulders of all involved, his nephews included. Yet only Cueball received a demotion, put to work stealing car parts from Rathbone Chevrolet Cadillac, with Seizer fencing the goods as Jim Rathbone collected the insurance.

Derrik was small potatoes, all said and done, Del assured Eddy. The club's objective had always been to establish smaller distribution centers outside major cities, never to conquer whole swaths of territory outright and defend them. They weren't a gang, didn't yet wield the manpower of area chapters — they hired reliable workers with broad local connections. Derrik might have cut a country road west through Jesutopia, but no one expected him to pave a highway. In other words, there were hundreds of Derriks out there, it just meant more work for Mickey, whose job it was to find them.

He then let Eddy know that Cueball's Nova was now his to use — for runs only.

"They took away his car?" asked Eddy, befuddled. "Can't they just fine him or something?"

"This is less radical than other punishments one might imagine, given the offense," offered Del Ray.

"Will it just be me out there, driving alone?"

"Until we figure something out, yes. But I don't see this as long-term. I think we'll have our boy back soon enough."

Cueball had finally done something he couldn't scapegoat away, to Del's mind, and if a small measure of restitutional subservience helped iron out the kinks, well, the young buck might be better for it. People had trouble respecting Cueball, Del said, because he didn't respect himself. He lacked faith—in anything. Eddy scoffed, and that's when Del Ray shared his doctrine of self-obligation: *Inside each person is a god-shaped hole, and some people fill it with God, and some fill it with pills, but most burn quietly with the ache of its hollow. If you can't learn to care for yourself, don't expect anyone else to, either. We all got pains and fears, but how we manage them defines us. It takes courage to look inward and wrestle with existence, and that earned confidence is how we can suffer the whims of a tulpa god who daily ignores or even promotes the suffering of billions, and still find reasons to love.*

Driving home, Eddy played out the drama of being on the road alone, suffering Cueball's absence. Their on-road banter and jokes helped mitigate his anxiety; otherwise, any cars keeping pace would undoubtedly strike him as cops or federal agents psychically attuned to bad-guy frequencies. At his most arrogant and combative, Eddy saw himself hitting the pipe hard, itching to test a radar gun.

The whole enterprise felt unsustainable, his unease the early rumblings of an earthquake.

Gin was home watching a british show on human evolution, finding herself in conversation with a skeptical-looking woman who argued that the human species peaked with the advent of industrialization, and had since entered a period of rapid decline—culturally, ecologically, and with regards to plummeting birth rates, biologically. *You won't hear any argument from me*, Gin thought. This opinion was immediately countered by another academic surrounded by her books, who held that such fatalistic theories failed to account for the resilience of Mother Nature and humankind's historic adaptability. Whereby Gin cocked her head, coffee cup extended, saying, "I appreciate the optimism."

Upon hearing the VW Bug's motor, she sat straight up on the couch. Eddy's meeting with Del Ray had been important enough for him to mention, hence these hours spent on a carousel of instant coffee and frenzied housework. She eyed the broom in the kitchen pantry, wondering if she should bring it over, to show she'd been working and not worrying.

Eddy appeared drifting in the open doorway, adjusting to a room darkened by blinds, the cool winter sunlight at his back. Then tossed his keys on the table and folded beside her on the couch.

As she went to say hello, he cut her off.

"Cueball's out," he said, whistling in a few bitter sips of her coffee. "That's disgusting. They got me driving alone."

"Alone? I don't like that," said Gin, killing the TV with the remote. Her job, in this moment, was to keep the focus on him: his welfare, his choices. Their lives.

"Del says it'll blow over if he keeps his nose clean. Got him on another job already."

"Sounds like he got off easy."

"Easy?"

"What he did was reckless and stupid."

Eddy faced her. "His dad *beat* him."

"I know, and that's terrible too!" said Gin. "Two wrongs don't make a right. But Cueball almost got us all killed. You weren't downstairs when that crazy shithead was waving his gun around!"

"To be fair, if it wasn't for your mom—"

"*What?*"

Beyond the open door, several small birds played hopscotch on the front lawn. Eddy imagined plucking out their delicate feathers until they were as bald as thumbs.

"Are you actually blaming my *mother*, who he called a *cunt?*"

"I'm just saying—"

"Are you high right now?" asked Gin, incredulous.

"Really?" Eddy asked, delighted. "You wanna check me out, doc?" He offered up the various orifices he might insert drugs into, pulling up an eyelid, slapping his ass. "I told you, I just smoke a little weed here and there. Is that a fucking crime?"

"Actually, yes, yes it is," said Gin, folding her legs. God, couldn't they just have a conversation?

"Whatever. Rehab's for quitters." He sighed loudly. "What a fucking nightmare. That Derrik was a goddamn psycho. Try to be a good worker, what's that get me? I still think we should go after him."

Gin focused on diminishing her anger from the wild intensity of a Cat-4 hurricane that demolished whole towns to a dust devil content with scandalizing trees. She searched for the best way to mention her relief that Eddy wasn't in any trouble himself, without exasperating the situation.

"I'm glad you're okay. I'm glad he's okay. But have you thought more about what we talked about? Asking for a different job?"

"Like hustling car parts with high school dropouts? No thanks."

"Maybe just something less out in the open."

"Gin, I can't. I'm stuck doing what I have to right now. You don't like it? There's the door."

"Oooh, *nice*. Is this a dare? Are we in the daring stage of our relationship? Okay, here's one: I dare you to quit. Drop out. Find a normal job. I dare you not to come home fucked-up every night. I dare you to give a shit about us again. Or, hey, just start with yourself—"

"I had a *bad day*, Gin. Things are bad all around right now and I just want to sit here and pop a beer and watch some fucking TV, okay?"

"And I don't have a problem with that! But you come in here all agitated, and if I offer any solutions, you dismiss them. I'm just asking for a little respect—"

Eddy's face grew maudlin with a sneer. "You know, I work with guys who'd kill for that very word. Why don't we make a deal—here's the *dealmaking* part of our relationship. How about you lay off the grief, we'll sit here for a while, all quiet like, and when I'm asleep, you can be a *bitch* all you want."

Gin reached over and slapped him. Without thinking, Eddy scooped under her legs and forced her toppling sideways over the back of the couch.

The regret was instantaneous. He scrambled around, apologizing as Gin scooted back on her hands. He raised his palms in helpless contrition, but Gin was already reacting—reaching over, she grabbed one of his mother's pewter clowns off an end table and bashed it over his head.

Eddy collapsed and Gin leapt up, scrambling for the bedroom, yelling terribly, "You'll never own me, you son of a bitch!"

Eddy bobbled on his knees, eyes clenched, sucking air through his teeth. His fingertips came back wet from his head, which was filling with light. The fear in Gin's voice was divine. Honing his rage, he quickly scanned the living room, spotting the broom in the open pantry.

He rushed over and took it up. Stepping back into the hall and cocking his arm, Eddy hurled the broom spear-like through the air, where it pierced the bedroom door and swung sideways like a down-turned eyebrow.

The fact the door was thin and cheap didn't register to Eddy—he'd *willed* the broom through its target—giving credence to a strong belief in his newfound powers. All he had to do now was walk down the hall, kick in the door, and stop the world mid-spin with his bare hands.

Time elongated to a near standstill.

Instead, he snatched up his keys and left, carrying forever into his future the pure animal sound of Gin's moaning.

Surfing the red-eyed wave of shank, Eddy violently sped up and braked his way through a labyrinth of backroads until he could surge along a vacant stretch of US-1, enraptured and glorious, charged by an unmitigated sense of betrayal. The steering wheel felt weak in his hands: malleable, crushable. His eyes trampled everything—buildings, dogs, cyclists—and edged from the landscape its very integrity. His heart beggarly, berating itself with memories of her already corrupted by the subtleties of rage. He cranked the heater and rolled up the windows, sealing himself in the inferno. His plan was to explode.

The hot air worked a different remedy, though, draining his energy as he turned sad and pitiful. He parked along the northeastern shoulder of the Eau Gallie Causeway, nerves shot, unable to eat or drink, snorting lines off his hand as he stared out across the water at Dragon Point, the tip of an island peninsula where, until Eddy was twelve, the concrete sculpture of an enormous dragon once oversaw the split of the Banana River off the Indian. All that was left of the razed sentinel that had once infused his childhood dreams with fantastic possibilities was a greenish slab of rebar and ugly stumps along the rock shore. This was a land of ruin. He recalled driving over this very causeway with Gin after leaving Bird's party, that special first night on the beach, and now imagined the trunk of Gin's Buick opening for a suitcase as he broke down and wept into his palms.

Come dusk he drove out to Snake Lake.

Lost on mud-pocked trails, Eddy eventually caught wind of voices, the bonfire glow hovering a sea of palmettos. Parking along a separate trail, he popped the glove box and took out the fifth of Jack stashed there and downed three hard swigs, bringing tears to his eyes.

News carried fast. Best to prepare.

There was a distinct possibility he'd be chased back to his car and beaten, so he left the driver-side door unlocked. He double-checked that his Glock's safety was off, then pushed it under his seat. He was too nervous to carry it into the crowd.

It was a small party of thirty or so bodies, people howling along to Dylan's stoner classic, "Rainy Day Women #12 & 35."

Right off the bat, Eddy noticed Mickey chatting up Jim Barns over on the periphery, preparing to leave. Acting like old friends, two players in the game, dark knights. Eddy kept to the shadows until the pair rode off together, then approached a few other people he recognized from other parties. His eyes kept wandering over to Colt, though, resting on a log, whooping and clapping to an impromptu dance performed by drunk women spinning in circles.

She caught him watching, and smiled. He was safe.

Still incredible how much the daughter resembled the mother: same hair, same eyes. Not worn-down, exactly, but more substantial looking. The kind of woman you couldn't guess what she did for a living: cruise ship jazz singer, news anchor with a wild side. Chimera. Chameleon.

"Eddy, hello," she said, tipsy, swinging an arm to his shoulder. "Where's baby girl?"

"Didn't you hear? We split up."

Colt kept her mouth open too long, head thrown back. "No! I thought you two was in *love*," and Eddy half expected her to laugh. "Aww, that's too bad. Really. A shocker."

"You talk to her?"

Colt shook her head no. "She don't call much since you happened."

"Derrik's not here, is he?"

"Oh, the asshole that tried to kill us all? I thought it best to put some space between us. No, I'm with this fool here," she said, referencing a man in an astronaut helmet spraying gasoline on the already enormous bonfire. They watched as he flung the can to the side, backed up for a running start, offered the sky an uproarious yawp, and launched himself through the wall of flames.

"You have a type," said Eddy.

"My beau. He's a stickman from Reno. No pun intended. Hey, is that little peckerwood Cueball here with you? 'Cause I wanna give that little shit a piece of my mind."

"No." Eddy lifted the bottle of Jack. "Care for a sip?"

"Aww. Who said son-in-laws were worthless," she cooed, unscrewing the top and tilting the shaft toward her cup. "I'm sure you two'll get back together soon. A man can't live without a gal telling him which ball to scratch, and a gal can't live without someone reminding her how truly sick her daddy was."

They drank together, casually, while about them a full-fledged bacchanalia paraded by. Shirtless women in stretched-out leather pants, faces ruined by sun exposure, were transformed now by masking firelight into coven sisters celebrating some stygian Sabbath, having crept out from their wooded haunts to tantalize and claw their sweaty counterparts, bearded trolls who danced lopsided with shoulders high, clutching their sex, revelers of some collapsing infernal civilization, draped in ashen smoke and bourbon and pheromones, jangling chains and dog tags and hooting calls that returned like amnesiac owls over the placid lake beyond which mirrored the moon's dumb countenance, promising eternity.

The craps stickman swam out from the dark to feed Colt a pill and whisked her away, into the melee, and that's when Eddy spied Gumby watching him from across the flames, seated in a squat. Eddy's throat constricted as he pretended not to notice, but the hit man was already rising and approaching.

"What you hunting, boy? Bit of mischief?" Gumby asked, stealing a seat.

He'd last seen Gumby at Bird and Charlotte's party last summer, when Gumby sliced up Jim Barns' face with a knife. Since then, the biker had gone underground. What he did for Seizer enjoyed all manner of speculation, including a rumor that had him roaming the countryside as the club's Enforcer, inhibiting competition and brokering deals using whatever tactics of persuasion he held at his disposal.

Eddy asked what he'd been up to.

"Oh, a little of this, little of that," Gumby grinned, flashing that single canine tooth filed to a point. "Garbage detail and the like. I heard you boys been doing some sightseeing."

"It's a big country," said Eddy. "Figured I'd have a gander before somebody nukes it."

Gumby clucked, massaging his chest. "I also heard your buddy Cueball wrecked a deal."

"All lies. Fella's a saint. Saved a busload of blind children from a waterspout just yesterday."

"Shit, ha!" cried Gumby, dancing his feet in the dirt. "Way I heard it, he stood up to a man twice his size and leveled him with his own pistol. What sort of animal spirit you think dwells in a boy like that?"

Eddy side-eyed the crazed individual. "I couldn't guess."

"He ever done anything like that before?"

"Not to my knowledge."

"Fair enough," said Gumby, stroking his black goatee. "Best be heading on. Leave you to your game." He winked, then pushed up and vanished into the night.

The stickman finally did something moronic enough for Colt to regret their pairing, a fistfight that left him careening headlong into a motorcycle gas tank, where he lay incapacitated amid great cheering.

Colt rolled her eyes and sauntered drunkenly toward the lake.

Eddy found a trail that hooked through the woods in roundabout fashion, hoping to find the right angle of approach and pierce, like a spacecraft, that tiny window of opportunity, lest his plan be obliterated. His heartache would not subside, he knew, unless he did something truly abominable, something to sever all ties—something unforgivable.

He found Colt stretched out on the lake's shoreline. She raised her eyebrows as he approached. He held the whiskey bottle up to the moon to show her the amber glow, noticing her naked thighs emerging from frayed jean shorts: alabaster and shapely as a teenager's sense of women's legs in old war novels.

"I half the worse taste," she slurred, taking a swig, "in men."

Leaning back on her palms, eyes rolling slightly, her jacket slipped over a shoulder. Eddy pulled it up slowly, his fingers brushing her skin.

When he went to kiss her, she retracted involuntarily. He mouthed her shoulder as she watched from some internal distance.

"Fucking kill you," she whispered, but gave in a little when he moved on to her neck, tonguing the muscles and collarbone. "Dammit."

He wasn't sure when Colt passed out, while he was trying to work off her jeans, or when, unwilling to follow through, and noticing she fell silent, he failed to tug them up completely. Her smooth hip shined in the moonlight, a thin strip of underwear pressed into flesh. He felt nothing, and considered masturbating, but there was no desire behind it; he was now but a body, emptied of spirit.

Envisioning Gin, his stomach churned with revulsion. He leaned to one side and pitched forward, tremors in his elbows, waiting for the heavens to quit spinning so he could leave or vomit. He pressed his fists into his eyes, praying, *Don't pass out, not here.*

He'd crossed the line, claiming a wickedness he knew deep down he'd carried all along, grateful now for the proving of it, and rent with its finality.

God damn every aspect of his being.

Whatever he'd had with Gin—it was over.

Eddy woke the next morning to a deserted campsite.

Someone had buried a hunting knife in the sand between his thighs. Back at his car, the inside smelled of urine. His gun was missing. The glove compartment yielded six pills in an orange bottle and he swallowed half of them.

Daylight filtered through his consciousness in highlights of confusion and disrepair, the landscape shimmering. Stumbling into a music store, he was soon thrown out by two clerks after biting down on a jewel case just to hear it crack. Then spent the next few hours curled up in a speedboat slung under a river wharf's gazebo. He had no idea where to go or what to do. Nobody could see him this way. Pretty confident he didn't want anybody's help anyhow, he swallowed the rest of the pills.

Lucidity found him startled awake on a floating dock, supine, dehydrated, surrounded by white sails against a blue backdrop. The gurgling mouth-sounds of seawater lapping fiberglass knotted his stomach. His best guess was the Melbourne Harbor Marina. He recalled a conversation with a dyspeptic beach bum in Indialantic who kept hawking up bile and covering it with sand. But now . . . where was his car?

A child's squeal broke the spell, and he turned toward the curious gazes of a towheaded boy and his overweight father. The child knelt over Eddy before the father yanked him hindward. Laying boot to pelvis, the man forced Eddy rolling onto his back. A stern command sent the child scrambling for the marina office, the father flipping open his phone.

Eddy spent the night in a holding cell at Sharpes jail, interred with a colorful gaggle of likewise miserables. Held under the Baker Act, he now awaited someone from Circles of Care, the local drug treatment center, to come retrieve him. His throbbing, sober morning was spent watching soon-to-be inmates get ushered through booking. When Draco came through, surprisingly, flanked by corrections officers, Eddy raised a hand, but Jesse's brother refused to acknowledge him, turning away.

A guard stepped forward and motioned for Eddy to stand. Taking him by the elbow, he led Eddy down the hall and placed him in a short line of shivering addicts and potential suicides positioned before a short black woman in uniform with a clipboard and *don't fuck with me* eyes. The white guy before Eddy kept switching his weight between feet.

"Are you currently medicated?" asked the jailer.

"Medicated?" asked the addict.

"Are you on any prescribed drugs?"

"Ma'am, for real? I'm always somewhere between geriatric and Jerry Garcia."

Soon they were on a bus, and Eddy spent the next full day trying to convince various doctors at Circles of Care he wasn't homeless or a junkie lunatic looking to off himself, just a poor sot who'd lost his best girl and decided to raid the old medicine cabinet. He sat through group meetings and one-on-ones with counselors and nodded, yes sir, no ma'am all the way. I am a victim of my own moral turpitude.

He was picked up by Jesse a couple days later, driving one of his brother's rebuilt Cadillacs. Neither spoke more than a few cursory sentences until they'd halved the distance to Palm Bay.

"How you feeling?" asked Jesse, quitting the radio.

"I need a beer," said Eddy. "I saw Draco inside. He made believe I wasn't real."

"Nothing's real to him anymore. The wires upstairs are all chewed to shit. I can't even bring him up, Mom just starts crying. It's no use bailing him out, 'cause he'll go right back in. I even offered to, but he just laughed at me over the phone."

"What'd they get him on?"

"Robbing a pharmacy for Oxy. He's headed to prison, for sure."

"Jesus. That sucks," said Eddy. "Man, I need a bed."

"You can crash at my place," Jesse offered.

"Do you mind? Just for a few days? I can't go home. I need to clean myself up. And Gin . . . I don't know if she's there or not, but I can't see her."

Jesse reacted. "I don't have anything at the house, so you know. After that Derrik mess, and Draco's stealing meds, nothing but beer comes through that door."

"Got any smokes?" asked Eddy. Jesse pointed to a carton crushed between the seats. "Alright, so what's the damage. Am I still playing for the team?"

Jesse leaned back. "Well, the long and short of it is, I don't know. But Cueball's gone. Split. Left me a voicemail, said he's never coming back. You should check your phone."

"I have no idea where it could be. Shit, I need to find my car. What else?"

"The good news is, Gin's put out a restraining order on you, so there's that. She won't tell anyone why. Colt wouldn't even tell Charlotte what she knew, so it's been a bit of a mystery."

"Excellent. And the bad news?"

"Bad news is, you've got a record now, which I'm guessing You-Know-Who and Bird won't be happy about."

"Beauty of the Baker Act is they don't file charges," said Eddy. "No record. And besides, I swallowed the evidence."

"Goddamn compadre," said Jesse, shaking his head. "Whatever you had to get out of your system, I hope to hell it was worth it."

PART III

THE MISSION

Deprived of his Nova, Cueball made the three-hour trek down to Miami in his old red pickup truck. The rusted beast sputtered and fumed, but made the distance. He curbed it six blocks from bayside, opting not to suffer the pretentious glares of valets, should there be any.

Feeling under his seat, protected by night, he took hold of the glass pipe and fiddled with it in the dark. There was nothing to smoke, but Cueball liked its heft, the possibility. The struggle to cut back had him clenching his jaw and searching online for home remedies for TMJ.

He checked the address written on the back of a Walgreens receipt. The streets looked run-down, but the waterside towers were definitely new money, skyline condos that brought to mind cocaine deals and porn shoots, as fashioned by his own late-night viewing habits.

Not that he required more reasons to be apprehensive. He'd never been alone in a big city before outside of Orlando, which didn't count, being minimally exotic. A kicked can knelled out his location as his Converse shuffled quickly down the dark sidewalk.

The residence was twenty flights up and stacked like square china, blue glass and white wraparound balconies. Biscayne Lofts West. A Mercedes drifted from the parking garage as Cueball leaned against a palm tree and texted. He felt dehydrated and hungry but practiced an upbeat mood; no reason to drag his problems south. He didn't want to come across as trouble, or needy. Just an old high school buddy down for a mini-vacation, up for anything, and in no way a burden.

Kid Kaos erupted from a side door, arms raised, a Red Stripe in each hand.

"Cueball! Oye, llegaste!"

All the way to the elevator, Kaos didn't stop talking, which put Cueball at ease, relieving him of having to dodge any thorny questions.

Kaos was pissed. Turned out Alex had pulled Kaos from his Mission post—no more security detail—to install him at the dance club, brokering minor distribution deals. According to Alex, it was a promotion, but Kaos knew the score—this was a power play—as Alex was also pressuring Kaos to disband the Puerto Rican Posse, forcing members to pledge Los Toros if they wanted to keep their jobs. *Consolidation, like a union,* Alex explained. *Everyone pays into the same pot, receiving the same protections.*

"Fucking bullshit, is what it is," spit Kaos. "The Posse is mine! He likes me having nothing!"

Despite the new job sounding better to Cueball, he chose to hug his beer over his duffel bag and echo the disappointment: he too had been exiled from a lofty position to some rinky-dink assignment—fencing car parts—all because he'd acted in self-defense. He quickly gave Kaos a rundown of the Derrik fiasco, making sure to swap out *father* for *boss,* before the elevator dinged at the penthouse suite.

"They rather you dead?" asked Kaos, tugging his chain. "Whatever. You and me, we dangerous, bro. We'll get ours."

The doors opened up to a sparsely furnitured condo with vaulted ceilings and blank white walls, an interior of marble and glass. Kaos made him take off his shoes.

"Yeah, Alex got like four of these, but this one's mine. I stay here, free of charge."

Kaos confided that Alex lived in a mansion on Hibiscus Island, while keeping a personal condo by the Fontainebleau hotel on Collins Ave. But the bragging was entirely lost on Cueball, for whom Miami remained a largely unexplored territory. His local experience had been relegated to the backwoods Mission drops; any sightseeing jaunt into the city proper with a work vehicle had never crossed anyone's mind.

"Thanks for letting me crash, I'm happy with a couch," said Cueball.

"Couch, nah," said Kaos. "We got four bedrooms, two facing the water. The big corner one's mine, and this here by the bathroom's Julio's, so—"

"Julio?"

"That little motherfucker," said Kaos, pointing his beer. "My cousin."

Curled up in a white leather chair by the TV was a young boy with his headphones on, reading a book. He seemed oblivious to them.

"Punk ass showed up here last week. Left New York all sparkles in his eyes and shit, hearing cousin Alex was some big guy, so he hopped a Greyhound, nobody, not even the driver said shit, just let him on. Ay bendito. I'm sending him back maybe, I don't know. I'll show him a good time first, make a man out of him." Kaos pointed a finger straight at Cueball's head. "No telling Alex, though, a'ight? He'll lose his shit."

Cueball agreed. "I'm happy not to see anyone, if I can help it. I'm just here to chill."

Kaos nodded respectfully; then a grin crept up. "But I'm not gonna let you sleep."

Then Kaos walked over and lightly kicked Julio's legs, startling him.

"I'm going out. You gonna be okay by yourself? You can order whatever—"

"I'm coming!" yelled the boy, dropping the book, headphones flung asunder as he rolled off the chair and bolted straight to his room.

"What'd I say? All eager and shit," said Kaos, sliding the duffel bag off Cueball's shoulder. "I got some people to see. You're coming with."

It wasn't a question. Cueball felt himself ceding control, and gave in, thankful.

As Kaos and Julio got ready, Cueball wandered onto the balcony. Across the bay the carnival of Miami Beach enacted a mute performance of prismatic lights along the strand. High-class hotels, bespoke shops and classy restaurants. Rich people's playground. The cool wind layered with anticipation. The dark waters magic, small boats drifting, islands pricked by streetlamps and glowing emerald pools and wide mansions. A patina of acquisition, achievement, encased in quietude, that elegant solemnity, which roused in Cueball a certain ambition, an urgency, the lure of full gratification. This penthouse suite alone was worth two or three mil, easy. Rapped his knuckles on the railing. Wealth was a difficult thing to wrap one's head around until you sat in its graces, charms at your disposal, marveling at its easy comforts, all within your grasp.

"Kind of a dump, yeah?" said Kaos, pulling over a white hoodie. "Alex took down all the art. But wait till you see the beachside place, overlooks the hotel pool. Thong kingdom."

Julio swayed back and forth behind his cousin, eyes clocking. "Good looking kid, right? Yo, look here, this is Cueball. He's family. You mind him or I beat your ass."

Julio scoffed, angling a glance, then spun around and danced away.

Kaos grimaced playfully and hiked a thumb back. "Fuckin kids these days, live in their own world." He gingerly slid the glass door closed and a pipe appeared in his hand.

"Wanna hit this?"

Boy did he. Goddamn, more than anything, but Cueball was in the middle of a silent battle to pump the brakes on his drug use, beating an indignant retreat away from words like *infantile* and *irresponsible*, uttered one time or another by his father.

"I'm good for now, bro, thanks. If I do any more I'll be up all night."

"More for me," said Kaos, lighting up. "This my reserves," he wheezed, holding in his breath. "Stash everywhere low."

"Product's moving faster than ever. Business is expanding, big-time."

Kaos squinched an eye. "Says who?"

Cueball froze. It was absolutely imperative that Kaos never find out his dad was part of the duo running this show. He shrugged. "Del Ray mentioned some new camps, to keep up with supply. They got a massive shipment headed to the Mission here soon. I was gonna run it before I got the boot."

Kaos nodded, blowing out the smoke. "Maybe I stop by and stock up. What day?"

"Same as always, third week of the month, Thursday drop-off probably," said Cueball. "You score straight from the batches?"

Kaos' face collapsed into his neck. "Man, I don't pay for shit." Then, knuckle-itching his chin, said, "You hungry? I bet you're hungry. I'm fucking starving."

They cruised the dense harmonic streets, Cueball riding shotgun in

Kaos' Beamer, music cranked up to heart flutter. Their first stop was a busted apartment complex, then the backside of a veterinary clinic. Cueball figured Kaos was collecting money, he didn't know. Hell, he could be making side deals.

With Kaos gone inside a corner bodega for rolling papers, Cueball glanced back to find Julio had brought his book with him, reading by phone light. Cueball angled to see the cover—husky mountain dwarves and menacing trolls, snow-clotted peaks, a diving serpentine dragon.

"That any good?"

Julio peered over the book.

"You ever read the one where the kids walk through the closet into another world?"

Julio soured. "You really not remember the book's name, dumbass?"

Stunned stupefaction was Cueball's reply, softened by a throat chuckle. "How old are you?"

"Eleven."

"Well, you look six. And your face is too small for your head, which is too small for your body."

Julio looked slapped.

"I was just gonna say," continued Cueball, "that most kids got, like, a Nintendo DS in front of them, and here you got a book, which is cool. Reminds me of my friend back home."

Julio clicked his tongue. "Don't lie, you aint got no friends."

Kaos returned with two Matervas and a Dr Pepper for Cueball. Then sat in the car quietly catching up on a barrage of texts.

"Your cousin's a little shithead."

Kaos tittered under his breath, eyes on his phone.

"You're pretty busy," said Cueball.

"I'm necessary," said Kaos, pocketing the device. "Okay, let's go have some fun."

Fifteen minutes later they were in Little Havana. A street festival shut down Calle Ocho and brought the community out in full force with live music and street vendors.

"You promised a club!" Julio piped from the back seat. "You said you'd take me!"

"Change of plans," said Kaos. "Why you fussin? Just fucking chill, we'll grab some food, I got people to talk to."

They parked in a church lot and walked the short distance, slipping into a river of people swarming into a musical vortex outside a venue called Ball & Chain. A dense aromatic aura of fried foods enveloped the block, yuca and red snapper and plantains, with folks sipping steaming cafecitos from tiny blue and white cups. Catching sight of an ice cream shop, Julio reeled, but Kaos dragged him away, *Later, chamaco. Business first.* Up the block past the Bay of Pigs monument Kaos located some friends hanging around a tent selling pastelitos as Cueball hung back, watching the crowds with crossed arms, feeling out of place. He didn't know Kaos actually knew any cubans, but then thought that was a weird thing to think. Julio hung back too, weaving around in a dance of boredom.

This scene would play itself out over the next couple weeks: Kaos off doing his own thing while Cueball chilled with Julio. It was clear the young boy worshipped both his cousins, asking for a full account of everything when Kaos returned: who he'd talked to, what they were planning, could he help? Kaos would cast a huckster shine on his escapades, only to let Julio know he wasn't ready. *Look at you, still painting your shoelaces all rainbow and shit. What, you wanna be my sidekick? This aint* Pokémon, *bitch. You can't fight.*

That first night, though, Cueball used Julio's predicament to help dial down his own discomfort. Here was this mouthy, penniless kid, a runaway from New York, entirely reliant on a banger cousin consumed by ambition, eyes on the prize—like, where did he even fit in?

"Hey little man, you ever shoot targets?"

Piquing Julio's curiosity, Cueball pointed over at a red kiosk, its walls lined with stuffed animals. Instead of answering, the kid simply trailed lack-lusterly behind.

"I'm honestly surprised this is still legal."

Cueball dropped three bucks on the counter, went down on one elbow, picked up the metal air rifle, and proceeded to fire away in spurts. The goal was to cut a red star from the center of a white target. The sites were off, but he shredded all but one corner emptying the chamber, and was about to go again before catching Julio's big eyes.

"You wanna give it a go?"

Julio's first attempt was dogshit, but Cueball taught him the trick. First, don't aim dead center trying to peck out the red star—the paper will just curl back around, and if any red is left, you lose. So you wanna shoot a circle *around* the star, so that the paper falls away. Second, don't just rapid-fire your hundred bb's—take your time using short spurts and single shots.

Neither of them won, but after five rounds, they were friends. Cueball was even awarded a high five.

"Little man got himself a sensei!" said Kaos, strutting over to pluck a shambled target from Julio's hand, holding it up high.

"I'm hungry!" whined Julio.

"Calm down, little bro, I got'chou," said Kaos, waving over a chubby guy carrying two deep-set containers loaded with chicken and rice. Cueball recognized the fellow from the Mission, a worker named Frio who often helped unload the furniture. When Frio nodded a wassup, something in his demeanor informed Cueball he'd been the topic of conversation. Kaos would later say Frio was a friend from Kissimmee, a former PRP member who pledged Los Toros to keep his job. Kaos called him a *halfie*, with blood ties to older cuban families, which Cueball took to mean mafia.

"Who takes care of you?" said Kaos, watching Julio devour his dinner on the curb.

"Boy's a shark," said Frio.

"I'mma bring some folks back to the crib," Kaos told Cueball. "You don't mind, right? Play some *Mass Effect*, smoke out?"

Cueball nodded his face full of rice.

But on the drive home, Cueball quickly faded. The night's events were almost enough to derail his anxiety, but once fatigue set in, the phantoms returned. The image of his father waiting for him silently in the dark, following his near-death experience with Derrik. The memory of blinding sunshine, the river below and Eddy beside him, high on pills and leaning off the wrong side of the Melbourne Causeway, laughing triumphantly as car horns blared behind them.

He pushed these away like smoke.

Six guys from Kaos' Posse showed up to play video games deep into the night, Cueball nodding during introductions. Not much later Kaos caught him dozing against the wall.

"You walking dead, cuz," Kaos said, taking him by the shoulder.

Cueball blinked. "I wanna hang, but I'm crashing."

"It's cool. Get some sleep. We got whatever forever."

Cueball dropped his voice. "Hey Antonio . . . eh, sorry . . . I just wanted to thank you again for putting me up. I'll get you back."

Kaos swatted this away. "I got you, bro, go crash out, I'll catch you in the a.m. Hit this kick-ass joint for some huevos. Shower's through the door, towels in the closet."

Slinking away, Cueball caught sight of Julio asleep on the couch, beer propped between his legs. Smiled to himself—he actually liked the little brat.

When Cueball woke, Kaos was gone. So was Julio. There was nothing in the fridge but ground coffee. In roughly an hour, he would learn his truck had been towed, having parked in front of an emergency clinic. And later, that his father had discontinued their shared phone plan, likely out of spite, hence no texts or calls from Eddy or Jesse or his mom.

But for now, at least, there was coffee.

Pulling over the bag of grounds, he assessed the previous night's damage. Bottles everywhere. Weed roaches stamped out on the marble island countertop. No wonder Alex took down the art.

He began cleaning. A ripped brown paper bag was spread out flat on the island. Cueball picked it up, wiped beneath, and flipped it over. On the back was a crude drawing in pen—the blueprint of a building. A rectangle, with hastily drawn circles and arrows.

They even labeled the thing: *Mission.*

It was a simple plot of land abutting a wildlife sanctuary, but as far as Eddy was concerned, it was heaven.

No internet, no engine noises or diesel in the breeze, nothing but uninterrupted Georgia woods filled with hawks and gophers and skunks like this one, wandering right up to the back porch, where Eddy shook under a filthy greatcoat, his chapped hands curving a warm mug, the tremors cramping his neck mere aftershocks of a larger quake only hours in the rearview.

Duke leaned over in his rocking chair, holding a grape. "They go crazy for these, watch," he said, and pitched the grape toward the skunk. The creature reacted tentatively at first, but having danced this twilight ritual before, sniffed and rolled the ruby pearl in its paws, chowing down.

"This is living," said Eddy.

"Certainly one of the better ways," said Duke.

The physical hurdles of recovery began manifesting immediately after Eddy's court-ordered stint at Circles of Care, where he'd been able to score some Adderall, which seemed to have staved off the withdrawal symptoms. Beleaguered with regret, and making all the sad promises people make in such situations, he agreed to hand his entire recovery effort and hapless existence over to Jesse, the only soul he felt withheld judgment.

Sorrowful, contrite, Eddy settled into a sleeping bag on Jesse's couch for what he imagined would be a slow, arduous recovery—but the cravings mugged him in the night, his clothes soaked and the sleeping bag stripped off by morning. Jesse kept him hydrated with coconut water and Pedialyte popsicles as Eddy chewed his nails to the ragged quick, unhungry, fingers tap-dancing his kneecaps. But always back at the fridge, staring blankly into cold brightness. Old Turner Classic movies were a welcomed distraction, watched through the night, as sleep proved impossible: his body woke from nods in spastic reanimation, pores weeping. Come the third day, he could finally handle toast and broth. Then chicken and rice. His teeth ached. His tongue felt sprained. Detoxing was like the flu, but with sledgehammers.

When Eddy showed he could hold a meaningful conversation, Jesse packed him up and drove him out to the hilly regions of Georgia, where the Twins were hunting wild turkey and fishing for warmouth.

The aged cabin they occupied wasn't worth the price of demolition, looked like, but it had a rustic charm and a flourishing grapefruit grove out back, an oddity but a reality, with branches shook each morning for breakfast. Eddy again took the couch for reasons of visibility, praying he wouldn't die here. Jesse wasn't even around a full day before Bird called him back, thus entrusting Eddy to the generous care of the brothers for a week. Without cigarettes, though, his level of discomfiture shot from manageable to migraine.

The back porch became his grovel haunt, a place to be alone, peering beyond the grove and into the woodlands, as one expecting a traveler, perhaps. As the sun dipped low, Duke returned through a screen door and handed him a cup of coffee adorned with a single floating marshmallow.

"Why don't you drink?" asked Eddy, suspicious of silence now, as it gave people more time to despise him. He felt vulnerable, and didn't wish to be vulnerable alone.

Duke sipped his mug. "Alcohol was never my thing. I like to be in control."

Eddy cleared his throat. "I wanted to apologize, and thank you. I know I put things at risk. Jesse said you went to bat for me with your uncle. I appreciate that."

Duke shrugged, an impossibly gracious response, Eddy felt.

On their drive up to Georgia, Jesse caught Eddy up on more events that had transpired during his brief incarceration. Seizer was flaming pissed, apparently—more than Bird, even—as the boss had no real patience for workers who couldn't keep their extracurricular activities in check. Del Ray argued that Eddy was a good kid who'd let a bad breakup ruin his judgment, but it was Duke who unexpectedly reminded his uncle that Eddy alone kept Derrik engaged at the welcoming party, despite its outcome.

Three weeks off for drug recovery and a month's docked pay was the meted sentence, along with a nonspecific probationary period, for which Eddy was entirely grateful and relieved.

"It feels good to have someone in my court," Eddy said.

"The Nova won't drive itself," Duke said flatly. "Plus it got us a couple weeks' vacation."

"You did me a solid," said Eddy. "You're a mensch. Take the compliment."

Duke stopped rocking, wood planks yielding mid-squeak. "To be upfront, I don't trust you. And we lack the time to vet and train someone new."

"That's fair. I deserve that."

"Yeah, you do," said Duke. "And don't get all sorry sap, I can't hear you whining about what you deserve or don't. You need to pull yourself together. There's people's lives at stake. Namely, my brother's. My vouching for you keeps everything running smoothly, but if I don't see rapid improvement, that changes."

"I'm not trying to be combative," said Eddy.

"It's nothing personal."

"I'll get there. I'm close."

Duke was silent, then leaned in. "You like this job? Honestly."

Eddy wasn't sure he was still in the sharing mood, but nodded, blowing into his hands.

"I don't believe you. I think you're here for Cueball. You got no real passion for this. No goals, am I right? So why not quit?"

Eddy could have touted a number of excuses. Instead he turned to Duke, greatcoat falling away, and spilled his honesty. Told how his mother had left him in debt. How his joining up was, yes, a service to his best friend, but he never slouched at a job. Yet now he felt lost, offering up blunt, bald disclosures so Duke might absorb his brute honesty without suspicion or pity. Maybe even absolve him, somehow, priestlike, arms full of amnesty. When Eddy was finished he tossed out his cold coffee, done with it and everything else, tired in his center, longing for bed.

Duke stared into him. "In all that, I didn't hear one word about personal goals." When Eddy didn't answer, he continued: "Your mom's gone . . . okay, mine is too, but I'm not crying. And Cueball's run off, so where's that leave you?"

"He'll be back."

Duke stifled a guffaw. Rose to go, but paused. "While you're in there digging around your insides, maybe figure out whose life you're actually living."

The screen door slapped shut behind him.

Expecting a morale booster, Eddy now felt like a scolded child. Considered setting fire to the hunting cabin, with Duke in it. He was too tired for either self-reflection or self-loathing—he wanted to atone and be forgiven in exchange for his capitulation. *I give up, goddammit.* Sinking back into his chair, he accepted this easy drift toward depression.

Even after Lisbon returned from collecting wood and got the fireplace going, Eddy kept to the cabin's back porch, well past sunset, forgiving the mosquitoes their stake in his penance.

With certain mental states, the world feels like it's constantly accelerating—no inertia, no plateau—a racing current where one's only fear is the roadblock you know is coming, the halting moment that collapses everything.

So you push into unbridled activity, avoiding lulls—*yes, but now what*—recruiting fellow midnight shape-shifters and lost-a-lots to ensure the ride never stops. Snort or chug whatever, Fireball and Jäger shots, salsa beats and psychedelic rock, eat fast, fuck weird, binge fantasy shows with expansive plots and world-building concepts that fractal out like kaleidoscopes, shooter games all guns and get going, text the crew and hit the club, chasing down who's the where what's next . . . to drop suddenly into nothingness, gauge on empty, falling through your bed, because in those cavernous seconds between nonstop frantic funtown and blackout sleep live the hellhounds of stark accountability, skulls at their feet, and in their howling high notes your failed obligations and guilt and fresh duress.

Luckily, Cueball was a gifted suppressor of what he could not rationalize, and never remembered his dreams.

But it was actually Julio who kept him grounded, out of his head and busy, while Cueball helped the young runaway stave off despondency by exercising his curiosity, if only for a short while.

When Julio first arrived, he thought he'd hit heaven. Kaos slapped his ass, told him, *This aint the big time, Macho Camacho. You gonna live with me, you gotta know the rules. You got chores, yo. It's better you learn how not easy shit is, there's crazies out here.* And then proceeded to throw all-night bashes. So Julio stepped up his game—showed up the next night all swagger and drip and attitude, a pint-sized imitation thug. Talked a ton of smack, hit the bathtub bong, then told a woman twice his age to suck his dick—and when she slapped him, ran off crying to his bedroom. Cringy as hell, but the boy was still Kaos' cousin, so when he returned, a red-eyed sourpuss flashing that goofy grin, all was forgiven.

Cueball hunted the opposite, avoiding the limelight while trying to keep sober.

Regardless, he too got swept into a fast orbit around Kaos' world— three long weeks lived as a single, inexorable day. It certainly paid to be the king's cousin, as Kaos treated Miami like a tasting menu, a conveyored assortment of delicious bite-sized canapés at a high-end fusion bar. The PRP crew partied till all hours, half wild on shank, or so smoked-out nobody could stand, smiling from their slumps in VIP booths and couches. Everything magically paid for, a moveable feast, and even though Cueball had pulled out a grand from the bank before leaving Palm Bay, he'd barely spent a dime.

It was the mornings that nearly did him in.

That's when everything slowed to a pulse, and reality crept in. Kaos was usually gone before Cueball woke, off on some errand for Alex, abandoning him to the white walls and silence of the condo. But not just him—he'd find Julio lazing on the couch, reading a book or playing video games with headphones on, as Cueball fiddled with the espresso machine. Here his mind would wander: to his father's anger, his mother's likely disappointment, the guilt he felt with leaving Eddy in a tight spot. Most days he'd opt for scrambled eggs and straight back to bed.

One morning, though, he stepped from his bedroom to discover Julio splayed out face down on the floor next to a spilled bag of chips.

Rushing to his side—positive the kid OD'd, given the amount of drugs around the house—Cueball flipped Julio over to find his eyes open, staring back.

"I'm bored," said Julio after a beat.

"What the hell?"

Julio's face scrunched. "Why you look mad?"

Cueball grabbed the child's foot and dragged him across the glossy white floor.

"Hey stop why!" screamed Julio. "What'chou doing?"

"I'm throwing you off the fucking balcony," said Cueball. "You almost gave me a heart attack."

Later that morning Cueball took Julio on their first field trip.

Some days they'd bus across the MacArthur Causeway and walk the beaches, scoping out girls and sampling taco trucks for new combinations— mango al pastor, kimchi barbacoa. Or they'd grab hot dogs and stroll the waterway bridges, searching for dolphins and jellyfish. Eventually Julio began to open up. He missed his friends back in Brooklyn, but especially his mom—a fed-up, hardworking, ass-slapping ninja who'd chase him down with wooden spoons when angered. Julio wasn't a bad kid, not really, Cueball thought—of the three cousins, he was the only one who didn't head up a street gang. The only thing Julio ever led was his middle school's marching band in a fancy parade alongside Central Park.

Cueball began sharing as well. His dad was a prime-A asshole, but he missed his mom. Her name was Charlotte, and no, he hadn't talked to her in a while. Nor his best friend, this guy Eddy. *You remind me of him a little. Actually, hey, you ever been to an art gallery?*

It was a spur-of-the-moment impulse, an intuition—Julio needed to see art. Needed to engage with something outside the norm. Not that Cueball knew the difference between a gallery and a museum, but he wasn't going to let that stand in the way of adventure.

After searching for places online, they pushed through the glass doors of a building downtown to enter a quiet, boxed space with somber lighting. A well-dressed woman behind the counter flashed them an intense smile.

"Is this worth anything, for real?" asked Julio, moseying around the first sculpture: an entire car smooshed into a cube, resting on the concrete floor. "Shit, pay me and I'll crash your whatever."

"They usually have a wall thing to read," Cueball whispered, avoiding the assistant's pursuant gaze as he failed to find a plaque. He was mostly on Julio's side regarding the artwork—but he also understood another side of the experience existed, and wanted Julio to know another side existed, and not just give in or shut him down, like a parent: "Maybe there's . . . a *history* behind this we don't know about. And this is a reaction to that history."

Julio regarded him as deranged. Then leaned over and flicked the sculpture, which rang out through the gallery as the assistant shrieked.

Cueball got them out fast and into a cab headed back to Wynwood, trying to explain to the cabbie what they were looking for, showing him pictures on his phone. Eventually they found it, a small park enclosed on three sides, each wall of which served as the canvas for colorful, odd, magnificent murals.

Julio was out the door before Cueball could even pay, rushing toward a wall depicting a fantastical anthropomorphic blue truck floating on waves, full of yellow and brown-skinned revelers, immigrants perhaps, in motley clothes and hats made of houses. Each section allotted for a different artist, and Julio skipped along pointing out his favorite dreamlike creatures and overly happy, possibly drugged flowers, before moving on to a bandana-masked young man poised to hurl a bouquet of flowers shaped like a Molotov cocktail, and a woman sunning herself beneath a newspaper that read "Are We Betraying the Planet?"

Cueball finally caught up to him, the boy standing silent before a cut-out sketch of a woman wheat-pasted onto a building next door. She was older, a mother perhaps, with hair strands hiding her face, anxiously clutching a cache of documents. From the extensive folds of her clothing flowed a vast cityscape: buildings, people, shadows, an entire subway track bending around a curve in what was unmistakably New York City.

"This," said Julio, "more like this."

Luckily there was another gallery nearby, where a latina artist was selling prints of her work, an image of a woman lifting up a man's head to view a single star. Cueball purchased a small print of the work for Julio, and as the artist signed it, she complimented Julio on his shoes, which he'd colored himself with magic markers.

On their walk home, Julio was animated, launching into an impassioned defense of an anime series Cueball hadn't yet seen and scolding him as uncultured. Cueball was in high spirits too, amazed a person could just walk outside any old day and be surprised by life.

As they were heading home, though, Kaos called—and suddenly all that heart-to-heart junk flew out the window.

Kaos swung by in his car and swept them off to a hot wings joint, where his boys were already face-deep in depraved sex stories. Evening arrived and turned the city into a giant slot machine again: roll deep with the PRP, back rooms with bottles, strippers grinding your kneecap as everyone hollered for that *dolla dolla bill, y'all.* Didn't matter this kid tagging along wasn't old enough to shave—money softened everything. Money was tender.

Cueball sulked internally, but said nothing, knowing there was no good place for a child in a drug cartel. But Julio was convinced he could prove his worth, and Kaos was slow to disabuse him of this notion.

Later that night, Cueball caught Julio praying.

As the condo groaned with drunken revelry, Cueball spotted Julio staggering toward his bedroom, following behind to make sure he was okay. Half awake, the boy stepped out of his shoes, fell to his knees by the bed, put his small hands together, and bowed. Cueball waited by the door, feeling not great. Maybe even a little bewildered and sad. As if you could just ask for a thing and get it. As if anyone deserved what they got.

In that moment he considered calling Julio's mother.

But he wouldn't. He simply couldn't accept responsibility for anyone else's life when he was barely managing his own. He hadn't even bothered pulling his truck out of impound, because why? It was a piece of shit, and he wanted to focus on the future. Maybe even stay in Miami and join forces with Kaos, an idea Kaos brought up the very next night.

"Absolutely I could use you," Kaos said. "Head you up a crew of white boys selling at hotels and golf courses."

They sat at an umbrellaed table beside a long blue swimming pool. A house party, but chic, exclusive—fifty or so professional-types dressed for the Oscars, and Cueball in black jeans and a borrowed salmon polo, mimicking Kaos. Cueball had no idea who these people were, what neighborhood this was, or why they were there. Julio was at the condo, set up with pizza and Netflix DVDs—Kaos made it clear he wanted to hang with Cueball alone.

"This is what Alex keeps from me," said Kaos, swirling his champagne.

Cueball didn't understand—they were literally sitting right here. To him, Kaos had everything.

"These motherfuckers, they're all for sale," said Kaos. "My cuz got dirt on lots of them, because he sells to them. And he can use the ones he got to get at the others. So he got everyone."

Cueball sipped his water, too nervous to pull a drink from the waiter's tray.

"Alex sends me out here to show my face, chat up the regulars," Kaos continued. "I represent the club. I represent him."

Without warning, Kaos tilted his glass sideways, slowly spilling his champagne to the patio floor.

Only a few people noticed, as most were beyond the pool, standing by the house or inside. Cueball sank into his chair as a waiter retrieved the empty glass and took Kaos' order of a whiskey neat.

"My ideas are too big for him," said Kaos, not missing a beat, motioning Cueball close. "Listen to this, tell me this is bullshit. So they got these liquid drugs you can put inside aerosol cans, right? So I say we start a publishing company. Books. Legit. Print the classics, stuff in public domain, nobody has the rights. What we do is, we spray one page with drugs. Just one. Page 69, page 420. Tuck that page in, bind it with the others. Prisoners order the book, guards check it—it's just a book! But our guys inside tear the sprayed page into little tabs, like acid. Sells twenty bucks a pop. Guess how much, one book? Eight grand!" he howled. "I know, right? Big ideas! But Alex, he thinks they're like . . . daydreams."

"That's a solid idea, bro," said Cueball.

Kaos leaned back, his face assured of this.

"He may ride your ass," ventured Cueball, "but man, this shit feels like a promotion to me. I mean, look at this place! These people! And you're right at home, not even sweating it. Maybe over time—"

"Over time *what*?" shot Kaos curtly, tugging his shirt. "Over time you're dead. Nah, now's the time." His voice dropped again. "We need to level up. I know a guy who works the Carnival cruises: Bahamas, Puerto Rico, Trinidad and Tobago. I got guys in hotels. Concierge, guest services. People everywhere looking for a good time, all the time. And you . . . you know guys who do the drop-offs."

This sent Cueball back in his seat, unsure where Kaos was headed. "Yeah, well, those aren't guys you can talk into turning a blind eye—"

"Oh yeah, why not?" asked Kaos. Finding Cueball slow to respond, he waved this off. "Okay, so maybe we start with the Mission. Get Frio to skim a little, not enough to miss. We hustle that through the Keys, build our clientele. I got a guy in Marathon with a houseboat who can store it! We start with bars, keep it small—" Kaos' speech raced to keep ahead of Cueball's expression, pulling away. "Or maybe we hit the whole stash! Show Alex how weak his security is! Then bring it back the next day, the whole thing. He sees I can plan, organize, adapt . . . that I got the fucking *balls*. He needs to understand I can work my own group! The Posse is mine!"

Kaos slapped the table in frustration, leaning back to pull wrinkles from his shirt.

Cueball paused, struck by a memory of that first morning following his arrival. The scrawled blueprints of the Mission on the kitchen counter. He had told Kaos about a big shipment heading south, and inadvertently fed him this idea. That's why Kaos drove him and Julio down to Little Havana instead of the club that night, so Kaos could meet with Frio and hash out a plan with his PRP buddies.

Fuck. Were they already stealing from Alex?

"Listen, Antonio," said Cueball. "I get your cousin treats you like shit. I get it, and fuck that noise. But man, what you're talking about doing is . . . crazy."

"I don't gotta convince you," said Kaos, gathering something back into himself, glancing about.

"That's true . . . I just don't see how you get away with it," said Cueball. "And besides that . . . dude, look around. People would kill to be in your shoes."

Kaos exhaled loudly, flicking a leaf off the table. Cueball waited in silence, hoping he'd been persuasive.

"Nah, you're probably right," Kaos relented. "I just got these ideas, you know?"

"Solid ideas, bro. And one day soon, I'm sure, you'll be in a position to make them happen."

Cueball offered nothing more. His friend was obviously eaten up by a need to prove himself—the irony being Julio was responding to Kaos the way Kaos responded to Alex.

Kaos abruptly rose and walked over to greet a group of people he recognized, leaving Cueball alone. When the waiter rolled by again, Cueball ordered an old-fashioned, playing games on his phone. Occasionally he'd turn to find Kaos involved in some intimate conversation, or charming a group of attractive listeners. The image of a powerful young man—how could his friend not see where he stood in all this?

An hour later they arrived back at Kaos' place. Julio had passed out on the couch and Kaos gingerly scooped him up, blanket and all, to deposit him in bed.

Cueball thought he might get a reprieve, but no—ding went the elevator, followed by PRP members drifting in loudly, half-baked, under the power of some curse, forcing into movement the rusty cogs of this interminable goddamn party, grinding out the minutes.

Despite all promises made to himself, Cueball accepted the pipe again, chasing shank hits with shots of tequila to wash down the taste.

He soon had trouble focusing, but Kaos was in his ear, hovering, elastic, criminal, saying it was their time to shine. Alex was holding him back, just like Cueball's boss was, two brutes of a feather. Hadn't he been humiliated enough? Ass kicked here to China? Maybe he shouldn't take anything lying down no more. Maybe it was time to man up.

Maybe, Cueball agreed, it was time his dad learned what a gut punch felt like.

"Tell me this plan," slurred Cueball. "Your plan. Tell me. The Mission."

They were together on the balcony, overlooking the dark water and beautiful lights, slipping into that deep-mood part of the drug experience.

Kaos ready with the closing pitch: of course they'd return the drugs! The very next day, absolutely! And no violence. Fuck no. They'd work everything out with Frio, who'd work it out with guys on the inside.

Next thing Cueball knew, he was bent over a toilet, hacking up dinner in a widening plume.

Beside him the door opened. Through tears he saw Julio, barefoot, rubbing his eyes. Barely awake, but his expression registered as judgment. Or disgust. Or maybe he was just a little bewildered and sad.

Eddy woke to the smell of coffee from a percolator going on the old O'Keefe & Merritt gas stove. Lisbon plopped down next to him on the couch, scribbling a sentence that let Eddy know he'd secretly hidden a pack of Camel Lights behind the firewood. Eddy thanked him with prayerful hands and a slapped knee. Then Lisbon scribbled out another word: *turkey*. Eddy assumed he meant *bacon* until Duke appeared dressed in full camo, carrying three rifles.

He set the rifles down nearby and poured three coffees, walking them over.

"I wasn't trying to be a dick before," he said, handing Eddy his.

"Must come natural," said Eddy.

Lisbon chuckled. Duke's expression warmed as he sat before the coffee table. "I know this isn't easy. We're rooting for you."

"I'm rooting for you," said Eddy, "rooting for me."

Lisbon was enjoying Eddy's dance around his brother's parenting. Duke continued: "Seriously though, if you can power through this mess, and not backslide, you'll be rewarded."

Backslide. That old Christian reprimand. And this talk of personal responsibility and reward: Duke truly was his uncle's nephew. He wasn't aiming to be mean, though, so Eddy kept it civil.

Duke picked up a rifle, leveled it flat, and presented it to Eddy. "You shoot?"

They drove out to the property edge and set up in a deer blind. Lisbon had boiled chicken noodle soup, which they drank from thermoses in the early frost. Eddy realized he was becoming friends with the brothers, who'd school him that week on everything from roosting trees to crankbait lures to the sullen ghosts of the Carolina foothills. And whenever the jonesing tore at him or the stomach twists started in—gun oil proving a noxious trigger—they'd give him the necessary space to handle it.

Several deer wandered by before any turkeys showed: four of them, with giant fanning feathers. The creatures were bluer and pinker than Eddy would have imagined—alien even. The rifle, though, felt magnificently dumb in his hands, so he watched elated as the brothers eased into their conviction and training, steady with their shots.

The Twins each bagged a bird that first morning. He watched Duke slice one open with a single stroke, undressing the feathered breast as if unzipping a hoodie from a child.

It was a week of new experiences. Eddy practiced the calming effect of boxed breathing. Learned when hunting how to see between things—high grass, peach trees, animosity, shame—while swearing to himself, *Never again*. He partook of baked fish and grapefruit, and when he could stomach more, a full meal of turkey and dumplings. Turned out Lisbon was a helluva cook.

The final day of his enforced furlough began at a farmers market, where they sold ten birds to a butcher who deducted their lunches—pork chops smothered in hot honey, collard greens, and jalapeño biscuits—which they took down to a lake near the cabin, setting up on the dock. The fresh air was nice but did little to quell Eddy's anxiety: his one wish was to remain at the cabin, avoiding forever the people he'd hurt. He had said and done horrible things, things that now made him wince. He was sick, or he was the illness itself, corroding all he came in contact with.

Eddy watched the brothers strip down and dive into the lake, swimming for a platform buoyed by floating drums at lake's center, where they challenged each other to breath-holding contests. Returning, Duke was fast but Lisbon faster, and it was good to see the younger take the prize, smacking the dock planks in good cheer.

This became a daily meditative practice, facing his faults and mistakes head-on. Eddy was unable to envision Gin without experiencing a deep, gut-level remorse. Or her mother . . . jesus, it was criminal. He scrolled through his phone, pulling up Gin's number, running through his apology, only to drop the phone to the wood dock and tug his ball cap over his eyes.

He didn't deserve to feel this good, the sun's heat upon his cold, folded arms. Didn't deserve forgiveness. He deserved not knowing if his best friend was safe—yes, he deserved that. He deserved Del Ray finding out about Colt and doling out a proper ass-beating. But not this warmth and slight chill, feeling hopeful.

He would keep away from folks for a while—especially women—until he could figure out how to be the kind of man who didn't harm them.

Sometimes the paranoia rose up like heartburn, sensing a terrible event had befallen Cueball, beyond the disconnected phone line, which Del Ray promised was Bird's doing. His friend had plenty of money, and was likely holed up in some squalorous beach motel, renting cable and blowing through sex workers. And maybe, just maybe, Eddy imagined, he was detoxing—clawing his way back to normality.

Duke finished drying off with his towel, pulling up a lounge chair folded back. He hummed a little tune and let his fingers wander into a greasy paper bag.

"It's ungodly how much I miss biscuits," he said. "That's how come Florida isn't the South: lack of proper biscuits."

"I want all of it," said Eddy. "The cabin, the skunks, this lake. I want the weird blue chicken eggs the farmers sell . . . everything."

They watched Lisbon take up a fishing pole and hike down the shoreline.

"I wouldn't be in this line of work if I was just clocking hours," said Duke. "It gives me a sense of purpose." He twisted onto an elbow. "Did Lisbon tell you I bought this place outright?"

"What, the cabin?"

Duke nodded. "Straight cash, off the books. Not even in my real name."

Eddy was impressed. "Congrats."

"The property's worth less than a new F-150 truck, but hey, it's chill, huh?"

"Greatest place on earth."

"I got a deal for you," said Duke. "You stay straight, tough it out a full year—no backsliding—and it's yours."

Eddy swiveled his head. "What do you mean?"

"Just what I said."

Eddy squinched his eyes. "Man, there's no reason to be an asshole."

"I'm not joking," said Duke. "The cabin, the land, this lakefront . . . the whole shebang. You can drive up whenever you want, your very own little getaway."

Eddy looked hurt. "Why would you do that?"

Duke stretched, fingers laced over his head. "Incentive. Motivation. Protection, for my brother. It's not all that luxurious, bud, you're just poor enough to appreciate it. Besides, everyone deserves a second chance. A second act, they call it."

Eddy blew through his teeth. "Thanks for having me. I feel a lot better. But I'm not looking for a handout."

Duke dropped his sunglasses. "People don't actually work for money, do they. They work for what money buys. My gut tells me you want more options, and a clear sense of purpose. To be your own man for once. Am I wrong?"

He wasn't. Eddy cleared his throat to speak, but didn't know what to say, so chuckled instead, so as not to own the possibility of believing any of this.

"Goals define a person," said Duke.

Beyond them, Lisbon toyed with a too-small fish nibbling his bait.

Duke closed his eyes, so Eddy did the same, bringing his ball cap low again. The cold was creeping back into the wind. He wondered what kind of fishing boats they ran on the lakes up here.

A phalanx of cars split the pine woods, fanning out before the warehouse bay.

The security guards aimed their weapons but recognizing the intruders shouted instead and were left hyperventilating, gripping their bloody stomachs.

The intruders carried automatics and leapt onto the loading dock, lifting the enormous metal door on rollers to fire haphazardly into the darkness of the warehouse. The return fire kicked up concrete and spun razored shards over the heads of a second wave of boys ducking behind the loading dock wall, guns raised and firing backwards.

Inside, the echoing pops were soon replaced by pleas in spanish as the attackers swam up and over the platform and into the void.

The rear door of a BMW opened to a kid all of eleven, bandana fluttering as he clutched a 9mm with both hands, fearful he was missing out on the action. A concerned voice shouted after him, but Julio's short legs moved quick. He hopped to balance himself on the ledge and lifted a leg to roll onto the dock, passing queasily the gutted men at his feet, only then thinking to slouch.

Falling from the passenger's seat, Cueball kept low and shuffled quickly to the warehouse's side as a final barrage of gunshots crackled nearby. The sound of cars peeling out reeled from some unseen distance out front. He peered cautiously around the corner, ready to fire, heart hammering, metal siding hot on his shoulder.

From the boxed darkness of the warehouse came a pathetic whimper.

Kid Kaos stepped into the light, blushed in rebirth, lugging by the collar a man twice his age who was, boots to bowels, a thing of blood. Kaos dragged the muttering corpse to the dock edge and without pause unloaded a single round into his temple.

Cueball raised a hand, body hidden. "It's me! It's just me!"

Kaos' dead eyes fell upon him, gun limp at his side, and returned within. Cueball scurried up a set of metal stairs, careful to avoid the bodies. He'd never seen a dead person up close, and now they were everywhere.

The misshapen body of Julio was spread out across the lowered tusks of a forklift. He saw no blood, but it was clear the child was dead.

Beyond him, their man on the inside, Frio, crawled sluggishly across the floor, trailing slime.

There were maybe five or six dead Toros, identifiable by their orange clothing. Two members of Kaos' team were down as well, with friends tending to them, while others knifed apart couch cushions in the main office, pulling out bricks of dope wrapped in brown paper like schoolbooks. They argued whose fault it was that some Toros had managed to escape, but quieted when Kaos howled.

Kaos knelt to the forklift and raised his young cousin into his arms, propping the child over his shoulder, anguished as he whispered, "Oh shit, little man. I'm sorry. Fuck, I told you, I *TOLD* you!"

Cueball flinched as someone unloaded another round into the body of a competitor. Frio had stopped moving but no one seemed to care. They were celebrating, tossing back and forth bricks of shank, already recounting their roles in the ambush.

Cueball marveled at the atrocity. Like one suffering a nerve-scalding burn, he was for the moment immune to pain. A tingling sensation coursed through his extremities and he felt lightheaded.

They think this is the end of it.

They think they've won.

Lisbon sat beside Duke in a cushioned white booth behind a round table, the small room shrouded in blue light, dark as an aquarium. They'd only just returned from Georgia to find themselves swept up by a tornado.

Lisbon strained to hear the conversation; the strip club music beyond the closed door was muffled but booming. This was what his uncle called a *safe* room, which implied the existence of *unsafe* rooms. To calm himself, Lisbon tried to picture himself among the grapefruit trees and funky straw smell of the outdoors, but it was already gone, as were his nails, chewed half to splinters.

"I'm not saying it's not disrespectful," said Bird.

"Then what exactly are you saying?" prompted Seizer.

The discussion was not going well. His uncle was clearly angry. So was Bird. Whenever Del Ray spoke, he used his hands mostly. Gumby laughed when others didn't, which was weird. Corey Buffalo stood by the door, arms crossed, looking tough. Duke was pretending not to listen, and was writing in the wrong crossword answers—maybe not wrong, but perpendicularly unconfirmed.

Lisbon and his brother were working the *New York Times* crossword puzzle by the light of Duke's phone. Pen no pencil. Nothing frustrated Lisbon more than writing over wrong answers, always making sure to have at least two perpendicular clues corroborated before filling in a word. Tonight, though, Duke kept writing in guesses, and Lisbon noted at least two errors resulting from his brother's distraction. To calm himself, he focused on the next crossword clue. Five letters: *Scalawag*.

"They might be lying!" barked Bird. "These kids are looking for someone to pin it on!"

"It's possible," added Del Ray, opening his hands.

Lisbon wasn't entirely sure if Bird's shouting was actual anger or him pitching his voice over the club music. He guessed both. Words and feelings ran together in Lisbon's mind when talk got heated. It became harder to parse what people meant from what they were saying.

"They have witnesses!" shouted his uncle.

"Who we don't trust," said Bird.

"I trust Alex, and Alex trusts his men," said his uncle.

Then Bird turned and punched a hole in the wall.

Parts of drywall hit the floor as he pulled out his fist, and Del Ray yelled, "Whoa there, brother!"

Gumby's laughter seemed inappropriate.

Gumby wore a black leather jacket and Corey Buffalo wore a jean jacket. Gumby's vest hid knives and Corey's jacket hid a gun that Lisbon caught sight of when he flipped it back to brace his hands on his hips. Duke had a gun too. These were the weapons he knew of. He had no gun, himself, because he wasn't allowed one.

"You can blow all your fuses, but it don't change the truth!" shouted Seizer. "Now, let's focus on getting your boy back here before Alex gets a hold of him."

"I'll go down myself," said Bird.

"I need you here," said Seizer. "We got other business to take care of."

"Sir, I'd be happy to find Heath for you," offered Corey Buffalo. "If he's with this Kaos guy, they're somewhere close. These kids aren't gonna abandon their families. They're probably holed up in some motel outside town, scared shitless—"

Gumby laughed louder this time.

"The Head of Camp Security must remain at the camps, but thank you, Corey," said Seizer.

"Yeah, thanks a bunch, Corey," said Gumby.

"Okay, let's cool it," said Del Ray, bouncing his hands like he was trying to calm the air.

"Maybe Camp Counselor here don't understand whose job he hopes to assume," said Gumby.

"Gum, c'mon now," said Del Ray.

"Why the fuck is this babysitter even part of the conversation?" asked Gumby, causing Corey Buffalo to clamp his jaw and intensify his posture.

"Because there's a real good likelihood these punks might think to hit us again," said Seizer. "We hear this Kaos joker's got family in Kissimmee, which is only a half hour from Camp Heron."

Lisbon watched his uncle approach Gumby, standing close. "Buffalo here is your new best friend. I need you both in hourly communication."

"Ten-four," said Corey Buffalo.

Gumby seethed.

"Everybody out!" growled Bird, flexing his hurt fist.

Del Ray guided Gumby gently toward the door with fingers to his back. Corey Buffalo watched the pair pass, eyes not meeting Gumby's glare, then followed them into the strip club.

Scalawag.

Lisbon knew the word. Pirates entered his mind. When he glanced back up, Bird was alone with his uncle.

Bird was much, much larger, and wearing no shirt under his leather vest. Lisbon admired the tattoos covering his body: it was like a treasure map. Duke falsely studied the crossword, his eyes fixed and glossy. Lisbon loved Duke this way—primed to act while pretending not to be.

"Let's not make this personal," said Bird, stepping up to Seizer. "When my son returns, and he will return, he will have a place in this club."

"He lost us territory *over a dog!*" wheezed Seizer. "And now he's gone and jacked a shipment from an ally? Are you blind to the trend here?"

"If in fact he was there . . . I'll reimburse you for your cut, entirely. Plus an extra fifty."

Seizer, stone-faced, mulled this over. "Fine. Throw money at the problem. But how can I ever trust the boy again?"

"I guess you'll just have to reach down a little deeper," said Bird with more severity.

"I'll take free money," countered Seizer straightaway, "or whatever honorarium I'm owed for enduring this level of disrespect, but nossir! my decisions are mine and mine alone!"

Glancing over, Bird caught Lisbon watching, and Lisbon disengaged. The room was vibrating. Duke was quite rigid.

"He's my boy," said Bird slowly, importantly.

"Let's pray he's not your downfall," said Seizer.

Bird pointed at Seizer's chest: "This is settled."

Leaving, Bird shot another glance their way. Lisbon understood that Bird knew he and Duke were part of the package. There was no Seizer without his nephews. The club music rushed in as Bird exited.

Lisbon elbowed Duke, signing under the table, so his uncle wouldn't see. When Duke kept guessing wrong and loudly, he pulled over his writing tablet.

CUEBALL IS PART OF THE PACKAGE, he wrote. JUST LIKE US.

Lisbon chose these words carefully, knowing Duke would know what to do with them. Duke tapped his knee and rose and walked over to their uncle. "He's afraid you'll go after Cueball."

"As he should be!" barked Seizer, still fuming. "This kid's looking to find out the hard way what happens when you cross the boss. The stink of weakness pervades."

"It's his son," said Duke. "If Bird ever threatened one of us, you'd be furious. Unstoppable."

"Boy's a live wire . . ."

"We allow for rehabilitation. You taught me this. There has to be a way back in, or this *will* become the wedge you're afraid of."

"He's gonna end up getting somebody killed," said Seizer.

Duke shrugged. "Cueball is part of the package."

Seizer exhaled loudly and clasped his bald head. "Yeah, I know."

"*Lord, forgive my iniquity, though it be great,*" said Duke.

Seizer clopped Duke's shoulder, a grin creeping up. "That so?"

"If you retaliate . . . guess what's next."

"No, you're right, I know, but all I see is red right now. It's gonna be a while before that boy is welcome near me, but you're right, I'll talk to Bird. This is family."

"His payoff makes for a quick turnaround on usable funds," said Duke.

"There's a positive spin," said Seizer, chuckling. "Should I be thankful?"

Duke raised an eyebrow. "Maybe we kick something Alex's way. A good-faith offering, maybe help settle that cousin issue of his. Keep it all in-house."

"Cooler heads prevail," said Seizer, taking Duke's hand and patting it. "How'd things shape up with Wildeboar at the cabin?"

"Better than expected," said Duke. "He's repentant. Ready to get back to work."

Seizer huffed. "Now we pull inward. See who's standing on the outside."

Rogue was the answer to the crossword clue. Lisbon lacked the two perpendicular clues, but he knew he was right. He waited patiently for Duke to return to show him, as puzzles were never fun without someone to share them with.

Music emptied from the end of the Black Road, a vacant stretch of asphalt run through dense woods and blinded by a cul-de-sac.

A grunge classic trembled from the Bug's speakers. Heads close and shoulders touching, a painterly account of brotherly love, Eddy and Jesse watched the pine treetops bleed from auburn to dark emerald.

The Black Road was Eddy's spot, just up the street from his house, the asphalt erasing a bike trail he'd taken to Southwest Junior High as a kid. The paved road sat empty a full year, no streetlights or houses built, before Eddy and Cueball brought machetes to slash out a camping spot for themselves, digging a fire pit and sprinkling broken glass about the perimeter to ward off animals and perverts. They befriended Jesse shortly thereafter, a mouthy surfer with a buzz cut, dragging in tow his nerdy younger brother, Draco, so smart he'd skipped a grade. On the weekends the gang cooked sirloin steaks over the fire, enjoying pilfered beers and cigarettes, curled up in sleeping bags as they traded ghost stories and evolving philosophies of life.

That young kid couldn't have imagined Eddy's life now.

"Remember the half-pipe we built?" said Eddy. "We'd skate *all day*."

Jesse did. "Launch ramps, a PVC rail. Shit was fire. Until the cops made us tear it all down. Assholes didn't realize it was all we had."

"How else would we have discovered Coors Light and Mad Dog 20/20?"

"Ha! I threw up gallons of that pink shit."

Camping later gave way to high school parties, when the Black Road became the premier teen hot spot, packed with kids ingesting cheap vodka, bogarting roaches, complaining of early shifts and handsy bosses, and fabricating whatever earnest lines might get them fingered or sucked off in the coolness of the blue woods. The police raids that followed were more or less agreed-upon training sessions for Palm Bay's finest: Broncos crashing through palmettos, cruisers flying down the block. Bottles were emptied, drugs "confiscated"—but never any arrests, as paperwork was a hassle and most of the kids were white.

As fast as it arrived, so it ended. One night a cheerleader from an encroaching, hipper crowd caught herself on fire after attempting to hush a lit match in a near-empty mason jar of pure-grain alcohol. That story made the nightly news, and all that remained of the Road's once-glorious past was the charred seat of an SUV resting in the bulb.

"Where'd everyone go?" asked Eddy.

"Got jobs," said Jesse, emptying dip into a soda can. "Got married. Got dead."

"Leaf McKenzie OD'd, you hear that? Forrest's little brother?"

"Tragic shit."

"He painted that big mural behind the Wal-Mart. Animals with human faces. He was in that ska band that did covers, Op Ivy, Bad Religion, with that drummer who got shipped off to Afghanistan?"

"The Panoptiskans."

"That's right!" said Eddy. "Damn. They didn't realize Leaf was gone till the lights came up."

"Dude, your hand."

Eddy raised his trembling fingers above the dashboard.

"Still goes off sometimes, like a little alarm. Little wake-up call. I can't thank you enough for helping me, seriously."

Jesse chuffed. "No man left behind. You'd do the same for me."

"You know I would," said Eddy. "I owe you. I feel ridiculous."

Jesse slapped his friend's chest, meaning, *Let it go.*

Upon returning from Georgia, Eddy moved back into his mother's house, which felt somehow smaller. The bed pillows had sopped up Gin's fragrance, so he washed all the sheets and rearranged the furniture, piling her forgotten toiletries into a garbage bag. The shank urges weren't completely gone, but their grip had relaxed enormously. If copious amounts of coffee didn't abate the cravings, he'd call Jesse, who could talk him down like a champ, or he'd head over to Duke and Lisbon's to watch eighties horror flicks. Duke surprised everyone by lowering his defenses a smidge, showing himself to be a jocular, intelligent guy, if a bit reserved, which in turn freed Lisbon to be the grandstander he was. They even had him trying new cuisines: thai, german, salvadoran. The secret thing nobody could help Eddy shake, though, was the guilt of having hurt Gin.

Through the grapevine, he learned she was renting a mainland bungalow by the river. Keeping a promise to himself, he would not contact her. Would not dwell upon the loneliness, nor the hapless depths of muttering depression, stripped of all but wishing.

"I could ruin a glass of water," he spoke into the night.

"What?"

"You think me and Gin—"

"Forget it, bro," Jesse scoffed. "Way out of your league."

"How's that even possible? We just broke up."

"She was out of your league to begin with."

"She said I didn't *own* her," mused Eddy. "But I never said anything like that."

"You didn't have to, dude," Jesse said, shaking his head. "Anyhow, it's probably better we stay single. We're never home. Can't talk about work. Why put someone through that?"

Gin had left one voicemail on his landline, while he was out-of-state, conveniently. She was trying something new each week, to keep upbeat— picking oranges at Harvey's Groves, a trip to the zoo. She apologized for slapping him. She didn't want him to call back, shouldn't have called in the first place, probably, but she'd heard something odd on the radio, which led her to a car dealership in Viera. There she watched average people battle fatigue and dehydration for the chance to win a used car. Whoever kept their hands on the car the longest, won it. They weren't allowed to sit, and each restroom break was prescheduled. Gin considered their misery a testament to willpower overcoming hardship, clapping alongside the judges as one by one the contestants shriveled and peeled away, bemoaning lost motor skills and swelling ankles. *I'm not completely sure why, but it helped,* she said. *I just hope you find help too. Something sustainable. I mean . . . I hope you find happiness.*

Eddy played the message four times before erasing it.

To cheer him up, Jesse took him to the Cocoa Beach Pier for a night of reggae at *Jamaikin Me Crazy*. Libidinous drunks, glued at the sex like love-bugs, danced in sweaty abandon as strobe lights pounded the chill ocean waters. It only made Eddy more depressed, and he left to go brood on the beach. His signals felt crossed, the wires corroded. Something inside him had died. No, that was bullshit. There was a path forward, he believed, he just needed to trust himself and focus.

He hadn't told Jesse about Duke's offer to sign over his cabin if he could stay sober for a year. A part of him worried his friend might misinterpret the gift as an undeserved leg up.

"Cueball call you?" asked Eddy.

Jesse shook his head. "I'm sure he's fine. He's always been way too sensitive."

There were rumors that Charlotte and Bird were separating, or were at least sleeping apart now. Eddy felt for what his friend might come home to.

"You ever worry about the DEA or ATF crashing the party?" asked Eddy.

"*Prison's just another word...for...nothing left to lose*," Jesse crooned. "If I start worrying about that shit I won't sleep."

"I feel like karma's right on my ass," said Eddy.

"Maybe try putting some good back in the world," said Jesse. "Pay it forward. Buy the coffee for the person behind you at Starbucks. Volunteer at some old folks' home, or a soup kitchen or something."

Eddy turned to him. "You know, that's actually not a bad idea. Maybe we could do it together."

"Shit," said Jesse. "I'm not paying for anybody's fucking coffee. I earn my money." He tapped the radio clock. "We should jet."

Eddy turned the ignition key and spun the car in a circle.

Traffic was light. Eddy found himself entranced by the passing street-lights, pregnant with insect carcasses. Creatures of devotion, drawn to a powerful light, which summoned from the infernal recesses of his subconscious a familiar figure. A short, bearish man—one who might prefer boxers to briefs, gelato to froyo, newspapers to the internet. A man whom his father would have said put his pants on one leg at a time. But also a collector of men; leader of an anonymous army. Seizer's appeal was the lure of the religious icon, a warrant against death—in its vicinity, you felt allied with greater mysteries. But on his bad side, every room with him in it was a trap. Which was why Eddy had wanted to stop off at the Black Road before heading to the meeting: to regain some confidence. They'd been summoned for an unspecified purpose, which his gut told him was bad news.

Also nagging at him was what Colt may or may not have told Del Ray about what had occurred at Snake Lake.

The small VW bumped over railroad tracks on a vacant stretch near the Harris complex, lurching to a halt under a white sign: LIBERTY STORAGE.

Jesse got out and punched in the gate's security code as Eddy clicked on the high beams and hobbled along the thickly wooded drive.

The old packinghouse had wired windows and corrugated metal siding, blue in the moonlight. One of an unknown number of tax fronts for Seizer, this facility was special, serving as the club's main postproduction holding facility. After the ice form of shank was cooked and processed at the labs, it was brought here, rechecked for purity, weighed, separated, and bundled into furniture for transport.

Headlights found the Twins' moving van parked by the concave pit of a settled sinkhole. An unfamiliar sedan with dealer plates rested nearby.

As the engine cut, the woods came alive—a place rent with ghosts and bullfrogs imitating ghosts. That's when Eddy spied, hidden in the bushes, a sleek chopper with high handlebars, a human kneecap welded to the front. It was Gumby's. Eddy had mentioned to no one his run-in with the Enforcer at Snake Lake, and was now genuinely afraid.

Jesse produced a handgun from under his seat, hiking it down his pants.

"You think that's necessary?"

"Where's yours?"

Eddy couldn't say it had been stolen from his car, likely by Colt. "At home. You worried?"

Jesse glanced at the building. "Seizer doesn't strike me as impulsive, and he doesn't do unscheduled meetings, right? Listen, last month a camp worker disappeared. Supposedly he was stealing. Maybe Seizer thinks I—"

"It's not you," said Eddy. "It's probably me."

Jesse considered this. "Maybe. But whatever, I got your back. If it's nothing, the mouse stays in its house."

They moved in tandem, scanning the darkness. Jesse located a panel by a door on the building's far side, punching in the code. As the door squeaked open, they were bathed in the radiance of a small sun.

"Seriously?" Jesse insisted.

Someone snickered. "Gotta make sure you boys are properly sterilized."

Locating the dimmer, Jesse brought into relief a sunken, windowless room. A table rested center stage, at which a league of gentlemen huddled over hands of texas hold'em. Mickey tilted a cup of tepid coffee toward his shabby face. Duke turned his ball cap around and reached into a donut box as Lisbon watched them descend the stairs with the intense, preternatural gaze of a lowlander. Gumby tilted in a chair at the room's far end, leafing through a wildlife magazine, seemingly oblivious.

"What's the word, jefe?" said Eddy, taking the seat by Mickey, who looked scary gaunt, his white arms peeking out from under a leather vest. "Dang, man, you're skinny as a beanpole."

"Got me a head cold," Mickey replied, scratching an ankle. "Haven't slept right lately. Seizer's got me running ragged."

Which was true, according to what Eddy cobbled together from overheard conversations. Seizer had Mickey operating on overdrive, apparently, with good results. Within a year the biker transformed from useful messenger to that high-end recruiter his boss anticipated, which wasn't necessarily reflected by his title. Yet "Fleabug" made sense to Mickey: hopping between cities, attaching himself to fringe groups in order to mine potential workers. From district Heads with distribution networks to Pushers with apartments to street Dealers, Mickey helped Seizer stack bodies between himself and the product, while ensuring the club's enduring presence in a region. The bureaucracy cut into profits, and opened itself to thievery, but there'd always be another bust, another kid who got *got* hustling a stepped-on quarter ounce through the projects—that was life. If a situation turned thorny, they'd send Gumby.

Seizer had a reliable Fleabug ferreting out subordinates with surprising enterprise and a viral product that would not quit, disseminating its message of chemical utopia to whomever would listen. All was going according to plan. But somewhere in the dregs—pitching to club owners and I-bankers and restaurant workers and cyber-moonlighters with dark web credentials—Mickey had become infected.

"See that car out front?" Mickey offered. "Perks, Brooklyn-style. I'm done with bikes for the long hauls."

Duke flipped something to Eddy across the table. Holding up the plastic case, he studied the nine-grade Nolan Ryan rookie card within.

"This for me?"

"Shit no," said Duke. "Gift from the Granger boys in Atlanta. We let them use the cabin for a weekend. Turns out their old man owns a sports card shop. Mick picked it up on the way down."

Wasting no time, Lisbon pulled out a Hank Aaron framed in glass. No corner rounded, not a scratch. Wearing that famous cheshire near-grin, as if already anticipating a run at the white man's most treasured record.

"Why you gotta one-up me?" Duke asked. "Scam artist. He only got that 'cause they think he's brain-damaged."

At a diner one night, while Lisbon was in the bathroom, Eddy finally inquired about his silence. Duke shrugged—Lisbon *could* talk, yes, he just chose not to, as it sounded funny. Turns out Lisbon was born with a tongue the size and shape of a grubworm, a grotesque and fascinating appendage he displayed thereafter in quick, random flickers, much to the disgust of Eddy and delight of Jesse, who when inebriated called upon the brother to amuse the gang by sending an unforgiving waitress or stingy barkeep deep into their own pitiable failures of vocabulary. As a boy he would call forth the tongue like a snake preacher, dancing about, hands raised and eyes lolling like the ecstatic. But puberty capped that fun quick, and Lisbon soon found himself belittled by those he'd formerly entertained, which kept Duke hugging his side like the thorny protrusion of a flower cultivated by evolution to ward off predators. Duke confided to Eddy his opinion that, while in the womb, he'd likely stolen valuable nutrients from his brother, which he recompensed by shouldering the brunt of a world hell-bent on crushing its own enigmas.

Mickey swept in the playing cards and reshuffled. "I'm headed to Arizona next week for the Hopi Fest. Got some natives interested in a score. Hey, Gum, you ever been out to Zions?"

Gumby flipped a page of his nature magazine.

"That man sure do love his animals."

"Anyone know why we're here?" Jesse asked.

"Business meeting," said Mickey. "Assets. Claims adjustments."

"What exactly needs adjusting?" asked Jesse, shifting so the gun slid up his spine.

Mickey dropped his cigarette down a beer's neck, staring out across the smoke. "Hell, I don't know. Claims?"

"Whatever it is, it's important," said Duke, setting the stage. "Our uncle woke us up at three a.m. the other night, asking if we'd heard from Cueball."

Eddy's heart jumped. "He say why?"

Duke grimaced as a motor settled into a cough outside. They waited in silence as Mickey dealt a hand. Then the door swung open and Del Ray took the steps cowboy-like, gripping a helmet shiny as a cosmonaut's. Keeping low in his seat, Eddy avoided Del's eyes, worried to find out if Colt had shared anything with him. The biker looked wildly unsure of things as he proceeded directly to the bathroom, muttering, "Got me a mean case of the montezumas."

The mood perked up a little after Del returned. He dropped a twenty in for chips and flashed Eddy a grin—a huge relief.

"Jesus, Mick," he said. "You got cancer or something?"

Mickey threw his hands up. "Everyone keeps asking and I keep saying: I'm working out. I'm sick."

"I call bullshit, partner," said Del Ray. "Looks like you're on the Jenny Crank diet."

"Hey, we all party," said Mickey, cool but enraged. "I do my job, so fuck off."

Pretty soon they were as quiet as a group of rabbits waiting out a storm. Mickey undid his watch and set it on the table, studying the time. Flops came and went, until an off-suited deuce on the river ruined Mickey's all-in flush draw, causing him to spin around and kick a dent in the drywall, which sent Del Ray, the winner of the hand, into a laughing coughing fit.

Bird arrived soon after, patting the dimmer and raising the lights to blazing. All but Gumby welcomed him as he fell in behind Jesse, gripping his shoulders. "Boys. How's the road been treating you?"

"Pretty good," said Eddy cautiously. "Last week we were able to drive the full sixteen hours without stopping."

"I heard. Let's not do that again. A person isn't as sharp after that amount of time. Besides, we don't want Lisbon murdering any more guardrails."

This yoked a nervous chuckle from the group.

"It's not that big a deal," said Duke.

The group moored for reaction, but got none. Bird, with bigger fish to fry, hollered to Gumby tilted back in his chair. "Any word on Jim Barns?"

Gumby offered his voice for the first time. "MIA."

Eddy ignored Jesse's shoe-tap under the table. He didn't understand what was being communicated, but if they acted like a pair, they'd be treated as such.

Bird sniffed loudly, dug for his phone, and stepped back outside.

Eddy hadn't seen Jim Barns since the party at Snake Lake, and before that, when Gumby damn near sous-cheffed the man's face off, following a racial aspersion. Jesse mentioned the haggard old creep was now working the camps as a Foreman or something, bandana under a ball cap, filling drums with waste and stacking pallets alongside the men he managed.

When Bird returned, Seizer was with him.

Seizer flashed a hyphen grin and pocketed his driving glasses as Bird bolted the door. The pair then circled the table like a magician and his famulus, primed for some opening act.

"Paving these boys' way to the poorhouse, buddy?" Seizer joked, patting Lisbon, who pridefully palmed his winnings. "Hey, Mick, you playing with no chips?"

Del Ray roared.

"I just can't catch a break with these fuckholes," said Mickey.

Seizer winced, the language hard on his ears. "Well, that's how it goes, trusting luck," he mused, then glanced at Bird standing opposite him. "Okay, enough chitchat. It aint pretty, so let's get down to it. Ray, why don't you start this up, tell 'em what you told me."

Eddy and Jesse spun to Del Ray, a spy in their midst. Del braced for the attention, sitting up, one eyelid drooping lazily as he searched for a beginning.

"We got a call two nights ago from our boys in Miami. Alex says about three-quarters of our last shipment got hijacked, early morning daytime. Says gang kids, call themselves the Puerto Rican Posse. But there's a twist. This Posse is led by Alex's cousin, one Kid Kaos, whom you boys are familiar with."

"Sure," said Eddy cautiously. "Cueball's friend. Antonio."

Bird spit on the floor and caught Seizer's glare. There was no mistaking their exchange, as if all the disappointment and bitterness that could rise up between a military general and his failed aide-de-camp was now present in the room.

Del continued: "Anyhow, it's been heating up down there, territory-wise. We've got word this Kaos punk moved his entire operation north to Fort Lauderdale. Now, Alex and the Toros are trusted associates, they'd lose more than they'd gain by stealing from us, as they handle our port deals and all rail traffic—"

"Ray, if you wouldn't mind sticking to the topic," said Seizer.

"Understand," Bird added, arms crossed, "that none of this leaves this room."

"This *posse* hit the Mission," said Del Ray, point-blank. "Primary warehouse for the Toros. As you boys know, it's boondocks out there. Tight security. Not a place you stumble across looking for a campsite. Whoever hit us knew where and when to strike. This was a particularly large shipment, meant to be housed for one day only. Had it on the books for weeks. And though we've verified at least one of these Posse fucknuggets worked there, familiarity with the size and timing of this drop-off was restricted.

Kaos was off the warehouse job, so the only folks besides us privy to these details were Alex and two of his higher-ups." Here Del Ray paused. "And you fellas."

Jesse snorted. "Well, shit, don't look at us."

"We know you didn't do it," Bird said, cracking his knuckles. "But there's no doubt this was aimed to cripple us."

"Who do you think it was?" asked Eddy.

Bird frowned. "Anyone heard from Heath?"

The emotional weight of the insinuation anchored Eddy to his chair as he searched everyone's eyes for meaning, thinking, *That stupid son of a bitch.*

"Alex's boys—the ones that *survived*," spit Seizer, "recognized him from your drop-offs. Said these kids came out guns blazing, shoot 'em up! Cocky, like I know that boy to be!"

Bird swallowed the insult. "I don't give a flying fuck if these spics wanna kill each other off in a turf war. Their blood is not my blood. But their business, when it intersects with our business, becomes my problem. And though Heath may be my son and my responsibility—"

"No! Now, Bird," Seizer fumed, pounding and gripping the table, "the problem lies well beyond that!" Rocking back and forth on his heels, he collected their startled faces. "You are your brother's keepers! You've failed each other and endangered your superiors! Ray, I fault you personally for being unable to handle your team. I expected a sight more from a man of your experience, much less a Jesuit."

Del Ray sucked a tooth.

"Dang it!" Seizer cussed. "No one's clean on this! Maybe I handed out too much responsibility before anyone could earn it, and now the South's gone the way of the West! It's like history all over again!"

Seizer's scrutiny found Eddy, who cowered as he approached.

"But now there will be law . . . and order . . . and consequences. So you tell me . . . where's Cueball? Is he with these kids?"

"I don't know," gasped Eddy.

"Have you spoken with him?"

"I was told not to," he said, glancing at Bird.

"And you expect me to believe you of all people listened?"

The subsequent silence slowly constricted about Eddy's throat.

Duke raised from his chair. "Sir, Cueball bears this responsibility alone, sir. It was his decision—"

The force of the slap split Duke's lip in two, upheaving the chair and sending Duke to the floor, where he lay glued save for his chest, which struggled for air.

"Your elders, son! I was not *speaking* to you!" Seizer postured grandiosely above his nephew, ribald in his fury. No one moved to help the young man, sensing a conclusion could only be met by absolute stillness.

"Now come on, get up." Seizer dropped a hairy arm, which Duke half-guessed before taking. Raising his chair, Duke gripped the table as Lisbon crouched beside him, wide-eyed and lost. Del Ray returned from the bathroom with wet paper towels, but waited. Then Seizer, suddenly protective, embraced his nephew from behind, an act so tender Eddy had to turn away. Taking the towels, Seizer dabbed his nephew's bloodied face as Duke's defeat transformed into a distant stare, a systematic way of dealing with such violence imprinted upon a child's mind long ago.

"My sister, she died in a car accident," Seizer said by way of apology. "Some drunk bypassing the interstate at Kernersville. We're kin, so of course I . . . All of us here, we're in this together, as . . ."

Not able to configure his thoughts properly, Seizer uprighted, the steel returning to his mien as he eyed them all judiciously. "If anyone hears from Cueball, I know before God knows, ya'got that?"

Seizer ushered Duke up the stairs and out the door. Lisbon followed, ducking and weaving like a broken mule strapped to a trace chain.

Del Ray cocked an eyebrow after they left. "Now there is one legitimately fucked-up family."

"It's how it should be," countered Bird. "And watch your fucking mouth." Ignoring Del's raised hands, he called out to the figure in back. "You satisfied?"

Gumby dropped his magazine to the floor. "I think I sussed a fair account of things."

Eddy had forgotten about Gumby, which now seemed an indefensible mistake—he should have been watching the hit man the whole time.

"Jesse, talk to Mick," Bird said. "We're switching things up. And if any of you hear one iota from my son, or Jim Barns, you call *me*. Don't go bothering Seizer."

"What's this talk about Jim?" asked Mickey, worried about his drinking buddy.

Bird replied with silence, climbing the steps. After he left, Del Ray reached into his boot and brought out a knife, eyeing everyone. He snapped it open with a wrist flick, then slowly closed it.

"What's that look for?" Mickey asked. "If Seizer wants to run around pretending he's a goddamn den mother, that's his right. I don't know diddly-squat. But what's this about Jim missing?" Mickey didn't dare glance back at Gumby, in case things were real bad. Instead he watched Del Ray keep at it with his knife—snap, snap, snap. "Hey Kemosabe. Why'nt you quit that fucking racket."

"This bothering you?"

Gumby's chair hit the floor, catching everyone's attention. "Hey Ray, that one of them limited-edition Delicas? You get that out a catalogue? I hear they split a gullet real nice."

Del Ray let the blade snap back with extra importance. "Gum, you can be a downright creepy motherfucker sometimes, you know that?"

Eddy walked out. Gone were all personal worries, stamped out by this ludicrous notion that Cueball had joined up with a bunch of wannabe gangsters who'd hijacked his father's stash. And yet, he was also reminded of the beating Cueball took by his father, and Del Ray's story of the penned-up dogs who, once freed from their cage, tore out the throat of their abusive owner.

A bit later, Jesse joined him outside, somehow in good spirits. "Dude, I just got promoted! I'm interim Foreman until they find someone else, but then . . . no more camps! I'm going on the road with Mickey!"

Eddy flicked his cigarette to the bushes. "Super."

"Are you kidding? I'll be traveling, making connections . . . how fucking cool is that?"

"Were we in different rooms?"

Jesse shifted his stance. "No, bud, same room. But seriously, who steals from Seizer? What kind of moron? No, for *real*! Cueball's fucked in the head, man! Did you catch that people *died*? Because he threw a *temper tantrum* over a *demotion*?"

"W-we don't know that!" Eddy sputtered. "You don't think some bangers wouldn't make this shit up to cover their ass?"

"No," said Jesse. "I don't. I think Cueball made a choice—against us. Against all of us. And I bet he won't even get punished for it."

"We're supposed to help each other out!" pleaded Eddy. "You helped me get better, and now we gotta help him! No man left behind, right? Or what the fuck is any of this brotherhood talk about?"

Jesse cinched his lips. "It's a bigger brotherhood now, *right?*"

Eddy couldn't believe what he was hearing. Turning toward his car, he spat, "You know what? This isn't a business, or a club . . . it's a fucking *gang*. And chock-full of yes-men, apparently."

He rushed pass Gumby's motorcycle, the bony kneecap shining in the moonlight, and wondered how Jesse could watch Seizer attack his own flesh and blood and still believe Cueball might be afforded any special consideration. Everyone was on edge, and the tension between Bird and Seizer palpable.

He also wondered why Bird kept bringing up Jim Barns—what did that old scumbag have to do with Cueball missing? Twice he'd mentioned the guy, and neither time in Seizer's presence. But maybe that didn't mean anything. The whole of it was baffling.

As he made his way through darkness, Eddy pictured Cueball at the Mission.

Saw the bloody bodies at his feet.

Saw the courtroom, his best friend's lowered head encased in light. Watched the jury come in, one by one. Then came the verdict, loud as day, as the families of the wronged clamored for his death.

Gumby's canoe cut a narrow path up through the golden-green blades of sawgrass jutting from the inky waters. Above him, the heavens split along a seam—one half bruised a purplish yellow, where an amorphous cloud fell off a cliff of its own creation and swept the eastern sky with rain; to the west, a vision of unending grasses swaying eerily beneath a flawless blue.

By late afternoon he had left the snaking inland river and dragged the canoe ashore a small island hammock, avoiding the chickee outposts and trail ends as best he could. Heaving a backpack to his shoulder, he trudged awkwardly through the unforgiving mush and gelatinous banks of the lower basin to set up camp where the land thickened.

For two days the hit man paddled these opaque waters, alone and into the wild. By the third he reached an uninterrupted slab of solid earth and abandoned his canoe to a hidden enclave to go about on foot, and by the fourth picked up the trail of a cat—a dark scrape mound consisting of soiled pine needles and black dirt covering a heap of scat, the feces wet and smooth and free of hair or bone, indicating a recent snack on organs, likely raccoon. When the animal fed weekly on the larger white-tailed deer or feral spanish boar, the shit came long and thick.

Gumby prodded the heap with a knife, crouching close as he chewed hard bits of jerked gator tail. He sniffed the soil, sinking his hands into the mud beside the tri-lobed teardrop tracks, undulating his body to emulate the stealth of a creature perusing the land as a king among the commons. It was the panther's presence of mind he wished to inhabit, the feline regard and prowess. Gumby toddled this way on all fours for a quarter mile before he lost the tracks to water and found them again heading northwest along an opposing bank, where he settled in for the night.

Without device or dog he hunted one of the last hundred of its species, to strip from the golden panther its pelt for an untested black-market value. He had ventured deep into the Everglades and up into Big Cypress for this and other animals in the past, but had yet to claim a panther, as had anyone, reportedly, since wildlife prohibitions began protecting the big cat under law. Befitting a personal belief that hunter and prey must stand on equal terms, Gumby brought only three knives and his blowgun for its magnificent claws and fangs, and little food so that they hunted in a sense conjointly. Keeping without a fire, he opened his last remaining can of tuna and spread the crackers on his bag as the smeared dusk gave way to chanting insects and the yawning deep regret of space in wide exposure.

In sleep he dreamt of nothing but the chase. When conscious, he stripped the land to an empty expanse barren of all but two creatures in rapidly closing distance.

His eyes bulged with ache as the fifth day baked him in a damp furnace where the marshes met prairies and pine rockland. Thankfully the skies grew overcast, and by late afternoon, a cool wind swifting through the palmetto carried to him the cat's first tortured scream.

Gumby froze there on the pond bank, clutching a makeshift fishing pole and watching his earthworm curl about a hook fashioned from plover bone. The cat wasn't but a mile off, but it was growing dark, and without a single fish to scale for dinner, Gumby lacked the energy for a night hunt.

He awoke the following morning to wet tracks circling the camp and long claw-grooves scratched into the phalangeal trunk of a cypress. There were even signs of the creature bedding down, seemingly at ease. Gumby bowed his head against the base of the cypress and wept into his shirt. It was clear what led the animal to him was mere curiosity.

By noon he had thrown all but one of his precious knives into the marsh and began to starve himself. This ritual required more from him, it seemed, than he'd bargained for—it wanted total debasement. For Gumby was beyond all other aspects a true child of nature and a militant animal advocate, someone who casually threatened children that menaced creatures at the zoo. Perhaps the most telling example of his devotion came when another biker, a Hun from Connecticut, brought a living possum into a saloon in Del Rio, Texas. The biker hung the creature by its tail from a wire of Christmas lights behind the bar while his friends hurled nuts and pizza crust at the hissing question mark until they grew bored and began throwing darts. Entering the scene, Gumby snatched up a bar towel and covered the fraught and furious beast and conveyed it swiftly out the back exit. A week later the police found the Hun strung upside down from an overpass; one of his kneecaps had been gouged out by a claw hammer and one eye sliced through, though he lived.

Come morning of the Sabbath, Gumby stripped bare to his sex, crazed with pain. He rubbed thoroughwort and fleabane over the bulging insect welts on his skin, unsure if the plants held any medicinal properties, but hoping for the best. He padded himself with mud to mask his flourishing scent and dipped his bedraggled T-shirt into a grassy pool, eyeing for gators, before wrapping it about his head to keep cool.

Upset at failing to undo one life in a span wherein a surly god had created all, Gumby kept himself only in jeans ripped off at the thighs, a backpack, and water shoes, now dried to mud-caked prunes. He had run out of time. He had to turn back now or risk being lost to the wilderness.

Hunger and mania drove him to switch gears and pursue a series of boar tracks, which would have to serve as the cat's replacement. This was how all of his previous hunts had ended, with a lesser sacrifice — deer, boar, black bear. Yet Gumby soon discovered with the boar's gruesome disembowelment and partial burial that he'd unwittingly stumbled upon the panther's trail again. The kill was not a day old, and there were more tracks and more shit. He was actually relieved to be free of having to confront a boar, as they were fierce creatures when cornered, equipped with sharp, sometimes chipped tusks. Once, on a hunting trip he was forced to attend as a child, he'd witnessed such a beast use its snout gear to crucify a dog to a tree.

After hacking away a section of the boar's ribs, he built a small fire in the earth and cooked the meat, knowing predators often return to a large kill and hoping the scent would carry. He stripped bare again to air out his soiled shorts on a brace of palmetto. A low-slung twist of strangler fig hugging an oak would serve as his sleeping post, twelve or so feet up. It had loops he could climb and flattened out broadly along a branch. Not exactly safe, as the cat could climb, but it gave him a slight advantage.

The ribs were greasy, and he'd just finished folding the meat onto a platter of leaves when a sharp wailing filled the woods, sounding for all the world like the spirit of a butchered child.

Gumby instinctively calculated the distance, snatched up his backpack by a strap, and scurried high to his perch, clenching the scalding meat in his jaws. There he withdrew a hunting knife fashioned with a gut hook, along with a foot-long shoelace, and laid them on a flat section of the fig. Next came the blowgun and three darts, each tipped with wax and sheathed in cotton. He tossed the backpack down near the fire pit, balancing his naked ass on the limb, and strung the large blade flush against his thigh. Then carefully assembled the interlocking parts of his custom-made blowgun, loading a single poison dart into the tube and snapping the other darts into a carrier on the weapon's side. As he waited, he slowly tenderized the boar ribs with his saliva, his mind a cradle of nerves. Upon finishing each rib, he spun a grisly bone to the fire pit.

The time was fast approaching. The sky grew overcast again and a new chill blossomed red in his cheeks. Eyes closed, the wind gave Gumby all the landscape he needed, the gusts providing a kind of sonar, wrapping about trunks, riding fast overhead and funneling out low pathways between palmettos hidden to him. Here the hit man employed the talents of his grandmother, a veterinarian made blind by rubella, when "viewing" her rock garden during storms. She would sit at the open window and listen to the rain's patter and skips, visualizing the objects' revealed dimensionality, having once described space as *sound scraped from shapes*. He allowed the utter hopelessness he felt after her death at the hands of a surprised burglar to resurface, held that bitter rage in place for a moment's regard, then immediately suppressed it—forming a molten coolness that invaded every aspect of his logic. The wind swept under his genitals as he shriveled sloth-like into a hug, gripping the murderous fig. The camp smelled of smoke and candied muscle, and he internally visualized the cooking pit, a hole brimming with ash and fire.

Hole is the name for a lack of something. Not a thing, but an absence. This is why Gumby hunted—to will within himself a nothingness into existence. Though he cherished the land's rich and diverse fauna, finding in them natures better harmonized with greater truths, he lived in a human world, and believed its reign in the hierarchy supreme. To kill a man, he would need to first sacrifice what he loved beyond all else, which would in turn deliver upon him the blank dispassion necessary for the act.

The first drops of estuarial rain fell sharply on his naked back and he clenched his muscles to avoid reacting.

A *hole is a no-thing*, he thought, beginning the ritual with a mantra of bastardized scripture he'd memorized and repeated many times before. *It's no loss, but an opening. A way into and through. A rite of inner emptying. Destroyer of the wisdom of the wise. A celebration of rivals and the deadening voice.* A soft image of the pit jumped before his mind's eye, and he continued. *It feeds upon whatever is cleared for it. It loves not. Wants not. Is nothing but the necessary and hollow heart of God.*

Gumby remained locked in meditation until the smell of woodsmoke mixed with the unfamiliar brought him back. He did not open his eyes but listened to the drumming of the fronds, rain droplets battering the earth with spoon-pocked impressions. He let it all pulse through him, shaping the hollows.

That's when he heard the prolonged giving way of a palmetto frond before it swished and rustled back into place.

He drew the blowgun pipe under his chin.

When he opened his eyes the panther was there, and larger than he'd imagined. Slunk down with its long tail raised and bent slightly at the top, its beatific golden face broad and darkly embroidered, ears perked. Gumby knew one shot was all he'd earned in this life. The rain fell harder and suddenly the panther began trotting toward him, taking refuge under the shadowy dominion of the very tree he crouched in. Taut muscles roped under its skin as if on pulleys.

The claws would gut him as the canines caught his throat, prying out his esophagus, emptying the jugular.

Its gaze settled on a patch of saw cabbage and he understood it would head there next. He raised the pipe, took the breath into his rattling lungs, and set his tongue behind his teeth. Imagined himself as always spitting a watermelon seed through a straw.

The dart sent a twitch like electricity through the puma. Hopping sideways on stiff legs, its fright gave way to a roar. After making three wide circles, it began purring. Gumby hadn't expected that, the purring, and the crushing shame of it corroded his heart. When the panther approached the brush, its back legs suddenly wobbled and collapsed.

Gumby could have let it die without the sight of him, but all things he felt deserved a reckoning with the cause of their demise — the face of an armed thief or the lights of an oncoming truck or the enlarged snapshot of rapidly dividing cells.

The emptiness within him surged, and Gumby leapt howling from the tree.

After washing his puffy face he lay in bed, wearing only the extra pair of jeans he kept stored in his motorcycle's saddlebags. Glass shards of a destroyed motel mirror lay about him. The long cuts on both arms were still bleeding, acts of self-mutilation, a kind of vengeance he imagined pacified the spirit of the sacrifice. The emptiness he felt flowered and wilted in turn. It was a harsh guilt, and he cherished its departures. He knew it would come again when needed.

Headlights flashed the curtains. He waited for a knock at the door, the cold bite of handcuffs. This was a game he played, knowing full well they never caught you until you no longer wanted to be caught.

He woke to the phone ringing, unaware that he'd been dozing. His eyes lit upon the panther's pelt spread out over wax paper on the adjacent bed, fleshed and salted and drying. The smell, coupled with the burning incense, was atrocious.

He pushed up and went over to the bathroom and made sure the ventilator fan was still on and working. Then returned and sat on the bed. The phone had stopped ringing but he knew it would come again, and when it did, he lifted it from its cradle.

"Gumby."

"Yeah."

It was Bird. "Did you get what you were after?"

"Yes."

"Good. Any luck with the cat?"

"Mm-hmm."

"Ho my god, you serious?" Bird twittered. "Well I'll be damned. You're the best there is, brother. My god. The big catch. Must be some kind of big price out there to be paid for it, no doubt."

His self-loathing flashed as heartburn, but Gumby mashed it down. "No doubt whatsoever."

"I'll miss having you around. How you feel?"

"Don't."

"Eh?"

Gumby stayed silent.

"Well, the big job's waiting for you. He's still out there and nobody's heard anything since. So I'm asking . . . can you get it done?"

"I can find him."

"Alright, but I'm asking if this is a done deal. The whole of it."

Gumby picked a shard of glass from his navel and pushed it under a fingernail. In his mind he saw the pit smoking, the animal blinking in the rain.

"Yes."

Eddy didn't know where to file a missing person report.

The Palm Bay Police Department was out of the question, as the station was located directly behind his house, way too close for comfort. Melbourne or West Melbourne PD would probably do, but they might ask why he didn't try Palm Bay first, given Cueball lived right up Minton Road. Eventually he settled on the sheriff's department—deputies were a different breed of cop, more laid-back he found, with a broader jurisdiction.

Eddy dialed the 800 number but chickened out when someone picked up.

Now he was sitting in the parking lot of the sheriff's office, seat reclined, trying to build up the courage to walk in and speak to a deputy.

He knew what he was doing—or thought he knew. He went back and forth, imagining the possible outcomes. Filing a report could put the club at risk, along with everyone involved. Seizer and Bird for sure. Charlotte, who didn't deserve it. Duke and Lisbon. If Del Ray found out, he would never forgive him. Nor would Jesse.

He had no idea what Cueball would say—his phone number remained inactive. Maybe this was a dumb move, but what was he supposed to do, *nothing*?

Bad news just kept coming down the pike: apparently Charlotte had moved out after getting into a big row with Bird at a friend's birthday party, and who could blame her? Word was, she was staying with Colt while searching for her own apartment.

A sheriff's deputy emerged from the station and Eddy slunk lower, opening a browser on his phone. He typed in "how do I become a deputy?" in case the dude stopped to ask why he'd been parked out front for so long. Soon after, though, the officer's green-and-white cruiser drifted away.

The truth was, Eddy had failed Cueball. Perhaps the sabotaging was an unconscious effort, feeling undervalued. Had he tried harder, Eddy definitely could have coaxed Cueball downstairs to hang with Derrik at that party, absolutely. But maybe some part of him wanted to watch Cueball catch flak from Del Ray, who could rattle his friend's cage and get his ass back in line.

How'd that tough-love plan work out, hombre?

Ducking gunshots and a beatdown from Bird. And now Cueball was out there doing god knows what with a bunch of half-baked, homeless goons.

It was also possible that the reports out of Miami were wrong: a case of mistaken identity, or a ruse to shift the blame from Kaos to Cueball. Or maybe Cueball was holed up in a no-tell motel in Orlando, binging pay-per-view and donuts and vodka, a dirty swab of human failure. He'd pop back up soon enough, shameful and sober, entirely unaware of the charges against him.

Another pressing question was what Seizer was plotting behind the scenes. It wasn't clear that Bird could save his son from whatever punishment was required for his insubordination.

Another officer stepped outside and Eddy lifted his phone as if speaking to someone.

Are you going to tell them everything?

No. You're just reporting that a buddy of yours hasn't been at the pool hall lately. They'll ask Bird if he's heard from his son, and he'll say he hasn't. No big deal, as kids don't always keep in touch with their parents.

How long's he been missing?

Not sure. My job keeps me pretty busy these days. (Don't mention your fucking job.)

Do you have reason to believe something's happened to him?

Not really, nothing specific. He just doesn't have many friends, and I haven't seen him in a bit.

Well, there's not much we can do. We'll put out an APB, see if anything turns up.

Or at least that's how things typically played out on TV.

Eddy stepped from his car, shutting the door mechanically. He crossed the open lot like a man on death row, terrified, yet thankful his wait was over.

The station lobby was cold as a meat locker. Vacant seats, dustless, smelling of lemon cleaner. Before him stood a long counter manned by a hard-jawed thirty-something deputy, who upon hearing footsteps raised his blue eyes, the very menace of authority.

"Can I help you?"

"W-where would I go to report a missing dog?" stuttered Eddy.

"A missing dog? Was it stolen?"

"No no, he just ran away."

"Um. We're not really set up for that. I'm not even sure if local PD is set up for that. Let me ask . . . I think we send folks over to the Humane Society now."

The officer raised both hands above his paperwork, trying to figure out where to start. He touched the phone.

"What about missing people?" asked Eddy.

"People?" The deputy reset his hands together. "Is someone missing?"

Eddy's sweat production ramped up, his heart pure thud. "Oh, no . . . no no no, I just thought there might be a special department for missing . . . *whatevers.*"

The blue eyes kept him framed—didn't budge, and yet searched every part of him. Then came a smile broad as a river.

"We have several divisions but sadly not one for lost pets."

"Okay, well, dang," said Eddy. "I guess I'll be stapling papers to telephone poles, then. Ha! But maybe I'll check the pound first. Sorry to bother you!"

Eddy swung around and beelined for the door, only to hear the calm, firm voice reach across the empty room. "What kind of dog is it?"

Eddy spun back on a heel without stopping: "Small one! Thanks!"

Outside, he waited a beat, catching his breath. There was a problem— he'd stoked curiosity in the man, he could feel it. The officer would have him followed, and soon discover who he worked for.

Eddy crept back inside. The pale blue eyes across the way rose up, pen raised.

"Sorry to bother you again, sir, but it's not like *illegal* to staple signs to phone poles, right? I wouldn't wanna be breaking the law or nothin."

"You should be fine," replied the officer. "Just don't go crazy."

Eddy chuckled, raising a hand. "Oh no, I won't!"

Lisbon sat beside his brother in a tufted diner booth surrounded by arcade games, eating pizza. Eddy sat across the table, but Lisbon's attention hung on a young girl in a red sequin dress playing Skee-Ball in an adjacent room.

Another child was bothering her, a boy, offering to share the tickets he'd won, but it was clear she wanted to win her own tickets. Both appeared to be deaf, their signing having caught Lisbon's attention. He admired the girl's intractable stance, chubby face full of indignation. When the boy stole a ball from her ball return and rolled it up her lane, she shouted at him, and Lisbon rose from the booth, ready to intervene—but stopped himself. This wasn't his fight. It was hers, and she was winning.

Heading back from Philly, Duke located a duckpin bowling alley with a stone oven outside Silver Spring, Maryland. Lisbon was thankful for the accommodation—he ate pizza for most meals, as pizza was delicious and squishy, apart from the crust, which he avoided. With his malformed tongue, hard foods that crumbled were choking hazards. Lisbon also enjoyed arcade games, especially *Donkey Kong Jr.*, which played an 8-bit version of Bach's "Toccata and Fugue in D Minor," the escalations and de-escalations at times mirroring his own internal music. He liked seeing himself in things, as it made him feel less alone.

"No coffee till I've put down a Gatorade," said Eddy. "Then only decaf. I'm getting my energy back."

"Lost those bags under your eyes too," said Duke, folding his pizza slice. "Naw, you look healthy, bud. You still feel okay driving alone?"

"It's a cinch," said Eddy, picking his eyebrows. "No complaints."

Lisbon wasn't sure he believed Eddy, as he associated eyebrow picking with anxiety. He watched Duke produce from his pocket a baseball card in archival plastic—'56 Mickey Mantle, PSA 8—sliding it across the table.

Though he found it hard to read people, Lisbon believed he knew what to expect from Eddy.

"You asshole," beamed Eddy, flipping it over. "Is this real?"

"I couldn't give it to you at the meeting," said Duke. "You were already kinda on thin ice, and my uncle thinks of tips as kickbacks, which translates to owing someone a favor. But these folks we're helping, they're just thankful. You know how many people would be unemployed right now if it wasn't for us? We're job creators."

Lisbon returned to the children. The Skee-Balls were grapefruit-sized, but that didn't matter to the little girl, who used both hands to whip them up the incline. The boy stood nearby, moping, then stole another one of her balls, holding it to his chest. When she chose to ignore him, he reached down and ripped her line of winning tickets from the machine.

"Mine!" she shouted, pushing him with her tiny fists.

Lisbon had twisted some red coffee straws into a little man, and was now squeezing that man, his knee pumping under the table.

"Tell me if this is too personal a question," said Eddy. "Is the reason you don't drink because your mom was killed by a drunk driver?"

"I mean, maybe?" said Duke. "Subconsciously? It's really just not my thing. I'll have a whiskey now and again, but I don't like losing control. I can barely ride an elevator. And you'll never get me on a plane."

The little boy had disappeared with the tickets. The girl continued to play alone, new tickets spooling about her tiny red shoes. Lisbon wanted to speak to her, sign with her, but he'd been warned against such things before.

"Can I ask another question?"

"Shoot," said Duke.

"If it turns out Cueball really was at the Mission, what will your uncle do to him?"

Duke smacked the crust dust from his hands. "Okay, let's do this. I figured it was coming. First off, Cueball was very likely there. The info we got was solid. And if he wasn't there, we have bigger problems—namely, one of our largest distributors lied and stole our product."

"I hadn't thought about that," said Eddy.

"But to your point," Duke continued. "Everyone wants Cueball home safe. My uncle has people on it. But it can't be done *loud*, you understand? Alex can't see how important Cueball is to us—who he is—or that opens a whole other can of worms."

Eddy nodded. "But what happens when he gets back?"

"My guess? He takes a long vacation. Maybe goes and stays with his mom for a while."

Lisbon had heard Charlotte was gone, which was sad. He liked her— she would rub his back when she spoke to him. He often wondered what it would be like if his own mother was still alive. If he was Cueball, he would go live with Charlotte.

"My turn," said Duke. "Hasn't your boy burned you enough? Why you still acting like his caretaker?"

"How's that lip?" asked Eddy.

Lisbon felt the heat rush to his cheeks. In his mind he saw his brother on the floor, the blood in Duke's teeth as he grimaced while their uncle stood over him, broad and pugilistic.

But Duke was smirking, licking the raspberry bump. "You think I didn't deserve this."

"You do?"

"My uncle worked his ass off for decades for this opportunity," said Duke. "He endures the lion's share of the risk to provide jobs for people like you and me, and this numbskull here," jabbing Lisbon with his shoulder. "If he shows *any* weakness, bad things happen."

"Worse things, you mean," said Eddy.

"Use your imagination," said Duke, sipping his soda. "But listen, I didn't expect him to interrogate you like that. The meeting was supposed to be informational—"

"Wait a sec. *Dude.* Did you already know about the hijacking before the meeting?" Eddy's accusatory glare spiked Lisbon as well. "And you didn't tell me?"

One of Duke's eyes went large. "It wasn't my place to say. We only had a day to figure out how to respond. And from my uncle's perspective, you likely knew something. Cueball's your best friend and you'd want to protect him, right? But your so-called protection stops us from finding him, and could end up getting him hurt. When I stepped in . . . I became an obstacle."

Eddy crossed his arms and slumped into the booth.

"We'll find him," said Duke. "We got good people on it. Your focus right now should be on your own recovery."

Eddy chewed his lip.

The little boy had returned, fists balled, and immediately tried stealing the new tickets. When the little girl slapped his hand, he retaliated by pushing her so hard she toppled over.

Lisbon slid out from the booth.

"Where you going?" asked Duke. "Hey, grab the check."

Lisbon swerved between gaming towers and consoles, missing small bodies. Not stopping to speak, he simply grabbed the little boy by the shirt and dragged him away in a horse collar. The boy cried out chokingly and the girl wailed and Lisbon felt the heat but didn't care and came upon the restroom door and beside it another door marked *Employees Only.*

That second door opened to a storage closet, and he swung the boy inside. The boy tumbled once and stabilized, then leapt away, clawing the rear wall lined with mops and liquid containers, terrified. When he glanced back, Lisbon signed, "No leaving for ten minutes or I'll break your ankles!" Then yanked the door shut.

Back at the Skee-Ball lanes, the little girl was gone. Nor was she at the ticket redemption desk, shopping for plastic trinkets or stuffed animals. Stepping into the bowling alley, he found her among the seats of a duckpin lane, pulling at her father's arm, a very large man indeed, signing some very serious accusations.

Lisbon rushed back through the arcade.

"What the heck's going on?" asked Duke as his brother arrived in a panic, but Lisbon halted only to slap a fifty-dollar bill on the table, beckoning them to follow as he raced toward the EXIT sign.

The beaches of Fort Lauderdale differ from other beaches along Florida's eastern coast. Daytona for example resembles a melting creamsicle, with blinding-white sand and patches of orange coquina. Cocoa Beach is cinnamon-gray and hard-packed, while Miami Beach retains a pearlish quality, flecked with coral reds. Lauderdale, however, consists mainly of crushed microscopic seashells and quartz granules dredged from the ocean floor and spread out in a lustrous, gray-golden hue. Over the years, trucked-in sand and hurricanes have altered the composition, and in this way, the shoreline is in constant revision, much like the city itself.

Here the elderly hunt coins and lost watches with halo-headed detectors as rollerbladers zigzag the wavy seawall. Come night, the barrier lights wink on, guiding couples along the oceanfront promenade toward restaurants and fancy nightclubs, where sunset women arrive in elegant, curve-hugging dresses and men with low-fade barber cuts linger curbside, strutting like ballplayers in decadent italian.

It's a city of stacked social echelons and eclectic zoning. Pushing out beyond the harbor mansions and luxury condos lining the canals and boats anchored along the Intracoastal Waterway, the glamour quickly fizzles to sprawling subdivisions and lots of tangled overgrowth, pawnshops with barred windows and dive bars whose loitering clientele suggests locals-only.

Kept from the promises of downtown, one senses a stirring latency in these less affluent neighborhoods: some cohering power, fitful in hibernation. Here the dusk wind can surprise you, carrying spices so distinct they refuse to congeal into one fragrance, but like groomsmen greet you individually as you pass. Laughter carries from behind screen doors as generations cook together, TVs on full blast. Kids launch bikes off plywood ramps and shoot hoops in their driveway, as a man leans under a propped hood in his garage, a light clipped near his face, searching for the 10mm socket.

On this particular evening, under a streetlight, a punk kid sporting a green mohawk and a chain linking septum to nipple hurried past another dressed in chinos and a wifebeater. Neither spoke, though each was fully aware of the other. They disappeared as a tricked-out Malibu barreled around the corner, hopping past a haunt of tangerine and banana trees cloaking a broken fence, where in the shadows a cigarette cherry glowed briefly brighter.

Cueball slouched upon his hidden throne of cinder blocks, eavesdropping on passersby who rattled on expansively in a language he spoke poorly.

Each night he'd arrive at the safehouse carrying a backpack of clothes and Taco Bell. He slept on the beach now, and his truck remained impounded, as he feared withdrawing money from a bank would alert people to his whereabouts. Plus he'd have to return to Miami, which he could never do again.

Around eight or so the women would arrive, young girls mostly, waving fingers as they passed or holding his chin cutely in their hands, calling him Beach Baby or Niño Blanco, *Why you always thinking so much, you make me sleepy.* Before long the safehouse was bumping, the stale creep of marijuana tracing the air. Yet Cueball would remain vigilant at his outdoor post until his anxiety gave way to exhaustion, halting the waterwheel that incessantly raised to his mind's surface one of a hundred horrible futures.

Everything was coming to a head tonight.

Cueball's dread had a canine grip on him as he struggled with what he hoped were false premonitions. Part of him was relieved. He was tired of sleeping among the dunes, sick of always looking over his shoulder—but also literally ill. Quitting shank was proving a rough go, made tougher by the drug's ubiquity. While fighting off migraines and stomach cramps with Excedrin and rum, Cueball hatched his escape plan.

As soon as he got his share of the stolen shank profits, he'd leave Florida—buy a bus ticket to Austin or Portland, because people talked about these places. He'd change his name and work a laundrymat until he could save enough to start his own business—a record store maybe, or a studio, cutting albums for the better local bands. With that money he'd

open an exclusive Hollywood-style club, all glitz and glam, with DJs spinning over a bar serving expensive cocktails, with famous patrons in the
VIP section waving him over. When these dreams grew too preposterous
to cling to, Cueball wallowed in his failures. Thinking of Eddy, his heart
sank. There was no world in which his best friend wasn't hurt by his leaving. And he couldn't call his mother, either, because he didn't have her
number memorized—following the warehouse catastrophe, he'd smashed
his phone and divided the parts between trash bins, convinced the club
might triangulate his position, like on *CSI*. Maybe it was ridiculous, but
Seizer felt capable of anything.

Across the street a group of dominican boys played wiffle ball under a
streetlight, mimicking Pujols in their stances, roping imaginary homers into
the upper deck. Opening Day wasn't till next week, but it had been draft
season out here all month long.

New blood, Kaos called them. *Fresh off the boat, big-eyed hope.* Kaos'
crew, scouting bodies, zeroed-in on kids like this, easy marks to move product. Maybe they'd arrived hoping for a better life, but Cueball knew the
depressing truth: that whatever personal hell you escaped, or proud nation-
ality you claimed, whatever sly-ass con man's pitch brought your family here
with their Disney dreams . . . you hadn't made it to America. Once your feet
touched sand, you were instantly Floridian, and god help you. The state was
shaped like a limp dick for a reason—or a funnel, pick your metaphor—a
sinkhole that sucked down the worst of the country's lunatics. And if you
hung around too long, you'd get chewed up by desperate friends or manipu-
lative family members or sweet-talking strangers sniffing out your paycheck.
A year of this shit would reduce a boy with heady daydreams and zero guidance to an organism of basic logic whose sole interest lay in ferreting out the
next score.

How long before one of their young buddies rolled up in a shiny new
Mercedes, sunglassed and Guccied, quoting whole passages from the
hustler's bible?

Cynically, Cueball imagined the boys were already in on the game.

Clawing its way back to his forethoughts was the image of Julio's lifeless body, splayed out on the warehouse floor . . . which meant it was time to go in, let the night have its day. His legs all pins and needles as he rose from the blocks and loped out front.

The safehouse lifted its ambience from a music video: a raucous coterie of gangsters mingled and cavorted as voluminous reggaetón and hip-hop resounded off the walls. In the kitchen bodies crowded a table of take-out chinese. Cueball always felt supremely underdressed among the dapper puerto ricans—kicks to lids, he was the shaggier option. Men with guns stuffed in their pants reclined near open windows, drinks in hand, occasionally peering out beyond the dead shrubbery to the street.

Cueball grabbed a Negra Modelo from the fridge and collapsed on a sofa. Daddy Yankee pulsed from the speakers, and soon a girl with cat eyeliner was needling his arm with her long acrylic fingernails, asking about his ride, where he was from. Though she was kind of a hottie, his focus drifted.

The warehouse job loomed large. It was supposed to be a quick hit, flash bang and they're out. No violence—a stickup job with a guy inside. Come the following day, Kaos promised, they'd return every ounce of stolen dope. It wasn't even stealing, not really. They were like hackers undermining a company's security system. It was about respect, proving to both Alex and Cueball's boss that they weren't worthless whatevers, but formidable. He watched Kaos' eyes light up: *We gotta do this shit, man! Think of their faces!*

Though Cueball never agreed to help—it was going to happen, regardless—he did ride with Kaos out to the Mission, partly to watch over Julio, who wouldn't be left behind. But he'd also failed to call up his father and alert him, which, no matter how he minimized it, made him an active participant in what went down.

Kaos' plan went like this: Frio would lure the Mission soldiers into a back room with two large pizzas from Anthony's Coal Fired, then lock them in. Once Kaos received the text, the PRP would drive up, grab the drugs, show their asses, and skedaddle.

Easy fucking peasy.

But when they rolled up, Kaos and his boys tore loose on a different mission—one that required blood.

Jesus, don't lie to yourself, you piece of shit. You knew. Some part of you knew.

When Cueball spotted the guards stationed on the bay, everything clicked. Why would anyone abandon their post for a slice of fucking pizza? Kaos' plan seemed suddenly ridiculous. Why would Frio stick his neck out for such a stupid ploy? Alex would have all their heads severed and sent to their mothers on Sunday. No, Frio was looking for a payday, same as Kaos. Likely with the backing of some cubans making a move against Los Toros.

Turned out Kaos believed jacking a big score from his cousin's largest supplier would ensure his own distinction as a legitimate rival, with the added benefit of making the Toros appear vulnerable. *Who's the bitch now, bitch?* He needed people to know he was a fucking badass, a human cock tornado, el rey de reyes. If he robbed the Mission and no one got hurt, he'd be seen as an opportunistic punk, a wannabe gangster waving a gun around. That's not a rep; that's a target. As head of the PRP, he needed to set an example, lest he invite speculation he was a gutless pushover, a walking ATM.

All that dreamland bravado dissolved the moment Julio got shot.

The scene was never far from Cueball's thoughts. Watching the young kid charge the warehouse, gripping a gun filled with blanks—Kaos' idea, since Julio wasn't supposed to leave the car. Then finding Kaos inside, sobbing over his cousin's limp body. *Corpse.* Julio's small hand tapping Kaos' back as he was carried away. The absolute shame Cueball felt for his own complicity. A shotgun blast to the face wasn't deserving enough. A Hellfire missile shot right up his ass and into the side of a mountain, perhaps— complete evisceration. Cueball and Kaos remained aboveground while Julio died. Is life fair? Go ask Frio the snail, trailing along his slimy guts as his so-called friends danced around him.

That one night he caught Julio praying—what a fucking joke. Life wasn't governed by any high-up godforce, Cueball knew, but by powerful, ruthless men, whom naive boys were apt to follow. Find that niche, cop that piece, get that tat. Ownership papers. Growing up where men are soldiers, alphas and betas, and the women afterthoughts, baby mamas and side chicks. Flip the place, race, legality of the hustle—be it Miami or Washington, DC, it was always about power.

"You slow or something?" a girl yelled into Cueball's ear over the music. "You hardly talk or nothing!"

Cueball felt the urge to pull her by the belt and kiss her. Take her into one of the back rooms, where they'd fuck the rougher parts of each other to a wet polish and lay about like beached orcas.

Dale, papi, que estoy suelta como gabete!

"I need another beer," he said.

"Do I look like a bartender? Take y'ass to the kitchen and get it ya damn self."

"I wasn't asking you to get it for me."

"Wha'eva," she mused softly, placing a hand on his neck, which felt comforting. Through the haze of smoke Cueball spotted one of the lookouts doing shots. "Hey! Hey, man! Aren't you supposed to be outside?"

The boy rolled his eyes. "Chill, maricón, it's a party."

Which was why Cueball now slept on the beach. The Posse was highly unorganized, operating with no methodology or core values. There was no discernible plan, no long-term goals or even a clear designation of roles. Kaos kept a few trusted Officers by his side, but the rest of the boys just flipped between selling, stealing, and safeguarding. Nothing like what Alex or Seizer had implemented. The gang's "treasury" consisted of a safe in a bedroom closet, a cash-counting machine, and a smartphone calculator app. Anyone here would absolutely turn state's witness if pressured—there wasn't any real loyalty he could detect—so yeah, it was a party. Kaos enjoyed having his face out there, arriving at nightclubs in-step with his high-heeled, teetering flock of models, more concerned with brandishing his playa rep than securing new product. Unable to keep his money clip pocketed, he put the PRP at the mercy of any beat cop with a notebook and a passing interest.

It didn't help morale that Alex had banished the PRP from Miami under threat of death. To some members, this meant abandoning their families and full-time jobs, all in exchange for a fairly unromantic version of thug life, wholly reliant on drug sales. No more Sunday football potlucks or family

BBQs at the park. When Kaos wasn't around, some talked openly of leaving. But no one did, for good reason—Alex wasn't bullshit. He was a G, a real gangsta, his will be done. Took his lumps early, working up through the Toros' ranks to fashion himself as a shrewd businessman with community ties and ambitions extending beyond the streets. Owned cops and a judge, some said. Golfed with the assistant DA, yeah bro, that deep. Any outsider could see who'd be left alive if this so-called war ever heated up.

Kaos lacked experience, manpower—and brains, honestly. Nerve he had in spades, but following Julio's death, he surrendered all leadership qualities to make a real go at self-immolation. Moped around barking nonsensical orders, undercut prized workers in front of their peers in bigger-dick contests that bred hostility. As old contacts ghosted him, Kaos was forced to scrounge up leads in Lauderdale and Hollywood by offering steep discounts on the stolen product, with buyers requiring assurances of confidentiality—Alex could never know. *All these dumb fucks scared of him, bro. And now with these cubans reneging on their promises to buy, 'cause Frio went down. . . . But whatever, fuck them rich-ass Republican bitches. Inside they white as you. I'll get mine, though, you watch.* Now everything was butter in a pan—a slow slide. Security was lax. Every day a new car passed the safehouse at a crawl, or a guttural motorcycle zipping up the block. Cueball figured Alex hadn't bombed the place yet because he was still in mourning for Julio, waiting for the right moment to do the job himself.

Cueball checked the time—Kaos and a small crew had driven out to a meeting with some local buyer, trying to sell off the last batch of stolen shank. Come morning, Cueball would leave for Savannah, because they had a big river in Savannah and cemeteries like gardens and cheap rent. He tried to convince Kaos to leave Lauderdale as well, but Antonio curled his lips arrogantly, saying: *This city mine. This the holy house of Kaos.* With disaster imminent, the captain bid his orchestra play on.

After the flirtatious woman grew bored and left, Cueball wandered into a back room and opened the clip on his gun, checking the rounds. It was a new compulsion of his, like confirming a stove was off.

Back in the living room, he approached a thin man, stoned elf eyes half shut, a woman with hoop earrings on his lap. "Gato, man, you hear from Kaos yet?"

The thin man paused mid-sentence, looking around as if startled awake. "Nah, but he should be here soon. Supposed to roll in with Deziz. Maybe check outside?"

"Can I see your phone?" asked Cueball.

Gato huffed, fishing his phone from his pocket. "It's dead."

After some financial negotiation that left Cueball with only two twenties in his wallet, the woman with the hoop earrings let him borrow her phone.

He stepped into the darkness of the yard, trying to recall Kaos' digits. Across the street, in the dark, an elderly woman stooped to pick a few meager wildflowers from a yard in passing, her hands like papier-mâché. Not just then, but in other small moments like this, Cueball realized growing old was something he'd never do.

Kaos was supposed to return by 8 p.m.—it was now 9:30, and he wasn't answering his phone. Cueball didn't trust Deziz, an indian-rican bouncer with a great wealth of flab, spirit, and humor all stuffed into a leather jacket. Out of nowhere Deziz had introduced himself to Kaos at a club, offering his services as an intermediary who dealt exclusively to corporate suits. Kaos was new to the area and eager to make connections. He said he had Deziz checked out, but Cueball doubted that, and now they were out playing with Cueball's last bargaining chip at a better life.

The banana trees didn't provide the best vantage to watch the street. Cornering the building, he noticed an old television antenna braced to the roof; from up there, he could view the whole neighborhood. So he gripped the metal pole, setting his foot against the stucco wall, and walked his way up, shimmying over the top.

Positioned cross-legged on the shingles, lost in silence and agitated reverie, Cueball searched for any good thing to hold on to . . . and so drifted into a place he rarely allowed his mind to go . . .

He'd found himself wandering South Beach a couple weeks back, looking for something to do—exactly what, he wasn't sure, still unaccustomed to the big city. The next day Kaos would surprise him with plans to hit the

Mission, but tonight the gang was partying at a club called LIV, which Cueball ditched for the seaside strip just south. In truth, the PRP crew merely tolerated him—some white high school buddy of Kaos', an unemployed tag-along—and Cueball didn't mind playing the role. Nobody, not even Antonio, knew he was the son of their biggest supplier.

South Beach was turning into a bust. Turns out Ocean Drive was a shitshow of drunk tourists and peacocking club promoters, so he wandered over to Lincoln and walked the shops. Which was fine. More of the same, clothing stores and shoe stores. But then, just off the thoroughfare . . .

A gay bar. Tall posters of male strippers, larger than life. He felt a rush of excitement, some forbidden thing provoked, tantalized, teased. *What can I get away with?* But he wasn't . . . he was just . . . he couldn't explain it properly to the imaginary person he explained things to in his head. There would be no outright acceptance, and so no proper clarity, just a kind of oblique impulse to delve into all manner of proclivities, an impulse summoned by the men in these posters, glossy as gum wrappers, and hilariously posed.

This some dumb shit.

He figured he was probably too young to get into the club. Nah, he was for sure too young. They'd laugh him out of line. So instead he found a neon diner and settled into a booth by a big window. Mostly vacant, the coffee was freshly brewed, and they even brought him ranch dressing for his fries.

Another problem with Kaos' safehouse was the complete lack of privacy, so Cueball decided to hit up a jerk joint later—slightly depressing places, forlorn music on repeat and floral alcohol smells, untrained masseuses who tenderized with knees and elbows. But he often found the women affable and jokey, like doctors, for whom the body wasn't some deeply flawed carrier of matters but a body, scars and pimples and three oily minutes of hard stroking caught in a hot towel. Relief, and afterwards, light conversation. The appeal of hairdressers and priests, a certain attentiveness and change of perspective, then out the door.

Sipping his coffee, he caught sight of a woman slipping into a booth beyond. Dark-skinned latina in a tight shiny dress, hair like a waterfall off one side. He'd only glanced, but she'd caught him.

Looking back again, she smiled.

She was very pretty and, to his mind, obviously a man in women's clothes. Or a transgender person. These weren't terms he'd properly sorted yet.

"Hello, sweetie," she cooed. Not loudly, respectfully. "We alone tonight?"

Cueball couldn't help his broad grin. "Oh, I'm just out here . . . enjoying my vacation."

She tapped a long nail on her cheekbone and pointed. "Can I come over there?"

"Um . . . sure, okay."

She smoothed out her dress when rising, and in those few steps over, promised Cueball everything before sliding in across from him.

A waiter set down her coffee and left.

"My name's Tita," she said, lowering her head to stare up into his eyes. "You alone tonight, baby?"

"How much you cost?" asked Cueball.

"Oh! Well then . . . a man who knows what he wants," she said, unfazed, flashing perfect teeth.

Cueball rounded his arms, fingertips together. "I fucked with a guy before."

This seemed to catch Tita off guard. She paused, as if gauging the true meaning of his words, then let out a cautious "Oh?" in place of a chuckle perhaps.

Cueball didn't know why he was telling her this. He shouldn't be telling anyone this.

"This guy, Jamie . . . his sister Suzie, she gave me a handjob," he said. "Then *he* did . . . later."

"Okay . . ."

Cueball waited for her to speak, but the seconds grew longer. And longer. "Does that make me pathetic or disgusting?"

"Hmm," said Tita, eyes a little wider now. "Hmmmm." She was letting the thought roll around a little. "Neither."

"Bullshit," said Cueball.

"Okay, I'mma let you be," she said, feeling for her purse. "Looks like you got a lot on your mind."

But as she stood to leave, she stopped. Cueball was trying and failing to hold back the tears that had abruptly, hilariously erupted from him. He wasn't even embarrassed—they had sprung up so naturally and effortlessly he hadn't the time to do anything but laugh as Tita rested on the seat's edge, casting her eyes about the diner.

When her eyes found him again, they narrowed.

"Honey, let me share with you one thing. If you ever want to be happy in this . . . *brutal* fucking world, you gotta be yourself. Not what people want from you. Not what they expect. But the person who knows what they want, and goes after it."

My father would literally kill me, thought Cueball.

Tita scrunched her mouth bitterly and tapped the table with her finger-tips, then left him to sit there under the weight of it all.

Cueball wiped his eyes with his sleeve, shocked to numbness by the sudden depth and quickness of the conversation. Like, what the hell just happened? He recalled Eddy saying Gin admitted to kissing a girl once—for which absolutely no one gave two shits.

What he oddly wished to confess to Tita just then but couldn't, as it required too much explanation, was the reason his father didn't call him Cueball anymore. They'd arrived at a bonfire party on a beach, him and his parents, and his father was introducing him to some random biker, a name entirely forgotten. Hearing his nickname, the biker's face erupted in delight. "Cueball? Like the Dick Tracy movie? What a great flick! Well, all the men but Dick were screaming queens, but I do love them old cop shows."

And that was it—the mere suggestion of queerness put his father off the name. Likely because it reminded him of the time he'd caught Cueball holding hands with a boy in kindergarten. They were sitting together on a bench after school, each waiting for their parents, singing songs and swaying their legs . . . and holding hands. That night his father tanned his hide so hard, Cueball couldn't sit for dinner or even breakfast the next morning.

He dug for his wallet. He had to leave. Paying the bill fast, he followed the ugly carpet out.

Back on the roof, this memory of Tita, engaging as it was, diminished before his next vision—Julio's dead eyes and bouncing head, slung over Kaos' shoulder, bloodying his shirt.

Cueball ran through his options again. If he wanted to do some real damage, he could shut down the club's whole operation with one phone call. It was an unnerving realization, because if he'd considered it, surely Seizer had as well. And Seizer had men in jail. If Cueball confessed to any crimes and got booked, they'd find him raped, shanked, mutilated, and bound to a toilet bowl. Neither Eddy nor Jesse could help—they'd sworn allegiances—and Cueball now understood what it meant to be a deserter. It meant abandoning all sense of security, your friendships dissolved, where any stranger's hello triggered suspicion and reinvigorated feelings of regret. And some nights, it meant a child's mangled face screaming you awake from nightmares.

He tried Kaos' number again. Nothing. If he didn't get his share of the money by midnight, he'd leave town without it.

By 1 a.m. Cueball was in an absolute frenzy, pressing redial. Most of the partygoers had left. Gato and some others were now out looking for Kaos after receiving a call saying Deziz's car had been spotted in Sistrunk, miles away from the outdoor mall where the deal was supposed to take place. On the phone's fluorescent screen an antenna radiated concentric circles from its center as if charting the rippling evolution of a single event gone awry, tracking the shock waves.

A sound erupted behind him, and Cueball crouched low on the roof, parsing blindly from the darkness the softer tones and shapes set apart by moonlight. The door of a shed burst open, spilling onto the lawn a drunken couple, giggling and tired with sex.

At the same moment, from down the block, an approaching engine clicked like a cooking timer, headlights forking the trees. Cueball quietly inched closer to the TV antenna, half expecting someone to open fire or shove Kaos' body out the door.

Instead, the white sedan parked along the street and killed the lights, its rims spinning like asterisks.

The two occupants spoke in low tones. The driver shrugged, stepped from the car, and lumbered up to the house, where the porch light showed his face. It was Deziz.

"Cueball!" he called out into the night.

Cueball pressed himself flat against the gritty shingles, praying: *Please don't ring*. His fingers searched the cell's raised numbers and hit the power button. Then came a terrible sound—his gun sliding down the roof, landing in the backyard. He winced and held his breath as the front door opened and shut.

A minute later Deziz appeared out back, approaching the couple in the grass. "Has visto a Cueball?"

"Quién?"

"Cueball."

"No. No he visto ningún cubano desde que nos fuimos."

"Cub . . . *White* boy!" But the kid was half asleep. "Shithead. How 'bout you? You see him?" The girl let out a little grunt and curled into her lover.

Deziz waited a few more seconds, slapping his thigh rhythmically with a gun. He left by pushing through a side gate.

Back at his car, Deziz spoke through the driver-side window. Cueball peeked over the ridge. An arm extended, handing Deziz a phone. A new voice filled Cueball's ears, one that registered with distinction, a voice he knew well. Deziz argued with the man noncombatively, as one does a higher-up, suggesting but never demanding.

"If he's not at his beach spot, and he's not here—"

After the sedan drove off, Cueball didn't move for five minutes, listening to the couple's breathing while focusing on places a sniper might hide— under cars, behind trees, rooftops. When he finally moved, it was to inch himself over to the antenna. Shimmying down, he crouched in the dirt. Then took off at a sprint down the sidewalk, giving up his gun for the possibility of living.

They'd sent Gumby after him.

• • •

The next morning Cueball was having coffee in a diner outside Boca Raton when the cell phone he'd borrowed vibrated across the table. He'd spent the night walking the beaches and bridges heading north and his hair was windswept and the corners of his eyes caked with salt and sleep. He waited for the waitress to dip back into the kitchen before answering.

"Who the fuck is this?" shouted a woman's voice. "You stole my phone, motherfucker!"

The more he told her to calm down the louder she became.

"Listen, *listen!* Let me talk to Kaos. Just shut up and put Kaos on the phone!"

To his surprise, there was silence.

"Kaos? He dead."

"What."

"That fat fuck Deziz was all tight with his cousin. But ya know what? Fuck them niggas. Now when you planning on bringing back my phone, you sorry-ass bitch?"

Gin had spent the bright April morning furniture shopping with her new friend, Kathy Junger, a holistic orthodontist from Port St John whose patients' records Gin was helping digitize.

Kathy was excited to be retiring her old gray filing cabinets, as they conjured the rather un-fun and overall antiseptic feel of other dental offices. Her practice was on the smaller side, requiring only three rooms and one bathroom in a subdivided Victorian. The waiting room oozed tranquility, soaking up the burnished light of late afternoons, and Gin would sometimes sit in there with a book on slow days, losing an hour or two. She adored the wraparound porch and grand teak staircase and the painting of the pointer dogs they'd picked up from an antique shop in Vero Beach. In truth, she enjoyed many aspects of Kathy's life, and immediately signed up for courses after her friend strongly hinted that good assistants were worth their weight in gold, and a person could get certified in under a year.

Gin enjoyed her friendship with an older woman, especially one with strong opinions and good taste. Kathy registered the world completely differently, like when describing a rosewood armoire—*clean lines, hefty, sensual . . . elegant.*

Presently she was attempting to convince Gin that a mid-century danish lounge chair with stiff cushions and tapering legs would open up her entire living room.

"And it'll retain its value. Enough to recoup the investment, if need be."

"It doesn't look like a spider to you?"

"Oh stop, it's perfect," said Kathy. "And your place needs some sprucing up. I'm terrified one day I'll find you smothered to death by a malfunctioned futon."

Gin laughed and ran her fingers along the cushion. "I've never bought anything like this before."

"It's a good beginner's piece. You can build a whole room around a chair like this."

Gin heard the echo: a whole *life*. She was taken by how a piece that appeared so insubstantial could carry such heft. The purchase felt like a small accomplishment.

After dropping off the chair at her apartment, Kathy suggested an early dinner at the Strawberry Mansion, where they ordered the day's catch and a few cocktails, followed by slices of perversely sugared peach cobbler. They agreed to catch a movie together later that week, when their workloads had cleared up a bit.

Back home, Gin toed off her shoes by the door. Glancing up the hallway to her bedroom, she noticed a glass of water resting on her recently purchased chair.

But she had not left a glass of water on the chair.

She chose the kitchen knife with the strongest handle. Creeping cautiously down the hall, Gin found it difficult to remember which wood slats creaked.

In her bedroom she discovered a filthy, sweat-soaked Cueball wrapped up in her covers, asleep. The window screen had been sliced through and a bra strap hung from a half-closed drawer, her things obviously picked through. She let none of this faze her. If she maced him or called the cops, he'd only run away and return later. Perhaps with a grudge.

She gently set the knife on the dresser and tiptoed quietly over. After a deep breath, she leapt onto the covers, trapping him.

Cueball bolted upright and gasped, blinking awake.

"There's a reason they invented doors," said Gin, playing like she greeted all visitors in such fashion, her nights rife with spontaneous moments like this one.

"I-I-I tried the door, but it was locked," he explained. "I had to go around back, your neighbor's dog kept barking. I couldn't wait outside. I'll pay for the screen, I-I promise."

He seemed embarrassed, unwedging himself sideways to retrieve his shirt from under a pillow and fisting his sunburnt arms through the sleeves, the tropical smell of aloe rising. Then, heaving Gin aside in a flash of white buttocks and torn boxers, he hurried jeans over his spindly legs, apologizing. He seemed—though the heat in Gin's cheeks told her otherwise—to be much more distressed than she was.

"Hey! Stop. You need to tell me why you're here."

"They sent Gumby after me," said Cueball. "Fucking clown. A blowgun . . . who does this? What kind of man . . . where do you get such a . . . skill?"

"Gumby?" She had never met the hit man personally, but people told stories. "I haven't seen him. I haven't seen anyone since Eddy and I broke up."

"I didn't know about that," Cueball said, looping his belt and fastening it. "Sorry to hear it."

"It's not your fault," she replied, unsure of the statement's truth. "Are you in trouble?"

"I've been away," said Cueball, ignoring the question. "I got your address off the library internet. They got your picture on a doctor's website. You should check into that, stalkers and whatnot."

"Well that's . . . upsetting . . . but why are you here?"

"I don't know, I was hoping . . ." he said, unable to find the words. He leaned against the wall, squeezing his arms. "I fucked things up, Gin. So fucking bad. I'm sorry I broke in, I know you're mad, and you should be—"

"I'm not mad," she said, touching her chest. "This isn't right, but I'm not mad. Can't your dad help you?"

"No fucking way," Cueball snorted. "I wanted to call my mom's cell," he said, gesturing at the house phone on the dresser, "but 311 don't give out those numbers. I had to dump the phone I had."

Gin wasn't sure if Cueball knew that Charlotte had left for Tennessee, according to Colt, who'd helped her pack.

Cueball's bottom lip suddenly began to quiver, fingers laced behind his head. His weeping came in breathy, staccato hiccups. It wasn't the kind of hurt you moved to comfort, and Gin hoped it remained in the realm of self-pity rather than morph into something destructive.

"Tell me what's going on," Gin said, fearing for her own safety now. She needed to know if she had seconds or minutes to rush him out the door.

Cueball knew better than to lay his secrets bare—the fewer people involved, the better—but felt an impulse to speak, to share in his affliction.

"I was down in Lauderdale, with these guys," he began. "There was this kid. We didn't shoot him, but we sure as fuck killed him. WHY DID HE GET OUT OF THE CAR?! Because he had to prove himself! Show us he'd die for us. Because that's what we were about, and he wanted to be about that too. Fucking CHRIST!" he yelled, slamming his elbow into the wall and plummeting to the floor.

There he sat, releasing his defeat in tremoloing breaths as Gin waited tensely on the bed. When his eyes opened, they were bloodshot. "The funny thing is, this is exactly what Dad wants. To make me into a survivor. I bet some part of him's even proud."

"I'm sorry, but I don't understand. Somebody died?"

"I fucked up real bad, Gin. I don't know if they wanna shoot me or pat me on the back."

Walking the beaches north for six days afforded Cueball time to think. The way he figured it, the severe punishment Alex enacted upon his own cousin would likely ensure nobody would try pulling a similar stunt with the Toros any time soon. Meaning Cueball had inadvertently helped out his father, by creating a temporary window of security for the club's shipments south. *What a hero!* Gumby's presence alongside one of Alex's spies was evidence the partnership remained intact.

"Maybe it's in my blood, you know? Maybe I *was* born for this shit," he spoke into the dark room. "I helped get a kid killed. He didn't know shit about shit. Should've been in school. Reminded me of Eddy a little, you know? We'd be partying, and he'd be reading a book. But these guys . . . one night they brought back this girl with braids. And pushed him into the bathroom with her. And they wouldn't let him out, until . . . and he kept trying to get out! And we did that to him! I did! We forced that shit on him!"

"Cueball—"

"That's another thing, right there, that name!" he said, running a finger under his nose. "You know how I got it?"

She shook her head.

"I was maybe, what, eleven, twelve? Dad got me a job spraying out Stop-N-Plop toilets, the blue ones, at construction sites? Wanted me to learn about work the hard way, always the hard way. Nastiest job I ever heard of. But afterwards, he'd pick me up, take me down to the pool hall with him and his buddies, sneak me a beer or two. Well, one day these four black dudes come into the bar and get a table, 'cause, you know, management don't care, money's all green. And they're playing, but my dad and his crew start talkin shit, calling 'em *boys*, getting 'em riled up. One big asshole finally gets around to using the N-word, and this black dude, he can't handle it no more, he throws an eight ball and hits this guy Carb right in the head. Carb goes straight down, bang! My dad, he leaps up and breaks a chair over this guy's back. Wham! Blood coming out the side of his neck where the leg caught him. Some serious shit. And these other n . . . these black guys, they know it's time to beat cheeks or go hard, so they stand up and fight, which was respectable. Like just now, *look!* You've never heard me say the N-word before, right? But it's in my head, it pops in there, 'cause as a kid I said it all the fucking time! Everybody around me said all this terrible shit! I'd say faggot, fucking wop chink spic-ass motherfucking cunts like it was water! Eddy was the only one who ever gave me shit about it! But in my mind, when I go back, all that trash is waiting for me. It was *put in me!* By THEM! And Julio, he had all that shit put into him by US! It doesn't fucking stop! It doesn't quit! It spins and spins, waiting to pop out! You have to actively say, *Don't think this, don't say this shit, this isn't you, be better.* You understand what I'm saying?"

Gin nodded, no longer watching him. She was staring at the thin-legged chair by the door.

"All hell broke loose. One black guy takes some brass knuckles to the ribs. Another crushes the nose of my dad's buddy Wayne, he's blubbering on the floor. Dad sees this and just starts whaling on this, this black dude. Then—nobody's paying attention to me, I'm just some kid on a pool table.

This black guy's yelling, *Call the cops, they gonna kill us!* But the bartender's back there on the ground somewhere, so the guy runs over by me and grabs a pool stick and breaks it in half, holding out the pointy end. I mean . . . what am I supposed to do? Next thing I know, I'm lifting a pool ball off the table. Without even waiting I just whip it as hard as I can at his head. Crack! Dude goes limping around, just dazed. Bye-bye. Dad runs over and breaks his jaw. End of story. I get a nickname. End of story."

Cueball exhaled as if to expunge it all.

"They told me," he said, face torn through with resentment, "that the white cueball controls all the colored balls. Who would say that to a kid? Called me a survivor, bought me ice cream. Said in life, if a white ball ever falls in a pocket, it gets put right back on the table. But only the wealthy and powerful win the game. That's the goal, who they wanted me to be. But I was just a kid, scared someone was gonna hurt my dad!"

On the bed, Gin felt something uniformly herself and spirit-like slip out from her—felt the cloth of the bed give way, felt her knees on the floor, and then, just as it was about to touch Cueball, retreat back into her body.

She picked up Cueball's glass and refilled it with water from the bathroom sink. He thanked her, holding the glass in his red hands like someone brought in from the cold.

"I'm sorry to bust in on you like this," he said, wiping his eyes. "I'll fix that screen. I didn't know where else to go. I know you never thought much of me, but you've always been kind. I thought maybe Eddy would be here. Anyhow, I might be heading north. Maybe Virginia or somewhere. Find me another job spraying out toilets," he snickered. "Shit."

"Did you need money?" she asked.

"I wouldn't take your money." He smelled his shirt. "But I could use a shower, if you don't mind. I've still got some junk in my system I'm sweating out."

"Of course," Gin said.

He nodded. "I am sorry to hear about you and Eddy. I don't doubt it was his fault. We're a pair of regular fuckups, I tell you what. If you threw us in a barrel of titties, we'd come up sucking our thumbs."

Gin pursed her lips. "We make our beds."

"That's a nicer way of putting it."

Down the hallway, the front door clicked shut.

Cueball nosed the air, waiting for Gin's response. She wanted to blurt out *Go! Now!* but there was nowhere to run. The footsteps arrived casually, the visitor apparently familiar with his surroundings. Gin flew to the bedroom door but was immediately snatched by the neck and thrown to the floor.

Turning, she watched a whirlwind in black leather yank Cueball off the ground and whale on the boy with slaps to the face before hurling him onto the bed, where Cueball shrunk into a ball and kicked furiously at his adversary.

But Gumby was relentless. With remarkable speed he butterflied a knife open, forcing himself through the kicks to hop atop his prey and hike the knife under Cueball's chin, laying poised there face-to-face like a lover. He tapped the knife's point on his false teeth, then pulled Cueball up to standing, slinging an arm around his neck.

Gumby rocked him toward the door, extending the knife at Gin like an index finger.

"Sweetheart," he said, nodding the weapon so that she understood. Then stabbed the danish chair, dragging the blade through the seat cushion with a satisfying rip. Flicking his wrist, the blade retracted into something the size and shape of a candy bar.

After tipping an invisible hat, Gumby marched a squealing Cueball down the hallway.

Cueball kept his good eye half-closed, playing possum. The windows fogged with their commingling breath. One of the bungee cords binding him to the passenger seat had rubbed his neck raw, but he couldn't adjust himself, as Gumby had him bound in the sweltering chrysalis of a sleeping bag. The cocky bastard even kept him riding shotgun.

"Old woman used to live upstairs from me," began Gumby, "said in her heyday they'd go down to Sebastian and watch folks shoot up aerial bombs to mark the sunset. I told her once in Merritt Island I seen them self-destruct a rocket over the ocean. I was eating blue crab at this outdoor joint and suddenly the sky lit up bright green. This old trucker next to me thought it was the Second Coming, I shit you not. Nearly choked to death on his fries, up shouting and waving for Jesus." Gumby snickered and sent a finger corkscrewing upward to imitate a soul's ascension. "You have to figure if a Savior ever came, doubtful he'd come flying over the Assembly Building. That's rock star thinking. Naw, he'd find the poorest, foulest soul in browntown, send him to the river docks with a cast net and the good word. I figure he's a word-of-mouth kind of guy. Hell, he's got the time."

Though Cueball had maybe heard Gumby utter a few thousand words his entire life, it turned out the assassin was a regular chatterbox. Yet Cueball responded only to questions, waiting for the one opportunity all doomed men anticipate, the flaw in the plan that would allow him to escape.

"I sure wish you talked some," said Gumby. "You know I aint gonna kill you."

Been saying that too, ever since they'd stopped off in Valkaria for vending machine chewing tobacco at a shady motel known for its mirrored ceilings and hourly rents. He'd already apologized for the eye wallop, claiming it wasn't intentional, but Cueball's gaze fixed on the hands at the wheel—the curve of a blade tucked in a leather wristband, glinting in the dash glow. In all likelihood the man's bones were made of metal. Any flashlight demanding license and registration would find its veins opened.

"You recognize this car? Got a good deal on it."

The spinning rims were unmistakable: it belonged to Deziz, the traitorous banger in Lauderdale. Deziz must have been double-dipping to get this sort of treatment. Or maybe Gumby just needed to erase himself from memory. Cueball just hoped whatever happened to that fat fucking turtle, it took a while.

Heading south on US-1, Gumby suddenly hit the brakes and veered onto the opposing shoulder, pebbles crunching underneath as the car sashayed to a halt. He quickly shifted into reverse, cut the wheel, and spun down a trail he'd overshot carved into the riverside palmetto, moving beyond sight of the road.

The hit man cut the engine, got out, and circled the car as Cueball watched, his pits sweaty and stomach churning as his heart pounded in the silence. The passenger door clicked open and swung wide, and here Gumby danced a little jig, maybe to get the blood flowing. "Okey-dokes. Here comes the fun part."

He gave the sleeping bag a hard yank, rolling Cueball out and onto a floor of white shells and splintered boat resin, the sharp rot of kelp flaring in his nostrils. Craning his neck, he found Gumby proud owner of the night sky, towering among constellations, ponytail hung loose like a firecracker wick and tonguing his sharpened eyetooth.

As Gumby prodded him, Cueball tried making himself heavy, and when that didn't work, he began to scream. The tip of his ear split open with a slash, a yelp catching in his throat as Gumby clamped his nose and mouth shut.

"Can we not, partner? I don't want to have to drag you."

Cueball went limp, and to his surprise, Gumby began unzipping the sleeping bag, but left the bungee cords wrapped about his elbows, restraining all upper-body movement save for his lower arms. Cueball was raised to his feet, ear gash singing. Gumby quickly rerolled the sleeping bag and pushed it to Cueball's chest.

"After you," he said, nodding up the moonlit path.

Eventually they exited at a cove where a cut of solid earth jutted into the river. The jagged wood stumps of a collapsed dock poked from the dark waters. Mid-river Cueball could make out the axe-headed outline of Underwear Island: twenty-foot-high cliffs gradually descending to water's edge. Cueball knew it well. They called it Underwear because, come midnight, that's all any teenage camper would be wearing. The Black Road crew partied there on occasion, mixing Wild Turkey with Continental Cola to charm the tongue with a flavor they called Orange Tic Tacs. It was best to get drunk fast and pass out early or be reminded the island was populated by rats the size of tomcats, well-fed off god knows what.

Gumby searched the muddy bank for something, a song under his breath: *Whatcha gonna do when the creek runs dry? Sit and watch that crawdad die, ho-ney, bay-a-by, mine.* In this escape scenario, Cueball imagined Gumby catching him at the highway and opening his guts to the asphalt.

There came the knock and ease of wood, the whisper of a skiff guided over water by a rope. Gumby motioned for Cueball to climb into the boat and take a seat, but in the darkness Cueball tripped over a thwart and landed ass up, like an inchworm, cold stale hullwater shivering up his shirt.

Gumby didn't bother to help him up, positioning Cueball's legs on the sleeping bag and shifting his head onto a life jacket the shape of a urinal seat, with a reek not dissimilar.

A boot squawked and the skiff rocked unbalanced with Gumby's standing as they coasted past the shallows. Cueball was able to twist his face to catch the faint shore lights dreaming in the wake of an oar.

Midway to their destination, Gumby quit rowing to lower his fingers to the black water. He typed the surface using minimal splashes, like Morse code. Out of nowhere a sleek wheel like the tire guard of an old automobile rolled past, a hole up top, as if freed from a carousel, its rubbery fin snaking under.

"That's godawful beautiful, come right up like that. Friendly species. Smart too, and dangerous if provoked. Kill sharks with their snouts, if you believe it—ram 'em in the gut and drown 'em."

Gumby tried calling again, but none came. For the rest of the trip he kept silent, leaving Cueball to imagine another failed escape, catching an oar to the ribs while trying to flip over the side.

Lapping wavelets foreshadowed their docking, where half-submerged mangrove roots rose up like an enormous mandible to meet the hanging dogwood branches.

Gumby hopped out and dragged the skiff high up the beach, then unstrapped the bungee cords as Cueball's bloodless arms smacked the boat's bottom like wings made of needles and stone. Moments later he was hoisted up to stand on the island bank.

"Walk thataway," breathed Gumby, pointing toward the crosshatched darkness. Cueball was pampering his swollen ear, blood on his fingertips. "Aint but a nick, boy, now get a move on."

They waded through vine and branches, using roots as upward steps. Leveling off, the path cut deep into a thicket of thorny underbrush sagging with pits. Whenever Cueball stumbled, Gumby snatched him up, pushing ever forward, guided by memory or incredible vision. If the plan was to draw out Cueball's hope to its finest, most insufferable point, it was working.

The unseasonable smells of early autumn found them—soiled bark and thin air imbued with musk and heat and thirst. Cueball tilted his glance to catch any half-light peripherally, a trick he'd learned stargazing. From beyond a maelstrom of kudzu came a transitioning darkness with slightly amber tones. He was beginning to sweat, the memory of sitting before campfires. Behind him, the stern nudging of Gumby's silent inertia.

A path of crushed shells emerged, piles of calcified fossils, chunks of aerated coral and porous limestone—bones of the earth; nothing passes into the next world. They came upon a small camping area backed by shell mounds, with a fire set before two tents. There Bird sat open-legged on a log, grimacing and stoking the fire contemplatively with a broken spade handle. He peered up only to acknowledge it was those he was anticipating. Cueball did not speak. No words could summarize what the scene told in its bare rendering. The flames chewed at the firewood like some creature pinned and writhing.

Using the spade's cherry end, Bird motioned for Cueball to drop down. There was a cooler next to a first-aid kit and Cueball needed water but was afraid to ask. Gumby left him and circled the pit as Bird reached behind the log and hoisted up two hard-shelled creatures—antediluvian water spiders, with spiny red helmets and long dart tails—clung together in coition. He ripped them apart at their sex and tossed them to the flames.

Gumby coughed, disgusted; they weren't to be eaten. Bird, catching his expression, jabbed the spade into the crabs' bellies, releasing their blue blood, and tossed them aside.

"Happy?" he asked, but the animals were already ruined. He huffed and turned to Cueball: "You may be my son, but your life now belongs to this man," he said, motioning to Gumby, who spat. "I told him it was his choice to bring you out here or drown you in the river."

Cueball stayed silent. Sap popped, showering outward, and one ember plummeted dizzily down to land on his father's naked arm and died there without so much as a flinch.

"You moved heaven and earth trying to fuck over your old man, didn't you?" he started. "Undermined my authority. Embarrassed some important contacts. Got, what? Six people killed? Made it pretty difficult to manage this outfit for a bit. And I won't even go into how your mother's taking it," Bird confided, and Cueball felt it. "I'll be straight with you, I had half a mind to say forget it: little shit made his bed. If Alex or his Toros had any inkling you were my son, we'd of lost South Florida and a whole lot more." He spit into the fire. "You have any clue how many Toros chapters there are, nationwide? How many kids they got on the streets? Whenever Alex wants, all those heads turn in our direction. The only reason he agreed to keep doing business with us is because we helped shake that cousin problem of his."

Cueball struggled with composure as Gumby, squatting, drew shapes in the sand with his hunting knife.

"You happen to see Jim Barns down there?" asked his father.

"No. Why?"

"If you had, you might be dead."

Cueball shivered, hugging into his knees. For the first time ever, he understood the practical imperatives underscoring his father's decisions as a leader, and felt all at once stupid and afraid. "D-d-did you send him . . ."

"Seizer gave the order behind my back," his father hacked. "You should thank your lucky stars he sent that nitwit instead of this fella here."

"That ball-sniffer couldn't track down a hot stone in hell," quipped Gumby. "I forget—who was it got him that job at the camps?"

"Don't fucking start!" Bird growled. "If it wasn't for me, he'd of had your ass locked up! Made his face look like a damn side of beef. But when I get my hands on him, believe you me, he'll wish he kept his old job fishing for turds."

Bird dug into his front pocket and unsquared a piece of paper and held it up to the firelight. It was a drawing of a palm tree, rendered tribal, yet different from the Armstrong Crew's.

"It's a Royal palm," said Gumby. "All the rage. A new symbol, under a new leader."

Bird watched as Cueball understood at least one thing. Then another.

"Did Eddy do that?" Cueball asked with a burst of confidence, feeling he might actually survive the night.

Bird, however, dropped the hatchet. "Now, you may be thinking this is some big opportunity for you. It isn't. This is the end of the line. If you run, you can never come back. Simple as that. This guy here," he said, jabbing his own chest, "isn't your father when you're out in the field. He's your boss. Get it? You do anything this fucking stupid again, you best change your name, son, 'cause it won't mean just another whoopin." He paused to let the point hit home. "So here's what's gonna happen: one Saturday not too far from now, you're gonna get up around four a.m. and take a ride with Gum over to Seizer's. When you're done with the job, you'll take what's left of him down to Billy's Nursery off Malabar Road. Billy's got a shed out back. I'll meet you both at Sally Ann's for breakfast. You'll get paid fifteen for it. Put a little money back in your pocket. And if this doesn't come off as clean as I'm saying . . ." he said, letting the tension hover. "Now, I hear you're pretty good with a rifle."

"What? I guess so," said Cueball, thinking, *This is insane.*

"Gum tells me you can peck out a bull's-eye from fifty yards back."

"How would he know?"

"He's seen you do it. Rifle and Pistol Club, out there in the woods."

"But I only go out by myself."

"How good are you with a handgun?"

"I'm better from farther back," said Cueball. "I don't know why."

"Well I know why," Gumby interjected. "It's because you're gifted, and because you're a chickenshit. You like seeing things fall from the sky like they're nothin. But we'll fix you up. Get you to meet the enemy eye-to-eye, like nature intended."

Bird gripped his knees. "Do you understand what's being said here?"

"I think so."

"Helping you will be Gumby's last job for a while. He's going on sabbatical."

Cueball didn't know what that word meant but nodded.

"I disappear and take the heat off," said Gumby. "Folks need to think there's someone out there hunting down Seizer's killer."

"Given Lauderdale, how hard it was for this man to track you," his father continued, "that says something to me. You might think we've got folks a sight more dangerous than you for this job, which is absolutely correct. But I need you *at my side*. We'll be losing contacts when we clean house. Certain jobs require a specialist, and you might not like me saying so, but nobody'd suspect a runt like you for this work. You'll get your training. And all that shit you've done in the past—son, that's a different person. That was a boy, lashing out. What I see here before me is a man."

This was no ultimatum Cueball could have foreseen. His father was offering him a major role in a regime change. But the thought of actually killing a person seemed wholly outside his range of reason or ability. Everyone feared Gumby to a point of reverence, but that didn't mean anyone wanted his job.

Still, Cueball couldn't outright reject the offer, or seem too eager—that would just confirm he'd made up his mind to run away.

"I guess I don't know what to say."

Bird jutted out his bottom lip, eyebrows raised. "Wouldja lookit that? Already we're getting the truth." Then he laughed unexpectedly, hooting: "You almost brought down the house, boy! Shit, who'd of thunk it? And now you'll help clean up this mess. Make me proud."

"We're just talking about Seizer, right?" chanced Cueball. "The Twins, they're not a part of this."

One of his father's eyelids fluttered in exasperation. "You get to ask zero questions. That old coot let me rot in prison, and he thinks I owe *him*? Claps his hands and I do my little monkey dance? He holds the past over my head like a goddamn chainsaw! Gum, you remember what he used to pay us to run his weak-ass junk?"

Gumby considered this. "Room and board. Spending cash."

"I earned my keep and more! Every day was my ass on the line. I did hard time protecting that ungrateful midget, I don't owe him shit! And now he's back to his old ways, cooking books and skimming money."

"He's stealing?"

"From all of us."

Cueball picked his fingernails, letting the popping campfire overtake the silence.

"Dad, I just wanna say—"

"I don't care," said Bird. "We're beyond sorry. This here's the hard way."

Cueball was relieved to hear it.

"Now, we need to cover up that old tattoo of yours," his father said. "And well, shit, I forgot my equipment. Guess we'll just have to make do."

Gumby didn't hesitate. Rising swiftly, he yanked the spade from the fire, grabbed Cueball's arm, and plunged the red-hot tip into the fleshy base of his wrist, where it flowered.

ddy had passed by Big Mike's Tattoo a thousand times over the years. The shop was a staple in Downtown Melbourne. Big Mike's custom designs were hyper-detailed, borderline 3-D, and world-famous—Top 10 inker on the East Coast, if a certain online magazine was to be believed. Eddy recognized his early work on dozens of bikers, before Big Mike raised his prices. Why this guy with a supposed TV deal in the works chose to remain in Brevard County instead of moving to a major city was something Eddy would ask, should the moment present itself.

Eddy withdrew a rectangular black portfolio case from his Bug, popped a mint, and strolled eagerly but professionally up the sidewalk.

He was nervous, but that's how you feel when you take control of your destiny. He silently thanked Duke for his patience and instruction, but god-dammit, he'd had enough. With his best friend and closest confidant still missing, everyone busy, and no hobbies to keep his depression at bay, Eddy needed a change—an infusion of purpose.

A bell chimed overhead as he entered the shop.

The walls were decked out salon-style with neon signs and framed pho-tographs, a panoply of famous clients sporting awe-inspiring tattoos. There were five vacant cubicles in back, the walls short enough to glimpse art-ists working on their human canvases. To his right, in one such cubicle, a strawberry-blonde woman in cutoffs was up on her elbows on a padded table covered in white paper, face sweaty but mascara holding, as a bald man bent over her lower back, focused intensely on keeping his lines straight. Eddy stepped to the counter and waited. There was a silver call bell, but he didn't dare. Half a minute later Big Mike appeared from a back room, walking up the aisle and stopping briefly to inspect his protégé's work. Eddy imagined him making mental notes, things one mentions only after the client pays and leaves.

They locked eyes and Eddy felt a jolt of nerves.

"What can I do you for, brother?" asked Big Mike, approaching. "I didn't think we had any more appointments today, am I right? Did I mess up? Where's Kat?" He turned to the artist. "Jimmy where's Kat?"

"Grabbing cheesesteaks," said Jimmy, not looking up.

Big Mike's face scrunched. "You have an appointment?"

"No I don't," said Eddy, and that's when Big Mike noticed the enormous portfolio case in Eddy's hand.

"Oh, okay," said Big Mike. "Listen, I don't do on-the-spot critiques, and we're currently not looking for new talent at the moment, bud, sorry. But we do have a program, sort of a workshop we do in the summer, and I'd be happy to take your name and email—"

"Oh sure, no problem," said Eddy, already backing up. "A workshop?"

"Yeah yeah! We take the top six or seven portfolios we see, really try to pin down specific strengths and weaknesses, and do one-on-one sessions with artists, to beef up areas of improvement—"

Eddy's palms were slickening; something about the legitimacy of the establishment unnerved him. The designs on the walls made him feel inadequate, a poseur. This was Big fucking Mike.

"I-I-I've only been inking a few years," he interrupted, willing himself to speak. "Maybe worked on fifty people? I know I've still got a lot to learn."

"Oh me too, brother!" Big Mike joked. "That's why I call myself an amateur professional. I'm a lifelong student. There's always something new out there: new techniques, styles, fads, new tools. It's a vocabulary, you know? The art form grows . . . you learn more . . . and you grow."

"That's exactly right," said Eddy. "I just wanted to stop by and . . . hey, I just love your work."

"Thank you."

"I saw this shaded eagle you did once . . . blew my mind."

"Eagle?" asked Big Mike. "On who? What's their name?"

"Bird?" said Eddy, feeling a rush of trepidation.

"Oh yeah! Wow, yeah, the biker guy. Big bear. I was an infant when I did that one, shit. My style has evolved . . . dramatically. But hey, I'll tell you what . . . why the hell not. Bring your stuff back to my table, let's have a look."

"Really?"

"Yeah, sure. I'm here for another hour . . . gotta eat. We're driving to Tampa for a conference. I'm not promising anything, but if the work looks good, maybe we can talk more about this summer program. You do piercings?"

"Once," lied Eddy.

"What's your name?"

"Eddy Wildeboar."

"Michael," he said, extending a hand.

"Big Mike?" asked Eddy.

"Whatever floats your boat."

Big Mike's station was all the way in back. Two chairs and a black table, more pictures and magazine covers, along with an old pink photo of a woman Eddy guessed was his mother.

"Go ahead and set it on the table," said Big Mike, and Eddy set down the black case and unzipped the sides. Big Mike wasted no time, flipping through the plastic sleeves to study the drawings with a keen intensity. These were images dreamt up in class or sketched at a drafting table well past midnight, and Eddy was silently ecstatic—the consideration made tattooing seem like an actual occupation, beyond the ranks of pipe dream or side hustle.

"These are solid, my man. Wow."

A burst of pride rose up in Eddy.

"You've got a real talent for shading. These pop. Even the minor filigrees are phenomenally well articulated. Good tones, linework . . . you self-taught?"

"Mostly."

Big Mike mugged an impressed face. "You got your realism, tribal. Got some goofy stuff, which is good, as people will always dig *The Simpsons*. Here's some weird-ass sci-fi. Not many will translate to skin like this, exactly—but still, nice. You've got a *decadence*, is what I call it, for unnecessary flourishes.

But decadence is just your true style in an immature phase. Your voice grows as you grow. It's clear you intuit flow well, and you got a graphic sensibility that's popular right now."

"Thanks," said Eddy. "I don't know what to say."

"I'd say take a class," said Big Mike. "At the very least. Might even move you up, 'cause yeah, you got it."

Eddy was almost on his toes. He couldn't be more elated.

Flipping the next plastic flap, Big Mike paused. Then sniffed, glancing up front. His fingers spread out and tented on the table.

"What's wrong?"

Big Mike sort of laughed. "It's fine to emulate other people's designs, my man, but you really shouldn't include them in your portfolio."

"Um. I didn't," said Eddy, unclear of his meaning. "These are all mine."

"All of these are yours," said Big Mike with a sad sort of smile.

Eddy studied the large cream sheet covered in berries, cherubs, flowers . . . and a Sabal palm. He caught Big Mike glancing down to his wrist, and withdrew his hands behind him.

"Okay, listen kid, I don't want any trouble."

Eddy shook his head.

"This a shakedown?"

"No," said Eddy, his face warming. "I'm just looking for a part-time job."

"A part-time job. You got another part-time job?"

It wasn't something Eddy could respond to.

"Kid, I'm asking if you're here on business. You trying to hire me? Or move in."

"I'm just looking for—"

"A part-time job, yeah."

Big Mike sighed heavily, his gaze again flashing up front. He casually flipped the page to the next board. Another sigh. He stabbed his finger at one image. "You drew this. This is yours."

It was an accusation. The symbol was a green pineapple, nothing special.

"Yeah, a pineapple, so what—"

"The shit you're selling kills people. You understand that?"

"I don't sell—"

"But you work for them."

Eddy couldn't look up.

"Two months ago my little cousin Kevin OD'd on shank. Passed away. Perfectly good kid, made some bad decisions. But made a really bad decision at a nightclub."

"I-I'm sorry."

"This symbol was worn by some guys he hung around. Not good people."

"I don't know a Kevin," said Eddy. "I'm real sorry." Part of him wanted to lunge for the portfolio.

"Listen, I've inked felons and Girl Scout den mothers, whoever," said Big Mike, his voice lower. "And I'm no saint, god knows. But you happened to catch me on a particularly bad day. So I need you to leave, and I never want to see your face in here again."

"Wait, hold on," whispered Eddy. "I'm trying to quit my job—"

"Yeah? Good."

"But I need another one first."

"And I want my cousin back. Guess we don't all get what we want."

Eddy quickly zipped up the case. Head lowered, he swung around Big Mike and marched up the aisle.

He almost made it to the door before Big Mike shouted after him.

"Hey, kid, wait!"

Eddy stopped.

"Nobody's looking for trouble," said Big Mike. "But so's you know, I got an arsenal back here."

The tattooing artist nearby stopped wiping and eyed Eddy suspiciously.

"A fucking arsenal. You hear me?"

Eddy half-nodded and scurried out the door.

On the sidewalk he broke into full panic mode, chest tightening, ribs caving in. He hopped into his Bug, jerked out of the parking space, and spun away. Tiny spinning lights danced in his eyes as he fought to control his irregular breathing.

Zigzagging back streets, he chanced upon an indian restaurant and wheeled around the back lot. With the car running, he opened the passenger-side door and yanked out his portfolio. Checking for cameras, he walked the portfolio over to a green dumpster, raised the lid, and slung it inside.

Then jogged back to his car and sped away.

Gin recrossed her legs, sipping a matcha latte. She'd returned from yoga to find Del Ray sitting on a metal bench in the tiny garden outside her apartment. Gin was sweaty and wanted nothing more than a shower, but there was no avoiding this. She walked past him without speaking and he followed her inside.

Del Ray made himself comfortable on the couch, a plastic shopping bag dangling from his fingers.

"He didn't say anything," Gin said, dropping into a chair.

"I want you to know that Cueball's okay," Del started. "Nothing bad's happened to him. He screwed up, but everything's fine now. And, well, I hate having to ask you this—"

"Screw you."

"I understand you're upset. It's an ugly situation."

"That crazy, weaselly m-effer threatened me, Del!"

"Who, Gumby? What'd he say?"

"He didn't have to say anything, he pointed a knife at me!"

Del Ray pursed his lips. Then took a strap of bills from the shopping bag and placed it on the coffee table.

"I don't want that," said Gin.

"Well," said Del, lifting his hand away. "Did Cueball happen to mention where he'd been, or what he'd been doing?"

"All he said was his dad was mad at him. And used my phone to make a call. Wait, did that creep tap my landline? Is that a real thing? Or was he watching my house, which is actually worse."

Del apologized with his eyes. He glanced about the sparsely decorated apartment. Then took out another strap of bills and set it down by the first.

"Take it. Fix up the place, go wild. I really dig this old chair. I know someone who might can repair the seat cushion."

Gin clenched her jaw. "I don't want your money."

"What *do* you want?"

"I want to be left alone, Ray! You guys with your whatever, seems like all you do is dump on women and make bad shit happen. I have a life now."

Del Ray thought about that. "You talk to Eddy much?"

She looked away. "No."

"Good," he said, raising his hands. "I'll get out of your hair. Sorry for the mess." He put the money back in the bag and went to rise, but hesitated. "Mind if I ask how your mom is?"

"She's dandy."

"Ever mention me?"

"Sheezus."

"Never?"

Gin eyed him coolly. "All she can talk about is some vegan hairdresser she's fucking in Gainesville. Big dick, apparently. Says she's through with immature types playing cowboy on their motorcycles, but I'll be sure to mention you said hi."

But Del Ray was already out the door.

"That went well," said Del as he slid into Mickey's car, parked up the block.

"Yeah?"

Del Ray blew through his puffed cheeks.

Mickey drove them north up US-1. Motels for outcasts littered the wayside. Acres of citrus cleared for yet another vacant strip mall. Mickey said he didn't know what they called the wasteland between Titusville and West Melbourne, but it gave him the heebie-jeebies.

"Birdland," answered Del Ray. "I bet they'll even name a street for him, one day."

"I have to say, I think there's some serious trust issues at stake here," said Mickey, wanting it to be known. "You think Seizer actually put a hit out on Cueball?"

"I think that's irrelevant," offered Del. "The die was cast long ago. You can't have two generals operating the same territory, especially with an old grudge tearing at their hearts."

They hung a left over some railroad tracks and entered a decrepit quarter awash in the aftermath of some ultimate economic apocalypse. Stray dogs trotted headlong like wheelbarrows through overgrown lawns. A lone child at the end of a driveway sucked a homemade popsicle while kneading dirt with a filthy fist. The street names were all taken from the legend of Robin Hood: Little John and Friar Tuck, Sherwood, King Richard.

"I hope to god you're wrong about Bird wanting Seizer gone," Mickey confided. "Honestly, I don't know who to trust."

"Apprehension will keep you alive," said Del Ray, not making a thing out of it. "The fact is, we're always one tattletale away from total collapse."

"That don't sound like brotherhood to me," said Mickey. "We should be looking out for each other. Why the fuck is Bird telling us this shit? I don't need to know this shit. Who cares if the old man's skimming extra? Seizer deserves it!"

"We're taking orders, Mick. Observing the plight. We're gonna sit still and listen to the commandant rattle on about sacred bonds and individual potentials, and we're gonna smile and nod."

"Bird's got more secrets than the pope. I'm not sure he's got our best interests at heart."

"Watch yourself, jack," cautioned Del Ray. "Let's press rewind and play-pretend that thought remained unarticulated."

"Don't get all high-and-mighty on me, you've said as much."

"You just can't take a hint, can you?" said Del Ray. "We can yammer and bitch all day about our hopes and personal insecurities, but we're clock punchers, Mick, and paid well to toe the line. An overly ambitious tongue is an expendable one, remember that. Focus on protecting your own interests."

"You mean zip it. We can talk about certain things, but not important things. Great, that's just dandy."

"I'm saying this isn't our boat to rock." Del Ray slapped his shoulder, to show no judgment. "I need you here, Mick. We had our past, but look at us now! You protect my interests, I protect yours—we get ours together."

At the end of Warwick Road they followed a dirt trail hugging the railroad tracks and soon came upon a lone ranch house fenced in by bottlebrush and pine. Bird's Fat Boy curbed the porch of the safehouse, with a few motorcycles crowded around back. Mickey spotted a camouflaged man with a semiautomatic tilted against a tree, only after he moved.

"How are we supposed to act?" Mickey asked, staring at the safehouse.

"Pretend you've got a shovel in a cemetery," said Del Ray. "And every word out of your mouth is another bit of earth flung over your own grave. Remember that he's choosing to let us in on this. Otherwise we're just a pair of smokejumpers without backup caught between two walls of flame."

Mickey toyed with the image. "Man, I swear to god I only understand half of what you're saying."

Del smiled. "Hey, know what? I bet we see a little pay bump outta this."

But Mickey's expression didn't change. "You got my back, right?"

"Not only that," said Del Ray, reaching over and snatching at his face. "I got your nose."

"Maaaaan!" Mickey howled, scurrying out. "Why you always gotta be acting like such a queer?"

Del Ray made his laughter excessively boisterous. Watched the armed sentinel in the woods smirk and shake his head. *Yessir,* thought Del Ray, *don't pay us no mind. Just a jolly old bunch of fuckers right here. We aint got nothing to hide.*

Seizer was shaving.

At first light, he ambled naked into his bathroom and got the hot water going in the sink. Pulled a towel over his waist and located the cracked leather bag in the medicine cabinet, retrieving the white bowl and badger-hair brush that always reminded him of a hometown apothecary's mortar and pestle. Took his time with the lather. Liked shaving. Shaved as if the world were emptied of its hardships by this ritual. And always before showering; liked to feel the water pressure on his newly raw face. Finding the stubble grain with his fingers, he stretched the old rooster flab taut. Recalled running away at twelve to Carroll Gardens, Brooklyn, to live among the retired Mafia, old men skipping pawns at the cafés. That bathroom with the chipped travertine tiles, shower piping hot, the entire space clouding over as the mirror disappeared. The elegance of suds, the pampering of talcum. The strokes of a precise tool edging off the body's excess. His grandfather, crossing the ocean from a small harbor village in Wales, packing with him this very same straight razor, bone-handled, whittled from a hart's thigh. How in a cramped cabin at ship's bottom, endlessly rocking, eager to seek out prominence in a new world, he was afraid, perhaps, but never—and Seizer was sure of this—while shaving. A calm assurance married to a sense of replenishment, dripping sweat. His pink-yellow skin the first line of defense for the internals, so he cared for it, kneaded it, memorized its pocks and ravines, the moles delicately raised for trimming. Could have passed this on to a son; would have with Duke or Lisbon, but he'd been away, scheming, and when he'd returned, they'd already taught themselves. This is how a man ages, unmasked by this essential ceremony. Whole groups like the hasidim in Williamsburg and Lancaster amish announced themselves by their denouncement of the thing. The statuary beards of ancient assyrians and egyptians; the unkempt hippies; the goatees of american fifties radicals, couched in poetry and subversion;

Castro's Cuba, all music and cigars and the poor. And to strip that away, to reframe one's countenance with bald authority—the very trademark of finance and the conservative mind, a tie knotted firmly at the neck—this was shaving. But that was not it, he thought, tapping the porcelain's edge, wiping the blade on a hand towel. Not political. Not a matter of scruff or anti-scruff, as some would have it, but a daily confrontation with one's visage—the flesh dealt; the life chosen. How it teaches one to *take* one's time, as it were. He began at the earlobes, water bleating, a dense fog flowering in the chest like pride. The brazen moustaches of autocrats, the gunslinging narcos and leathered homosexuals. The biker's bold muttonchops. We make unto ourselves, ourselves. Facing all possible futures, to gain some incommunicable peace with this and many other realities, and to do it alone, this was shaving.

But Seizer was not alone.

Gumby watched from the slit in the door. He knew what he was interrupting, recognized the beauty of a ritual performed in steamy, ambient light. Focused on the exquisite bone-handled blade raised slightly beneath a hopping adam's apple. The object pulled at him, its craftsmanship unparalleled: stark white, with brown channels overlaid by a thin lacquer. How it swiveled neatly on a short pin. His intimacy with knives and a desire to own the most exceptional examples were perhaps a decrepit form of the longing Seizer felt for a blood heir, having some say in what survived you. All matter exists to be fashioned and refashioned. Knives, blades, shivs—all things fall under the cutlass of some horizon.

Gumby let the door drift open.

As Seizer wiped off the blade and again raised it to his throat, Gumby pounced, yanking him back by the arm, the razor spinning red in the porcelain sink.

But the room was too small, and Gumby's force too great. Entangled in each other's lack of balance they romped, waltzing, overturning a shelf of hygiene products on their way to the floor, where they locked together and wrestled like darwin's beetles. Gumby kept behind, securing his leg's grip under Seizer's rib cage, one arm around the boss' neck and the other beating his bald scalp with the blunt end of a hunting knife.

It was over in less than a minute.

Seizer lay motionless on the tiles. Gumby unfurled himself and scooted back into the hallway, where Cueball stood rigid by the door, palms on the wall.

"That old cat had some moves," huffed Gumby, out of breath. He lay flat on the floor, staring up. "You see how meaty thick his neck was? I had no idea. I had absolutely no grip on him." Rubbing his leg, he added: "Whew, I cramped up."

Cueball inched forward to get a better look at the bloodied naked man lying spread-eagle on the floor.

"Is he dead?"

"No, he aint dead. Not yet at least."

Gumby dug the hunting knife into the floor and spun to his knees, favoring a leg as he stood. He rewrapped his ponytail and dropped it down his shirt. Limped over and patted Cueball's shoulder, offering him the hunting knife dangled between two fingers.

"Well, I guess that about wraps up my end. Feels weird to be the guy helping out, I don't know what to do with my hands," he said, balling and unballing a fist. "Here, let's get him in the tub."

"I don't think I can do it."

"You can," said Gumby, forcing the knife into Cueball's grip. "Just remember what we talked about. Reach back for the sacrifice. Find that hurt and let it swell up easy."

During his month of rushed apprenticeship, which doubled as rehab— not so much scared straight as scared stiff—Cueball learned a great deal about knives and close-quarter melees, but nothing prepared him for this moment, the actual execution of his instruction. It was like learning to drive stick and then forced onto the track of the Daytona 500. They'd sat in Gumby's kitchen going over diagrams, eating sparingly, training when they weren't sleeping. Gumby had no TV and his books were all survivalist guides, weapons catalogues, wildlife magazines. Cueball submitted without much outward reluctance to the drills and memorization of combat techniques. *First of all, there's no such thing as a knife fight—there's the person doing the cutting and the one* getting cut. *You'll have to think on your feet, as you'll only get a few strikes in before they wanna wrestle. A thrust up through the lungs stops the screaming. Tuck the knife under your forearm like this, blade out, so you slash when you punch. Artery here. Harder to knock away, and once you're on the ground, dig into their stomachs.* They slept in hammocks on the back porch and cooked broccoli tofu rice and halloumi in a pan over gas. Gumby disappeared and returned at night without warning, carrying off boxes of dart frogs, tanks of snakes, cages of alligators, and a potted plant from which he extracted the deadly curare poison—cleaning house, while keeping Cueball's nerves on-call. They discussed the blowgun once to dismiss it: Cueball would be the son of blade and bullet, as each person must find the particular style of weaponry best suited to their nature. But blade to begin with, as Gumby demanded his student's first hit be carried out eye-to-eye, and messy, so it registered.

By far the strangest thing required of Cueball, though, was this *sacrifice* Gumby insisted upon, based on a questionable assertion that held that by killing something you loved, of cosmic lesser value than yourself, before killing something you didn't, of equal or greater value, one might somehow salvage one's humanity. And worse: you had to keep sacrificing new things, as the soul built up tolerance.

But Cueball went with it, pondering what he loved, which sadly wasn't much. He finally settled on his collection of Garbage Pail Kids, a series of grotesque and humorous stickers culled from old-school bubble gum packs picked up over the years from yard sales. His idea was to burn one for each kill, or leave them as calling cards. The novelty of the fantasy amused him.

Gumby responded by slapping his face into a wall.

You think I'm some kind of psychopath? Out here killin for fun? Well, I got news for you, this is real work, and a fright bit harder than it looks. He unclenched his nails from Cueball's neck and paced the kitchen's linoleum. *If I'm the psycho, what the fuck's that make you?* Cueball couldn't guess, and that satisfied Gumby enough to change his tone. *Son, these people we hunt, they aint good people. They're in the game. Now, killing is like feeding, and if you're not careful, it'll poison you with regret. You gotta feel nothin doin it, nothin at all, or it* will *haunt you. I can walk you down to the VA hospital if you wanna see what that looks like. You need to find something beautiful you stole from the world for selfish reasons. Something that yanks you down at the center. A suffering that no two ways, you know in your heart, you're responsible for. And own it. Once you own up to it, you can cage it, and keep it. And when time comes, it will protect you, because the thing you're doin next isn't as bad as what you already done. Got it? So what is it? What's a thing you loved and sacrificed for selfish reasons? Be honest.*

Cueball didn't even have to think about it: Julio was already there in the room. From that point on, things became both easier and harder.

Gumby stood over Seizer's body, flicking his own nipple, which Cueball guessed helped him think. "Grab him under the feet."

Cueball slid around the doorjamb, catching a glimpse of the bloody razor in the sink. Saw the fresh red leaking from Seizer's neck and scalp, watched the steady but shallow breath-beat. Gumby twisted a towel into a snake and wove the snake between Seizer's armpits for handles. Cueball balanced the hunting knife flat on the sink edge and pulled the shower curtains back on the lion's claw tub and together counting they hoisted laboriously the slumberous boss into the basin like a dolphin.

"Thick old son of a bitch," said Gumby, puffing his cheeks. "Okay, I'll wait for you outside."

"What you mean outside?"

"In the hall?"

"You said we were doing this together!" cried Cueball.

"We are. I'm complicit," said Gumby. "I don't have any blinders on, I'm helping you kill this man. But I won't be around for the others, and it's important you do this part alone." Sensing Cueball's continued reluctance, he said, "Here, hand me that shortblade from the sink. Just remember, people die all the time. Think of our boys in Afghanistan, popping the brains out the back of the Taliban."

Cueball fished around the sink and produced the straight razor. Gumby took it and sat at the edge of the tub. He poked the soft flesh of Seizer's chest and stomach, reiterating the internal damage to be done by striking various body points. Cueball picked up the hunting knife, turning it over in his hands. He found it hard not to watch Seizer's eyes for movement, the blood from his cracked dome leaking down in a widening rivulet.

"Pay attention."

"I am. I'm going over what we talked about."

"Good. Keep it fresh. You been practicing with that rubber knife? Good. Now, just like with the punching bag."

"I'm not sure I can do it," Cueball said, sickened by the blotchy skin and purple cheeks, the hirsute sprays of hair. "A knife seems . . . so awful. Like you said, I gotta find what I'm comfortable with. And I think I'd just rather shoot him, if I had to."

Gumby didn't know what to say. Whipped his ponytail back, staring away. The absolute nerve of this kid. "Fine. You wanna be a pathetic little *murderer*, with no honor to it, no way back . . . then you go right on ahead."

"Wait don't leave."

"This shit'll eat you alive, but you do whatever—"

Seizer came alive, catching Gumby's arm.

Hoisting himself up, the boss swung bearishly without aim, flailing and catching his side on the tub's edge, which stole his breath. Gumby tried grappling with him but Seizer rolled over and put Gumby in a headlock. Trying to stand, but slipping, they fell sprawling from the tub and into Cueball, who elbowed and kneed anything close, the hunting knife spilling from his hands as they all went to the floor together.

The old man's grunting abruptly stopped, replaced by a hoarse groan and wheezing.

Cueball unsquinted his eyes to find Seizer lying at his feet, gulping air like a stranded fish, the hunting knife pinched between ribs. His blood came out gushing, liquefying Cueball's socks and shoes.

Seizer's eyes rolled back as Gumby kicked him in the head repeatedly until finally the labored breathing cinched in his throat. Then Gumby fell swiftly to one knee, and with the man's own razor opened a wide slit at his throat, whereby the old boss gargled the last hopes of himself onto the white tile floor.

Cueball's arms went rubbery and shook as he pitched aside and retched beside a small radiator. Before he knew what was happening, he was being dragged from the bathroom by the shirt collar and rolled onto his side.

Straddling him, Gumby rubbed his back and blew on the nape of his neck. "Deep breaths, partner," he whispered. "Let it go now. Let it go."

Cueball couldn't imagine ever describing this to anyone. He felt like a rising balloon whose insides had suddenly crystallized, and succumbed to the plummet. Gumby slipped off to look him square in the face. "You're famous, bud. You did it. I told you. Let it take you where you're going. Breathe."

Cueball tried to concentrate on breathing, tears in his eyes, his sinuses clogged with vomit.

"You've come out the other side, little man. I knew you could do it. Your pop said pick the craziest son of a gun I knew and I told him, that boy of yours—he's a live wire. Beat a man twice his size with his own pistol. I've worked around enough poison to smell it."

"I can't breathe."

"That's the adrenaline. Feel your stomach. Feel the air in there? You're a dust ball on the wall, you're so light."

Cueball imagined himself a dust ball on the wall.

"Believe it or not, you're handling this better than I did my first time. Just know this, little buddy: you don't have to fear anything ever again. Never again. I'm so proud of you. Seriously, I couldn't be more proud."

Cueball wanted to say he didn't do it. That the knife fell from his hands and spun on the handle as if attempting to locate some true north, and that Seizer had simply fallen on it. But he said nothing. What happened was either fate or magic.

And then, just as Gumby promised, Julio came to him.

Expressionless, cast in light. That boyish grin. A true loss. A greater loss. A deeper hole. Much deeper, by comparison. Every single day, firemen and cops and doctors saw the dying and let them pass. Nothing to it. Nothing special. Cueball welcomed the numbness.

Gumby smiled, unveiling the vampiric tooth as his hand smoothed the pallid, sweaty face of Cueball, comforting a child with a fever, his voice quiet now, soothing as a lullaby: *You did it, boy. You did it. My boy. You know what you've gained here, son? You know what you now possess? The multitude. The whole world's yours to lean on.*

Mickey surveyed the motel hallway before rapping twice on a door at the far end of the L-shaped building: Room 101.

From here he could see every car entering the parking lot. The pool was supposedly closed, but he spotted a towel draped over a recliner, a glass of ice tea nearby. Also, the front office was closed for the afternoon — and it was these types of inconsistencies that preyed on Mickey's paranoia.

When the room door opened, Mickey was immediately neck-cuffed and yanked inside.

"Hold up!" shouted Jim Barns. "He's a friendly!"

The arm relaxed and let loose, pushing Mickey into an armchair.

Mickey recognized the strangler as Corey Buffalo, from the camps. By the bathroom sat two boys with automatic weapons in their laps, eyes glazed over. Barns sat on the bed wearing nothing but boxers and a soiled T-shirt to save them all from embarrassment, a remote in one hand and daytime soaps on the TV. The slashes under his eyes and bisecting his chin were little more than pink threads now, but still distinctive. The room smelled of stale man funk and cigarettes. Buffalo moved back against the wall, snatching up a bag of Doritos.

"There's beer in the cooler," said Barns.

Mickey reached over and lifted the lid. Twisted the cap off a bottle and leaned back, not necessarily thirsty but wanting to make a good impression. He examined the two boys: shank-heads, no doubt, paid in dope to be their henchmen, as even Jim's own motorcycle club couldn't help him now.

"How's it hangin, Corey?" asked Mickey, showing no grudge for his manhandling.

The muscleman gripped his biceps. "We're sitting ducks."

It was odd seeing Buffalo among the present company. Vouched for by Del Ray, Buffalo kept mostly to himself, and Bird had nothing but praise for the guy. Whatever deal Corey struck with Barns must have been pretty big for him to undercut such relationships.

"How many weeks you been holed up here?" Mickey asked Barns.

"Who's counting?" said Barns. "Thanks for coming. I expected maybe a grenade through the window."

"Well I won't lie to you, Jim, they're gunning for you."

"You think I don't know that?" said Jim, tracing his knuckles with a finger, his cantankerous face fouled by hatred. "But what they don't know is that I'm coming for them too." Barns let his jaw hang in a silent chuckle as Mickey guessed at his meaning.

"Seizer's gone," said Mickey. "I don't know all the details."

Barns swung his frown to Buffalo. "Yeah, we figured it'd be sooner rather than later. Thanks for the heads-up. Any more good news?"

"Gumby's supposedly out there looking for the killer, but the truth is he stepped aside. Came into some money and disappeared. I stopped by his house to make sure—all the animals are missing."

"Ho-ly shit!" Barns yelped, frightening the boys from their trance. "That is good news! That'll make it easier for me to sneak up on the bastard some day and choke him to death."

"Only if you beat me to it," chimed Corey.

"Who they got coming after me?" asked Jim.

"I don't know."

"There's somebody."

"To be sure," said Mickey.

"Bird is in the wrong here," Jim countered. "I never went after that idiot son of his, but no one seems to care! And now Bird's the fucking boss!"

"You saying Seizer didn't order a hit on Cueball?"

"Shit, it wouldn't surprise me none. That boy deserved it, if what you said is true," said Jim. "That's plain good business. Seizer mighta paid off a few of them spaniards to go after him, who knows, but it wasn't me. But you *know* if them nephews jacked a haul, Bird would have 'em face down sucking swampwater, no questions asked. Tell me I aint right!"

"You're not wrong," said Mickey. "But you *were* down south."

"Mick, shit, I never denied that. I got a lady friend lives in Homestead, right by Miami, rents out these Airstream trailers to fishermen. I even put in for the days off beforehand, ask Corey! I'm gone a week and I get this call from Bird, and he goes, *Jim, I know what you're up to.* I was like, *the fuck you talkin 'bout, partner?* He asked where I was, I said visiting a friend. He goes, *Where?* I say, 'Hell, man, that's *my* business.' Then he accuses me of being in Lauderdale—on Seizer's behalf, no less! Don't even mention what for, but says if I ever came home, they'd never find my bones. I got a house I aint been to since. Now, I didn't know if it's who—Bird or whoever—but somebody's playing me for a patsy. And if Seizer's out of the way . . . well, shit, I guess that answers my question."

"Sounds like it," Mickey confessed.

"He wants you to run," added Buffalo. "It makes you look guilty."

"I told Corey about it, and he saw the writing on the wall. Figured we'd get ours before everything went to shit."

Mickey's hands were beginning to shake a bit and Barns noticed. "You jonesin?" he asked, then turned to one of the boys. "Toss me a bag."

Before Mickey could deny anything, a gallon freezer bag hit him square in the chest. It took a moment to register that he was holding roughly a hundred thousand dollars' worth of pure shank.

"What's this?" he asked calmly, but he knew. Jim would often hook him up with an ounce or two from the camps—which was funny, because apart from Bird confiding in him and Del Ray about the supposed contract hit put out by Seizer, he'd also mentioned Barns was skimming product, which Mickey knew to be true. This bundle of treats, however, proved Jim now had his hands full-fisted in the bossman's cookie jar.

"No one's safe under Bird," Barns said. "He'd knife every one of us to save his own hide."

Mickey fingered a sharp corner of the plastic bag. "He's got an army, Jim."

"He aint got shit. That there's what buys an army."

A new pressure was building in Mickey's chest. A decision would have to be made before he left the room.

"This is the best offer you'll get," said Corey, donning his hat and pointing two fingers at the boys. "Lunch break's over."

The boys zipped their weapons in a duffel bag and followed Corey out, closing the door behind them.

"This aint no life for old-timers," said Barns, picking his teeth with a chewed fingernail. "Corey's got a whole bunch of them kids loyal to him. He's our golden ticket."

"And you trust him?"

"Hell yeah, we're buds. He's the one got them boys looking up to me. Decent sense of justice, bein in the war and all. Pissed off too. Lost out on some big payday with Seizer, apparently. He was hoping to make Enforcer, but Gumby raised hell over it. Anyhow, his son got that disease where the muscles get all flimsy and he can't swallow right, pretty expensive stuff. All he asked was that we keep Del Ray aboveground. I said, 'Hey, brother, my beef's with Bird and the vampire.' Unless you know something I don't . . ."

"No," said Mickey, glad to hear Del Ray was getting a reprieve. "If Bird finds out he'll string us up."

Barns nodded matter-of-factly. "So let's get ours and blow town. Here's the deal: we strike all three camps at once. Corey's boys will open the gates and we carry out every last bit we can muscle. We funnel the dope through your contacts and split the money three ways." He watched Mickey's hangdog face get more tired. "There's other jobs, Mick. Now I've known Bird for years, and that man couldn't keep a cleanup crew in work after a hurricane. He's no boss. There's something in him likes to hurt people. And he'll burn it all down if it suits him."

Mickey lifted the plastic bag and shook out a few small shards of dope, then zipped it back up and tossed it on the bed.

Barns, to his surprise, tossed it back.

"Signing bonus. We need you on our side, Mick. People trust you."

Mickey didn't have the words.

"I'm talking brotherhood!" said Barns, his pudgy face suddenly swelling with disdain. "The real kind, not this fly-by-night shit!"

Mickey cradled the bag to his stomach like a lost puppy. "Did you know I used to be a stagehand for Guns N' Roses?"

"No shit?" said Barns, scratching his balls. "You know I used to be a plumber?"

When Duke wasn't working, he was at Seizer's ranch, rummaging through his things.

Two weeks had passed without a word. Duke spent the first week tearing the place apart—ransacking drawers, unscrewing light fixtures, uncrumpling papers from the waste bin—searching for any clue that might explain his uncle's sudden disappearance. But there was nothing. The house looked clean and unlived in. A head of lettuce wilted in the crisper. Newspapers piled in a soggy teepee by the door.

Heaping upon himself a lowering nimbus of despair, Duke stayed drunk all weekend—which, for a nondrinker, kept Lisbon busy feeding him bowls of chicken noodle soup and Gatorade. Once he got that out of his system, he returned to the ranch, this time to pore through his uncle's journals.

Within Seizer's greenhouse was a large hardwood desk surrounded by towering, leafy plants. Hidden beneath a red maple bonsai was a small safe, and in that safe twenty blue journals—two decades' worth of his uncle's most intimate thoughts and plans. Duke pounded coffee and read through the journals until his eyes wavered, attempting to narrow down from a long list of potential enemies the one his uncle had failed to protect himself against. Come sundown, he'd lock up the journals, set the bonsai back in place, and trek the drainage canal to a bicycle he'd stashed in the woods.

Bird called several times. He felt Duke should be aware of a trip Seizer was scheduled to take. The club had recently connected with a certain south american diplomat in exile—a corrupt narco-affiliate hoping to offload a stockpile of pseudoephedrine, a drug-making compound rumored to be stolen from a notorious Juárez kingpin. *I know I can trust you*, said Bird, *but keep this under your hat. I don't like the smell of it.* The diplomat had originally negotiated a sale with a Nuevo Laredo cartel, but last month a sizable portion of that cartel's foot soldiers—a federation of local street gangs and mercenaries—were ambushed by a rival syndicate's paramilitary forces and slaughtered in a two-day war that mobilized federal troops and braced the city in a violent lockdown. Having lost his buyer, and short on time, the diplomat was forced to reach out internationally.

Seizer was set to travel to Monterrey, Mexico, and seal the deal, but when the time came to finalize plans, he vanished.

Bird's own investigation had come up short—no airline tickets, no ransom calls, no scrawled messages left in a mailbox. It was like the old man had simply upped and disappeared. *I'll tell you what I know, you tell me what you hear.* Bird had his men on the job, with Gumby at the fore, and would exhaust every resource.

The story was just specific enough to keep Duke from accusing everyone around him of collusion, insurrection, and murder. The cartel wars were all over the news, yes, and his uncle was indeed shopping around for more pseudo in bulk—old pipelines dry up—but never would Seizer travel outside the US without security detail, and never without sharing his plans with Duke.

For unbeknownst to most, Seizer kept strict counsel with his nephew regarding all aspects of the family business. When the time came, it was Duke to whom he'd bequeath his empire—the real estate and small businesses and, most importantly, his stake in the club. It was Duke who followed the flow of capital, studying weekly reports generated by Seizer's zealous record-keeping, and Duke who knew what shell companies were being used to launder funds, and Duke alone who understood Seizer's long game: *Our only real hope for the future is legitimization,* his uncle would say. *All criminal enterprises eventually get what's coming to them.*

And maybe that's what happened—he finally got what was coming to him.

But if so, Duke wanted a name.

So whenever he wasn't on the road, he returned to the greenhouse and read through his uncle's private notes. Seizer had made a slew of friends and enemies in his lifetime; if you ever crossed his radar, your name went in the journals. The sheer amount of information recorded was overwhelming, yet Duke took pains to categorize potential suspects under three likely principles of motivation—financial gain, reward of status, or revenge— chipping away like a diamond cutter set on extracting a perfect shape from what first arrived in raw, insinuative form.

Power relied on the extension of its threat. The journals stretched back decades. Who had his uncle underestimated?

This here's made-for-TV living, Seizer once said, and Duke believed it. Nothing seemed implausible when dealing with folks whose freakish realities were often exploited by daytime talk shows. *Rare is the soul who makes an honest living. You work for Mickey D's, you're supporting deforestation. You clerk up at Wal-Mart, you're ignoring the well-being of ten-year-old factory workers. From top to bottom, we're scavengers and parasites. You must do well by yourself before you can hope to benefit a family or community. To become a philanthropic Buffett, you gotta start as a money-grubbing Kennedy. So sell whatever form of hooch you can get your hands on, 'cause people will forever pay good money to help them forget themselves.*

But this wasn't brewing corn mash in a still: most shank ingredients were illegal and difficult to obtain. Any attempt to buy pseudoephedrine from a US manufacturer got you red-flagged by the Feds; even small-scale meth cookers had to sign forms at the pharmacy for their Sudafed. And distribution was just as dangerous, and not just because of the Law—trade was rife with competition.

Convinced they were next on some hit list, Duke hammered out two sturdy cots of plywood and he and Lisbon took to sleeping in the garage with camping lanterns. They ordered takeout, never from the same place twice. Duke stashed an AR-15 behind the washer and pissed from the back door step. Considered praying. Prayed. Cleaned his gun and installed floodlights. And on those days he wasn't driving, snuck back over to his uncle's to scour the journals.

Lisbon had begun making this weird nasal sound, a whine like a pup's whimper, his suffering dangerously transparent.

"You need to calm down," said Duke. "We can't stick out like sore thumbs." When Lisbon signed his own suspicions, Duke was straight with him: "Maybe, but we need proof."

On the road, Duke barely spoke, frustrating Eddy, who spent hours alone in the Nova only to be met with his friend's brooding dreariness and distance.

"Not hungry?" asked Eddy, noticing Duke's untouched burger.

They sat in a café in Charleston, South Carolina—a slight detour off the main drag following a successful run. Duke watched his brother balance an angled saltshaker on a few measly grains. Onstage a young woman dressed for Burning Man butchered an Ani DiFranco cover.

Eddy nodded her way. "Maybe afterwards we go say hi. She's cute, yeah? Get your mind on something else."

"My mind's where it should be."

"Just because I suck at helping doesn't mean I'll stop trying," said Eddy.

Duke closed his eyes. "You can't help with this."

Duke had always known his uncle to be a private man, yet the journals yielded something unexpected: the old bruiser had been writing a memoir. There were passages that read like brief history lessons, like how Bird had been arrested in Los Angeles in 1980 at the age of twenty-five, following a drug raid on a Tijuana-based outfit that served as Seizer's main narcotics supplier. Duke was surprised to learn Bird was just fourteen when Seizer found him pickpocketing hippies in San Francisco's Haight-Ashbury district, an underfed runaway. In the young upstart Seizer discovered a protégé, someone to help boost sales from his small-time marijuana farm in upstate Mendocino County, a front called Marble & Tile Industries.

The kid moved product like gospel, wrote Seizer. *After he took up with the bikers, that gospel spread.*

Marble & Tile soon branched out into coke and heroin after the Flower Power zeitgeist lost its brakes and crashed headlong into disco. When Seizer caught his workers snorting speed during breaks, amphetamines were added to their supply menu. To help Bird handle a growing list of responsibilities, Seizer hired on two other kids: an affable, long-haired Berkeley dropout familiar with weed strains and a quiet biker friend of Bird's who dressed in all black and smoothed out touchy situations with cutlery.

With Del Ray and Gumby on board, everything clicked. The start-up quickly evolved into a mid-level enterprise, selling product out of forty or so tienditas along the Pacific coast—between San Diego and Seattle—small-town grocers carrying a little something extra behind the counter for their customers. Seizer became a minor drug baron seemingly overnight.

Then one day the Law came a-knockin.

It was a low-key affair—a regular Saturday afternoon pickup in Venice Beach. Bird went into the butcher shop alone, sending his Wingman off for ice cream. One minute Bird was smoking a cigar, counting cash, the next he was face down on a cutting table, gritting his teeth.

The Feds were relentless, generating a sweeping net of litigation under the RICO Act. The racketeering charges were later dismissed, but the drug charges held up, so off to San Quentin for a decade went Seizer's main foot soldier, effectively leveling his enterprise. Marble & Tile Industries went bankrupt, with assets sold and proceeds swept into offshore accounts. Marijuana plants were set ablaze and harder drugs cut to a fraudulent impurity and muscled through the streets.

Not once during the backroom interrogations or court proceedings did Bird mention his boss, and in return for his fidelity, Seizer quickly eliminated the mexican informant granted asylum for his testimony.

It was the end of an era. Seizer quietly disappeared, while Del Ray returned to college and Gumby pivoted to mercenary, advertising dirty deeds done dirt cheap in the classified section of *Soldier of Fortune*.

Duke's name first appeared in an entry marked "Jan 1986," when Seizer received word his sister, Annabelle, was killed in a car crash, along with her boyfriend. He immediately returned home to Greensboro, North Carolina, and adopted her infant twins. For three years he took up residence in Annabelle's house, caring for his nephews, while living off earnings from two strip clubs and a brief foray into adult mags (*Love Jugs, Hog Honeys*). But Seizer was hounded by ambition, and yielded—leaving his nephews in the care of Dag Nasty, a good-humored neighbor and family friend who taught creative writing at UNCG. Seizer's notes argued another reason for his departure: kidnapping was far more common than folks realized, and he feared his nephews may become a weakness exploited by his enemies.

Back in California, with time served for good behavior, hell-on-wheels left prison and went legit. Reuniting with his old girlfriend Charlotte, Bird traded the arid heat of the West for the beaches and wetlands of the Space Coast. Soon after, the biker began receiving money orders in the mail, which he used to start a carpentry outfit, and later, a moving company.

Seizer moved about sporadically, settling on Chicago to begin his research into drug cartels and pharmaceuticals. His dream was the formulation of a perfect drug—inexpensive, addictive, class-fluid—something that would sell in both dance and country clubs.

The first inkling of a coherent plan arrived at the dentist's office, flipping through magazines: an article on the failing War on Drugs, chronicling the dangers of meth. Here Seizer learned how ephedrine was originally isolated from the *Ephedra sinica* plant in Japan in 1885, synthesized as amphetamine in Germany, and crystallized into meth around the end of World War I. From the 1930s and beyond, these formulations remained mainstays in the marketplace, sold largely as decongestants and pep pills. But it was the historical chart that caught his attention. An armchair economist, Seizer spotted something altogether lost on researchers: namely, that amphetamine consumption appeared to spike at the onset and decline of nearly every recession in the US over the past sixty years.

This was a revelation. Here was a cheap drug as market indicator. The pattern wasn't perfect, but it made sense, given how users, many of whom were poor, felt the pinch of a slowing economy well before Wall Street analysts did.

Seizer began reading everything about amphetamines he could get his hands on. He discovered that "crank"—a shitty meth fix once relegated to bikers—had rivaled coke as the preferred stimulant for sixties party people bored with hallucinogens. The abrupt drop-off of more traditional drugs was certainly influenced by new federal drug regulations, like Nixon's Controlled Substances Act, but meth's rise also anticipated the country's first recession in eight years. From the mid-1970s to early '80s, at the height of Marble & Tile's reign, speed reemerged on the scene like a heart arrhythmia, in rampant fits and starts, as rising oil prices, stagflation, and mass unemployment produced three recessions inside of a decade, sending the country into a financial panic. Yet demand for amphetamines dwindled in the prosperous mid-eighties, when an influx of prescription and designer drugs hit the marketplace—including crack, which was suddenly everywhere.

Crack was everything Seizer envisioned a superdrug could be. Cheap and addictive, it sparked a wildfire of media coverage and took the country by storm. The manufacturing process was giddily simple—add water and baking soda to cocaine and heat it up. Any two-bit distributor with mediocre contacts could make millions.

So what if he did the same with meth? Bought the raw materials, cooked it, cut it, and distributed it—then collected the money and laundered it? What kind of earnings could be had with such vertical integration?

Unfortunately, his DIY daydream was too prescient.

As another form of speed—Ritalin—enjoyed a resurgence alongside punk rock and white suburban malaise, an entrepreneurial family of mexican brothers in their twenties began importing hundreds of tons of indian and thai ephedrine into Mexico, which they used to create the world's first meth superlabs. Seemingly overnight, the Americas were flooded with cheap, high-grade product. It didn't matter if the US economy was booming or tanking—meth spread up the Pacific coastline like poison through a vein.

Beaten to the punch, his dreams on hold, the would-be czar returned to Carolina and nephews who couldn't have picked him out of a lineup.

The Twins were in third grade, living a comfortable life with Dag, and Seizer saw no reason to upset the balance by moving them in with him. But that didn't mean he'd remain hands-off. He became instrumental in their education, grand technician of their inner lives: scoutmaster, mentor, tutor, instructor of etiquette, godfather, and up through their early teens, warden, a firm believer in the belt.

Here Duke set down the notebook, off to brew another pot of coffee.

He'd run across Rutha Mae's name and needed a break.

Women came in and out of Seizer's life, but there was only one Rutha Mae. Late twenties, with short-cropped hair and a wide smile, Rutha was the only black grad student at the Quaker school studying criminal justice. She worked part-time at Tate Street Coffee, which served the best italian sodas in town, and Seizer would flirt with her at the counter, embarrassing the teens. Rutha was kind and fearless with her heart, which wed the Twins quickly to her side. For movie night she brought them gifts: a chess set, a bent nail puzzle, books of sudoku. And for a time, it seemed their uncle was truly happy, content to spend his days fixing and flipping old houses, nights with Rutha Mae and the boys.

Folks found ways to mention their differences in race and age, but the two seemed unbothered by this. When they kissed, it was always too damn much, like starved children let loose on a buffet.

Here was something Duke didn't know: it was Rutha Mae who'd introduced his uncle to molly. She liked to dance, liked to feel the rainbow lights wash over her body; he did not, but the popularity of the drug interested him. *I asked her, what's MDMA feel like, and she says, "Just try it, we'll melt into each other." Still I declined. Honestly I'm amazed I keep her interest.*

Rutha Mae Poteat passed away unexpectedly in a furniture store one bright Saturday afternoon. She was testing out mattresses, lying down on each to sense their relative firmness or plushness. When five minutes became ten, an employee went to wake her up, but she was already gone. Doctors said stroke, likely caused by sickle cell, and were adamant she felt nothing.

Duke had never seen a person suffer such anguish as befell his uncle. It was terrifying and persistent, as if his very being had been punctured by a pipe and left to drain.

Neither brother blamed him for leaving again. Dag Nasty, full of grief for his friend, agreed to continue his guardianship as the boys entered high school.

Seizer sank back into his life's work, a hermitage of death and capital, accompanied now by the ghost of a woman he loved, leaving little room for anything else. The millennium was fast approaching, and though stocks were on the rise, clinical reports on drug abuse indicated a meth market turning bullish.

Portland, Oregon, welcomed him. Here was a town invaded by meth—a junkie mecca. The youth camped outside his hotel begged for cigarettes and donuts, brazenly hitting their pipes. They turned Seizer on to some college students pressing pills in their garage—"ecstasy," they called it—MDMA mixed with caffeine, meth, and other substances, creating hybrids. Gone were the days of drug mules swallowing condoms—these kids were driving product right down the coast, just like old times, motorcycles replaced by an armada of Honda Civics.

The millennium flipped its page. The Towers fell. The dot-coms imploded. A waterfall of capital swept into gold and real estate. The country entered into a protracted war with Iraq, then Afghanistan. Seizer left Portland for the East Coast, and over the next three years haunted New York, Boston, Philadelphia. *Managing my criminal Rolodex*, he wrote. *Hope to one day meet the Sacklers.* He'd show up in Carolina for holidays, but the Twins never expected him to stay: this was a lost soul chasing his white whale.

Then in 2005 a report surfaced: an admissions study showing amphetamines had, for the first time ever, overtaken heroin as the preferred drug among addicts checking into Los Angeles rehab facilities. Oregon was already ahead of the curve, and this development began to trend east, state by state—a kind of reverse manifest destiny, with implications equally insidious.

I'm not sure what's causing the tremors, he wrote, *but the worms are twisting right out the ground.*

It occurred to Duke here, where the narrative portion of Seizer's autobiography abruptly ended, that his uncle had failed in these many pages to confront the ethics of feeding a deadly poison to other humans for personal gain. Turns out he was a paradox like the rest—a hardscrabble everyman forging his own path, but a deceptive opportunist as well.

The final journals covered the last five years—newspaper clippings, obits, vignettes of submerged truths. A conspiracy project of hermeneutic artistry—side notes to history, which are history's origins.

Platte land, Osceola County—Sep/Nov ARM foreclosures

Obetrol, magic of rebranding—Adderall, "A.D.D. for All"—lucrative child
  and young-adult market

Ezekiel 33:2–6, Nahum 1:9

Mick treatment options?

forgive, reconcile, move forward

Parsing the coded impressions of a man incapable of trivial speculation was exhausting, but Seizer had taught Duke the value of patience. Taught him the importance of black coffee and greenhouses full of light. Crumb-cakes and herb gardens. This is how a boss lives. They did a study once: a man's lifespan could be determined by which section of the newspaper he read first. Open to the business section, you're dead by seventy; open to the funnies, you'll outlive your peers but not your wife. Eat lots of fish, take daily walks. Don't jog, jogging's bad on the knees. Learn to interpret poker tells; bodies aren't good at lying. Find a hobby. Collect something only you consider valuable, like my sugar cubes. This one here? It was on JFK's breakfast plate the morning of the Bay of Pigs. Be demanding of your time, as nothing is more precious. Be aggressive with your heart and money, as both will fail you without warning. Invest heavily in group morale. The threat of violence is often more effective than violence itself. The more commonplace violence becomes, the more it's deemed acceptable among the lower ranks. Be the sheriff. Draw up the laws, define a code. People will look to you for how to act.

Every Sunday uncle and nephew met in the greenhouse, running through the weeklies, a large fan breezing nearby. Lisbon was never invited, learned to sleep in. If he was jealous, it went unmentioned.

His uncle's wry smile, ready for questions. Obviously proud. But tired too, aware of his limitations, grunting his throat clear as he ran his fingers through thinning white hair.

Duke remembered the day everything changed.

It was August, and Seizer was passing through Greensboro on his way to Knoxville, where he had chemists testing out various drug combinations and reductions—meth with cannabinoids, meth with ecstasy—maybe two weeks before they concocted the formula for shank. Duke and Lisbon had moved out of Dag's place and were renting a small apartment off-campus, Duke ready to begin his senior year at UNCG, while Lisbon built desktop computers to sell.

Duke was eating cornflakes at the breakfast counter, going over scenes for an acting class, and Lisbon half-asleep playing *Call of Duty* in his underwear when Seizer barged in wide-eyed and clutching pages, calling for Lisbon to bring over his laptop.

Following his uncle's orders, Lisbon searched YouTube for "Jim Cramer Bear Stearns Bernanke debt meltdown." Seizer grinning like someone with a winning lotto ticket in their back pocket, dropping the loose pages before Duke.

"What's this?"

"Treatment center admissions data, brand-new, year to date. Check the chart."

Duke scanned the pages as he ate. "Didn't you say these numbers peaked and dropped already? Why're they headed back up?"

"If what I just heard is true, these rates are gonna skyrocket."

They spent the rest of the morning watching videos of talking heads repeating the same phrases: *subprime loans, mortgage defaults.* Seizer was convinced his market indicator was flashing red, with dire days ahead.

It was time to get the band back together.

"What kind of people are they?" Duke inquired about his uncle's old California crew.

"Worldly and working class. Bikers."

"But they're not, like, giant racist douchebags, right?"

"There aint no other type of white," said Seizer. "We're out here sorting skill sets."

"Well I don't know what that means, exactly," said Duke, "but I guess I'm asking if they're okay people. I mean, I understand what we're doing—we're the tobacco company—but I can't work with folks I don't respect."

"You work with what you got," replied his uncle flatly. "I trust them and they trust each other. Seed the pot. Once the first shoots come in, we can branch out and diversify, build a proper garden."

The ephedrine hydrochloride would come from China, stockpiled in a climate-controlled warehouse in Orlando. The safrole oil, which led a saucy double life as an aromatic, came from Cambodia. They'd train-in the cannabinoids from Washington State and the coloring from a plant in Jersey. Florida would host his superlab—the East Coast his big slice of key lime pie. Everything done through partnerships. Once they grew large enough, they could drift into the western border country and corkscrew right up into the Heartland.

Duke dropped out of UNCG and Lisbon quit his job. Seizer traveled to Florida for clandestine meetings with Bird to hash out the details— *Reunions,* he wrote, *that started off as sparring matches and ended up as prayer meetings.* He searched for places to set up camp—unincorporated, centrally located hamlets with cheap wooded acreage and small police forces. The wrist tattoos were a concession to Bird, as Seizer didn't want their names out there but understood the need for symbolism. The Great Recession was fast approaching. When the time was right, he'd hire on Mickey, and send his disciples upon the land to preach the good word.

Duke's tears smeared the text into illegibility. All this preparation—and for what?

Stop feeling sorry for yourself. What does the boss do? The boss works. So get back to work.

Duke reviewed passages of former homework assignments. Seizer had him memorize the rival gangs: Nuestra Familia versus La eMe, Crips and Bloods, the Aryans and Black Guerrilla Family, the US Justice Department and La Cosa Nostra. A history of broken bonds and airport swaps, alley hits and off-road burials. Bandana colors and flashed hand signals. How it all started in Chicago, where Capone hired from all races. How Jeff Fort and Bull Hairston united smaller street gangs into Black P. Stone Nation, the first mega-gang. Or in New York, with Hell-Cat Maggie of the Dead Rabbits and Battle Annie of the Gopher Gang—when the time is right, get the women in on it too. Expand the borders; soon they won't be able to recognize us in our suits. Gangs with national charters have built-in hierarchies and self-police, with bodies on the street—why buy when you can rent? Seek out the computer savvy; information superhighway, second only to I-95. Do the gruntwork now, son, bust your ass. Find a hispanic girl to help with the language, get in with the laborers. Seek out the underprivileged, people who wanna work. A man must build out of himself, so cut back on the booze, stay in control. Be fierce when people least expect it, and forgiving when you can afford to be. Set up several safehouses in every state, and don't bother rehearsing your death—things never turn out as you imagine.

Duke scanned the ledger of new and former employees: bank clerks and veterans and short-order cooks in diners outside Baton Rouge, Des Moines, Salt Lake. Be careful picking insiders, less than one percent should know anything. Information is power, so we don't name the club; when you stay out of the language, you stay out of the greater consciousness. If journalists give you a name, you hire someone to hire someone to hire a group of kids to pull a similar crime in a nearby town. Spray-paint that name on a wall, then make an anonymous call—there's these kids in an abandoned warehouse kind of thing.

And listen close—you never by god ever walk into a situation without three escape routes: the sky, the land, the sea. What's above you and about you and below. Because you are guilty, God will take two of the three away. The last will be His benevolent gift of mercy.

This is what made Seizer the Seizer.

So why the fuck would such a wily professional of the highest order hop on an international flight with no assurances or backup, without even a whisper to his closest ally?

Because he hadn't planned to leave, that's why.

Because he was fucking dead.

K-I-S-S, his uncle would say. *Keep it simple, stupid. Who would benefit most from having me gone?*

Bird.

Duke went to the streets and found a dealer who sold him an untraceable pistol. Using a rotary blade, he cut a small square out from under the moving van's dashboard. Made it so you knocked hard, the base dropped out.

They were driving out again on Monday. He watched Lisbon mash handfuls of potato chips into his mouth, laughing at a TV screen the color of ice, and felt insanely protective. Seizer's heirs by contract were set to receive a ten percent stake in the club's future earnings—a sum that needn't be paid if they were dead.

In the darkness of his garage Duke drank milk straight from the jug as the water pump clicked on, hummed, clicked off. He reclined on the hard cot in silence. The moon was there, and soon the crickets started in. And beneath these sounds, that patterned human thump—the only reason for any of it.

Feign respect. Be vigilant.

The sky, the land, the sea.

PART IV

SEIZER REDUX

It was snowing in Florida.

Curled white flakes with black, pull-apart souls—they arrived with a warm, westerly wind to filter slowly into town like leaflets from a warplane. Daylight smudged the smoky horizon red as a bad erasure. At night, the periphery glowed. When flames from the massive brushfires caught an updraft, neighborhoods were suddenly inundated with the stuff— lilting, leached, luminous—ash.

Residents stood on their lawns hosing down rooftops, deciding whether or not to comply with the evacuation. News choppers buzzed alongside the military's overhead. The grassy farmland between Melbourne and Orlando burned quick as kindling. Television and the internet were great sources of chaos and misinformation, routinely substantiating and refuting the very same rumors.

So began a week of scorched earth following a mild drought. Traffic slowed on I-95 for the sudden emergence of frightened animals streaking across the highway in odd pairings like some lost flock from the Old Testament, including homeless folks caught camping out in the woods. Herons sailed out wings ablaze, trailed by turkey buzzards, who abhorred their dinners cooked but made do.

The fire departments of Brevard and Osceola counties, well-equipped to handle the annual summer wildfires, collaborated now to contain a different beast altogether. It appeared the conflagration had separate origins, and soon the news was reporting arson.

Under a white bedsheet, Colt watched the carnage on a muted black & white TV, while Del Ray sat knees-high in a nearby armchair, naked, reading from books stacked on the floor: Burnett's *Florida's Past*, Bely's *Petersburg*, Spinoza and Camus, a heap of brokenhearted poets. Occasionally he'd glance up to study the news. When his eyes met Colt's, she pouted.

"I don't know why you're reading. All you really want to do is crawl back on top of me."

Del Ray flipped a page. "Coffee break."

"Come get some sugar."

"I need some me-time, baby."

"What for?"

"Regime change tomorrow," said Del Ray, flipping a page. "Bird crowns himself the new high and mighty. Trying not to dwell on it."

Colt twisted upright. "They stopped looking for Seizer?"

Slapping the book shut, Del Ray bugged his eyes, meaning: *Not a moment's peace.*

"First of all, it's none of your goddamn business. Secondly, you're leaving for god-knows-where tonight with god-knows-who, which is none of *my* goddamn business, apparently, which doubly excludes you from this privileged information." Nodded.

"I just came to say goodbye for a while," said Colt.

"And we'll say goodbye a few more times before you leave, I'm sure."

Del checked the spine on another book and drew it up, but couldn't concentrate. Watched Colt unfurl her naked body in a languorous stretch.

"You use men," he said blankly.

For a moment the air was still between them.

"You've used me and I let you," he said. "I cherish even being a bother."

"Are you joking?" asked Colt, squinting.

"I've seen the real you, baby."

"You don't know a thing about me, jackass."

"No?" he asked, smiling. "Day one, that grungy little St Augustine pub. There you were, wiping down mugs, them two suits paying five bucks a guess at your birthday. Made three hundred bucks in ten minutes. Told myself: now here's a heart burglar of the highest order." He leaned forward. "What's the frenchy word for *charming*?"

"What?"

"*Charming*, or maybe *lovely*? 'You're so *lovely*.' Go on, I know you know it. Give it your best froggy whelp."

Colt puckered her mouth to keep from smiling. What was he getting at? This was 221B-Baker-Street kind of fun.

"*Charmant.*"

"There it is!" Del Ray laughed, wishing for a big cigar. "All tease and bated breath! I recall you using that word on some jerk-off, stingy with his tips. When I heard that, I knew I wanted you for myself. Not to control, but to bear witness to. I knew you'd break my heart, but I also knew I could get you back."

"You don't have shit back, Ray," Colt said, not contemptuously, letting the white sheet slip to reveal a breast. "What makes you so sure you had anything to begin with?"

"You're like a lure, all shiny deliciousness—then comes the tug. *Charmant.* Who uses a word like that and doesn't deal in heartache? Two weeks I sat in that corner booth, hell or high water, dreaming up ways to evade your tactics. Held my coffee close and watched your whole operation unfold. Another night, another poor dumb stud."

"Wow. Creepy. You're a creep."

"And you're a collector of damaged men."

"Hey now. I had a little girl back home to think about," Colt said, propped on an elbow. "But you use people too, don't you, professor? Turn lost boys into drug mules. Your own little Pinocchios."

Del Ray mushed his lips. "I'd say I help fashion opportunities for the economically disadvantaged."

"Admit it, this is some kind of social experiment for you. An anthropological study."

"Hell no, it's a job. Supply and demand."

"Not for the faint of heart. No children under this height."

"No pregnant women prone to motion sickness."

"Or women period," said Colt.

"Not my outfit to command."

"Just biker sluts, periodically."

"You're a dying breed, baby, goddamn," beamed Del Ray. "Eyes wide open. A rubber angel—get dropped into the muck and bounce right back up to heaven."

"If Bird becomes Seizer, do you become Bird?"

"I have no interest in any such job," said Del flatly.

"No?"

"Zero."

"But if you were boss, would you hire women?"

Del Ray enjoyed this display of high regard. "I'm all for meritocracy, sure."

"Got no bad thing to say against creed nor color. Yes sir, no sir, mama's little Eagle Scout. A blee-din heart. A Demo-crat."

"I deal Left, but share the concerns of the fiscally conservative."

"Tell us your thoughts on gay marriage, Congressman."

"We are but one race and love according to our natures. We are what we are and love who we love, and are who we love, and I can't imagine denying that for another person would make me a better one."

"It's a shame how you waste your tongue talking," Colt said. "Deja de hablar y muerde mis pezones."

"God, baby, let it out. Share your truth." Del Ray rose slowly from his chair and crawled through the air.

"Probablemente morirás buscando sombras," she said, her voice not raised. "Eso es lo que quieres, no? Con esos niños a tu lado? Y sin mí."

"Love it. Love . . . it. How those syllables flutter up in the air and have sex with each other."

"Come on, Ray, let's just fuck. Slowly, comfortably, until one of us falls asleep."

Now he was on top of her, sidling her legs apart, stroking himself long. But she trapped him in her thighs and flipped him over and nearly off the bed. The blood drained to his head as he lay upside down wheezing, pupils floating in the whites of his eyes.

"This is all I ever wanted," he groaned. "Just one woman I kinda get who kinda gets me too. You're my chapel. I kneel inside you. Tell me I'm your one and only."

"You talk and talk."

"Maybe it's our moral obligation to pass on this affair genetically."

"You mean like a kid? I'd kill it."

"Ho-ly shit."

The look on Colt's face made him quit laughing. "You want a child between us, outlaw?" she said. "Let me take Zippo for a while. Show her the countryside. Let her run free. You can keep an eye on Gin for me, make sure she doesn't fall in with the wrong crowd. Namely yours."

Del Ray swung his head up. "Woman, did you just ask a red-blooded american male if you could *take his dog?*"

"I know what kind of man you are," said Colt pointedly. "I can't say it's been all sunshine and orgasms, but I won't deny what we have. And maybe with this kind of . . . *appreciation* we share . . . it's fair to take on some mutual responsibility."

"Goodness, did you almost say *love?* 'Cause I thought I almost heard—"

"With trust comes responsibility. And with responsibility, sacrifice." Colt got a slow, teasing rhythm going with her hips. When he tried touching her face, she batted him away. "You watch my child, I watch yours." Then, emphatically: "I don't want your boys anywhere near Gin."

Colt never told anyone what happened with Eddy that night at Snake Lake. Like so many secrets, her experiences were hers to deal with how she saw fit.

"I'm losing focus here," said Del Ray.

"Promise me."

"I can't watch them all the time."

Colt slid down his legs and crouched low, lifting his testicles to her palm. When he raised himself up to look, she pointed his cock at his face, squinting one eye like sighting a gun.

"Promise."

Del Ray threw his hands high. "Yes, ma'am!" he laughed. "Done and done!"

When Del Ray woke, Colt was gone.

He was briefly happy until he realized he wasn't. Walking onto the porch, he whistled for Zippo, knowing full well she was gone too. What were relationships without trust? Didn't he preach that to the boys? Lifelong bonds forever?

He showered hot and terrified himself with scenarios involving Colt splayed beneath the sweaty, hairy torsos of faceless men. To clear his mind, he fried up a grilled cheese and tomato sandwich and plopped down before the new TV in his living room. He considered color TVs a waste of space, not even furniture, whereas black & whites were antiques of some value. But cable news was a luxury a man of his position could no longer do without, and besides, you could hang them from the wall now.

The brushfires continued to spread, but Del Ray wasn't overly concerned—if any of the three shank labs were in harm's way, he'd of heard about it. Driving up I-95 the previous day, headed to IHOP for pancakes, he'd spotted the first blotches of smoke in the distance and phoned Corey Buffalo, who assured him the blaze was miles from any camp, though he was prepared to evacuate them, if necessary. Del's second call to a camp guard confirmed what Corey said, so he let it go—this was why you had employees.

Overnight, though, large stretches of farmland and savanna had been leveled with all the rage of a dead man's vengeance, the flames aggressively leaping roads and canals. Whether the work of a single arsonist or by concerted effort, the fire marshal couldn't say, only that the fires began at separate sites and were joined by a flare-up of winds.

Del Ray ate and watched as a vibrating red blob besieged Osceola County west of them. Central Brevard swam in an ocean of orange juice as the beaches and barrier islands pulsed under an eerie green miasma, air quality dropping across the board. He toyed with calling Gin to find out who Colt was leaving with, but that seemed childish. He should be content: he had nothing to give but himself, and still she returned.

The news cut away to an anchorman staring blank-faced above the camera. A breaking announcement—they were going live.

A set of images flashed on-screen: a school bus ripped open like a Boston cream; a long dirt road where slash pine met wetlands; pieces of camouflage tenting flapping in the wind. The correspondent lunged at the camera, unable to contain his excitement.

Del Ray fluttered off the couch as if electrified, rushing to his bedroom. Hidden behind a pinup of Jane Russell was a strongbox housed in the drywall. He spun the dial and opened the vault door, withdrawing a series of foldable maps stamped with multicolored flags marking drop-off sites and storage facilities, including the three production labs located between June Park and Holopaw.

The chucklehead on TV didn't know it, but he was standing smack-dab in the middle of Camp Crawdad, just north of Lake Washington. Del Ray recognized the exploded bus as the sleeping quarters for camp workers, last seen when giving Corey Buffalo a guided tour.

If the fire marshall was correct in his assessment of the second inception spot, then the club's smallest lab, Camp Heron, resting deep in the St Cloud pinewoods, was likely gone as well.

Someone's got our number, thought Del Ray, sweating through the paper.

Luckily no fires were being reported south of Highway 192, where their third and largest lab, Camp Sticks, remained hidden on an island where the St Johns fed into Lake Hell 'n Blazes. Were the flames to spread into the basin ten miles south, the club's whole manufacturing operation could be lost to the tempest.

Game over.

Del Ray phoned Bird—straight to voicemail. Cursing, he rang Corey Buffalo again—voicemail. Was he being set up? What the fuck was happening? His stomach plumbed the vacant air of a downward drifting fear. All kinds of dope was already lost, surely. He texted a few camp guards, typing in dog-whistle messages that signaled shit had hit the fan and call me, pronto. He worried about workers (survivors?) getting leaned on by the cops. Normally this concern might be shared with Gumby, but Gumby was not currently available.

Fuck it—grabbed a hand spade, pulled on some galoshes, and set off into his garden naked. He might need some payoff money, and kept a few bricks of large bills buried in plastic under the cantaloupe.

•   •   •

A couple hours later, Del Ray watched an alligator cross the road as his motorcycle puttered in the heat. The gator raised its head, jaw unhinging. Del Ray lifted a boot of polished green scales to show him who was boss, then circled around. The air was a caustic cloud of fuel vapors and woodland smoke, smelling like autumn had won the war on seasons.

Before venturing westward, he had tried sneaking a glimpse of Camp Crawdad, but Harlock Road was blocked by cops directing traffic. Water patrol units fought news crews for access to the fire-engulfed woods surrounding Lake Washington, so Del Ray turned around. Nothing but emberous ruins and federal agents in that direction, no doubt, so he headed back to Highway 192 and the other camps.

Two city workers manning the orange plastic barriers cordoning off the highway watched Del Ray pull along the shoulder. As they approached, he saluted them with two fingers, each wrapped in a C-note.

The vacant road to Orlando was barren and unrepentantly hot. Blackened pines were bent like radiator pipes, palmettos curled like the claws of hellions half-escaped from the underworld. Del Ray dug into the RPMs, picking up speed, thinking, *This might be your last day as a free man.*

On the charred and smoky trail leading to Camp Heron, he spotted fresh treads in the mud pits—whoever it was, they were using ATVs.

The camp was abandoned. Torched and ransacked—charred masks and melted rubber smocks strewn about the premises, a discarded bloody shirt. Del Ray wasn't too excited to inform Bird that they'd lost two camps—*at least*—in what appeared to be a slash & burn takedown. Perhaps it was Alex and his Toros, payback for the Mission hit, or remnants of Kid Kaos' group of reprobates hiding out in Kissimmee, continuing the score. Or hell, maybe even a pack of disgruntled on-site workers, seizing a genuine opportunity.

Heading back east, Del swerved before a short bridge, bumping down a sandy driveway.

The modest bait shop was situated along the banks of the St Johns, and the owner and caretaker, an elderly curmudgeon fit with black rat eyes, surveilled him suspiciously from his chair on a floating wood dock, surrounded by airboats. Del Ray parked his bike and skipped downslope to greet him.

"Hey there! Hey! You got an airboat I can use?"

The old man scowled, yanking a thumb hindward. "What the shit you think that is?"

Del Ray sucked his lip, snatching off his sunglasses. "I can see the boat, goddammit. I'm asking if it's ready to go."

"Yeah, she's ready."

"Good. You recognize me?"

"Maybe. Who you supposed to be?"

Holed up in his backwater shack, the surly old grump was prone to confusion. Yet he remained the initial roadside warning system for the club's biggest asset, Camp Sticks, which Del Ray made a mental note to fix.

Del wanted speed behind him but airboats made an unmistakable racket, and who knew what awaited him on the river. Spotting a dumpy metal canoe, he dragged it onto the airboat's deck, which made the old gent regard him funny. Fishing poles and tackle lay in the canoe's hull— a ready-made alibi.

Del Ray handed the old man three large bills and jotted down a phone number.

"You think they's a mole at camp?" asked the old-timer.

"Now why would you say that?"

"You look like a feller don't know whose side he's on."

Del Ray gestured at the smoky hour on the horizon. "Same man whose junk set fire to that sky. Pater pongo."

"Nobody I hears set them fires, least not on purpose," the old man said. "When they come back 'round, they says it was some sorta chem'cal accident."

"Who said? How long ago?"

"'Bout a few hours 'fore dawn. Jim and three them boys, with surg'cal masks strapped to their jaws. That's Barns' truck back there, with them four-wheelers," pointing to an overhang behind the bait shop. "Carryin gas jugs and garbage bags. Took some boats out."

"Barns aint allowed back there no more, you old frapping coot!"

"They told me he got hired back on! Been up here a week now, goin back and forth. I figured it was fine, since it was the regulars with him. Heck, I don't ask questions."

"Apparently!" Del Ray chided. He glanced toward the elevated bridge, seeing no cars. "You got a weapon up yonder?"

"Got a Magnum strapped under the billiards, and a two-barrel under the bar."

Del weighed the risks. Getting caught with a gun meant violating the state's Three-Strikes Law, and he already had two felonies in his pocket. But not having one might find him floating face down in a patch of swamp lilies.

"Rent me that shotgun," said Del Ray. He could always sink the weapon. "Hell, bring 'em both out."

The old man reluctantly obliged, returning with a sawed-off shotgun wrapped in doormats and the Magnum in a freezer bag.

Del Ray spent a few minutes disemboweling randomly the metal and rubber innards of Jim Barns' truck and puncturing the tires of the ATVs. With Seizer missing in action—did Jim know he was dead?—and Bird preoccupied with picking up the slack, Barns had pounced. Setting fire to the camps made sense, if only to implicate a certain disappeared landowner and his associates in the dealings of an organized drug cartel. But Barns wasn't necessarily a big thinker, so it was doubtful he was acting alone.

"Well, old man, I'd get back inside and call it a day. If you hear sirens, hit the buzzer and fake a nap. Oh, and another thing—if I don't return in two hours, you call that number and say so."

The elder squared up, spit out some chew, and hobbled back toward the bait shop.

Del Ray boarded the airboat and untied it from the dock, drifting out upon the tar-black waters. He would switch to the canoe a few miles from camp. Climbing atop the high driver's seat, he grabbed the rudder stick as the huge fan behind him cranked over and spun.

Seconds later he was whipping across a world of sawgrass.

The vegetative headwaters of the St Johns River were labyrinthine and largely uninhabited—a prime location for a superlab. Del Ray was the one who nicknamed it Camp Styx, which felt appropriate no matter how you spelled it. When scouting the area, the only evidence of human activity he'd encountered was a sunken houseboat and the stilted ruins of an abandoned homestead. Swamp living was hard going: apart from having to motor in for groceries, the waters inspired (or invited) a particular brand of madness, a belligerent isolationism. This was true to brand, the region being a proving ground historically for toothy creatures stalking each other into extinction—trod upon by mastodons and sabertooths and three-toed galloping horses; traversed by whales the size of bingo halls; and further back, beforetime Ur-vamps gorging themselves on the blood of unthinkable game. As the creatures appeared in Del Ray's mind, a pair of gold-flaked, prehistoric eyes watched him coolly before whisking back into the depths.

Del blamed dehydration and booze for the legends bandied about in local bars and fishing camps—tall tales of miniature beings escaped from a traveling circus a century before, whose incestuous progeny now sailed the river on rafts of lashed sugarcane. There was talk of a monstrous spawn of cracker and cow, whose bloodcurdling moohowls stalked nightboats along the foggy riverbanks. Or the vengeful spirits of massacred seminoles who wrestled young toughs in wagers for their souls. One fella even claimed to have spotted the ghost of William Bartram himself, out in a canoe with a tiny sail, collecting new specimens for his sketchbooks.

Some argue superstition is the bane of progress, our repellent ignorance made manifest, but Del Ray disagreed—it was human to create what we feared, from gods to bombs, and where would we be if we let those fears atrophy, dropping our defenses? Doubtful safer. Probably dead. Certainly dull.

And what was Del Ray's own contribution to the river's colorful crypto-zoology and returning dead?

Shank zombies.

Sent jittering in cruel, fixed focus were the fiendish camp workers, raised to labor thoughtlessly in a graveyard of blue drums filled with toxic waste—family men reduced to toadies, hooked on the product they produced. The chemists were mad-eyed goons in bug-eyed respirators, and the border guards sunglassed, expressionless minions clutching machine guns like guitars, This Machine Kutz Fuzz, with orders to shoot first and ask no questions. Which floated another possibility for the week's developments: maybe this wasn't a hit job. Maybe Barns cut a deal with the Feds, and these fires were the trailing breadcrumbs of a massive sting operation gone awry.

A couple miles out from Camp Sticks, Del Ray swerved into a watery alley carved from tall, stalky grasses. He killed the engine and dropped the cinder-block anchor, slipping the canoe carefully into the dark waters.

At the oars, Del navigated a maze of narrow channels. He watched moccasins glide by in parenthetic pairs as the summer heat fell in waves, drenching him in sweat. Soon the pathway opened upon the wide tongue of the lake, and for a short distance he rowed nervously in plain sight of any speedboat watchmen.

The distant whirr of a helicopter forced him to pick up the pace, thrashing swiftly toward the island, an arched passageway hacked from leafy overgrowth—wide enough for a pontoon, tall enough for an airboat. As the oars scraped the muscular shallows, Del hopped out and tugged the canoe ashore.

The island was densely wooded—witch hazel, willow, poisonwood—assailed by any wasping cinders from the sky, the whole of it would burn. Del Ray hid the shotgun behind a tree and hiked the Magnum down the rear of his pants. Entering the woods, he became the pupil in an ocular swarm of insects, swatting vainly at the hoards, as the sudden reek of cat piss struck him and voices filled the air.

Approaching cautiously, he found the camp fenced in by thick brush and concertina wire. Beyond the scrim, bare-chested men in jeans sat packaging dope on picnic tables. Others wearing smocks and gloves moved containers of hydroiodic acid into a cordoned-off structure, where two large brewing tanks were slightly visible behind an entrance of plastic slats. Del Ray dropped down and elbowed his way along a sandy path, heading for the enclave's far side.

There he spotted the body of Jim Barns—strung upside down to reveal a catfish belt buckle and large gut frowning at the navel. Half of him was a bloody mess. A leather jacket covered his face as he twisted in the wind.

Suddenly from behind him came a rushing through the undergrowth. Del Ray flipped over, knowing it was no deer, and whatever happened next, he deserved.

"Del?"

"It's me, Lord!" he choked, his final thoughts fluttering up like butterflies. He'd crossed over the waters of the damned to fall upon the elysian shores, untouched henceforth by sorrow, only to discover these butterflies were not messengers of hope but spirit guides in drag sent forth to usher his sorry ass off to Hades.

A thatched roof lifted gently in the breeze, floating occasional sun over Cueball's face. A handgun rested on the picnic table before him.

Del Ray mopped up the vegetable soup with white bread, his spoon clicking the bowl's side in approval.

"My compliments to the chef."

"He's gone," said Cueball, eyes vaguely inhabited, picking nervously at the gauze bandage on his wrist.

"I have a question," said Del Ray, wiping his mouth. "Are you *for real* back?"

"I got no choice."

"Aww, bullshit," said Del Ray. "You sitting here means you made a choice."

Cueball slumped inward. "Sometimes I think maybe I'm just unlucky. But then I remember them babies born with their hearts on the outside—"

"Jesus. Point taken." Del Ray caught the ladle in the black pot before him. The smell of stewed vegetables occasionally out-perfumed the camp's repugnant odor and he was glad for it. "I was informed you was in secret hiding."

"I aint hiding from no one."

"I just meant not showing your face."

"I'll show it to whoever wants to look."

Del Ray's expression darkened, taking stock of the young man before him. It was like Cueball had been put on earth for one purpose, to learn humility through suffering. Which was tiring to watch. It wasn't that Cueball never gave up—he did, constantly—but the world just wouldn't stop torturing him.

Del pointed his spoon at a clutch of barrels. "Were you present when that happened?"

Cueball shook his head gravely. "No."

Before sitting down to eat, Del Ray had spent five minutes looming over the emaciated body of Mickey, coiled unnaturally inside a blue barrel. He'd been shot through the chest and likely drowned, Del wasn't sure which first. They'd poured acid over his face and fingertips, ripped out some teeth, and tried burning off his gargoyle tattoo, failing in disgusting fashion. For the first time in a long while, Del Ray broke down. Even if he was a treasonous sonofabitch, a sarcastic shithead and an addict, Mickey had been his friend. All the dude ever wanted was to be part of something larger, a brotherhood, and earn his share. But when the time came to choose sides, he betrayed his keepers. Unfortunately for Mick, his fellow turncoats had different plans, Sherman-style, which no longer required his support.

Del Ray understood now why Buffalo wasn't returning his calls—this was a coup.

He cleared the lump in his throat. "I can't believe that fat fuck thought he could get away with this," he said, glancing at the swinging body of Jim Barns. "I don't know how to fix this, and I'm the goddamn Fixer! Why am I so surprised? Give these bastards an inch and they'd slit all our throats."

Cueball had more to tell: apparently Jim showed up to Camp Crawdad with some young guards, unannounced, while Buffalo was busy elsewhere. Sensing something amiss, the workers rebelled by locking themselves in the school bus with garbage bags full of cooked shank. Barns ordered them out, and when they didn't listen, he torched the bus.

"He set fire to people," said Cueball. "Actual people."

"How do you know this?"

"Ricky," said Cueball, nodding at the sprawled body of a boy manacled by the wrists to a boat trailer; somehow Del Ray had missed this body amid the other horrors. "We used to steal car parts together, but I guess he got himself hired on as a guard? Anyway, this morning he called me up asking if I could help him move some stuff. I had no idea. We showed up and found these fucking ghouls here mixing a batch up for themselves . . . but I don't think they know what they're doing. Ricky was wanting to steal whatever they'd made." Here Cueball paused. "When I saw Mickey, I lost it."

"You put the beatdown on your buddy?"

Cueball glanced back. "He'll be okay."

Del Ray chewed his soup luxuriously. "So Jim convinces Mick and Buffalo and some guards like Ricky here to haul away the finished product . . . but then Jim double-crosses everyone and sets fire to the camps . . . and leaves the equipment?"

"This was just a payday. Nobody wants to run a camp. They know Seizer's dead, or think he is."

"I wouldn't go making any big assumptions based on the word of some kid," said Del Ray, but backtracked: "He say anything else?"

"Apparently Mickey got in Jim's face about him burning those people. So Jim shot him."

A spasm of grief wrenched Del Ray. "Your boy say where they're hiding the stash now?"

"No, but it's probably already gone. They've been hauling junk out for a week now. I tried texting Dad but reception's shit. I think Jim came back today to tie up loose ends, maybe steal whatever else these fools cooked up. He brought a gas can and a blowtorch. And this gun."

"Where's Buffalo?"

Cueball shrugged.

Del Ray watched the workers go about their business, unhurried. "And you took care of Barns all by yourself? Li'l ol' you? And nobody put up a fuss?"

Cueball allowed a smirk. "Once I shot Jim in the leg, everyone kinda stopped moving."

"Then what?"

"Then they started moving again."

"My god, son, where'd you get the balls?" howled Del Ray. "I might wanna upgrade. Well, shit, this aint so bad. I mean it's bad, but. Lots of equipment left. Plenty of ingredients, looks like. And between you and me, we got an air-conditioned warehouse full of reserves. We'll be limping for a bit, but it aint a head shot. Plus now we got ourselves a patsy for Seizer. Just gotta deal with the Twins."

Cueball's eyes narrowed. "What do you mean, *deal with?*"

"Help them understand Jim Barns murdered their uncle," said Del nonchalantly, wiping his mouth, "and plotted this here uprising."

Cueball tilted back, as if judging the authenticity of Del Ray's words. What happened to this boy? Del mused. Operating with new machinery, apparently. Something like a conscience must have gelled down in Lauderdale.

Around the camp men worked various duties: mixing solutions, filling up plastic baggies with rock scrapings, draining liquids into large brown bottles. Del's one request regarding the camps was to set up some environmental protections, hoping to keep the St Johns from becoming the next Indian River Lagoon, polluted to the point of widespread fish kill and algae blooms. Despite assurances, he'd heard workers had begun dumping barrels of waste into the river just to see if it would catch fire.

Lake Hell 'n Blazes, indeed.

Away from them, two men relaxing on barrels were lighting a glass pipe. Sufficiently high, one took up a shovel and began to beat the flat end against the flabby stomach of Jim Barns.

Which brought Jim back to life.

Barns yanked the shovel away and swung blindly at his attackers, nicking one's arm and barely missed decapitating the other.

"Holy pig shit!" yelped Del Ray, leaping up. "You let that motherfucker *live?*"

"W-what was I supposed to do?"

"What is your job exactly?" asked Del Ray, eyeing the handgun on the table. "I'm not quite sure I fully understand the current nature of your employment."

After seeing Barns wasn't going anywhere, Del returned to his seat, muttering to himself, and reached into the plastic for more white bread as the men chased circles around the dangling figure swiping at them at every turn.

"This is a crazy fucked-up world," said Cueball.

Del Ray shook his head, yessir, full of all kinds of weirdos, from tax lawyers to street preachers. To survive you got to prove a might bit crazier than most, and fashion out of pure bullshit and guts your own fighting stance, so when they threatened your livelihood or your ridiculous soul, you showed them the horror of blood.

But the truth was, Del Ray admired Cueball for his decision not to kill Jim, which wasn't a good sign for either of them.

Raising the bread, he paused. "Jesse was working pretty close with Mick. We don't believe—"

"Fuck no," said Cueball, adamant.

"Agreed. Let's not bother him with this mess. Where's he at, Michigan? We need his head in the game, out there collecting leads. But c'mon now, let's get. This place isn't safe."

"What about all this?" asked Cueball, looking around. "What about Jim?"

Del Ray slipped on his sunglasses. "Some things are best kept simple." As Del ambled toward the workers, Jim's pistol appeared in his hand. "Hear ye, hear ye, you undead sons of Caliban. Get lost or stay put, I don't give a flying fuck. Sprawl in the pit's much mire or grab all the shank your shaky hands can carry. But before anyone leaves," he said, raising the weapon, "I need a volunteer."

Back on the river, Del Ray spooned soup from a Styrofoam bowl between his legs as Cueball rowed them back toward the land of the living. Forgoing the unmistakably loud whirr of the airboat in favor of the silent canoe equipped with fishing rods, they were now just a man and his best friend's son out to hook a few bass.

Tender-footed dragonflies tiptoed the knotgrass, as the quick snap of a fish tail rang surface patterns from the stalks. It made Del smile.

"I truly do love this land," he said, keeping positive, which was his way. "What is *wilderness*, really, outside the human heart?" Waited a beat, as if the question wasn't rhetorical. "You cross that river from Georgia, you're freed of any sense of shared moral certitude. Forget your old life, this here's a different kind of promised land, populated with the fodder of Late Capitalism—from child thieves to condo colonizers to serial killers, male and female. A whole town full of carnies? We got that. Mermaids in a tank? Sure 'nuff. Visitors catch a whiff of orange blossom and something in them chimes atavistic. Humors and lusts. Infallible beast or fallible man, makes no difference, stars above don't care. This here's the real Eden. We make laws to define the parameters of safety—but safe for who? The pale and moneyed. Maybe people are starting to wake up to the fact the old contracts don't work for everyone. Hell, it don't matter. Whole state will be underwater soon enough. And we might even deserve it."

Cueball stopped rowing to stare at him. Del Ray spit over the side. "What's the problem?"

"What *the fuck* are you talking about?"

Del Ray raised an eyebrow, picking his teeth with a fish hook. "Is this not what fishermen do, speak their minds in open contemplation?"

"We're on a fucking canoe, Del!" said Cueball. "It's hot as balls! There's fucking mosquitoes . . . everywhere! We just left a fucking *drug camp*! Mickey and Jim are fucking *dead*! There's probably cops galore at the bait shop just waiting to arrest us, and here you are talking about . . . what? What're you saying? It's *supposed* to be this way?"

"Cool your jets, princess. If the cops *are* waiting for us, you can't be freaking out."

Cueball pressed his palms into his eyes. "This is all my fault."

"No sir," said Del Ray matter-of-factly. "This mess began in California.

Power, machismo, revenge—old grudges. Seizer thought a measly thirty grand in scattered payments would offset ten years in prison, and bullied your dad openly like a child. No, this was never gonna end well."

They ducked as the sound of a CL-215 Scooper plane ruptured the air overhead, pushing north with over a thousand gallons of water housed in its belly. Cueball bent forward to re-situate the shotgun under the doormats, mumbling.

"What's that?"

"People are dead because of us."

"Yessir, and fuck 'em," snapped Del. "You're alive because you acted to preserve what is rightfully yours to safeguard. Take off the blinders, son—this is what elevated competition looks like. You've grown overly accustomed to the apex predator's creature comforts, but the rest of the kingdom plays for keeps. Country's chock-full of needledicks blind to that simple truth, selling off freedoms to feel a teensy bit more safe. Everyone thinks they're a mastermind, but most of us are yahoos, yap dogs, and Iagos. It's pandemonium out here, with Nature at constant war with itself. Listen here: without violence, which befits an organism struggling daily to survive, you wouldn't have its opposite, which is the nurturing and adamant, instinctively loving tug of our progressive selves. It's a harmony, which is not a relaxed, ambivalent state of being but a constant clash between opposing forces. We war to know safety, and cherish any opportunity at love."

"You're insane," said Cueball. "You're like some screwed up . . . jack-in-the-box . . . philosopher. With a broken spring and fucked-up music."

"You get mad like your dad does," said Del Ray. "It's a tiresome quality."

"Well thanks, Dick Ray. Go fuck your mother."

If Cueball was any closer, he'd have been slapped. Instead, Del eased back into his patience. They still had another mile to go, and drowning the young man wasn't worth dreaming up an excuse.

Instead he said: "From an early age, kids are taught that there are those who take responsibility for their own actions, and those who hold the world responsible. But the truth is, we're all responsible—for everything. If there's no holy god or whatnot pulling strings, then we determine the codes we live by, and are held accountable to them. Life isn't inherently meaningful, or a metaphor—it just is. And bud, let me drop some Knowledge on you—you're neck deep in *just is*. You want some advice? Seek out harmony. Balance the good with the bad. Practice forgiveness, for yourself and others. Adapt."

"You talk a good game, Ray, but I caught you on your hands and knees in the dirt, calling out to a god you don't even believe in."

"You see?" said Del Ray, dipping his hand to show decline, then pivoting back up. "And now I'm filling up my belly with delicious shank-head soup, passing on generational wisdom."

Cueball cursed and shook his head. Del Ray set down his bowl and stared out across the water. "We need to lock this down. Word can't get out, or more of them will come out of the woodwork."

"More who?"

Del clucked. "You got any clue what we're making here, champ?"

"Drugs," said Cueball tiredly.

"Not just drugs. *The* drug. The drug big leaguers used to call 'pep pills.' Jolts for the narcoleptics. Fuel for great american novels. What Hitler pumped into his veins at the end of the Reich—Vitamultin-forte. The only thing missing from our cocktail is crushed up peasants' hearts and bull testicles. Amphetamines are everywhere, in different forms. We might've added some touchy-feely for the club kids, but this country was built on speed."

"You make it sound all honkey dorey."

Del Ray snickered at the misphrasing and wiped an eye. "Listen, I'm not saying it's good, I'm saying it's historical, maybe even evolutionary."

"And that's supposed to make me feel better?"

"No. It's supposed to help you understand what kind of power you have in your hands."

"Nobody wants to be fucking Hitler, man."

"Hitler, shit," said Del Ray. "Hitler was a psychopath. But know there will forever be a top dog, and people battling for position. Hell, even Hitler didn't want to be a Hitler . . . he wanted to be a Caesar."

"I don't want that, either."

"Whatever. Not everyone has such simple expectations from life as you do. You need to put more effort into understanding the complexity of this situation. You're not stupid, but you keep pretending you're still just a boy in the woods, and that's simply not the case."

This struck Cueball as possibly true, unfortunately. "What do you want from me, Del?"

"Grow up. Take this seriously. Find something crazy to believe in. Cover your ass, 'cause when you cover your ass, you cover mine."

"Okay then, Preach . . . what do you believe in?"

But Del Ray was done talking. He took his time separating the floating green peas from the other veggies with his spoon, dumping the peas into the river. Carrots fared well alone, but green peas were the worst kind of bad luck, especially if you didn't have red onions to counteract them.

el Ray sat alone in his truck with his feet propped on the dashboard, a Bud Light in one hand and his other swirling the dregs of a popcorn bag.

Every so often he liked to visit the drive-thru movie theater, the last of its kind in these parts. Only three cars and his truck sat parked before an enormous screen showing a double feature of *The African Queen* and *The Treasure of the Sierra Madre*.

Two phones rested on the dash: one belonged to Mickey, the other to Jim Barns.

Jim's phone suddenly buzzed and Del Ray swung his legs down and caught it.

Corey.

He stabbed the answer button. "Yello!"

There was a long pause.

Del Ray waited. "I'm listening."

The caller hung up. Del Ray sniffed and dropped the phone in the popcorn bag. That was the end of that.

Wishing to test his psychic abilities, he stared at Mickey's phone, which he had forced himself to retrieve, fishing around Mickey's rancid body in the waste barrel.

I fucking dare you, he thought.

The phone danced around and played a funny little tune, like a robot humming. This time when he answered, he said nothing.

"Mick?" asked Corey Buffalo.

The flash of emotion Del felt wasn't useful; this wasn't the time to allow himself the privilege of feeling.

"Hey, Corey."

Long pause.

"Let's talk."

Shorter pause. "Half is yours if you help me move it," said Buffalo.

Del Ray weighed his response. On-screen, Humphrey Bogart's gold-hungry Dobbs, having shot his friend, was washing his face in a dirty pool of water when a gang of mexican bandits wandered by. *Hey, don't I know you from someplace?* asked a bandit.

"That's a generous offer, but I'll have to decline," said Del Ray. He had no idea how much stolen shank Buffalo had with him, but moving it would be quite a hassle, and fairly easy to track. Completely out of his depth, this guy. He wondered if Corey was now contacting the very men he'd helped imprison as a bounty hunter.

"Here's my pitch," said Del Ray. "One question, real simple, and if you answer honestly, I'll personally make sure your son finds a good home at a private facility. People who can care for him, indefinitely."

Another long pause. "I appreciate the concern, Del, but I'm more than capable of taking care of my son."

"For now," said Del.

"What's your question?"

"Did Seizer hire you to go after Cueball."

"Why would that even matter at this point?"

"Guess it doesn't, really," said Del Ray. "Just curious."

"No."

"No?"

"But I would have done it," said Corey, "knowing what I know now. Backstabbing son of a bitch. Jim said he'd never even met Seizer, not once. Bird was his contact, and he flat-out sold Jim down the river."

"And then Jim turned on you," added Del Ray.

"The fear got to him," said Corey. "If Bird can drop a boss, everyone is expendable, right? We're all just currency. I know you, Del . . . this sloppy shit's gotta have you worried."

"Hmm," said Del Ray. "Well, I suspect you should be gettin on."

"You coming for me?"

"That falls outside my job description and jurisdiction."

"But someone is."

"Oh yeah," said Del Ray. "Someone definitely is."

The line went dead.

"Happy trails," Del Ray murmured in his cab, dropping Mickey's phone into the popcorn bag alongside Jim's.

That was that.

Sometimes the Fixer job meant fixing things before they broke; other times, cleaning up the shards. Del Ray flicked his tinny beer can, sussing what came next. Bird was convinced Seizer had sent someone after Cueball—or so he wanted everyone to think. This meant Del could insert himself as the voice of reason, or let it go, and simply fall in line. In either case, Corey was right, there were no assurances.

He tilted back, raising his boots to the dash. This was the best part of the film, where all the gold dust the men had worked so hard to mine was swept up and carried off by the wind.

Eddy washed the ink from his arms above the gloveline, gazing out the kitchen window at a birthday party across the street.

Balloons tied to a mailbox. Kids on skateboards pulling tricks on the driveway's slight embankment. Five years back, he might have been one of them.

Another intrusive thought: these parents out enjoying the warm weather, pushing strollers and spooning sherbet, were secret shank users. The whole idyllic picture was a mirage—each glossy life a lie, teetering on the brink.

Come on, quit the bullshit.

He slipped on a new pair of nitrile gloves and began breaking down the tattoo machine, dropping the disposable tube to the trash and the needles to a sharps container. He'd just finished Jesse's cover-up, a Royal palm, erasing the Sabal that had always defined the Armstrong Crew. Though each member was being promoted and reassigned, they'd continue to wear matching insignias.

Jesse was now the club's newest Fleabug, inheriting Mickey's position. Hopping from city to city, he was set to visit Chicago this weekend, he told Eddy, to meet with a new district boss—whom he called a "Head"—in a trip he insinuated could double sales. Eddy wasn't jealous, exactly, but it was clear Jesse had risen above the rest in Bird's esteem.

Even this house spoke to his prominent position—gifted from Jesse to his mother. Located in a South Patrick gated community near the Air Force base, it was a far cry from rough-and-tumble Palm Bay—at night, security guards roamed the neighborhood in golf carts. With his mother off visiting family in the Philippines, Jesse invited the Crew over for brisket and baseball, testing out his Big Green Egg smoker. Eddy was glad to see him, as these hang sessions had become less frequent.

Yet the day's biggest surprise was now hunched forward in a wicker chair, eyes glued to the TV, a crumpled bag of salt & vinegar chips in his lap.

Cueball hadn't completed a full sentence since arriving, and Jesse offered no explanation for his presence. When Jesse peeked up grinning from his laptop at the dining table, Eddy followed his raised eyebrows to Duke, who sat starkly erect and deranged-looking on the couch, staring a hole through Cueball's back.

"Why's it so quiet in here?" asked Eddy.

Cueball glanced around to find everyone staring at him.

"I didn't think anyone wanted me to talk."

Jesse snickered. "When'd you start caring what people think?"

"Sounds like you ran into someone who taught you to keep your trap shut," Duke said bitterly. "Or maybe you saw some shit that shook you up."

Cueball ignored him. "I just haven't hung out with anyone for a while, is all," he said, itching the stubble along his cheek, his eyes watery and dark. Eddy thought he might be high.

But Cueball was sober as a bouncer. Before Gumby left, he and Bird sat the young man down to iron out the details of his story, which should be kept mundane and inconsequential, but not so vague as to arouse suspicion. Nobody could know he was the club's "special jobs" guy, the Hitter. (The baseball sobriquet being Cueball's own idea, and just to show he was a good sport, his father allowed it.) Cueball practiced his backstory enough to have it memorized, but it wasn't every day you were forced to chill with brothers whose uncle you'd watched die in a bloody, frothy mess on a bathroom floor.

All eyes upon him, Cueball gave the room a once-over. Egg-white and sparsely decorated. A huge hibiscus lithograph hung above the couch, pursed like an enormous vulva.

"Nice place, man. I bet your mom really digs it."

"Yeah, she's stoked," said Jesse, trying not to itch his tattoo, lubed and gleaming. "Brand-new washer and dryer, dishwasher. There's some water damage in the bathroom, but hey, they knocked down the price and Mom doesn't have to live out in the sticks anymore."

It made Cueball miss his own place. The red octagonal homestead on its acre of ranchland now belonged to his father, who refused him residence until Cueball could repay, through hard work, some undisclosed amount he'd lost the club. He was currently shacking up in a Cocoa Beach motel infested with centipedes.

"Wasn't sure when we'd see you again," said Eddy.

"Where'd you go?" asked Duke.

"Hung around Cocoa," said Cueball. "Hiked up to Daytona. Met some kids who let me crash at their place for a while. Nothing special. Slept on the beach sometimes. Got a tan."

"Your friend Kaos shot up the Mission and these Toros dudes said you were there," said Duke. "We had to put new drivers on that job. They refused to work with anyone associated with you."

"I heard," said Cueball. "But you guys met Kaos—dude was a joke. I mean, we hung out in high school, whatever. He stole from us and got what he deserved. Good fucking riddance."

"So you weren't in Lauderdale?" asked Duke.

"I mean, I thought about it. But I had to get clean, and the only way I could do that was alone and cold turkey," Cueball said, testing out his lie. "You guys saw me, I was a mess. Like I lost some part of myself. Had a lot of pent-up anger. So I had to bail, figure out who I was again."

"Shit!" Duke clucked. "That from some self-help book? They got shrinks hanging around these beaches in Daytona?" Jesse laughed, but Duke ignored him. "I was expecting you to say you left 'cause your dad kicked the shit out of you."

Cueball gritted and bore down. Without knowing it, Duke had given him the edge he desperately needed. Guilt gave way to umbrage. Nobody knew what he'd gone through, how he suffered. He didn't owe anybody shit.

"Listen, I know you're going through your own stuff right now," said Cueball, turning to face Duke, "but don't you fucking talk to me like that. I'm not proud of what happened, but I'm trying here. Yeah, my dad tore into me. And yeah I was pissed. But he was just trying to knock some sense into me. And truthfully, if I'd had a little more help from you guys, I might not have been as fucked-up as I was for as long as I was."

Duke shifted in his seat. Cueball went back to watching baseball, his ears hot. After a pause, he glanced over at Jesse. "I was real sorry to hear about Mickey."

"We've been in lockdown since," said Jesse, rubbing his bare feet together. "What that bigot did to Mick was the worst kind of evil. They kept the casket closed."

"I can't even," Cueball spoke softly. "When they find Jim Barns, I hope they cut his nuts off."

"We're still not sure it was him," said Duke, pushing his cold stare around the room. "All we hear is what they want us to." Sweeping up his soda, Duke slid open the glass door to join his brother by the pool.

Cueball waited. "He been like that?"

"Wouldn't you be?" said Eddy.

"Yeah, I guess so."

"Seizer isn't coming back," said Jesse.

"How do you know?" asked Eddy.

Jesse shrugged. "Think about it, dude. Mission gets hit right when Barns goes AWOL, then Seizer goes missing. Mickey discovers Jim's plans and gets an acid bath. The camps get torched and Corey and the guards disappear with the goods? This has major planning written all over it. Seizer's definitely gone. And if he's not dead, with the Feds for sure searching property records on those labs, he's not showing his face anytime soon."

Eddy turned to the Twins, legs dangling in the water. "It's been hell for them."

Cueball frowned. "But hey, I hear you fellas are getting promoted, is that right?"

"Jesse's got like three already," Eddy ribbed. "Me and these two, we're waiting on specifics. In the meantime, I'm still a Wingman—that's what they call us speed demons now. Every day it's something new: new routes, new tats, titles. This operation's blowing up. Or maybe not, I don't know—the fires got everyone spooked. Del Ray called it a supply chain issue. We're down to running once a week. But how about you? Your dad got you scrubbing toilets or what?"

"If I'm lucky," grinned Cueball. "He has me collecting piddly sales from golf caddies and bartenders. Yeah, I'm a gofer. He's just busting my balls for a bit. He'll come around."

"I'm making a beer run," Jesse said, pocketing his keys and putting on his shoes. "Stella and Sessions good for you fools?"

"Fine," said Eddy.

"Oooh, you boys got fancy," said Cueball, animated now. "Grab me a sixer of Coors. You got someone to buy it?"

"I always drop the dotheads an extra tenner," said Jesse.

As the door shut, Cueball eeked his face. "Why you think asians always hate on each other like that?"

Eddy swept a chair over and positioned himself directly in front of Cueball. "Alright, motherfucker, where you been?"

"I told you."

"You didn't tell me nothin that wasn't horseshit."

"You pissed at me?" Cueball ventured. "'Cause I get the feeling."

"*Hell yeah*, asshole! You know how much trouble you caused? We thought you were dead! Or killed someone. And now you're just . . . back?"

"I owe you an explanation."

"Didn't call once. Phone disconnected."

"Dude, I got this ten times over already from Mom," pleaded Cueball. "Dad stopped paying for my plan, and they wouldn't let me start another one without a credit card."

Eddy contemplated his friend's words, noting his demeanor — it was in his nature to sniff out inconsistencies. The defensive posturing and excuses were in character, but Cueball was clearly acting, as if pretending to be the old Cueball, which was strange, because that would mean he was someone else now.

"Okay, yes, I should have called you," said Cueball. "I just had a lot of thinking to do and . . . aww fuck it, okay . . . I went into rehab."

Eddy paused. "Like actual rehab? Like a facility?"

"*Not so loud!*" whispered Cueball. "You can't say anything! I don't want people thinking I'm a fucking basket case."

"But you got help."

The third-base coach on TV ran the batter through his signs. "Yeah, I got help."

This seemed to relieve Eddy. "Since we're being honest . . . I spent a few weeks drying out, myself. Lucky Jess and these two were around, or I don't know what."

"Nothing to be ashamed of," said Cueball, perking up. "Man, I missed you, bro. I felt bad for not reaching out, then worse because I'd waited so long."

Eddy picked his lip. "I even went to the cops."

"What?"

"*Shhhhh*," whispered Eddy, glancing at the glass doors. "I *almost* did! Seizer told us you and Kaos hit the Mission. Thought about taking off myself, actually."

Cueball rubbed his chin. "Why didn't you?"

"What, take off? Where would I go?"

"Anywhere. You've got savings."

"Fifty thou don't mean what I thought it did, man. Besides, I used most of it to pay off the mortgage."

"On your *mother's* house?" asked Cueball, unbelieving.

"I live there."

"But it's *her* house. Do you have anything left?"

"I'll probably clear six figures with my promotion," said Eddy. "I understand what you're implying, but I'm taking responsibility for things. I'm making amends."

Cueball could punch holes in this argument, but stuck to his father's plan—Eddy's trust was his way back into the Crew's good graces.

"I guess you heard my mom left," Cueball sighed. "Gone to Tennessee, living with my aunt. I understand why. She's been through all this shit before, you know?"

Eddy nodded. "You hear Gin and I split up?"

"Somebody, maybe Del Ray told me," Cueball said. "But that was a while back, wasn't it?"

"Not so long ago," said Eddy.

Cueball's expression grew sympathetic. "I heard Dad bought you out of the tattoo business."

Eddy ran a hand through his hair. "Yeah, well. I wasn't exactly rolling in clients."

A few weeks earlier, Bird had commandeered the tattooing business and dissolved their partnership with a ten-grand buyout, claiming tattooing was a low-level position, but his real motive seemed to be free labor, as he immediately tasked Eddy with designing a series of specialized tats for a ghastly array of lowlifes Mickey had plucked like fungus from the naked underbelly of America during his tenure. As the club expanded, so did its factions, each requiring its own telltale insignia—animals, symbols, fruit—like the pineapple design Big Mike discovered among his portfolio, which tipped Eddy off that other such groups existed. More strangers were showing up at Bird's safehouse, which no longer felt safe, and from their banter Eddy learned about the Wildcats, the Boondockers, the Slumdogs—all drug runners like him. He felt exploited, but what was he going to say?

"Guess I have to return the Nova, huh?" said Eddy.

"A day didn't go by I didn't miss my baby!" Cueball beamed, happy for this unexpected gift from his father. "But you'll be getting a new ride, right? No way you're driving that old VW up and down the interstate!"

Eddy raised a pair of devil horns: "Mustang, Sally."

"Hells yeah! The new ones?" Cueball raised a middle knuckle, which Eddy bumped. "Shit, pretty soon you and me'll be back giving those pole dancers up in Charleston the two-pronged attack! God, I need to get some pussy. Look, feel—my balls about doubled in size," Cueball said, rising.

Eddy snorted, drawing his feet up to kick. "Settle down, you nasty fuck."

Cueball's chuckle died as he glanced out at the Twins. "Those two sure are torn up about their uncle."

"It's the not knowing part," said Eddy. He pointed at Cueball's gauzed wrist. "Jesse said you tried burning off your tat?"

Cueball jangled his arm.

"Why'd you do it?"

"The truth?" said Cueball. "I didn't feel like I deserved to wear it anymore. It's healed mostly. I think it'll be ready for your design in a few weeks."

"Must've hurt like hell," said Eddy.

"It wasn't a pleasant experience."

They called them "suicides" as kids—a mixture of Coke, Mr. Pibb, Fanta, Sprite, Hi-C, and Barq's Root Beer. A tart, punchy sugar rush that hit the heart like a backbeat on a personal soundtrack, and suddenly your day was all roundhouse kicks and rainbows.

Jesse watched three black teenagers entangle their arms pushing gigantic cups toward different spouts. They wore blue blazers with red ties, shorts with high white socks—prep school uniforms. Paying at the counter, each said, "Thanks, Mr. K," and dropped a penny in the extra-penny tray.

And why did this inconsequential scene frustrate him? *Envy* was the answer he found, though that wasn't exactly right. Whenever these feelings crept up, Jesse didn't let them pass, lest they resurface later as aggression, the stacking of a hundred daily microhurts.

The podcasts all said don't make excuses. Wherever you started out was an accident of birth, but the rest was up to you. What these white podcasters talking about money couldn't see, or refused to address, was how someone who looked like him might face a harder uphill battle. To account for the variance, Jesse doubled his efforts. When they said, "Don't be controlled by emotions," he became a man of secrets. When they said, "Build high-trust relationships with powerful people," he made himself indispensable.

Jesse sensed his time was coming, so he kept his head down and disappeared further into his work. He needed to be necessary to *everybody*.

Eddy once called him a Company Man—well, so be it.

This was the only store that carried craft beers within a fifteen-minute drive. It wasn't even microbrews, just a few non-domestics. The floor was grimy, with tiles coming up, despite the entire place, *sheesh, these people*, smelling like disinfectant. Jesse gripped the thin handle to the refrigerator. A heat was in his chest. He stared at his fist. If he yanked hard enough, the entire glass door—screws, hinges, everything—would come off in his hands, he was sure of it.

Instead, he reached for the sixers of Stella and Sessions, then hefted out a twelve-pack of Lone Star, because fuck Cueball's Coors, he was the one paying.

Ambling back, his eyes caught his prized belly swaying under a Hawaiian shirt, a bulge of casual indifference that both accentuated and obscured his social standing. He'd gotten his wish—he was now Bird's party boy recruiter, a wrangler of men, a known entity. People said he was funny as fuck. He had a crab dance. He flashed a Stallone impression when arm wrestling. Able to outdrink nearly anyone, he would stir up a crowd with free booze, then pull a particular fellow aside, someone he'd identified as potential company material. A jolly, intimidating bear with a big heart, he used whatever it took to reel in new Prospects.

No longer able to see his belt, this too made him one of them.

He *was* one of them, right?

Mickey made him feel that way, for sure—regarded. The last time he'd spoken with Mick was in Pittsburgh, at the Squirrel Hill Cafe, aka the Cage, a townie dive with a colorful history that still allowed smoking and threw down the best meatball sub west of Philly, or so Mick promised.

Jesse had copped a booth in back, ignoring the crowd. He'd come from a house party thrown by a dealer who networked with university kids, and was still a little stoned, tearing through a hot sub and nachos before noticing he'd missed three texts. He bummed a Marlboro Red off a cutie at the bar on his way out.

"Hey there, partner," came Mickey's voice in the phone. "I'm sorry about this, but I'm getting pulled out of town, so I can't meet up."

"No problemo, hustler," said Jesse. "Workin man works. I, uh, already ate anyhow, I couldn't wait."

"Listen, we need to have a conversation. You alone?"

"I am."

"Seizer's gone missing."

Jesse instinctively moved to the shadows, surveying the street. "What does that mean?"

"I can't go into it right now, but you need to stay put," said Mickey. "I'll find you some leads up in Ann Arbor or something, but you don't come back till you hear from me, you dig?"

"Roger that," Jesse said, realizing he'd cherry-boxed the cigarette. He didn't know which questions *not* to ask. "Is everyone else okay?"

"Yeah, we're hanging in there. But buddy, you gotta trust me on this: If Bird calls, not saying he will but if he does, and he wants you to come home, you gotta tell him you're on some big lead. Let me take the heat. Can you do that?"

"Mick, you need to tell me what's happening."

"I absolutely will, but I'm still figuring it out myself. Just stay put, keep doin whatcha doin, and I'll have answers for you soon enough," he said. Then, striking a different tone: "How was that hoagie? Was I lying?"

Inside the convenience store, a frail white woman had scattered her change on the counter, using two crooked fingers to sort dimes and nickels toward a pack of menthols.

I should offer to pay, Jesse thought. Looking around, he contemplated buying her the whole rack of cigarettes. *Happy birthday*. Then: *I could buy everything here. All the pretzels and Skittles and hot dogs and car oil and these weird little gummy hands. Most def.*

Instead, he leaned over the lotto scratch-offs spooled under the glass. He purchased hundreds of dollars' worth each week, and whatever he won, he transferred that same amount to Draco's commissary account at the work-camp prison in Milton. Draco caught fifteen years after forcing an old man to drive out to an ATM by gunpoint, a known pedophile whose lawn they used to mow as kids. Nobody knew why, but Draco only wanted forty dollars, and once he got it, took off running into the night.

The white lady finished her purchase and shifted away. The clerk watched patiently as Jesse set down the beer and dropped a C-note on the counter. They stared at each other.

"Do you have . . . ID?"

"Aw, c'mon dude."

"No ID, no alcoholic beverages."

"Kareem."

"You look very young, like a baby. A fat baby, and I could get in very serious trouble—"

"Fuck off," he gasped, not unkindly. Kareem had already called him out on the fake ID once and they'd had a laugh.

Kareem stared at his beer. "Lone Star, this is not a good one. I tell you a secret. Very serious, I look this up. This beer was invented by the Texas government under George W. Bush in order to keep illegal mexicans from producing babies. I tell you, it will make you sterile."

Jesse let the expression provoked by this absurdity hang there a moment. "I fucking hope so."

Kareem chortled.

Jesse purchased sixty dollars in lotto tickets and tipped an extra ten for Kareem, who thanked him. Before walking away, he dropped a quarter in the penny tray.

Kareem caught him at the door with a shout. "Wait no, you forgot, I forgot to remember, your mother, her Sanka!"

"She's got cabinets full of that stuff. Seriously, she keeps them in business."

"You wish for me to be poor," said Kareem. "Yes, I understand."

Jesse wore a smirk as he loaded the beers into the saddlebags of his Harley, the air thick with mist and drizzle.

Try as he might, he couldn't shake the discomfort he felt watching those kids in the fancy uniforms buying their sodas. They just didn't realize how good they had it.

But hell, couldn't the same be said about him? Wasn't he blind to their particular situations, also? Goddamn. They might be in prep school, but they were still black, and no amount of money erased that particular target.

Everything these days felt all knotted together, all the social bylaws and economic stuff and racial strife, the constant grievances, and once you started questioning exactly who you were to people, it made you want to give up. He was tired of the dance, hoping to be seen as one man, not a member of any group, responsible for his own actions. Maybe that was small-minded, but the world felt too big to try and rescue. Or care too deeply for. Opening up like that only got you hurt. He needed to look out for himself. And that meant proving he was singular, reliable—devoted to the task.

For example, Michigan a few weeks back.

Corey Buffalo had called him up out of nowhere, wanting to meet at some bar—the Tap Room in Ypsilanti, a blazing electric martini sign outside. Why Corey was in Michigan, who knew, but he had some urgent story to tell, saying it involved Mickey. Then asked if Jesse knew anyone who could move a lot of product fast.

Jesse arrived early, sitting near the lone window in back. Nursing his beer and admiring the fake ID he'd picked up in Detroit, he listened to a nervous korean woman onstage read poetry soft-spokenly from her phone.

What happened next happened fast. Had Jesse reached for another tater tot, he might have missed it.

A puttering sound caught his attention and Corey Buffalo was suddenly outside the window, backing his bike to the curb, when a black van appeared. The rear doors of the van swung open and a man carrying a short pipe leapt out and struck Corey once in the head from behind. Four other men appeared and helped lift the body into the cargo, then returned swiftly and, using two such pipes fed through the bike's frame, hoisted Corey's motorcycle up and into the back.

And then they were gone.

Jesse spun around, wiping his sweaty hands on his jeans. The anxious woman onstage stumbled over a verse and apologized, beginning the line over.

After the claps died down, he purchased one of her chapbooks, then tipped the mexican bartender a tenner on his way out. This was how Jesse spread the wealth, ten bucks at a time, to folks like himself who were forced to redouble their efforts.

Outside the bar that day, he redialed Bird's number, convinced he'd made the right decision by reporting Buffalo to his boss. If the product Corey wanted to move wasn't a side hustle, which itself would have put the club at risk, it meant he was stealing, and Jesse wanted no part of it. It pained him to think Mickey might be involved too, but in the end, Jesse was in charge of his own self—his own fate—and everyone else could kiss his ass.

The Runners and their Wingman narrowed down their lunch choices to three spots in Greensboro, North Carolina: a thai restaurant with all-you-can-eat spring rolls, an indian joint with a buffet, and a cramped, arty café rife with university students engrossed in the types of conversations fueled by caffeine and higher education.

Eddy cupped his hands to the window. "College towns weird me out."

After dropping off their dope package at a barbershop in High Point, near the world's largest chest of drawers, they parked the van at a Harris Teeter, hopped in Eddy's powder-blue Mustang, and headed straight for the university. The plan was to grab some grub near campus and wait for Dag Nasty to get off work before heading over to his place.

It had been over a year since the brothers last saw their guardian, the jovial old biker who'd raised them while Seizer was off rebuilding his empire, and Lisbon seemed in high spirits, readying himself for Dag's jibes and wise-assery. Even Duke, whose glum disposition of late tracked mud through every conversation, was upbeat and talkative. The closest Eddy got to feeling sentimental was reliving that first drop-off in North Wilkesboro, not two hours away, where an elderly lady stepped onto her farmhouse porch and scared the bejeezus out of him.

Buoyed by the magnolia-laden, redbrick charm of the campus, the Twins took Eddy on a brisk tour of UNCG, summoning a few wild memories, to which they added another: while passing a study circle of young women debating under a crape myrtle, Lisbon plopped down to join in. A white student with unwashed dreadlocks bonneted with twine cleared her throat loudly, catching Lisbon's attention, as did her sea-green eyes. When he failed to get the hint, she extended her middle finger. The others laughed. Lisbon flashed a big smile—then opened wide and unloosed his quivering worm tongue.

Everyone jumped. One shrieked. The woman with dreads didn't budge, struck dumb by this disruptive force in her world. She kept her eyes trained on Lisbon's mouth, which made him very uncomfortable. "Do that again," she ordered, but he would not, and stood up. But she too was rising, following him, telling him to wait up, she was sorry, and suddenly they were running.

The car that hit him was only doing 15 mph uphill, but it was enough to lift Lisbon over the hood. Someone screamed as he rolled off, bounced up, and in a moment of pure adrenaline, raised his fists to the air like a gymnast executing a practiced display.

"You're a goddamn nutjob," was Duke's assessment, blocking his plate of sweet basil chicken as his brother forked stolen bites with a sheepish grin. "I still think I'm gonna die before you, against all evidence."

"You were this close to banging a lesbian," commended Eddy.

"She wasn't a lesbian," said Duke. "Girls just look like that here."

"No shit?"

"We knew some lesbians growing up. Dag's friends. They all had short haircuts and smelled good. Those hippie chicks all smell like foul-ass patchouli and chase the dirty dick."

After lunch they hit up Tate Street Coffee. Duke ordered a round of lattes, introducing Eddy to stories of Rutha Mae, their uncle's girlfriend who'd passed away. "She'd sneak us raspberry tea and cookies during her shifts. She was the absolute best. Life really is the One-Shot Olympics."

Lisbon wiped his eyes, smiling. Despite feeling a bit out of sorts all morning, Eddy patted his shoulder.

"One day maybe I won't be so busy, I can actually try and meet a girl," Duke said. "I can always come back here, I guess. Finish my degree. I only got fourteen credits left. Town smells like a hamster cage sometimes, but I don't mind. You ever think about college?"

Watching two pasty kids trade pawns at a nearby table, Eddy overheard one wheeze through a sex joke about the shape of bishops. Across the way, two freshmen argued mid-century south african politics. Then there was this other guy, a bright sunflower pinned to his black overcoat, whose dead eyes scrutinized Eddy with grave interest.

"The fuck you staring at me for?" asked Eddy in hushed tones, but the philosopher merely shifted his gaze. "My god, no way. Not if it means hanging around these tampon-sniffing freakazoids."

"You angry?" asked Duke.

"Nah," said Eddy, unsure. He did feel something, irritation maybe. "Maybe the food was too spicy."

Lisbon lowered his mug and pointed out a group of young women passing before the front window in their country dresses, sunlight ghosting the image of their legs. At bars, Lisbon's shy intensity often read as creepy, his pad and pen met with paralysis. But he was a goofy, kindhearted soul who Eddy had watched coax a giggle from many a waitress.

"Yeah, I know why you like it here," teased Duke. "But I do feel like I'm missing out on some things."

"You're not missing out on shit," Eddy said.

Duke raised his coffee. "Well . . . a proper education."

"You think these people know more about life than you?" asked Eddy. "They learn facts. Most don't even learn that. I've partied with college kids and ask what they've learned in school and they say the same thing: *nada*. Got stoned and argued about what greek god could beat what superhero in a cage match, and who wants to listen to that shit all day?"

"All right, bud, you've got your opinions," said Duke. "But it's definitely necessary for certain jobs. Like chemists. You need schooling to be a chemist."

"Nope. There's chemistry books to read."

"Even if people read books for that reason, it's not like anyone would hire you without a degree. School tests your knowledge."

"Whatever. I know a few chemists," Eddy joked. "Back home we got tests too. It's real easy to tell who passed and who failed. In a place like this, you go it alone. Nobody's got your back."

Lisbon drew out the words *YOU WILL DIE ALONE*. Eddy understood before Lisbon got it all out, but waited. "I know that, you scary fuck. You will too. But you bet your ass I'll be right there beside you when you do."

Lisbon smiled.

Duke's phone rang. *Where you at? 'Nother hour, you think? Yeah. Eggs and bacon's good. Hells yeah. Get the saltiest pork they got. Just for a night. These boys haven't had home cookin in forever. Okay, then. See you soon.*

They browsed the punk/ska/reggae stacks in a funkily decorated record shop and hit the corner convenience store for some hard ciders before strolling the few blocks to Dag Nasty's house, a two-story prewar Victorian nestled among colonial revivals. According to Duke, the old bespectacled white-beard used to teach as an adjunct professor at the university before last year's layoffs, and fancied himself a guitar player.

Dag rode in on a Heritage Softail, his pitted shirt stale with dried sweat and shoes peppered with hacked bits of cartilage and muscle, having come from the meat-processing plant, with a stopover at the butcher. He wore a beard like Santa, but orange near the nostrils. Duke and Lisbon shied away from Dag's generous hugs and handed him a present of Florida swamp cabbage, old-fashioned, heart of palm hacked at with a machete until the strips peeled back like the stubborn brain of an onion.

"You look like a curious young man," Dag told Eddy for no reason he could discern, but his smile was infectious. "You eat turtle?"

Eddy chuckled. "No, sir."

"All I got is turtle. Won 'em in a poker game, hundreds of 'em. Got a house full of terrariums. No wait . . . they all got stolen, along with the porch snails, strangely. You like ostrich eggs?"

"I've never—"

"Got a bunch of those too. Thing is, sometimes they got a fetus inside, and how you can tell is, you spin the egg counterclockwise, and if it wobbles, there's a baby ostrich in it. And the babies, if you nurse one and feed it proper, you can train it to run *real* fast. Then you sell it to these egyptian fellas up in Roanoke for the big bucks. They race 'em up there."

Eddy glanced back to the Twins, who were gripping their mouths. Dag snorted a laugh, his spotted head bobbing. Then started in on an embarrassing story where he'd once brought home buffalo patties, but after a younger Duke learned what they were, vomited them up. Dag was the type of person who missed out on all the advantages of anger by sighing and getting a mop.

"Helluva chopper you got there," said Eddy, admiring a second bike in the garage.

"I put that together when I was twenty. My first wheels, yessir," Dag said, whipping the chrome pipes with a scarf that hung from his pocket. "Parts I found all over. Sank every dollar I had into it. I used to take these boys out, made them wear their helmets even though I didn't. I was young, stupid, saw it as an infringement upon my rights. Doesn't make me much of a role model, you think?"

"You old scag," said Duke. "Don't make it sound like you was some badass."

"I'll get mean on you, you little snot!" chuckled the old man, bobbing.

Dag invited them inside, punting Lisbon's rear along the way, then shrugged off his shoes and puttered barefoot into the kitchen to start coffee.

Back on the couch, he pulled out a photo album as Duke rolled his eyes. "I know, but some of us get old," said Dag. "Blah blah blah. Not everything was good, per se, but I like to enjoy the times that were."

Dag passed around a picture of Duke and Lisbon at thirteen. Pig-nosed doppelgängers scowling under bowl cuts. Too-big clothes. A mountain river rushing alongside a trail to one side, a high country road on the other.

"Ye tik tha 'igh road 'n Ah'll tik tha lo road, 'n Ah'll be in Scootlan love a'fore ya!" Dag sang with a thick burr.

The longbeard reiterated how much he missed the boys. He'd been their mother's neighbor since before they were born, sharing a garden space of tomatoes, honeydew, sweet corn. During the course of one story, Eddy caught on that Dag was gay. Framed pictures of him traveling with other men lined the shelves. It turned out Dag was a failed novelist too, and a prolific backroom gambler before he finally settled down as a Presbyterian and part-time educator. Then came the layoffs. His dry, sardonic humor kept the brothers one-upping him with their own stories, and Eddy figured they could have done a lot worse for a guardian.

Over dinner, Duke mentioned that Dag was on his *second act*, having survived a long fight with alcoholism in his late thirties, to which Dag replied: "There's no second acts, just second winds. Same life, just take a deep breath and continue on."

What would a second wind look like? Eddy wondered. Was he into his second wind? Was there a third?

When Dag finally mentioned Seizer, it was as if in remembrance. A solemn period ensued, whereby nobody spoke and Dag lit a joint and passed it around. Eddy owned up to the possibility that his earlier irritation grew out of sensing what he would soon confront: a loving home, a stable childhood. The rest of the evening was spent in laughter, often to tears. Dag spoke at length on paintings and charcoal drawings hanging at odd angles on the walls, until Lisbon reappeared from upstairs holding a nutcracker—a german man in top hat and open frock, riding a rocking horse. The Twins proceeded to crack walnuts between the horse's saddle and the figure's ambitious cock, which acted as a lever. At one point Eddy pulled a notepad from the coffee table and began sketching the family lying together on the couch. It had been a while since he'd sketched anything not intended for the human body. Nobody called him a fag for doing it, either. Silently he reconsidered an assortment of personal beliefs. The old house creaked and settled as if breathing. A peace lived here, as within the cabin in Georgia. The branching paths of possible lives splintered out before him in silent reverie.

When he woke from his trance, everyone was asleep.

In that fleeting moment, as if trying to retain the emotions of an already dissolving dream, Eddy believed he could be happy again.

Eddy woke curled up on the recliner, tasting his own mossy mouth. Sunlight peeked from behind a curtain, sharp as a child's whine. Dag was curled up in his beard, feet pushing Lisbon off the other end of the couch.

Eddy pulled himself up and walked into the kitchen.

Duke was in there, head lowered, with an arm extended across the small table, holding his phone. Beside him, a folded newspaper and steam rising from a mug. The scintillating weight of some new information had compressed the air, the room's light made fragile. Eddy knew approaching meant knowing, so he hung back.

Shifting his weight, the floorboards creaked beneath him, and Duke lifted his head. His eyes were swollen—two shot glasses of blood in an empty refrigerator.

"Just say it," said Eddy.

"They found him."

Word got out a rager was blowing into town.

By early Saturday morning, Wickham Park was brimming with folks already on their third beers. Curious bikers and felonious nomads and 24-hour party people whose names appeared on a long invitation list all headed for the Space Coast en masse for a rowdy weekend of boozing and sport. Joining them, much to everyone's surprise, were solemnly dressed local citizens and veterans of foreign wars out to pay their respects at the Vietnam Veterans Memorial Wall, a replica in miniature being shepherded along the Southeast, park to park.

The grand collision was Bird's doing, never one to waste an opportunity.

With his home turf on lockdown, and the media abuzz with talk of wildfires and shank superlabs—the country's first, they were thrilled to report—Bird figured a surge of ne'er-do-wells into the region might dilute the pot enough to overwhelm the Feds and a sheriff's office out playing duck-duck-stomp-ass with every hood rat and barfly in Brevard County, trying to scare up eyewitnesses and former camp workers. Likewise, hosting Seizer's funeral service at Wickham on Memorial Day would allow them to send the old man off in honorable fashion, burying his ashes right under the noses of law enforcement and workers alike, as some invited were actually low-level employees of the club, ever ignorant of this fact, and of their benefactor's demise.

Regardless of the endgame, Bird felt Seizer deserved an appropriate tribute to his life's work. Duke and Lisbon agreed to the ceremony, so long as it was kept simple and respectful.

Del Ray was harder to convince. Although the defensive cordon of false documents Seizer had set up for his Lake Washington land purchase was now traceable to one James Brandon Barns of Palm Bay, a horde of ruffians with rap sheets coursing through town would not help dissuade investigators from targeting Melbourne as ground zero for an illicit drug nobody knew existed till last year. The explosion at Camp Crawdad and the Camp Heron inferno had journalists flying in from all over, and though Camp Sticks was properly dismantled and scrubbed by a midnight crew, it didn't mean the club was in the clear yet. Why tempt fate?

Bird countered by citing his concern for the safety of the Twins—paying off a data-entry schlub at the county clerk's to forge property records wasn't a foolproof act; it was best to put as many false leads between the Law and the young men as possible. Hearing this rationale, Del Ray relented, as it signaled the possibility that Bird's vengeance might end at usurpation, the sins of the uncle resting with the uncle.

There were spinning rides and carnival food and face painting for the kids. Sharing duties with twenty other local businesses, Bird was helpful in rounding up a few musical acts and organizing security. In return, he was granted the right to hold a brief ceremony near the lake for a person identified in his obit as an attorney for veterans and a founding member of Daytona's Bike Week, having in his youth worked as a cameraman on *Hell's Angels '69*.

Away from the larger festivities, Seizer's funeral opened with a song, "Shall We Gather at the River," his Harley-Davidson shouldered by the Armstrong Crew like a coffin under a lined salute of motorcycles run parallel each other, front tires raised and engines revving. Del Ray marshaled the proceedings with Seizer's own King James Bible and a sensible amount of platitudes. There were mourners Eddy didn't recognize. Dag sent along flowers, as he lacked the sick days to visit. No one was surprised to see Charlotte in attendance, arm hooked into her husband's on one side, Cueball's on the other. A small pit had been dug under a large oak and within this Duke emptied his uncle's ashes, then a red maple bonsai, closing the earth over. Lisbon set down a rose, of which he kept one petal. Del Ray lifted his voice in final prayer above the din of distant merriment, while Duke kept his open eyes focused on one man.

Afterwards the crowd dispersed, heading for the Wall or the music stage. Cueball spoke to no one, accompanying his parents to the food pavilion.

Jesse fell into conversation with several strangers, whom Eddy felt inclined to avoid, so he tended to Lisbon, knelt down crying over the bonsai. Eddy watched Del Ray pull Duke aside, whispering something in his ear. Duke leaned back with a hard look of disgust, offering a few words of his own, then strode quickly over to raise his brother up as Eddy followed them to his Mustang.

Back in the car, watching Del leave on Seizer's motorcycle, Eddy asked if everything was okay.

"Should've been someone else in the ground," Duke said bluntly. "Get me the hell outta here."

A heavy gale picked up just as the candlelight vigil commenced by the Wall. Overhead clouds clustered like great empurpled man-o'-wars, trailing long wisps of rain. Out came the umbrellas and garbage bags worn as ponchos, the candle procession ending at the stage where a southern rock band waited to stir passions to a frenzy.

It didn't take long. The brawl started in a beer line and quickly spread to the pavilion. Families sprinted off, holding hands and splashing mud. Then a gunshot split the air, making it official, after which a bullhorn activated an already nervous police force at the ready, unlooping their nightsticks to fall upon the crowd.

Those out-of-towners not ducked into cop cars quickly dispersed to nearby bars and local hot spots, the gunning grunts of motorcycles echoing from I-95 clear out to the beaches. And where they went, trouble followed. Street puddles flashed blue and red, store windows gone watt. Whiskey-heavy eyes haunted the dim and crumpled limelight of pool halls, the evening growing deeper into its promise. Raised drinks and lowered standards, as sex assured the living life was still worthwhile, at least for another night.

Here Bird's real inspiration behind the mega-invite made itself apparent.

Moving from bar to bar, backslapping and neck-gripping, quartering the jukeboxes and buying drinks, Bird stumped his card table and urinal campaign. His plan to draw potential recruits to his doorstep had worked, with Prospects Jesse had compiled in his brief but fruitful tenure suddenly all in one place. Unwilling to admit his true aims or position, the new boss merely insinuated he was a man to know, a middle-management liaison bowing to higher powers. *A sort of district Head, you could say.* The economy was bad and people were hungry for work. *You know Jess-boy? Yeah, well he knows me. What you good at? Well, hell, brother, today's your lucky day!*

He walked tall and proud, sure of himself, sure of his plans to revamp the organization's structure. Once he got the new labs up and running, with a host of new networks streamlining the stuff, he'd let his presence be known. No more of this decentralized hogwash. Who were they, ISIS? Power needed a face. Seizer couldn't even control his own men. Bird would run the enterprise top down, like a gang, flagrant and conspicuous, the tried-and-true Mafia method. People would recognize him, would know he held at his disposal a veritable militia of mercenaries.

And what would he do with them? Anything. Anything he wanted.

In the meantime, he would claim the name Seizer as his own.

Westward his future called: prairies double-daggered with telephone poles to the last unblinking expanse, carrying his message of cheap euphoria. An ocean of men angled at his will and sent forth like a flood. Seizer the father and Seizer the son who is made the father, as Seizer was made the ghost. The namesake felt predestined, a birthright—one must seize the Seizer.

After a long night out, Bird returned home. Now that he had the power, he could put it aside. He had men stationed in cars down the block, but he wouldn't think about them. Charlotte was asleep, nuzzled under his chin, a full-grown woman he cradled like a child. *Just like her*, he thought. Wept to sleeping. Not for Seizer but for the whole of it. Bird stroked her hair. She'd gotten homely over the years, but was always pretty when she cried. He felt his longing for her slipping away already. She'd be gone again soon. The world was changing, but not his lust for floundering, hard-hearted women with big tits and beautifully beaten cunts. God, he could taste the lovely salt of them. He recalled that night Charlotte returned home from one of her charity drives to find him drunkenly fucking a random bar slut on the couch. As she watched, he stared her down, and continued. This is who I am. Take it or leave it. Wasn't the first time, but compounded with all the other headaches, it proved too much. He was sure she still loved him, but love was never enough—partnerships required a submissive. She'd have to respect who he was now, what he'd won. Rocking in his chair, he massaged her head and looked out through the sliding glass doors into the rain, wondering if he'd sacrificed too much. A wife. A son that no longer resembled anything he'd known of the boy before, becoming the man he wasn't sure he wanted around. No use dwelling on it. What would be would be. Sipped his vodka and rocked slowly as Johnny Cash sang an ode to everywhere he'd ever been.

On the other edge of the glass doors, through the rain, Duke watched Bird from beneath a black raincoat, hidden among saw palm and tentacles of greenbriers, clutching a high-powered rifle. Beside him lay a finished box of pork lo mein and a silver flask. After hitting the take-out chinese joint with Eddy and Lisbon, he'd complained of stomach cramps, *Gas, most likely,* and lay down in the back seat. As the pair went into a convenience store for sodas, Duke crawled out and retrieved his rifle from the trunk, wrapped longways in a raincoat. His note, scribbled in blind pencil, read: *Had to Walk—Please get Lisbon Drunk. Meet you at your House later.*

It was a three-mile trek along the canals and brushy woods to Bird's backyard, where Duke camped out and waited.

After nursing the flask to near-empty to combat hours of internal head noise, roustabouts for his wrath, Duke heard the low pops of Bird's motorcycle in the driveway. He raised the gun to an upturned knee. But when the living room light clicked on, it was Charlotte in the scope's eye. Bird moved in and out of view as Duke watched intensely the interactions between the couple for further clues to his guilt. He wanted evidence, a confession of body language, something. He watched them argue, watched her bawling, watched them hug. Charlotte pulled vodka from the freezer as Bird stood staring out the glass doors into that boundless wet and howling darkness of which Duke's spirit now felt entirely comprised. Watched them down shots at the table. Watched her collapse weeping on the couch. Then Bird broke down a little too, a truly wretched moment that had Duke stroking the trigger. The scope fogged up and he wiped at it. He saw the future many times over—the crashing glass, Bird pinned to the wide rocking chair, a panicked Charlotte fleeing. With so many ex-cons in town, who could tell who was responsible? And if he was wrong about Bird, so what?

No, he told himself, *it matters. You only get to do this once, and then hold it forever.*

Duke folded back deeper into the palmetto, letting the drunk have its way. Mist and rain swept over his shoes and hardened his knuckles. He kept the scope poised as the couple rocked together. Family seemed like such a simple logic, so appropriate and right, so serene at times. But it often failed. At the center of family, something always weakened.

He passed out before the living room lamp clicked off.

In the morning's bluish eve, Eddy flipped the switch in his garage to find Duke hanging halfway through a side window, balancing on his stomach while simultaneously attempting to whip a raincoat over a rifle on the ground. Finally he just dropped onto the cement floor, rolled over and stood up, raising his shirt to inspect the red bars imprinted there by pressure.

Eddy lowered the chopping knife. "What the hell?"

"I didn't want to wake you."

Glancing at the gun, Eddy scratched his leg sleepily. "Where'd you go?"

Duke tried to remember his story. Hunting. What did these people shoot when they were angry? Raccoon, storks?

"Rabbits are fast as fucking zippers, man," he said. "I think I clipped one but it took off and I didn't feel like chasing it. And you know about the meat, right? If you don't plug 'em dead with the first shot, the adrenaline sets in. Tastes like rubber."

"That's squirrels," said Eddy. "That's what happens with squirrels."

"Yeah, no, you're right. I heard that about rabbits too, though." Duke took up the rifle and placed it on a workbench by a table. "Where's the cleaning kit I left here?"

Eddy gestured at a stack of metal shelves. Duke went over and picked up the kit.

"You expect me to believe you left the gas station without saying anything so you could go hunt rabbit?"

"I needed some time alone," said Duke, bending over the weapon as one preparing to reap the full benefits of ritual.

"Where'd you hide that thing?"

"I didn't hide shit, it was in the trunk. I put it there thinking I'd go out later this week."

"You let me ride around with that thing in my trunk! Fuck, man, is it even legal?"

"Yes, it's legal," said Duke. "Now would you stop making me feel like a criminal?"

Eddy's body was limp, but his eyes were wide-awake.

"That's no .22."

A single vein of fear stretched from Duke's lower abdomen to the top of his head, ballooning rigidly along his spine. He raised his eyes to his friend, hoping for an understanding to pass between them. "I know. But it's all I got."

"That's a pretty powerful gun to take rabbit hunting."

"I said it's all I got."

"Where's your flashlight?"

"What?"

"You went hunting in the dark with no flashlight."

"Huh, no. The battery died. I tossed it."

"You tossed a flashlight because it ran out of batteries," said Eddy, waiting. Then he shook his head. "I'm just gonna ask this once, and you say whatever you're gonna say—is someone dead?"

Duke stared at Eddy's knees. "No."

"Should I be packing clothes?"

"No," said Duke. "We're okay."

Eddy wanted to press more, but recognized the need to let it go. "Alright. Well, you missed a helluva party. We ended up at some strip club with this Medal of Honor winner. He went from getting religious about seeing himself mirrored in his buddies' names in the Wall to, like, telling Lisbon the government creates all the world's diseases. Fucking looney tunes."

"Can't be good at everything," said Duke.

"Did Cueball text you? He wanted to pass on his condolences."

Duke placed his hands flat on his knees. "I kinda need to be alone right now, Eddy."

"Okay, sure. But hey, next time, use the front door. I came out here expecting . . . I don't know what."

"Gotcha," said Duke, cinching his lips. "Wait, where's Lisbon?"

"On the couch."

"How's he holding up?"

Eddy yawned, resting his head on the doorframe. "He'll live."

The door shut quietly and Duke released his breath.

For the next hour he labored under a stark bulb, cleaning the rifle and ignoring the sticky underwear cling and stone-stomach malaise of beyond-sleep. When he finished he walked into Eddy's backyard and stood in the calm crispness. Birds were beginning to rouse. The night's grief seemed impossible to hold on to in the clear morning air.

Noticing the remnants of an old tree fort resting in the lower limbs of a pine, Duke hopped the fence and skirted the woodline. Climbing two-by-fours nailed into the trunk, he passed the waterlogged room to push himself onto the tar-shingled roof, overlooking woods and distant houses.

There he sat waiting for the sunrise, watching it all come alive.

At the funeral service, Del Ray had pulled him aside to say they'd found Jim Barns holed up in a trailer park in Tampa. After a bit of negotiation, the treasonous camp Foreman admitted everything, even giving up the whereabouts of Corey Buffalo.

"No one'll be hearing from either of them again," said Del Ray. "Trust me, they each paid a very lengthy price." Then: "Your uncle will be sorely missed. He was clever as a fox, bold and unrepentant, a true leader. He drew up deals between enemies and put them all to work. But his true legacy is you and your brother. I want to assure you, you'll be taken care of. We're all in this together."

That's when it crumbled, the whole facade, all the bullshit bearing down on him with a weight too great to bear.

"Your words," Duke seethed, "mean absolute shit to me. If we were in this together, my uncle would still be alive."

The sun was slow in coming as the air stilled in anticipation. Birdsong intensified, and he welcomed it. He considered interrogating Cueball—but not Eddy, who couldn't keep a secret; it would tear up his insides and wash into his face.

Duke wasn't going to run. He hadn't spent all this time learning the ropes just to hand over his uncle's life's work to a bunch of disloyal lowlifes.

It was time to have a sit-down with Del Ray. Lay it all out on the table. Even if Del was a quality liar, he was for sure a talker, and Duke felt he was pretty good at reading people. It was risky, but he had to do something— already his frustration threatened to shift the direction of his rage, seesaw-ing from a fiery, rightful vengeance to an inward-seeking chill of hopeless depression.

But all of this could be put aside for later. Now was a time for quiet, to sit alone with this idea of his uncle, in loving memory, contemplating a world gone by. The eastern sky lit up with the pale ribs of faraway clouds. The squirrels were out in the trees. And though the brushfires had long been put to rest, the air still reeked of the belly of the earth rent inside out.

Loitering in the parking lot of the Helter-Skelter, the only real music venue in town, Eddy made a telescope with his fist, thinning the hole until it pinpointed past the fat crotch of his palm and focused on a convenience store sign a quarter mile away. To his amazement, he was able to read the gas prices.

"Devil's magic!" erupted Eddy. "How's it work?"

"Cuts down on any excess blur, increasing the depth of field," Duke explained, leaning against a tour bus. "Maybe you're myopic."

Eddy balled both hands to his eyes, forming the mask of a superhero. "Behold to the Blind Orgasmo! Savior of virgins, maidens, and MILFs alike. He *sees* with his *fingers!*"

Duke snickered, despite himself. Better that than betray his true feelings, gearing up for the confrontation ahead.

"Try curling your fingers like this," he said. "See? That's the Bloods sign: b-l-o-o-d."

"Looky there," mused Eddy. "Where'd you pick that up?"

Shouts of melody and rapture erupted from the club's parking lot, where drunken kids with dyed hair and piercings stared down the barrel of their futures and laughed.

Duke checked the time. "I best get inside, catch this dude before the groupies get him." He leaned back to spy Lisbon napping in the Mustang. "Keep an eye on him."

"Make it quick, I'm starving."

Duke was meeting a kid named Ferris Yang, lead singer of the Termites, a punk band out of Ybor City. The Termites were in town for one night only, so as a favor to Jesse, who'd convinced Ferris the band could score a bigger payday by adding a few dealers to their guest list, Duke volunteered to drop off the band's earnings.

Yet Duke's intentions strayed well beyond this.

At that moment, creeping through the club's rear exit, Del Ray entered a steaming horde of sweaty punks wrapped in blue coats of smoke, their wan and ornamented faces luminous in black light. He gently pressed aside the liberty-spiked and shaved patrons donning skinny jeans among pool cues rising and dipping like dowsing rods attuned to bottom-shelf liquor. Over on the dance floor, hands thrust skyward, the disenfranchised amped on shank moshed together through private oblivions under converging gyres of stage lights while drum notes thumped to a Vandals cover—

Drowning in this toilet
of shit that they call life —
work like hell at Taco Bell
for $4.25 an hour.
No one gives a squirt of piss
if you fucking die,
so seize the day
by the balls
and squeeze until it's on its knees!

Del Ray pushed through an older crowd hugging the bar—obscenely droll, ironic types—to summon the bartender over with a twenty spot, yelling at his ear. An electric guitar sent the crowd leaping like water beads from a rutting gator, so Del Ray went up to his tiptoes. Finding Duke and locking eyes, he waved him toward a back room located behind the bar.

The office was small: a desk and computer, three chairs, and a filing cabinet. Pages of nude women cut from magazines of different eras papered the walls. Del Ray fell into the desk chair, clucking like a pimp surveying a precinct. Duke shut the door and sat directly across the desk. The room was notably well-insulated from the noise beyond.

"Welcome to my life," said Del Ray, pushing a pint of ginger ale Duke's way. "All this young hot tail just aching for a gentle ear, and I always end up locked in some claustrophobic room like this, strategizing." Rapped his knuckles on the desk. "Just can't win."

"I was thinking of you yesterday," Duke started.

"Oh yeah?"

"There's this guy in a documentary, calls himself an artist. Cuts animals into thin slices, like lunch meat, then mounts the slices in glass partitions, so when you step away, you see the whole cow again. But then you notice . . . it has two heads."

Del Ray frowned professionally.

"I thought it was the most disgusting thing I'd ever seen," said Duke. "And as soon as I thought that, I knew you'd find some way to defend it."

Del Ray dragged his longish fingers through his hair, a straggly nest of wasps. "You wanted to talk?"

Duke checked the ceiling for cameras, despite knowing these safe rooms were locked down and scanned daily for bugs.

"I'm here with a proposition," said Duke.

"You sweet on me?" asked Del, crossing his steel-toed boots. "Come to confess your innermost deviant desires?"

Duke placed a handgun on the desk.

Del Ray appeared undisturbed.

"My uncle made two million this past year. That's post payoffs . . . contacts, workers, special interests. It's yours if you help me."

Del Ray mentally ran through some calculations with the intensity of a man counting a four-deck card shoe.

"I'm gonna level with you, Duke, partly because you're my responsibility, and partly out of respect for your uncle. The number you've quoted is a gross underestimation of Seizer's cut."

"That's the offer," said Duke.

"I heard your uncle willed you boys a whole lotta land. Real estate — now *there's* a venture with a solid future in it." Del Ray's eyes darted around. "Do *you* own this place? Wait, do *I*?"

"All his land is under contract to sell."

"Which still leaves you and your brother ten percent of the club's business," said Del. "That's fuck-you money. You're the wealthiest twenty-somethings I know. And hell, you got the mags too, right? I believe I'm still technically an employee of yours."

"The magazines have been transferred to another party."

Del guffawed. "Am I being fired? In this economy?"

All ownership and operating privileges related to the magazines had been signed over to Dag Nasty, a gift that would allow the old-timer to live out his glory years away from the slaughterhouse's rank and file. Besides, Duke had no idea how magazines operated; he only knew how to run a drug cartel.

"All I need from you —"

"Some of those columns I penned for your uncle I'm actually proud of," Del Ray continued. "Sure, it was a means of laundering money, but it was just as much a literary pursuit, for me."

"Are you serious right now?"

Del Ray sighed. "We all have lives to live, Duke."

"You don't even wanna hear my request?"

Del Ray dead-eyed him. "Vengeance is a gnawing solitude wrapped in a false promise."

Duke's composure collapsed into a single emotion, with a demand he almost couldn't speak. *"You owe me the truth!"*

"Son, you're not hearing me," replied the biker, looking tired. "Vengeance does not bring nourishment, because it bears no good fruit. It's a contemptuous refuge for the weak of spirit. It unionizes a sense of injustice and suspicion and rage — now listen to me — in the service of one god, and that is itself. You cannot reconcile its logic, because it has none. It is a reactionary, emotional evil — an autoimmune disease that feeds off the very heart it aims to protect, without remorse. Take it from a man who once knifed a man over a woman: revenge will turn a healthy young tyke like you into a blood-hungry, stammering idiot in no time. And it might just get you killed."

"He was my uncle!" Duke spat, infuriated by Del's pontificating and the fathering he had no right to. "Look me in the eye! You tell me a drunk like Jim fucking Barns had the goddamn *gall* to ambush him! And why'd Gumby leave town so quickly, huh? And where was Cueball?"

"Now you're just throwing around names—"

"This is bullshit, Ray! And you know it! There's one person who aimed to benefit above the rest. Now I'm giving you the opportunity to be on the right side of this."

"Here's the thing," Del Ray said, running his thumb along the ridges of his lip, "your yelling . . . just irritates me. But I understand it. But I also understand some things you don't. First off, Gumby left 'cause he killed a big cat out in the swamps and banked a shitload of cash for it. Once that was done, he was done. Go ask Bird yourself, tell him I told you a whopper and you come to verify I was a stinkin liar. And I'll let you in on another thing: Gumbo is the one that tracked down Barns. As a final favor, for free. You should be praising his fucking name, not slandering it. Who you think cleaned up that Kaos mess for your uncle down in Lauderdale? Me? And as for Jim, *that* jackass helped turn Mick against the club. That's right, our good pal Mickey. And several guards, including Corey Buffalo, who likely helped Jim with the murder. Now I'm trusting you not to share this with anyone. But if it wasn't for some quick thinking on Bird's part, your uncle might not have been the last to disappear . . . I believe you catch my drift."

Duke didn't know what the truth was—just that this wasn't it, not fully. "Nobody alive left to question. Wraps up pretty neat."

"Just because it don't smell right don't mean it's wrong."

"You're not telling me everything," said Duke. "No one balks at two million. I have to wonder what's in it for you."

"You're under the false impression I give a shit who runs this enterprise," proclaimed Del Ray. "I'm a sidelines kind of guy, Duke. Ever seen a turtle in harm's way? *Ploop*, head right back in the shell. My main interest now is general security, for everyone. Now, I respect you bringing your concerns to me, rather than doing something stupid and regretful. I owed your uncle some debts, which by keeping this meeting between us I will now repay in full—Duke, son, you've gotta let this go."

Unifying claps erupted beyond the door, which reminded Duke he still had to track down Ferris before Eddy got bored and wandered inside. "I won't ever forget this," he said.

"No one's asking you to forget anything," said Del Ray. "But your uncle had targets laid over targets on his back. Mourn him, yes, but know he always, *always*, understood the dangers inherent in this business. And you should too. Had this line of inquiry met with a less understanding individual, you'd be in *terrible* deep shit right now."

"Duly noted."

"Well note this, bud . . . there's a *new* Seizer now. He—is—your—boss. And you will respect the privilege to serve under him." Here Del pointed to the door. "You have a brother out there who relies on you. *I* rely on you, goddammit. Duke, one day I'm sure you will inherit that lofty position for which you've been trained—oh yeah, I know about your uncle's plans—but first, you have a thing or two to learn about judgment. Patience, mercy, work—make these your virtues. Move on. Rededicate yourself to a fruitful existence. Don't go looking for enemies."

"If you knew it wasn't Barns or Buffalo, or wasn't *just* them, would you tell me?"

"Did you hear a word I just said?"

"I need to know who I can trust!" barked Duke.

"Am I not serving both our interests by driving down from Jacksonville to talk this thing through?" Del Ray asked, arms spread. "I quit a meeting we've rescheduled *three* times, with terribly important people! Folks with shitty taste in scotch, but important nonetheless."

When Duke spoke again, his words were hushed. "How can I be sure you won't tell Bird about this?"

"*Seizer*. Respect the title. The answer to your question is, because now *I'm* implicated in this mess," said Del Ray, wincing at the pure truth of it. "Listen, I don't want there to be any bad blood between us. This operation can't afford two men of delicate positions squabbling. God knows I've got enough on my plate. You've got good instincts, Duke, but I need you to pull your shit together and be the leader you were trained to be."

Duke gripped his mouth. "Can you promise . . . can you promise protection for my brother? That whatever happened . . . however it happened . . . that this is the end of it?"

"I've got you *and* your brother's back, wherever, when," Del promised.

Duke's voice hovered above a whisper. "I'm trying not to lose it, Del. Nothing makes sense. I'm so angry, all the time. I just need to know Lisbon will be okay. I'll find a way to swallow it. I'll go along. But I need to know this is the end of it."

The biker let the words hang in the air and accumulate significance, to honor them, in a way, before extending his arm across the desk, palm up.

Duke stared at the forearm. After a deep breath, he reached over and locked the grip, tattoo to tattoo. Then retrieved his gun. "I'll hold you to everything said here."

Del Ray nodded. "Reset those priorities, brother. Don't let the hard times make you forget life's actually enjoyed by some folks."

The door opened to a torrent of laser sounds and closed to muffled bass chords.

Del Ray stayed on, nursing his beer.

In his heart he was still upset at Bird for burying Seizer. It undermined business and brewed discontent, threatening Del Ray's own shot at a simpler life. Del could envision no world where Jim Barns was sent down to Miami to take Cueball out. Odds favored bad luck and simple opportunism—here was this mouthy, lazy hanger-on headed south on vacation, right when Bird needed a patsy. Sure, Jim was likely pilfering a few shank shards here and there, and Seizer likely skimming off the topmost layer of cream, but did either impropriety warrant death? Not in Del Ray's estimation.

Neither had he enjoyed watching a camp worker empty two rounds in Jim's stomach and one in the head, despite what the son of a bitch had done to Mickey. But in this business, once a plan solidified, you had to see it through, no matter how gruesome or hurtful.

So he lied to Duke about Barns being in Tampa and about Gumby hunting down Corey Buffalo, managing the timeline as he and Bird saw fit, while distancing Cueball from the crime. After Bird's threatening phone call to Jim, they expected the old sot to high-tail it out of state; instead, Jim bunkered down and convinced both Corey and Mickey to help him sack the camps, each believing, Del guessed, that with all former bonds of trust eroded, the club would self-implode. Such mutiny was stupidly foreseeable—if the second-in-command was blind to such allegiances, that blatant indifference tumbled straight down through the ranks.

Not that it mattered much now. So long as Cueball and Jesse kept their traps shut, Del Ray was optimistic that Duke could be held in check.

Mickey's death continued to sting. How even an honorable idea like *brotherhood*, that old shibboleth, contained its own blind spots and perils. Without mutual trust and social bonds, the world becomes the plaything of tyrants and barbarians.

Colt's face crept in there too. Check out this old couple reclining on beach chairs, watching the Gulf waves performing acts of memory. Zippo nuzzling his hand. It was a sappy daydream, but the ache was real.

Who would best, in the end, further his own interests?

In the movies, the last man standing was either the upright moral citizen or the most brutal bastard. But in real life, Del Ray knew, it was usually the most conniving.

el Ray found the newest Seizer in his backyard grilling steaks, an apron smeared with sauce tied to his waist. The prominent mound of flab once constituting Bird's impressive belly had noticeably shrunk over the past few months, leading Del Ray to conclude his friend had either stopped eating, period, or was dipping his wick in the company product.

The pair of rib eyes sizzling on the grill cut it back to one possibility.

"Hail Seizer and his glorious tongs!" cried Del Ray. "My stomach heareth the spit of sirloin and mine eyes smelleth onions. Behold his impressive grill, from which no beast doth return uncharred! Of all base natures, hunger is the most accursed, for its death can only assure its resurrection. I ask, good sir, have ye a departing slab of flesh for an arriving one?"

"Afternoon, shitface."

"I don't go by that anymore," said Del Ray, leaning into the meat smoke. "They call me the Artist Formerly Known as Fixer."

Bird spun the tongs like a six-shooter. "My mistake, *Maven*. Glad you could make it. I think you should reconsider 'Interlocutor.' It's a title with a legacy, has a nice ring to it."

"Yeah, that shit just slides right off the tongue," said Del.

Bird grinned, but grew serious as he wrung his hands through the apron. "So what did we learn?"

"He was just fishing for information."

Bird eyed him. "So he has to go."

"What? No! Duke had his doubts, he voiced them, we talked it out—issue resolved."

"I'm not convinced."

"This beef was between you and the old man. Enjoy the victory. Order is restored."

Bird clicked his tongs. "Alex buried two cousins and keeps asking about Heath. Any time Duke wants, he can lead that son of a bitch right to my doorstep. That weighs on me."

"Don't let it. Our boys on the inside will alert us to any developments."

"Maybe Duke knew about the old man sending Jim Barns down to Lauderdale to kill my son."

Del Ray threw up his hands. "Let's not any more with this conspiracy shit. No intelligent human would've trusted Jim Barns to change their oil, much less carry out a hit. There's no proof Seizer ever sent anyone after Cueball. It's total fantasy."

"Buffalo corroborated it."

"Corroborated, huh?" said Del Ray, still uneasy with how his friend was put down. "Terrified people say all sorts of things."

Bird frowned. "Ten percent of sales. Can you believe that? Rich little bastards."

"And as boss, you hold the lion's share. The Twins have zero reason to undermine the growth of the business. It only helps them."

The newest Seizer puffed his cheeks and flipped a steak. "Any word on Holopaw?"

Del Ray clapped, thankful to be moving on. "Camp Slimfast will be up and running in dos semanas. And you've got to see this place, brother: big old bomb shelter, great ventilation, storage, the works. Out in the middle of nowhere. We got one monster tank, looks like a mechanical elephant from some Man Ray painting. We got an updated formula, the very best *chefs*—it would debase their work to call them *cooks*. The whole process streamlined. I get a hard-on just thinking about it. Plus the Valkaria plant's on track to begin production next month. In the meantime, our stockpile's selling steady. Think rosy horizons and drinks with delicate umbrellas. Good times."

"It will be for you. Three mil, that's a jackpot."

"Let's not jinx it with talk. We'll see how the year goes."

"That kind of wealth brings new perspective," said Bird.

"I aint greedy," said Del Ray. "And don't insinuate, it gives me heartburn.

Just do me a favor, old buddy, don't let paranoia get the best of you. If we foster trust and respect, we can ride these boys straight to the finish line. Just like Jesse."

"Number one draft pick, that one. We should get him a tour bus. Six new cities locked down, tripled demand. Why am I still living in this shit-hole?"

"Settle the condos in Winter Park and you'll have legit funds to play with."

"Burns my ass thinking of what all cash I'm losing waiting for these camps. Dwindling supplies. Cops paid to do jack shit. Salaries I'm floating."

"You'd rather have folks in the unemployment line? Answering questions about previous work experience?"

Bird chuckled morosely. "Hundreds of thousands of dollars. Worse than taxes."

"We pay not to worry," said Del. "Focus on the five-year plan."

"Those twins copped a goddamn fortune," said Bird, not letting it go. He offered Del Ray a beer, twisting the cap off his own. "Do you see my concern? Why not take the money and run? If we had that kind of money at his age, shit. What's Duke hanging around for? What's he after?"

"He was bred for this," countered Del Ray. "He's a solid asset. And Lisbon isn't stupid. Honestly, we're underutilizing that young man. He's real good with numbers."

"Oh, I have no doubt he's keeping count."

"Are you trying to give yourself a heart attack?" asked Del. "Five years! Retirement! Buy an island down in the Keys. Buy two. Open a bed & breakfast for movie stars and magnate widows—"

"Sit back and let you manage labor, keep Jesse in the field? Have my boy working security detail?"

"Paradise! Get Lisbon running numbers, maybe create an upper-management position for Duke—"

Bird flung the tongs to the grill. "You just finished saying that little prick was gunning for me, and now you want me to promote him?"

Bird's temper was tripping memories of California, no doubt fueled by the new chemicals in his system.

"He's a born leader that knows the business," said Del Ray. "Use him. Give him a garden to tend."

"And how long before the Feds dig up something on Seizer, only to discover he's got living relatives right where the lab fires started? We gonna disappear federal agents? Or what if down the road Duke learns the truth about what happened, when he's got more power and some men under him? It's got so I can't sleep at night."

"These *issues* have *provisions* in place," said Del Ray, flustered and pinching the air to accentuate his meaning. "That person who exists on paper is a *ghost*. There are four people alive that know the truth, none of whom will talk. Don't show favoritism, or nepotism . . . get beyond the *-tisms*. Be their leader. Concentrate on directing the Heads and expanding your territory."

Bird knocked back his beer. "This shit aint easy, Ray. Every day I worry about which fuckhole will land me back in prison."

"C'mon, hoss, don't get gitchy," said Del, worried about his friend, noting the tremors, the inconsistent thinking, the gums a little darker now from lack of care. "Might wanna flip them steaks."

"How's my son holding up with his busywork?"

"Solid. No complaints."

"You beat a dog long enough, it learns to stay down."

"We'll just have to agree to disagree on that one."

Bird turned to the woods. "We'll only use him when necessary. Certain jobs, sharpshooter. We can't have his face out there with so many people wanting to bash it in. I got him in Orlando today on a private range."

Now there's a terrifying notion, Del Ray thought. Cueball honing his skills, with all that pressure building up inside. You push your beliefs onto a kid with too much force and one day you wake up to a human time bomb beset with the empty calling of a terrorist. Silence, exile, cunning. Gumby's twisted logic rising up in Cueball's subconscious like some guardian angel of misanthropes.

Bird yanked back the tongs, blowing on them. "Tell Eddy what to expect from the meetings with the Heads. Make sure he understands the runthroughs the day before are mandatory."

Del Ray squinted. "I'm not trying to be contentious, and I think Eddy's a smart chap who deserves a promotion . . . but he's not right for this position, in my opinion. He's a much better fit for the warehouse job, separating stock."

Bird raised a hand. "Eddy's smart, and capable, and one of the few people around here I still trust. I'm like a father to that kid. He's never back-talked me . . . not once. All he needs is a little tailwind."

"These Heads, they're big players—I worry they'll eat him up," said Del Ray, careful with his phrasing. "They might better react to a person with a temperament they recognize. Someone who knows the game inside and out. Someone raised for this very thing."

"You want me to introduce Duke to the very people who could topple and ruin me," said Bird. "That's your big plan."

"This is my team," said Ray, "and our core squad. Trust me with my job."

Bird sheared off a bit of steak, handing the fork to Del Ray. "How's that?"

"A little tough . . . and pigheaded, and unwilling to let bygones be bygones."

"Is that pepper enough?"

"You want another Mickey on your hands?"

Bird glanced at the woods encroaching at the fence line, saw where the movement was coming from—a snake rummaging through the undergrowth. "If I put Duke in charge of a smaller camp, would that shut you up?"

"Hell yes! Entirely fair," said Del Ray, knowing it was the best he'd get. "He'll be happy to prove himself. Get Lisbon organizing shipments with Elroy. Keep their minds busy. Trust will eventually reestablish itself—on both sides."

"I wish you were more on my side with this," said Bird.

"I'm never not on your side," said Del Ray.

"*If* we do this," Bird said, watching him, "you're training them. And Ray, if this backfires . . . if I hear anything that smacks of organizing . . ."

"We'll send them on their merry way. But you can't go into it thinking that way."

Bird rubbed his face, switching gears. "How close are we with a new Fixer?"

"Got my eye on a Marine, two tours in Iraq. A real hard-ass to keep people in line. Knows the territory, good with secrets. Family, two kids—very stable."

"Stability is good."

"Our plan is solid, brother. Employee upgrades and better products."

"This extended-release pill . . . it's like the future come early. Seizer got a few things right."

"*Better living through chemistry*. It's gonna sell itself, brother. And the new ice formula is pure crystal sunshine. Think Superman's hideout," said Del Ray. "And the best part of this new pill is, it staggers the effects, less of a hangover, people can work the next day. Shank becomes part of your daily routine, like that first cup of coffee. Amp up each morning, smooth out in the afternoon."

"Just in time for the Los Toros to be selling their own brand of junk shank."

"That's just . . . whatever," said Del Ray. "Alex promised once we got the new batch ready to go, they'll quit pushing the shake-and-bake. I mean, it's weak-ass shit, and he straight-up told you about it, which counts for something. All our reserves are headed north and Alex still has to make money."

"How long before we got people selling that knockoff shit in our own backyard?"

"You kidding me? That'd be a godsend," said Del Ray. "We shouldn't shit where we eat, anyhow. Some scrub kids making a measly fifty thou off this back-alley, stir-fry fucking cough syrup? Uh, *yes please*! I'd love a group to throw under the bus if the heat ever comes down hard."

"So I turn a blind eye. Lose even more money."

"Are we the cops? We gonna chase down every kid cooking up junk in their basements?" asked Del Ray. "This is our window of opportunity, hoss—right now. It's all we've earned. Even if it came to ceding Miami in the future—hear me out—what would we lose? Five, ten percent? Would you pay ten percent to stay out of a turf war? Do I have to remind you of SoCal? We have established distribution clusters outside twelve major cities *in less than two years*! If we were legal, we'd have our faces on *Forbes*!

Promote the Armstrong Crew and distance yourself from your subordinates. Be that invisible clockmaker."

"While my Maven tracks each of the club's subgroups and manages low-level operations," said Bird. "That right?"

"You'll receive weekly in-person reports," promised Del Ray, "so that *you* can focus on guiding and appeasing the Heads. Concentrate on the big boys."

"I can barely keep up anymore. Maybe I should buy some notebooks, like the old man."

"Research new avenues of investment," said Del Ray. "Enjoy some downtime. Buy a hammock."

"Maybe someday you'd like to be in my position," offered Bird.

"Bite your tongue," said Del Ray, spitting. "Seriously, I don't even like you joking."

Bird frowned a smile. "That everything on the agenda?"

Del Ray thought about it. "Well . . . just so we don't piss anyone off, it's just 'Los Toros,' not *the* Los Toros."

"What?"

"Earlier you said *the* Los Toros. Los means *the*, plural."

Bird sighed. "You know how to burrow right under the skin, don't you?"

"It's a vestige of my witnessing days," Del Ray said by way of apology. "Sometimes Jesus don't take right away and you really gotta grind into their hearts like a mad surgeon. All brimstone and hellfire, really terrify the shit out of 'em."

"Okay, *padre*," said Bird, hooking an eyebrow. "You want a steak or what?"

"Naw, I'm good," Del Ray scoffed. "You already killed those things twice over, cooking them so long."

Huffing, Bird lifted a steak from the grill and whipped it to the woods.

Eddy recognized the redhead picking through clothes piled up on foldout tables along the back wall of the church annex. Her name was Suzie Fuentes, and in a former life she'd been the valedictorian of Palm Bay High, meant for greater things—a cute goth nerd who won science fairs, but who could also kickflip a skateboard.

Suzie Fun-times, they'd call her. After high school, though, Suzie went on to become an internet camgirl, inexplicably. Eddy now watched her stretch a ruffled old blouse at arm's length, her hair dyed a haphazard shade of sunset, crowded by poor people and folks without homes.

This was the young woman to whom Cueball made Eddy promise to deliver a quarter of his drug earnings, should he die—which made no sense, as they'd dated years ago, in middle school.

There was nowhere to hide. Standing behind a walled counter in apron and gloves, Eddy had been assigned to the kitchen, ladling chunky vegetable soup into half-pint containers. His plan was to play dumb and hope Suzie didn't recognize him.

He'd finally taken Jesse's throwaway advice to volunteer at a food pantry, putting himself for the first time in service of his community, a spontaneous decision born of midnight internet surfing and shame. Eddy couldn't ask anyone else to join him, as that would require explaining his motivations. The experience itself was weird and deeply uncomfortable, at least for the first hour, before the uplifting feeling of doing unassailably good work kicked in.

A portion of his unease stemmed from the church's notorious reputation—June Park Healing Baptist was an ultraconservative sect known locally for hosting book burnings in their back lot and for antagonizing local patrons of gay bars with megaphones and crude signs promising damnation. The soup kitchen was seemingly the lone civic activity of worshipers who euthanized progressive ideologies by the pernicious score on Wednesday nights and twice on Sunday, yet on Saturdays apparently traded in their Old Testament God for the Gospels' Jesus. All this changed recently, though, after their hellfire-preaching pastor skipped town with the organist, which divided the congregation. In an attempt to revamp their image and stop the hemorrhaging of members, their web page now stated the church was "under the care and guidance of a new pastor" and "actively seeking young members of all orientations. Nobody can judge but the Lord."

Which spoke to Eddy, who understood the desire to offset past wrongs with karmic credits.

The rectangular building beside the church was subdivided into class-rooms and a narrow banquet hall, where a single door bottlenecked a line of hungry people. Foldout seats had been set up, but many just took their food and left. Donated clothes were restricted to two items per person, without real enforcement.

The vegetable soup smelled of garnished swampwater with a rainbow sheen, yet the patrons paid no mind, collecting too their servings of garlic bread, bean casserole, and meatballs. Eddy placed the plastic half-pints in a row, finding it hard to look folks in the eye during offerings of "Bless you," "God bless you," "Thank you, boy, this helps." He decided it didn't matter if the church's benevolence was the result of penance or altruism—hungry people were being fed.

Suzie went missing from the clothes table. She wasn't sitting in any chair, either, thankfully.

"Eddy?"

Shit.

"Suzie!" he pronounced too loudly. She was in line with her tray, arriving from his right. "Look at you! You go to church here?"

Which was the wrong question, given her down-turned expression. "Um, no—"

"Soup?"

"Uh, yeah, sure," she said, deflated, but offering a smile.

His embarrassment building, Eddy blurted out, "Hey, wanna meet up out front in maybe ten minutes? I've got a short break."

"Um, sure!" she said, somewhat over-enthusiastically.

Hanging up his apron, Eddy overheard an unwashed couple complain about having to sit through a sermon in order to secure a hot meal. This payment to a benefactor also felt deeply familiar, as Eddy realized debt came in many forms.

"Suzie Fun-times!" he called as he approached her outside.

"Oh, sheesh," she said. "That nickname got me in a lot of trouble over the years."

The day was bright and lovely, and Suzie was sitting on a wooden pole meant as a parking stop, food plate in her lap.

"How's the grub?"

"Look at these sad, dry little meatballs," she said. "No latina hands touched these. No italian neither."

"How's your brother?"

She shrugged, gauging perhaps what she could trust him with.

"Jamie and me don't talk much. He got a job selling tires down at AutoPlus, keeps him busy. You still with that pretty girl wears all those flowy dresses?"

"Long story," he said. "I rarely see anyone anymore."

"Not even Heath? You two were best friends."

"Yeah, but barely. A lot changed after school."

"For real. My whole world," she said. "Maybe you know . . . but college didn't work out for me."

"Same," said Eddy. "But who knows, there's still time."

Her eyes danced around. "I'm kinda in a financially *disadvantaged* situation right now. No big secret. I partied a bit too hard out the gate. Wrong crowd, heavy drinking, then harder stuff. Meth, shank. You know, fell in love with feeling good."

Suzie's casualness with vulnerability struck him straight through, as if pain were a twelve-step chip you flashed with your hello so people stopped asking. He'd seen this young woman spread out naked in a video Cueball had shown him online, eyes closed and masturbating with a vibrator whose speed alternated with the amount of prepaid tokens viewers sent her. This was the world they lived in. Watched as she swam her spoon through the soup.

"My dad kicked me out. And my brother . . . he didn't want me around his daughter. Guess I'm a bad role model."

"I'm sorry to hear it."

Wiping away a tear, she nodded. "Not what I expected from myself. My life. I've been clean for three months," she confided. "I don't know why I'm telling you all this. Maybe because I'm here with all these poor people getting free food and shit."

He laughed nervously.

"But I got a friend I'm staying with now, and a job at Starbucks, which gives me health insurance, luckily. I'm working my way back. I come here . . . honestly, just to be around people. All my friends are gone. Which is just depressing."

"You're sharing, so I'm gonna share," said Eddy, taking the stump beside her. "I hurt people I cared about too. Spent a lot of time feeling guilty." Her red eyes widened, her smile genuine—just a naturally good-natured individual. "Can I say something? We're still young. We've done dumb shit, yeah, but that shouldn't define us."

She shook her head no. "Maybe."

"Definitely," said Eddy. "Listen, Suzie, you're the valedictorian . . . *forever*. Yeah, of course I remember! And nobody can take that from you. You think you're the first highflier to stumble along the way? Hell no. Every CEO, astronaut, billionaire—they all have some crazy backstory. And later on, they *sell* that story. This is all just advertising for later! *Yeah, I remember Suzie Fuentes making fun of meatballs in a church parking lot . . . and look at her now!*"

"Oh god no, stop, please," she laughed, but her eyes were big and wet, ready to believe.

Eddy tapped his chest. "You think you're the only one fighting to stay sober?"

She pulled back. "You too? They got everyone."

"So drugs put you off your game, so what? Maybe you hurt your family. But here you are, working your way back. It's fucking . . . admirable."

"I've made some real bad choices," she said, an eek issuing from her cheek. "A friend of mine OD'd . . . that shit shook me. Something hydro . . . dome . . . something? I was like, what's in this shank?"

"Hydrocodone? It's not in shank," said Eddy, suddenly unsure.

"But you don't know that, right? Who knows what these assholes cut that shit with."

Eddy's nodding was convulsive. "For sure."

"I did some other things," she said, looking around, "people might recognize me for."

"Doesn't matter," said Eddy. "I don't know what you did, but think about it: in the future, every president will have sold drugs in high school. Seriously! Or have a sex tape. What matters is building off your lows. Platform after platform, working your way back up. You're the architect, building this house of You. But it's only as stable as you believe it to be."

"Wow," she laughed, wiping her eyes. "That's some shit to say."

"It's true," said Eddy, wanting to believe the words. "Listen, I gotta get back. But wait, come to my car for a sec, I have a bag you can put those clothes in."

They walked to the other side of the small weedy lot, Suzie clutching her roll of clothes. On the passenger side of his car was a grocery bag, but stuffed under the seat was two thousand dollars in twenties, a stash of go-money.

"Oh my god," she said, rubbing the hood of the Mustang. "This your ride?"

"Uh, yeah," said Eddy. "Dead uncle. I might sell it, the insurance is a lot."

He popped the door, took her clothes, reached down to open the grocery bag, and snuck the two grand into the pocket of some jean shorts without her seeing.

"Bag's not sticky or nothing, I checked," he said, rising out.

She thanked him and they stood there for a moment, trying to figure out what to do next, then hugged, laughing a little.

"Here's to staying sober," she said. "What a stupid thing to say."

"Not at all," said Eddy. "I hope you find your way back . . . to whatever it is you want."

They exchanged numbers. He watched her walk over to an old beat-up Corolla, waving as she glanced back.

After she drove away, Eddy rushed back inside. He dropped his apron on the used-clothes table and left without telling anyone.

What an absolute nightmare.

Someone had mown the small patch of lawn outside Ma Kettle's Saloon and it smelled green and fresh in the watery light. Eddy chewed pumpkin seeds and watched cars rocket down the Dixie Highway like pinballs. Anticipating his first stint in the Majors had him fighting all morning to keep his breakfast down. Whenever a vehicle turned up Malabar Road, he pretended to be perplexed by something he was reading.

Suzie Fuentes had clean run him over.

Her courage and tears had Eddy slopping about the muddied freshets of difficult emotions and moral obligations. There was no world in which Cueball could hear about their meeting—it would wreck him. Or worse, he'd track her down and try to help, a possibility rife with potential negative outcomes.

But Eddy couldn't think of Suzie right now—he had a job to do. A lot was at stake, and if he didn't focus, he could lose business for the club. Or maybe even get them all killed.

On his passenger seat lay six brown folders. Each contained the summarized rap sheets and bios of different Heads—district bosses whom Bird had hired to oversee multiple distribution sites within their regions, and whom Eddy would be meeting for the first time in under an hour.

Bird had prepared a list of questions he would ask Eddy during the meeting, thereby feeding the Heads whatever information he wished to impart. During a run-through at Bird's safehouse yesterday, with Del Ray acting as quizmaster, Eddy had nailed the memorization questions, an ace at cramming for tests, and did fairly well fielding anticipated counterquestions.

This prompted Bird to give him a hard side-hug, saying, "I always knew you'd be here, right by my side. Makes me proud. My second son."

These old words left Eddy feeling torn, unsure how he lived in Bird's mind these days. Was his boss actually proud? Or was Eddy just easy to manipulate? To move on, he chose to believe a familial bond still existed between them, that from the spinning vortex of their lives, a simpler path ahead remained possible.

The Heads all looked like you'd expect—well-fed and mug-shot worthy—felonious suits who'd agreed to work for a shadow boss they'd never meet. This "Chief," as the boss was known, was a fabricated character of Bird's own making, a way to show face without exposing the crown. Near the end of each financial quarter, moving forward, the Heads would file into Palm Bay for a sit-down with Bird, aka Seizer, who self-identified as a kind of undersecretary to the Chief. Eddy would act as the Chief's voice, his instructions—the First Contact—which brought to mind space aliens, though Del Ray suggested he try visualizing it in electrical terms. The role involved the conveyance of critical information in person, which meant he'd also be traveling. Sales figures and inventory reports could be encrypted, but certain sensitive requests required a human representative—it was, in some respects, a spin-off of Mickey's old job, before he joined the club.

One of the brown folders had him freaking out. It belonged to Alex, the Toros leader. A single photograph, grainy and enlarged, shot from an elevated distance. Would he recognize Eddy from the time they'd met last year at Alex's club in Miami? Luckily Cueball wouldn't be around, probably directed to some post hundreds of miles away. Several times the night before, noticing his composure, Bird assured Eddy there was nothing to worry about—there'd be wiggle room for error and improvisation, and Eddy would be forgiven a stumble or two. But it wasn't hard to imagine one of these brutes taking out a gun and ending his life at the table.

He checked his phone for the time.

After hot-boxing a smoke, he squashed it underfoot in the grass, locked the car, and made a beeline for the bar entrance.

The inside of Ma Kettle's was dark and boozy, bathed in the greasy stench of onion rings and burgers. The lady at the counter fixed her bra strap and nodded him toward the rear, where Del Ray sat alone in a screened-in porch nursing a pint and softly humming an old Sunday school hymn: *Father Abraham had many sons, many sons had Father Abraham.*

Then his voice went off like a gunshot. "There he is!"

They locked arms and Del nudged a chair over with his boot.

"How you feeling?" he asked. "Ready to go?"

"I think so," said Eddy. "Bit of a nervous stomach."

"Just remember how we practiced. If you don't know what to say, say nothing. Pretend it's confidential. And turn off your phone—if that thing rings at the table, you'll catch some eye shrapnel, if not a whaling. And if someone threatens you . . . you laugh."

"Jesus, is this your idea of a pep talk?"

"I'm here to keep us all aboveground and thriving," Del Ray said, pushing forward a decaf coffee. "I'd get you a beer, but you should be sober for this. Remember, it's like goat herding—if they look lost, just point 'em in the right direction."

In his nervousness, Eddy let slip that he felt deeply undeserving of this job. To his mind, Duke seemed a much more natural fit. Armed with a calm demeanor and potent self-assuredness, his friend would have shown up today with a bagel and a Big Gulp, yawning.

"There's a reason we picked you," said Del Ray.

"I don't look threatening?"

"Ha! Maybe. I was going to say it's because you think on your feet when people fuck with you, and these guys will fuck with you." Del Ray took Eddy's shoulder, his smile one of confidence. "Remember, I'm right upstairs, your eye in the sky. See this earpiece? You got nothing to worry about."

The Heads arrived soon after.

The meeting was relatively informal: seven men dressed for shuffleboard or bocce, elbows on the table, warming up with bad jokes and health complaints over iced whiskey and beers. Each Head was allowed one bodyguard, who had to wait in the bar.

Looking about, Eddy was relieved to find Alex had failed to show up.

The meeting started without fanfare. In the screened-in porch overlooking pinewoods, Bird presided dressed in a collared shirt—a first. He wore glasses and read from a notebook, going down a list. He even pretended not to know things. Eddy still found it odd to hear people refer to him as *Seizer.*

Halfway through the minutes, Billy Tan Wojahn, an ex-Army native with a face like a lunar landscape, requested a policy change following a serious screwup the previous month. Billy Tan owned a small chain of grocery stores doubling as distribution sites along the Gulf of Mexico, what he called the Redneck Riviera. His qualm was with the Packers, who were not his own employees but prescreened workers supplied by the Chief. Two stamped crates had been mixed up—"Catch this irony," he said. "You can't make this stuff up—*apples* and *oranges.*"

Oranges were oranges, Florida grown, but apples were crates of shank hidden in red wax replicas. Luckily a transport agent liked to snack on the drive, so the shipments were halted and returned before they affected some stock boy's inventory.

Billy Tan wanted to use his own men to crate the shipments, some of whom were admittedly undocumented workers, when Bird cut in: "We're not an equal opportunity employer, Billy. We can't be. This problem of yours seems managerial. Now, your guys label those shipments, correct? So you can't lay blame entirely on the Packers. Our staffing policy cuts back on thievery, plain and simple. If Chief's men pack it, that's fewer people we'd have to interrogate if something gets stolen or goes sideways. We can't take chances with illegals, 'cause if they get arrested, suddenly the Feds are involved. Not to mention, you might get yourself a spy. Just ask Django. Juárez has been sniffing around for months. We know for a fact they got Pumpers in Atlanta and Scouts in Orlando—"

But Eddy was no longer paying attention. The posturing and bickering was having a negative effect on his anxiety. He spoke only to regurgitate information, unable to shake the feeling that the DEA or local police—somebody—knew about this meeting, and being caught with anyone at the table would ensure the creation of a folder bearing his name in several governmental agencies.

For the first time, Eddy believed that he worked for a drug cartel. Not just a business, or a club, but a *cartel.* Duke and Lisbon and Cueball were the heirs and progeny of drug lords. He could even imagine who'd play them in the movie version of their lives. Jesse—that chubby prankster who once tied a younger Draco to his bed, spread out porn mags, opened some Vaseline, and shouted for their mom—was *actually* out in the world right now collecting gangsters. Gone too was the heavily tatted, backyard party king of Palm Bay—before him sat the mythic Bird of horror stories, substantiated. A true drug czar. The fucking Seizer.

And here Eddy was, a scrawny nobody, dropped into a den of drug pushers and strongmen, some of whom might even consider him dangerous—a hilarious notion. But the newest Seizer had vouched for him, which carried weight. It meant knowing that if any of them took a shotgun blast to the face, rest assured the next morning a score of men, acting on information from Eddy, would be out in the streets hunting down the responsible party. That's what they saw in him—loyalty, allegiance. They roamed pool halls and trailer parks looking for his kind—those hard-born, pushed-around, inconspicuous keepers of secrets.

"Hey, short stack."

Bird was watching him.

"W-what's the problem?" asked Eddy.

"He asked you a question."

Eddy swerved to a fat guy, bowling ball for a head, Luther, ex-mob, more sweat than shirt. "Any issue switching up the early October drop-offs? So we start with the ukraine's in Pittsburgh, instead of Philly, then another in Ravens Eye, West Virgina? Who's that guinea fella with the blue eyes?"

"Fiori, but they call him Fury," offered Bird, adding a jokey barb: "Might help to remember the names of your Holders."

"Uh, Chief said that'd be fine," said Eddy, flipping through his small notebook. "But we need extra coverage. We've received tips," he added, catching himself a moment before eyeing Bird for confirmation, "that the southern Pennsylvania border's being closely monitored. Some rolling mom & pop labs got busted a few weeks back. Chief wants an extra Wingman on any transport crossing the state line."

This was a complete lie—there were no such labs, no such tips, but the Heads demanded reassurances. Some had legit businesses to consider, families, mortgages, college tuitions. Bird created straw-men scenarios to publicly tear down, emboldening their faith in the legitimacy of the security he offered. And the safer the Heads felt, the easier they were to manipulate.

"That all you have for us?" asked the bowling ball, tonguing his cheek.

"Looks like," said Eddy.

Luther leaned over his gut. "Who's your boss, kid? Who is this *Chief?*"

It was a test. All eyes were upon him. Eddy was able to swallow the adrenaline spike before it registered in his expression.

"Never met him. All my checks come direct deposit."

The mobster fell back with a belly laugh, joined in by everyone at the table, who seemed glad to have the tension dispelled. "You must got some balls," he said. "Little shit. Who trains these kids, Seizer?"

"No one trains young men like this," grunted Bird, giving Eddy a look he'd come to cherish.

The afternoon fell to storytelling as the meeting adjourned and a final round of drinks came out. Eddy felt he'd pulled off the job okayly, but desperately needed a cigarette.

Unfortunately, a mexican-american Head named Django cornered him before he could get up. Despite the conversational tone, Eddy sensed he was fishing for something else.

"Gangs are shortsighted, they only see differences," said Django. "But us, we have unity. Cooperation. Gangs, they see tiers, top and bottom. Like this term 'drug mule.' These are people, not animals. They do scary work. We should pay them well."

An advertising exec and former coyote who transported illegal migrants along a route he called the "ACE Train," Django now worked scores between Knoxville and New Orleans, building off networks he'd developed among itinerant populations. It struck Eddy that Django was the new version of Derrik, the biker contact who was supposed to open up the West for the club, but instead shot up Jesse's house party. Del Ray was right, there was always another person to do whatever job necded done. Good for business, but it also meant they were all expendable.

"There's all kinds of gangs—latino, italian, black. Shit, polynesian. When I was a kid in LA, I got jumped by these asians, saw I had an asian lady on my arm—right there in front of the movies! Because their mentalities are narrow. Gangs are too much based on one thing: race, place, economic whatevers. What's their number one problem?" asked Django, holding up a finger. "Limited access. No whites in the barrio, no yellow in Hollywood, no chicanos anywhere but the kitchen, right? Now imagine this—a club that unites them all. We're talking real jobs, living wages. Most of my families, they got no healthcare. Even al-Qaeda gots healthcare. Obamacare? Yeah right, when I see it. My people, they starve to pay rent. And I'm supposed to watch them bail out these Wall Street pendejos while our kids don't eat? Uh-uh. No way. Access is key. Access spreads wealth."

"Absolutely," Bird chimed in. "My thoughts exactly."

"I'm gonna have a sit-down with the Chief," Django said, and Eddy understood he was being asked a favor. "Immigrants wanna work. If we break up the small-minded mentality, we can have our people everywhere, at every level. The customers aren't going anywhere! Well, unless the levees break again, right? Ha, I could teach a course."

As the Heads finished up their discussions, Eddy put on an affable look and made himself as small as possible until they all finally filed out of the bar.

Del Ray stomped downstairs and playfully slapped Eddy's face lightly before putting him in a headlock. "Goddamn, boy, look at you! Almost twenty and all growed up! You sounded like a union rep down here!"

Bird propped a pint glass before him. "Maybe you're too valuable to be left alone. These guys might try to steal you away." His back slap was heavy and jovial. "You did good work today, son."

The word hit like it was supposed to.

"Thanks," said Eddy. "Django was cool. He's got a lot of big ideas."

"They all do," said Bird. "Some better than others."

Eddy grimaced. "I'm actually kinda glad Alex didn't show up."

Del Ray leaned back and folded his hands behind his head. Eddy felt he'd made a mistake. Bird's grip on his shoulders seemed to confirm this. The aging biker slid over a chair and smiled like it was all Boy Scout fun.

"Alex is severing ties," said Bird.

"I wouldn't put it that way," said Del Ray, encouraging a hard look from his boss. "Well, I wouldn't."

"In this new position of yours," said Bird, pianoing the table, "you're gonna hear some things." Paused so Eddy understood. "Alex claims the FBI popped a few of his boys last week. Worried him enough to renege on a major deal, right as our new camp kicks off manufacturing. And just like that, Miami goes dark."

"He's keeping things in-house till things calm down," Del Ray clarified. "It's a solid move. We'll begin feeding him the goods again by December. We have his word."

"In the meantime," Bird continued, "they've got boys selling stuff you make out of a plastic soda bottle. Mix it up wrong and it blows your face off. So I have to ask myself—if you're gonna say fuck the heat and stay in the game, why put out an inferior product, when we've got the goods right here? Why would someone do this, Eddy?"

The question hung in the air long enough to move past the rhetorical. "Maybe he thinks we tipped off the Feds," said Eddy. "Or maybe he's just trying to keep himself safe. Maybe keep us safe too."

"Or maybe," nodded Bird, ignoring Del's smile, "there are no Feds, and this here's a bullshit excuse to cut us out. Maybe these Toros think they're the new Cocaine Cowboys."

Bird let the accusation sit as he left to pay the tab. Del Ray ordered two shots of mescal as some local patrons began to file in. Eddy protested, but Del ignored this, pushing the glass into his hand.

"To the First Contact. Work is the curse of the drinking class." He gripped Eddy's neck, staring into his face. "You, sir, are a *professional*. I hope one day you get that tattoo parlor you talk about, 'cause I wanna be the first one in that chair. You choose the design and I'll write you a little narco-corrido of an unassuming willow seed that blossomed into a venus flytrap."

Back in his car, Eddy's buzz all but evaporated.

Talk of the tattoo parlor disheartened him. The option didn't even feel like an option anymore, just a fantasy he played out before sleep sometimes.

His options felt reduced to one option—remain a club member in good standing, attendant to the needs of his superiors. He owed Bird that much, didn't he? This man who'd opened up his home when Eddy was essentially homeless? Who'd lifted him up from poverty?

Driving north, he passed a series of trailer parks, single-wides of prefab aluminum glinting behind the overgrown vegetation near Castaways Point. He was no longer scraping the very bottom, at least. Eddy wondered how long before the Heads got greedy and revolted, splintering off into factions. Hostility at this level seemed inevitable. In the meantime, Bird would string them along with promises. Soon it would be Eddy making the promises in Bird's stead, a toy soldier placed between two slowly advancing hydraulic presses. Or maybe he was paranoid, and everything would work out fine.

Back at the bar, the Heads had showed him real respect, and the dark nourishment of that pride lingered.

For now, he was safe. Cueball was safe. Duke and Lisbon seemed fine. Jesse was making bank. Eddy's mother was still being cared for and Gin was still better off without him. Bird had entrusted him with an important position with real-world implications and he'd proven himself worthy. Was this not one of the futures he'd longingly envisioned for himself as he was sweating out toxins at the Georgia cabin?

Yet a small, denigrating voice, some internal editor, was already hacking any future dreams down to size.

This parlor shit's a no-go. Don't forget that Big Mike rejected you, asshole. You've already visited a college town and discovered you don't fit in. And don't forget Suzie Fuentes and the countless others who suffer while you continue to benefit. You deserve no hope, sleep, or forgiveness, given what you've done.

He'd beat addiction—that was his, he owned that truth. As for the rest of it—he couldn't tell if he'd made good or bad decisions, he just knew when things hurt or didn't hurt. And if that were the case, why beat himself up over any of it?

PART V

THE
SKY
THE
LAND
THE
SEA

The side streets were barricaded for the Cocoa Village Arts Festival, an ostentatious display of fabricated Old World charm, with courtyard cafés and galleries and catacombs of kitsch tucked into several blocks of gingerbread brick and fern-strung alleyways.

A gaudy enterprise devoid of locals, but for once Cueball didn't mind the snowbirds. He'd grown to envy the quaint normality of their lives, their iced coffees and small dogs, the congenial banter exchanged as they browsed the paper-clip clipper ships and alaskan wildlife photos. What about them had he ever found so distasteful, so ominous, these middle-class americans with their thick glasses and terrible haircuts and varicose veins? What had he imagined they were lording over him?

From a park bench, Cueball watched a small girl quietly surrender her fight to keep her ice cream cone from dripping down her hands—a moment of loss so innocent it choked him up. Weird, but he'd been feeling slightly unhinged as of late, morose even, as if he were an outsider himself. His dreams lately plagued by a recurring nightmare: diagnosed with cancer, the CAT scan found his entire skeleton was etched with scenes from his battle-scarred life, like a whalebone scrimshaw.

His father had ordered him to lay low for a week, so he wandered the beach alone gathering shells or sipping Jose Cuervo in the shady overlook of his dingy Cocoa Beach motel room, watching the gray ocean swell and break behind sea oats. He was glad to be free of the golf caddy dealers, the off-duty cops at the range, but in solitude his mind tended to cannibalize itself, revisiting the past. TV only exacerbated this. Pumping gas one night, he overheard an older white guy call the clerk a *spic*, and considered following that man home and doing terrible things to him. He often returned to that night in Miami Beach, where the simplest of questions posed by a trans sex worker brought him to tears. He imagined sharing his secrets might open a space of acceptance, or drive. But it hadn't. The world chewed each promise to the bone, the leftovers raw and meager and sadly bearable.

In a search of purpose, he decided to get square with Duke and Lisbon. He considered stuffing their mailbox with bricks of two-dollar bills, or baseball card hobby boxes, something oddly specific that indicated a personal regard, yet cowered before the impetus pressing him to do so.

At the arts fair the snowbirds sorted, slurped, meandered, bartered, and smacked their children. A few even bought something. When a group of kids his age back from Afghanistan wandered by in pixelated fatigues, Cueball took cold comfort in believing they'd done some killing themselves. It was like a secret organization he'd been inducted into, where members operated under the public's willful ignorance and fantasy.

He milled about novelty stores selling bear jerky and tins of chocolate-covered ants. The magic shop had a wallet that caught fire when opened. Yes, I'm sorry for murdering your uncle, Lisbon, here's some fake shit in a can. Here's a clock fashioned from a tree stump, Duke, I hope it gets you through this trying time. Inside a New Age shop selling power crystals, he imagined leaping atop the glass counter and pushing a pistol into the roof of his mouth.

Instead, he ventured into an encampment of booths set up in a parking lot.

One such booth was staffed by a young woman with finely drawn eyebrows selling henna tattoos and jewelry. She wore an eyebrow ring, a nose stud, a tongue bar, and, in full salute beneath her tank top, two nipple rings shaped like half-moons.

Cueball stood silent before her wares as other shoppers trickled away.

"Ever try henna?" she asked perkily.

Cueball held up his wrist, a warped Royal palm covering a pink scar. "Got the real deal, thanks."

"Niiice," she said, drawing the word out cutely. "You here with your parents?"

He smiled. "Oh yeah, just me and the fam."

"Where you from?"

"Nowhere. Everywhere. I'm barely here now." Responding to her eyebrow arch, he added: "We take our camper around the country. What else you got back there?"

"Um . . . we got patches."

Out came a plastic case filled with an assortment of patches, bearing all manner of affiliation.

"I should probably eBay them, but I'm kind of a Luddite."

"What's this?" Cueball asked, holding one aloft.

"Army, baby! Eighty-Second Airborne. It belonged to my grampa. He used to trade with his friends up at the Cape. That one there's Military Police. And those, those are astronauts."

Excitement gripped Cueball. "Do you have anything with Armstrong on it?"

"Hmm, lemme check." As she bent forward, her shirt top pursed, but the nipple rings remained just out of view. "Apollo, right? Buzz is so hot. Oh here, check these out. It's got everything: the moon, the eagle, the earth."

"Is that a palmetto in its claws?"

"I think an olive branch. Like for peace?"

Even better, thought Cueball. "How many you got?"

"Maybe six? I can give them to you for . . . two bucks apiece?"

"Two bucks? Really? But they were your grandpa's—"

"He don't mind, he's dead. And you seem like a nice guy. He'd be happy they went to someone who cared."

"I'll give you fifty, for five of 'em."

"Oh, no—"

"I insist. That seems fair."

The girl smiled, clicking the tongue bar against the back of her teeth. "What's your name again?"

"Heath."

"Well, that's a very gentlemanly offer, Heath."

He smiled, crossing his arms, thinking yes it was.

It was probably just the enthusiasm of getting her number, but when Cueball stepped from his car at Indialantic Beach twenty miles south to meet the Crew, it was with a newfound optimism. The sun was high overhead and the beach dotted with umbrellas and bodies like jelly beans. He even found himself saying hi to passing strangers.

Duke and Lisbon were on their knees waxing surfboards. Eddy was piecing together fishing poles beside newspapered clusters of baitfish.

"Howdy!"

Duke looked up, befit with his usual scowl. "You bring beer?"

"Shit," said Cueball, deflated both by his forgetfulness and his lofty mood's impermanence.

"Jesse's bringing beer!" Eddy shouted over the wind.

Cueball stripped off his shirt and began applying sunscreen. As the boys resumed their work, he fell into a beach chair, waiting for the right moment.

"I have a surprise for everyone!" he bellowed, feeling instantly stupid.

Already their faces betrayed a gleeful group desire to attack. *You have a surprise for us? Oh yay! Goody!*

"It's nothing, really. Just I was down at the art fair, and I met this girl selling stuff. Got her digits too. She's got like an eyebrow thing . . ."

Cueball held out his simple offerings.

"They're from when Armstrong landed on the moon."

Lisbon hopped up from the sand and stumbled over, snatching up a patch to bring close to his face. Eddy and Duke each took one, inspecting the sewed ridges. The two traded smirks but Lisbon was ecstatic, slapping Cueball's arm before hustling back to his blanket.

"I know it's dumb, I know it," said Cueball. "Shit."

"Naw, man," Eddy replied. "They're beautiful! I will treasure this forever."

"Screw you."

Eddy turned to Duke. "Look, bro, it's even got *the moon* on it!"

With them off to the races, all Cueball could do was cuss and snap on his sunglasses and turn away.

A few seconds later, though, a shadow crossed his knees. Duke was standing there turning the patch over in his hands. His expression was serious, as if coming to terms with something. "These real?"

"The girl said her grandpa used to work at NASA, so yeah, they're legit.

And with the shuttles being grounded, I bet they'll be worth even more as collector's items."

Duke accepted this, peering back at his brother, who was hiding the prize in his shoe. "So we got two choices today, fish or surf," Duke said, pointing out a twin fin about Cueball's height.

"I don't know how to surf," Cueball confided. "I can boogie board."

"You used to skate, right? You'll get it. Let's practice by hopping up on the sand."

Before he could argue, a hand extended toward him. Pausing briefly, Cueball took Duke's arm, tat to tat, and raised up from his chair.

"Where'd you learn?"

"Carolina's got beaches too, man."

Out on the water, Cueball managed to stand a few times, and even kept his balance long enough to turn once.

Eddy held the fishing pole between his legs and watched, the line resting lightly on his middle finger as he zeroed in on the vibrations, drifting toward that place where the sea and the fisherman are like two siblings holding opposite ends of a string, each one's tug the specific cue of a private language, a simple discourse that managed to part the depths of each.

He was having trouble shaking some things Duke had said at a 7-Eleven earlier.

Arms full of chips and Slim Jims, he found Duke perusing a rack of magazines, stuffing a *Playboy* behind the dirt bike mags.

"Just a big old sausage fest," said Duke.

"Say what?"

"We've lost our women."

Eddy almost laughed. Lost where? But then Gin's face surfaced and split his afternoon along a clean fracture of regret.

"I can't remember the last time I hung out with a girl," said Duke. "I'm not talking about chasing tail, I'm talking about catching a movie, grabbing food—chillin."

Eddy wished he'd just drop it. "Man, I know for a fact you banged that black waitress at the crab shack in Columbus."

"I told you, man, I'm not talking about fucking!" exclaimed Duke, voice rushing to a hush. "She was nice and all, but I don't recall her name. I just remember she was born in Kansas, because who the fuck's born in Kansas? Seriously, when's the last time you hung out with a girl? A *female*." He let that point simmer. "When's the last time you saw your mom?"

Eddy hadn't spoken to her outside of voicemail since Christmas. Or Charlotte since Seizer's funeral, sharing only a hug and a few cursory words. Colt crept in there too, drunk forever under a barbarous moon at lake's edge. So much stacked regret. Gin's burning words. *Yeah, she slapped you, but you lost your goddamn mind.* To stave off the memories, he kept busy with work and masturbation and zero fucking drugs, unfortunately, drinking more these days than he'd care to admit.

"Busy people make sacrifices," Eddy mumbled. "I heard half the folks in med school get dumped before graduation."

"We're not in med school," said Duke pointedly. "They left us. Didn't want to be around us. Didn't think we cared, 'cause we didn't. Bird thinks they're weak. To him all women are Old Ladies or whores, but even the Old Ladies get treated like dirt. It's despicable. More than that, it's unnatural."

"I've never heard him say—"

"This is a cult. We're in a cult," said Duke. "We've been manipulated. Cut all ties, so all's we got to rely on is each other. Textbook military tactic."

"Alright, jeesh," said Eddy. "Maybe we can download some app or join a hiking group or something. There's plenty of places to meet chicks. Heck, we could double-date."

"Can you imagine us on dates?" asked Duke, grinning like a psychopath. "What would we talk about? Work? Know any cool new music? Me neither. Face it, man, we're not interesting. We're worker bees, with money."

Eddy cleared his throat. "Maybe I prefer it this way."

"Bullshit," said Duke defiantly. "You just accept it like the rest of us. Cueball's the only one who might prefer hanging out with dudes all the time."

"The fuck's that mean?"

Duke shifted the bag of chips under an arm. "You know."

"Know what?"

Duke cinched his eyes, trying to get a good read. "Because he's bi. Or closeted or something."

The sudden squeezing issue with Eddy's throat felt clinical.

"You see, this is exactly what I'm talking about. We don't confront shit!" cried Duke. "We've been molded into these little plastic soldiers. Dickless, green . . . disposable toys."

"Yeah, well, it wasn't exactly Bird who created this shitty cult culture, now was it?"

Duke stood flat-footed. "You're absolutely right. My uncle was a hundred percent wrong about some things, including trusting a bunch of backwoods assholes to carry him through old age."

In this moment, a ruthless thought entered Eddy's mind. Here was Duke, still positioning himself as an insider—but with his uncle gone, he'd been instantly demoted to Eddy's level. And knew it. *Actually*, given his promotion to First Contact, Eddy now outranked Duke, which felt bonkers.

But Duke had tears in his eyes.

"Shit, man, I'm sorry," said Eddy. "That was uncalled-for. You touched a sore spot. Your uncle was a good man."

Duke stood there, jaw clenched. "Was he?"

After an interlude of silence, they approached the counter together, but Duke swung back, poised by Eddy's ear.

"I can trust you, right?"

"Of course," said Eddy.

"I need a favor. You see me getting this upset, acting strange . . . I need you to talk me down. Lisbon and I, we have to keep our heads down. They'll come after us—"

"Who will? They got that guy—"

Duke was watching the floor. "I'm not always patient. The time'll come—"

"You planning something?"

Duke spun out of his reverie, wiping his eyes. "No, I mean, if we don't get these promotions . . . I may have to reevaluate staying."

"Dude, it's a done deal. Del already said once they get the second camp running, you're the Foreman. That's his word."

"Until then, Bird's got us running with a new Wingman each week. Most can't even remember the routes. It doesn't feel secure," said Duke. "Listen, don't tell anyone we talked about this."

"Of course," Eddy said. "Hey, man, look: we're family. You can trust me."

Duke slapped Eddy's shoulder on his way to pay for the snacks.

Back on the beach, Eddy woke from his meditation to something cold and wet sliding down the back of his shirt. He jerked up, wiping feverishly at his neck.

Jesse's big grin said it all, suntan lotion in his hands. Eddy grabbed a towel and chased him down, snapping it over his legs until Jesse turned and heaved Eddy over his shoulder, ending the skirmish.

The bronzed filipino had replaced his gut with what he called a "starter six-pack." Gone were the greasy jeans and beat-up Nikes—Jesse's new wardrobe consisted of guayaberas over white T-shirts, a silver chain, long shorts, and fancy flip-flops.

Once freed, Eddy retrieved two beers from Jesse's duffel bag. They sat watching their friends duck surfboards under the incoming waves.

Jesse held up a space patch like one tickled by the mangled reality of a child's drawing. "Is this for real?"

"It's funny, huh."

"Not really," said Jesse. "What are we, five? And why're we so far away from the bikinis? We look like a bunch of gay dudes celebrating our right to marry." He inched his sunglasses down. "No pun intended."

"Duke say something to you?" asked Eddy.

"No, why?"

On the waves Lisbon just missed decapitating his waterborne brother.

Jesse raised a hand as Cueball approached, stabbing his surfboard in the sand. "Cuuuueballll. Brotherman."

"Damn, boy, look at you!" Cueball said, extending an arm. "Hip to the hippity hop, motherfucker, you look slick! Where'd my fat teddy bear go? Are these muscle implants?"

"Shit," said Jesse, dodging Cueball's nipple pinches. "Duty called. Said Jess, you fat fuck, clean it up. These guys'll respect you more if you respect yourself. I have a hard enough time getting these dudes to believe what I'm offering is for real."

"Bet they think you're a cop," said Cueball.

"I hear that shit all the time. But usually I got one of Mickey's old contacts introducing me, so I walk in with some street cred. But that don't stop people from busting my chops."

"You must have some stories," said Eddy.

For certain, Jesse mugged. "How long you been fishing?"

"Couple hours," said Eddy. "Nothing's biting."

"Well I came down here to fish, and I can plainly see you're not interested in catching any."

"You wanna have a go?"

"You gotta learn to take a risk, my friend," Jesse said, and immediately stripped down to his boxers.

"Whoa!" cried Cueball. "Seriously, though, why filipinos always getting naked?"

Jesse took the catch bucket down to the ocean and submerged it and came back and began quartering the baitfish with a knife. Then dropped the chunks in the bucket, swirling the water until it was red and gruesome.

"You should get them out before you chum up the water," said Eddy, recalling the last time they'd bloodied the shoreline, only to hook a bull shark. Even after four hours on the beach, beer bottles jutting from every orifice, the shark continued sucking air.

"They'll figure it out," said Jesse, carrying the bucket downslope.

"Dude's fucking nuts," said Cueball, watching Jesse hoist the bucket over waves. "He's changed."

"Got his shit together. I wish I had his motivation," said Eddy. "Actually . . . I've been thinking about starting my own side hustle."

Cueball tilted his head. "You serious?"

"As a heart attack," said Eddy.

"Like what? You gonna get back into tatting?"

"Why not. Get my own shop."

Cueball shrugged. "Do you have the funds? Not to be a dick, but. Maybe try reaching out to Big Mike first. That guy's all set up—"

"Fuck Big Mike and his Ed Hardy rip-offs," said Eddy, spitting. "I want a stable of *real* artists. I may not have the time to ink every job myself, but I can spot talent. I mean, look at Jesse, he's got his real estate thing going."

Cueball jutted his lip. "Well, hey man, if you're serious . . . a parlor would be something I'd throw money at."

"Yeah?" asked Eddy. "A partnership? I'm down."

"Hells yeah, bud!" said Cueball, genuinely delighted. "You and me, Bonnie and Clyde! Let's do it! I'll be Clyde. Instead of gunning up banks . . . we'll make bank, gunning tats."

"Did you just think that up?"

"I just thought that up, straight freestyle from the heart, baby, that's how sure I am this can work!"

"It wouldn't be easy," said Eddy. "We'd need artists, equipment, clientele. You have to turn on the utilities and get insurance, all that mess." He glanced down the beach. "Yeah, we'll make it happen. When the time is right, it'll happen."

"Naw, man, don't do that," said Cueball. "God . . . *damn* it! *It'll happen. I'mma do it.* If you don't wanna do it, just say so. Don't make me part of some lie you tell yourself."

"What's your fucking problem?" asked Eddy.

"Don't you ever get tired of just dreaming? Commit to something, for chrissakes," said Cueball, shaking his head and sipping his beer. "Whatever. Two tears in a bucket . . . motherfuck-it."

Eddy held up his hands. "Why is everyone attacking me today?"

Cueball realized he'd put more strength behind the words than he'd intended. He pushed Eddy's shoulder and ducked to catch his eyes. "Don't listen to me, man. I'm just a hammer looking for a nail."

When Eddy didn't budge, Cueball raised his fist, knuckle out. "Don't come at me with that shit," whined Eddy, waving it off. But Cueball didn't drop the fist, and eventually Eddy huffed and reached over, knocking the knuckle.

Cueball smiled, raising his beer at the ocean. "Look at this idiot."

Jesse had blushed the water pink and was swimming around in the guts and filth. Bobbing up and down, he faked a shark attack, waving his arms for them to join him.

For most folks, Wet 'n Wild called to mind a family-style theme park offering crystal-blue wading pools and looping waterslides, but for Cueball it summoned a high-end topless bar off Orange Blossom Trail in Orlando, where white-collar patrons stopped off for a brewski and some jiggle after enduring the rigors of eighteen rounds of humiliation touted as leisure. Often these same men lined up out back prior to tee time, looking to score a little pick-me-up, something to narrow their focus and drives. Cueball would collect the club's take from management and stay on for the buffet and afternoon show, another side gig till Bird found cause to utilize his son's more special talents.

Headed back to Melbourne, no streetlights for a stretch, Cueball lowered his window and sipped black coffee, the pungent scent of skunks mounting the dark countryside. Not a wholly unpleasant smell—homey, actually—drawing out memories of earthen flats and white egrets and tire swings brimming with water. The lovebugs pasted to his windshield carried too some inkling of childhood, which he indulged as the night wind toyed with his mood soporifically.

The beach party a few weeks back felt reconciliatory, and his plan to slowly win over the Twins through amiability and distance appeared to be working. They'd even come to his nineteenth birthday party, a mellow affair held at a bowling alley, for which Cueball bought several rounds using a brand-new fake ID, a gift to himself. And though he hadn't yet followed up with the cute art fair exhibitor who'd sold him the patches, she was never far from his mind. The problem was, he'd never asked anyone out before; he only ever met people at parties. But things were changing, and Cueball felt upbeat and confident. He hadn't relapsed, and alongside Eddy, picked up his pool stick again, meeting up for quarter buffalo wings at the Golden Cue. He even invested in a polo shirt, and a few nights back, clutching his phone like a security blanket, walked into a gay nightclub far from home and sat down at the bar, nursing a beer as he watched sports highlights.

Suddenly his phone piped up beside him. As the caller's name registered, he smiled.

"Duuuuke. 'Sup."

"Where are you?"

"Headed back from Orlando. Why, you boys got some fun lined up?"

"We're dealing with a situation," said Duke tensely. "Our Wingman had a blowout."

"What?"

"Our *Wing*-man had a *blow*-out," Duke enunciated. "We have some friends waiting for us at a bar, but man, we're only a few miles from home, and I'm already pretty loaded."

It took a moment to understand what Duke was saying. "Blowout" was code that the Wingman had been pulled over by the cops, and "the bar" referred to their final drop-off destination. Apparently they were carrying a big shipment too. At least it wasn't a "blown gasket," which indicated someone was definitely headed to jail.

"Did you call your guy a cab?" asked Cueball, referring to whatever new point person was responsible for helping out if a run went sideways.

"Yeah, someone's picking him up," replied Duke. "We're headed to a diner now, waiting to hear if another friend might join. You wanna grab a quick coffee with us? If not, I'm thinking we might just head back, hit the sack. It's been a long night."

Duke wanted to return to the storage facility and unload the shipment, pronto, but his point person insisted they wait at the designated safety checkpoint for a replacement Wingman. Duke, clearly unhappy with this strategy, was asking if Cueball would come hang with them until things got sorted.

"Coffee sounds good," said Cueball. "Which diner?"

Duke ran through a series of false street names indicating a truck stop just off the highway, out near the dog tracks and former jai alai center.

"I can be there in fifteen," said Cueball, always willing to help, if only to further his foray into Duke's good graces. "Hit me up if your plans change any."

"Roger that," said Duke, and hung up.

Cueball turned on the radio. No cars in sight and empty cattle farms for miles. These new Runners, where did Jesse find them? No doubt getting pulled over scared the poor newbie nut-thwacker shitless; probably already back home with his doors locked and blinds drawn. The more Cueball thought about it, though, the more he felt his dad should be informed of the predicament.

Town lights fogged up the sky ahead. Cueball punched in his father's number, thinking as it rang that he should have called the business number. "Pop?"

"Heath? Can't talk, I'm busy."

"I figured you might wanna know—"

"I'm busy here, Heath—"

"I'm gonna grab a snack with the boys, so I'll be late for dinner. Looks like my buddies' Wingman had some car trouble, so they called in the cavalry."

The line went dead.

Cueball touched his phone screen. Yep, hung up. Weird. He dropped the phone in his lap and watched a train of red lights glide through the air. The truck stop sat just beyond the Interstate bridge.

His phone rang as he passed underneath it.

"Hello hello."

"Get your ass home!" Bird bellowed.

"Whoa! Calm down, why are you shouting?"

"Goddammit, Cueball! I told you never to use the landline for business!"

It had been years since his father last uttered his nickname.

"Get home, now!"

"Calm down, Dad! Are you on some new lipid medication? What the fuck?"

"Come here! Home base, not your hotel room, you hear me?"

"Okay, sheesh, I got it!"

But Cueball was already pulling into the lot.

The truck stop was comprised of a small diner attached to a convenience store with pay showers, both decorated with old holiday bulbs. The halogens were off at the pumps but the store lights were still on. Behind the complex, Cueball could make out the long flat side of a big rig, parked for the night.

"Where are you right now?" Bird asked.

"I'm here but I'm turning around."

"Where?"

"Here! At the diner!"

The other end of the line went quiet, but Cueball sensed his father was still there. The convenience store looked unattended, but then a clerk popped up and shoved a carton of cigarettes into an overhead bin.

"Heath," said his father. "Get home, son."

"I said I was!" shouted Cueball, hanging up. "Fuck *you!*" he spit into the phone, switching it to buzz and flipping it to the passenger seat.

Exasperated, he slowed before the gas pumps. Diner looked closed. If the Twins weren't waiting around back, he'd call Duke and apologize and head over to his father's safehouse.

The back lot was more spacious than he expected, and dark. Ten or so eighteen-wheelers and a few box trucks stretched out for the night. Cueball steered between them, scanning the empty cabs. He found the Twins' moving van beyond the final parking spot, set before the woods.

The van was turned around, facing the other vehicles. The cab lights were on but there was no one inside, so Cueball parked facing the van with a little space between them and waited, rotating the rearview mirror to peer back at the silent metal rigs glowing under a single stadium lamp. At one point he heard a loud clang, and what sounded like people arguing. He inched up and scanned the dark underbellies of the rigs for movement. Nothing. Back lots always made him uneasy. He imagined all kinds of ugliness happened in places like this.

In the rearview a silhouetted figure appeared. Cueball ducked instinctively, reaching under his seat. The gun's features took on a solid reality in his hand. But there was a recognizable affect to the figure's gait, an unhurried bob, shoulders out and elbows tucked as if holding something.

It was Duke. And he had nachos.

Duke rounded the Nova and set down the nachos and two sodas on the hood, then stared directly through the windshield at Cueball, who immediately dropped the gun. He put a hand up and stepped from his car into the humid night as Duke untwisted the Dr Pepper cap with a hiss.

"So this newbie dipshit got himself pulled over, huh?" Cueball joked with a tinge of superiority. "Poor kid. I bet he's already back home hiding under his covers."

"Or he's getting booked up at Sharpes," said Duke.

"Where's Lisbon?"

"Working on a fuse. We got a tail light out. Must've just happened, 'cause I checked them yesterday."

Cueball dropped his elbows to the car hood. "You see what he did to get pulled over?"

"I just saw the lights. But you don't have to do much in Melbourne Beach, those cops are ridiculous. One time we got stopped driving through the richie part by the causeway. Handcuffed me, talked some smack, the whole ordeal. They thought we were casing the neighborhood."

"What put you over in Melbourne Beach?"

"It's kinda strange, actually," said Duke. "We loaded up a big package from a storage unit off A1A. Don't ask me, your dad okayed it. But the cop was on us, like, wham, right on Fifth Ave. Nobody was speeding. Probably didn't help the new kid's not white."

"He black?"

"No, some rican kid up from Miami, one of the Toros. A good-faith gesture on your dad's part, I guess. If they have one of their own up here, it stabilizes things."

"Huh," said Cueball, scanning the lot. "Sounds a little sketch."

Duke followed his gaze. "Well I haven't seen anything, you know, *suspicious*. Other than the cashier giving me the stink eye. He was on his phone and I showed him the empty coffee pot and he was like, *Whatever.* So I ended up getting cokes instead."

There was that sound again—metal against metal, people talking. "Did you hear that?"

Duke squinted, his nose perked. "What's up?"

"Voices," said Cueball.

Duke glanced back at the moving van just in time to catch two police cruisers rolling out from their hiding spots in the woods, lights off.

"Oh sh—!"

Then came the sound of an engine turning over, followed by another. Then another. The parking lot erupted into a cacophonous chugging of big rigs, drowning out all else.

"Get in the car!" Cueball yelled.

Duke spilled soda over himself in the confusion.

Then came another sound—a metal door on rollers, flung upward. From the rear of a nearby tractor trailer, a swarm of dark abstractions spilled hunchbacked to the ground as if from a conveyor belt, landing crouched and rising, weapons in hand.

Cueball rocked back on his heels like a dog snapped by the leash, unable to choose between his weapon in the car and the sudden safety of the woods.

The air was unzipping, accompanied by music—a whispering of notes through dense blocks of space. Duke was out in the open, dancing, his thin hoodie flapping as a new wind tore through him, dropping him to the ground.

Cueball felt the guns upon him, but the shooting had ceased. Someone was yelling not to fire. *Not that one. Find the brother, the twin.*

Boots rushed past Cueball as he scrambled for Duke, now wide-eyed and gasping on his belly, his mouth a sunken bloody mess opening in prayer or a curse as he gripped the muddy weeds to steady his trembling.

More shots, single shots, and two men collapsed nearby, one clutching his stomach and another holding his destroyed jaw. High beams shot on and a voice rose up, howling weakly in strained volume, tempered by deformity.

Lisbon charged headlong through the gloom bearing the handgun Duke had stashed under the dashboard, firing haphazardly into the darkness. The return fire from invisible gunmen sent Lisbon's arms up like a marionette at the piano, and he too collapsed.

Cueball was suddenly up and running wild, his jerked movements more a scattered pulse than a sprint. Someone caught him by the knees and he landed face-first into a putrid gully. Gripped by his shirt and pants, unseen forces dragged him brutishly backwards as he punched and kicked in all directions. Screaming out, a knee caught him in the ribs, muffling him. Hands fumbled through his pockets, extracting his car keys. Twisting, he caught sight of Duke's dollish body being hoisted into the Nova's back seat, his blue-white face marbled by moonlight.

An overseer was barking orders. The assassins took turns nudging Lisbon's body with their boots. One man unzipped and openly pissed on him as others watched, proud hunters over a fresh kill. A machete appeared, a counterpart holding aloft the arm bearing the palm tattoo.

"Get away from him, you MOTHERFUCKERS!" Cueball squealed, and hungered for his gun.

The men carrying Cueball hurled his body into an open box truck, where a large unseen figure shoved his face to the cold metal floor and promptly sat on him. Beyond sight someone was violently retching and apologizing in intervals, having never witnessed such brutality before.

Cueball struggled to face the door.

One of the police cruisers pulled into the lot, stopping short of Lisbon's body. Emerging from the passenger side was a latino kid not but eighteen, white T-shirt and black jeans, and though Cueball had never met him, this nameless boy was undoubtedly the missing Wingman. His dumb innocent eyes filled with revulsion and terror like someone dropped into a pit of starving pigs, having been lured there by the promise of fresh bacon.

Double-crossing son of a bitch!

The cop from the second cruiser approached the scene from the rear. Without pause, he raised his weapon and fired a single round through the base of the young boy's skull, then proceeded to step over the body, drop the weapon, pocket his gloves, and meet his fellow officer leaning against the hood, arms folded. The man bearing the machete jogged over and lifted the boy's arm, finding the tattoo there.

The box truck door plunged down on its rollers, sweeping Cueball into a red metal cave, clanked shut and locked from the outside. He felt the engine turn over and clenched his teeth against the vibrations as the goon straddling him readjusted his weight. Outside, the loud big rigs set up to hide the sounds of gunfire grumbled through their gears. Amid the ruckus played a loud radio. The queasy undulations and intermittent dips tipped an already irrational Cueball over the edge and into a waking nightmare where he lay crushed and injured in the stomach of some enormous leviathan, the warped walls singing and flexing as he cried out for an end to it all, knowing he was lost.

Two exhausted and sweaty behemoths stared contemptuously down a full day's drive from South Jersey to find the newest Seizer's eyes alight on them in the manner of a conqueror whose grasp on the loose architecture of empire was now threatened at its very rivets.

"Did I stutter?" barked Bird. "We're done here! Go!"

One of the musclemen peered over at his colleague to confirm a proper shared response, which Eddy on the couch feared may require from him some final act of courage.

"But what do we tell Luther?" asked the one. "He'll shit fire if we come back without an answer from the Chief."

"We've lost men, goddammit!" Bird hollered, and everyone's eyes went to the telephone on the floor, which only a few minutes before had been attached to the wall.

Bird calmed himself. "You tell him . . . tell him yes. We can double the next shipment. The Northeast Corridor remains a top priority."

The men left under the watchful glares of safehouse guards stationed on the front porch. Bird made sure the door was completely shut before stabbing numbers into his phone and pacing.

Eddy had never seen his boss in such a state. Details of the last few minutes remained vague, even for those in the same room. One minute Bird was harshly criticizing Cueball in low whispers, which ended in the pounding, beating death of the landline; the next, he was terrifying anonymous contacts in a rapid series of calls on his cell, ignoring all else.

"Charlie! Charlie what happened?" asked Bird, lurching back and forth. "Are you sure?" He stopped and gripped his face. "Okay. Okay good. Any other casualties? Bodies. Where. Where'd they take them. Where *exactly*? Well find out!"

Eddy felt a chill envelop him, like with any 3 a.m. phone call, where the faces of loved ones rush by in paralyzing succession, waiting for a name.

"Make sure he's not messed with. And keep me updated." Bird flipped the phone to the floor and stared at the ceiling. "We got hit."

"Hit?"

Meaty fists flexing, Bird knelt before the coffee table, flattening his palms on the glass. A great relief spilled over him, injecting into his dark demeanor a surge of authority and calm.

"Almost there," he said. "Okay, Eddy. Things are about to get hairy. I need to make a few more calls, but then you and me are gonna have a heart-to-heart."

"Are we in trouble?" asked Eddy.

Bird cinched his lips. "Depends on how you look at it."

Del Ray stood atop the steamer chest in his living room, eyes closed and arms raised, wearing not a stitch of clothing. Small dots of paint, red and brown, covered his entire torso and lower extremities. Under his breath he murmured the language of ritual, tying his sexuality to ancestral forces imaginatively construed only hours before in an attempt to fling off his gender's bad rap as one of mindless trim hunters and megalomaniacs, and so embraced wholeheartedly the animus of a speckled hen, gleaning mojo from whatever cosmic spirit might possess him, psychosexually.

Beside him lay a rubber rooster mask. It was, as one might assume, his night off.

The gunning blast of a motorcycle in the distance woke him from his meditation. That, and Zippo barking in the yard. The front door creaked open slightly with the night wind.

The revving faded, only to return louder and more insistent before Del Ray recognized the pealing grunts as his ringtone. He located his phone under a biography of Caligula, but the caller had hung up. He'd also missed a few calls—a Head in Knoxville, a Head in Tallahassee, and two unknowns, possibly the same number. That was a lot of folks, but they could wait.

After setting the phone down, though, it rang again.

Del Ray answered as an annoyed speckled hen. "*Raaahhh.*"

"Ray?" It was Bird.

"Bossman! Hey, listen, it's my night. I need my night."

Outside Zippo continued her assault on whatever phantoms roamed the outer dark.

"Apollo's down."

Del Ray stepped off the steamer chest, feeling lost in time. "Was it the Big Guys or Little Guys?"

"Little, looks like. But there *were* cops involved."

The hijacking took shape in Del's mind as a TV crime show—a grainy overhead shot of Duke and Lisbon under sheets, a frenetic blur of police cruisers, a close-up of him clutching a shotgun, cowering in the corner of his bedroom.

"Did anyone make it home?"

"Let's focus on the more important issue," Bird said, airy as any circling hawk. "Honest opinion—let's say someone threatened your family, your livelihood, and the man whose sole judgment you relied on tells you not to worry about it. Do you ever trust this person again?"

Heat flushed Del Ray's cheeks as comprehension took hold. Here was the naked truth—so clean and stupid and concordant with Bird's nature that Del Ray felt ridiculous for having thought he might ever contain or counsel it. "You sorry, sloppy son of a bitch, what did you do?"

"Be straight with me, old buddy . . . did Duke promise you anything?"

The bastard wouldn't quit until he had destroyed every vestige of Seizer's legacy. Del saw a dark future already forming on the horizon, a legion of government agents in Kevlar vests, slouching towards the Space Coast.

"Those kids risked everything for you. Are you *insane?*" Del spit into his phone. "They put their trust in us! Up and down that fucking road every night, for us! Am I missing something here? Are you privy to information I'm lacking? Did a shipment ever *once* come up light? What the actual FUCK?!"

"I need men with fucking backbones!" Bird yelled. "People who can make the calls that need to be made, no matter how ugly shit might get!"

"Bullshit! You want dickless sycophants that parrot your every word. Those kids were our future . . . our insurance! Did you consider for a second what'll happen when the others—when *your son*—finds out you did this?"

"He'll do what I tell him to! And the rest'll follow suit, or I'll have their asses. So I need to know, right now . . . where's your heart? I'll let your poor judgment slide this once, but I need to know if you're with me on this."

Del Ray laughed, furious. "You and your bitter heart. You buried two of my brothers tonight. My wards! Put everything we worked for at risk, all because you couldn't police the ghosts in that thick fucking skull of yours. And I'm supposed to just go along with it? Are you *for real?*"

"I always figured when the shit hit the fan—"

"Nah nah, SAY IT! I wanna hear you say you're *for real!*"

"Gotta tell you, Ray, you're forcing my hand."

"Fuck your hand, you've hacked the feet out from under us," said Del, breathless now, his thoughts primed for new vistas, a backpack full of cash, some heavily wooded backcountry. A shuffling noise came from down the hall and he waited, listening.

"Leave me high and dry. Just like the old man."

"Game over, partner," said Del Ray, lowering his voice. "I'm surprised the Feds aren't here already. First the labs, now this? Watch your back, old buddy, 'cause you've unleashed the tide. Nobody will ever trust you again."

"Del, you asshole, I never needed anybody's trust. My god. My men need to fear me."

The line went dead, leaving Del Ray gripping his phone in a confined room growing increasingly smaller. If Bird was willing to murder the Twins and dangle every other underling before the authorities like offal to the wolves, Del Ray knew he was but a short skip from the gallows himself. He shouldn't have shown anger—that was a mistake. Instead of being cautious, he'd been reactionary. He should've let Bird think he was still on board.

The front door creaked open.

Del Ray turned, peering reluctantly into the void.

The lifeless body of Zippo flew through the air and skidded to a halt at his feet, the poor dog's eyes gone wide and glossy, tongue out. Del Ray yelped and flew back over the trunk.

Hovering in the dark was a wiry blue electric smile. That disappeared. Del Ray raised the phone but had no chance. A pair of toothy prongs shot across the room and struck him in the chest and down he went, onto the couch.

Holding the shooter end of the electrical umbilicus, Gumby danced into the room and hopped lightly over the ruptured dog to leap upon his incapacitated prey. The shock of the taser left Del Ray stunned, though his eyes swarmed in their sockets.

Gumby was giddy with joy. The excitement of the ambush and Del Ray's exotic body art thrilled through the hit man a deep and glorious commingling of natures.

"What is *happening* here, old son?" Gumby asked, poking the paint dots with his skinning knife. "Are you supposed to be some kind of toad or something?"

Then he spied the rooster mask, lifting it high on his knife tip.

"Bless me, what's this? Oh my lord. I always knew you was a crooked stick," Gumby chuckled. Then he rested his cheek against Del Ray's, lifting the taser before them. "Lookee what I picked up at the flea market. Makes me feel like Spider-Man."

After an hour spent enduring every pothole and surface change, Cueball felt the box truck slow to a halt. The obese stranger rolled off him as a latch popped and the metal door swung high. Someone grabbed his legs and dragged him out and walked him a short ways before shoveling him into the back seat of his Nova, where Duke's body lay slumped against the opposite door. The large man scooted in beside him, pinning Cueball in the middle. His hand brushed Duke's arm and found it cold, hair prickly wet with blood. The driver must have brought along his dinner, as the car reeked of garlic shrimp.

The worst possible thing had happened and absolved all pretense. The world was no longer something to explore with the senses but an emotional holding pattern of nauseating defeat. When the car stopped again, Cueball hoped for a quick death. Instead, rough hands snatched him by the neck and guided him marching up under the frazzled front light of a stuccoed house. He was pushed through a dark kitchen and into a stuffy den with wood paneling, lit softly in purples and tangerine.

A woman in a bikini top and flimsy cotton shorts lay asleep on a corduroy couch, the dead cigarette in her hand poised like an ashen fishhook. Two men, one large one skinny, dropped Duke's body on a ratty sofa opposite her.

A third man, the apparent leader, spoke up: "Dexter, your chick's not looking so hot."

Dexter, gangly, a stud in each ear, squeezed his way through and tended to his girlfriend. Rummaging around the table, he held up a hypodermic needle between pinched fingers. "Lisa baby, get up baby, c'mon."

The girl's eyes slit open and she slapped him away. "Why you gotta do that?"

"Don't scare me like that, baby. You can't keep doing this, alright?"

The girl brought a pillow to her face as Dexter petted her shoulder, snickering self-consciously under the disapproving eyes of his counterparts. "Hon, you gotta go."

A fist caught Cueball in the kidney, meaning for him to walk. He stumbled past the woman and Duke's crumpled body and folded into a loveseat beyond.

Dexter gave up trying to wake his girlfriend and the three men pushed back into the kitchen, beer cans popping, and soon the men were talking openly, as if fresh home from a jobsite.

Why'd we bring the dead one? came the voice of the big guy from around the corner. The leader answered: *Charlie said hold him, it's supposed to look like a kidnapping. Lure any others out.*

I about shit myself seeing the pigs roll up like that, said Dexter. *You reckon, what? These kids were planning to hijack a load?*

Just some dumbasses got on the wrong side of a bossman, sounds like.

Well, someone's looking out for him. If we didn't get that call from Charlie . . .

The leader stepped back into the room, flashing his glare at Cueball. "If you try anything stupid, I'll shoot you, I don't care who says what." Then ducked back in.

That body's gonna start smelling up the place.

Shit, for this kind of money I'd stack the whole house with bodies.

You see that one guy's jaw?

Shit was de-stroyed. Fuuuuuck.

And what was that machete all about? Were they going after their tats? God help me.

Cueball's heartbeat swelled in his ears and his stomach eased to putty.

Despite the atrocities addiction had wreaked upon her body, the girl had shapely hips and nice thighs, sprawled out sweetly awkward on the couch. Cueball was glad she was here; together they inhabited a space out of time, her gauntness a kind of triumph of biology over desire, a body weathering an endless storm of debauchery. Whatever brain recovery process now fought to manage Cueball's trauma settled on a calm need to push everything away. Self-pity, fury, guilt—later gator. He would clear his mind of all the professed righteousness of the world, all the *stuff*, to make room for the darkness.

He cried without much expression. Lisbon was dead—mutilated. Clearly the work of his father, a thought beyond disheartening. Unforgivable. For a moment he toyed with the possibility of the hit coming from a rival gang. But then why save his stupid ass? Why these three redneck idiots holding him hostage? No, it was obvious. The puerto rican kid was a pawn. The cops paid off. First Seizer, then the nephews. A certain slow-to-stew retaliation that seemed his father's trademark.

Who next? Who not next. Whatever it took for total control.

Cueball had tried so hard to change. To become that trusted friend. That good worker. That son.

In the kitchen his enemies cracked jokes.

He found the hypodermic on the table and returned to the loveseat. They would never let him be anything but what they wanted him to be.

I heard it had something to do with Jim Barns' lab going up in flames and him getting shot by them guards.

Naw, this reeks of a lover's quarrel. They was all fuckbuddies.

C'mon now, he's probably in there listening.

Listen to you two fucktards. This was payback, Charlie said as much. But that mess don't concern us. Dex, you need to get your whore outta here.

She aint no whore!

You dropped your load in the first twat that spread for smack and now she's the Virgin Mary.

Why you gotta go say shit like that, Leonard? You know I can't hear shit like that.

Cueball slid a finger along the wet needle. Then rubbed the tawny substance down the bridge of his nose like a child applying war paint. Every time he ran, they caught him. Whenever he fucked up, he got promoted. His father demanded he exist in a limbo of aggression, like Gumby, who off duty must have languished bored and restless as a ghost in a shuttered asylum. But a cold-blooded murderer he was not. What

Gumby mistook for killer instinct was Cueball's impressive capacity for loss. He could lose everything, at any moment, and consider it a blessing. He never expected much from life, so whenever something good dropped into his hands, he distrusted it, because if you didn't, the world just kept breaking your heart.

If God did exist, It would understand there were times when the only way out was giving up. If God made everything, It made everything from Itself, which meant every day small pieces of Itself gave up, like Jesus had, when asked to forfeit his life to save the world. And isn't realizing you're going to die, yet refusing to stray from the path, the same as suicide?

Cueball flicked the needle like he'd seen done in the movies. He didn't know why people did it, but they did, so he did it too, and there was a proper explanation for everything he'd ever done.

A surge of readiness caught in his throat.

Beyond him, Duke's arm slipped from the sofa.

You noticed? Yeah, I use bump fire stocks. You can pick 'em up at Swampdog Ammo off Minton. Turns a regular rifle into an automatic. I'm surprised they're legal, to be honest.

Might not be for long, with this black sumbitch in office.

Well, he aint all bad.

Good lord, what news you watch?

My mom got cancer of the lung, you know this, and they took care of her medication and everything.

Man, I just hope they stop filling up my division with these scrubs. New day, new people. And some of them aint right in the head.

Well, put in for a transfer, bud! Come work the camp with Lenny and me. There's no bullshit with Greco. You do your work, he'll treat you fair. Hell, he even paid for drinks last week at the Purple Porpoise, then took us all out to the titty bar up on Sarno? There's this brazilian chick with tits like bowling balls, and what she does is, you slip her a twenty, she'll let you eat her!

That aint true.

Go down there!

Damn that's special.

Another thing about Greco . . . he wouldn't do us like these boys. He'd come talk to us.

You sure 'bout that?

Sure I'm sure. What you think, no?

You looking for job security? Hazard pay?

I'm sure it had to be done, but . . . you know, what if it was one of us?

It wasn't. And there's your fuckin answer.

Cueball pulled Duke's shoulder to see his face—a swollen eye peered back, crusted red at the rim. The sudden cough spooked Cueball, who nearly stabbed Duke with the needle.

"Lisbon," came his whisper.

"Shhhhh," Cueball said. "I'm sorry. I'm so sorry."

Duke's good eye welled up gleaming as he trembled. When his breath arrived, it was loud and wet. "I can't breathe."

"I'll get you outta here."

Duke clenched and wheezed, gripping Cueball by the wrist. With all the sad effort he could muster, Duke dragged the hypodermic toward his neck. There was no mistaking the intention.

"Just let me think a sec, hold on."

Duke's eye went momentarily wide. "Mom?"

This sent Cueball to a lower level. The next retch brought up blood and a horrendous gargling. He glanced at Duke's grip on his wrist, the scar and Royal palm. Pulling close, he drove the needle into Duke's elbow pit, plunging half of the liquid into him.

"I'm sorry, man," he cried softly. "I'm so so fucking sorry."

Duke snatched his arm back. His one eye found Cueball, and something materialized there before he curled away. It could have been anything—resignation, hatred—but Cueball believed he saw something softer, human, forgiving—or so he needed to imagine.

He waited with Duke until his breathing stopped.

That cop straight-up shot that kid.

What're you pussies so worried about? The pigs are on our side!

I'm saying who's got my back?

This here's a risky business. You want out? There's the door.

Shit, I got your back, man.

Well, there you go! This little crumb eater's got your back! Now you feel safe?

Cueball wept. What was done could not be undone. A dark star formed and collapsed at the center of him, and he let the gravity of it take everything away—the harsh thoughts, the emotion, all the fear and shame. There would be no more falling in line.

Julio came to him.

The hole is a no-thing, Cueball thought, crawling across the carpet toward the sleeping girl, the hypodermic in his hand. *Not a loss, but an opening into emptiness. My inner right. Destroyer of wisdom. A celebration of the deadening voice. It feeds off love and leaves you, like God.*

From the kitchen came the sound of a plastic baggie being flicked.

Look here, try this. This here's the good shit.

Holy cow, look out! Maybe just a little, I don't do this shit no more.

I'm gonna check in on her.

You gotta get her outta here.

That's what I said! Damn, you're on my last nerve.

Am I now? The very last one? You scrawny little white trash fuck.

Don't look at me. I think you're both full of shit.

Ha! Look at him go. I tell you what, god's honest truth—we're survivalists. We take what we want, when we want it. And if you get in our way, it's your butt.

Fuckin outlaws.

You make the gun laws stricter, we'll buy more guns. Don't pay us a working wage—fuck it, we'll make our own money, and lots of it. You say there's no POWs? Fuck you. There's this thing we call loyalty to our fellow countrymen. No man left behind.

Fire and ice. Go on, get some more. This here's some pure American Dream.

"L-L-Leonard."

This fucking jerkoff. WHAT UP, DOC?

"LEONARD!"

The big man beat Leonard into the den to find Dex staring back at them ominously as Cueball held a gun to his head.

"Aw shit," said the big man, drawing his weapon. "Where'd he get that?"

"I had to," said Dexter, "he was gonna stick her."

"Shut up!" ordered Leonard from behind the doorframe. "Drop it, man. Or shoot him, hell, it don't matter."

"No wait WAIT!"

"Shut the fuck up, Dex!" shouted Leonard. He rounded the corner fully, .45 in hand, sights leveled. Cueball responded by pulling back on the gun's hammer.

"Dex, you stupid motherfucker," said the big man.

Dexter yelped as Cueball forcefully arched his back, an arm around his neck. "Throw your guns over here!"

At first they didn't respond, but Dex was so blubbery and indecent that the larger man tossed his weapon out of pure humiliation. Seeing this, Leonard did the same, cursing, "You fucking cowardly fucking shitheads!"

Cueball motioned the two men to one side, walking Dexter past them and out through the kitchen. They followed slowly as he skipped backwards toward the hall. The front doorknob gave with a click and Cueball stepped out into the night, pausing at the threshold.

"You aint goin far," Leonard promised, half-hidden behind the kitchen wall.

Cueball placed the gun flush against Dexter's skull. Then imperceptibly raised it. The gunshot exploded and Dexter bellowed gibberish.

Leonard caught Dex on the run and yanked him around the corner, twisting him to the kitchen floor. When he was sure Cueball wasn't coming back, he drove a fist into Dexter's neck as the young man stumbled to stand, dropping him again, attacking his stomach and face, over and over, then raised himself above the whimpering idiot and leapt away to bolt the front door.

Breathless as he wandered back. "Whew-wee, that boy's got balls. Hulk eggs. No wonder."

"Should we call someone?" asked the big man.

Leonard couldn't say. The whole thing had been mishandled to the point of tragedy.

From behind came a yawn as the sullen young woman moved sleepily into the kitchen, rubbing her eyes.

"Why's everyone have to yell?"

"Well now, good mornin, darlin," said Leonard, sending another brutal kick into her boyfriend's stomach. "Nice nap?"

Gumby's knees dug into Del Ray's pelvis, the knife's blade poised at his throat. Del Ray would be gutted like a goat, the walls smeared with his intestines or some such awful savagery to keep the cops guessing, and his carcass wrapped in bedsheets and tossed into a swamp for the gators. The waiting game was a torturous affair Del was willing to endure for the granting of a single wish: that Gumby remain in the living room.

"You're a sick monkey, Ray," Gumby taunted, his one chiseled tooth hooking a lip. "Some would think I'm doing the world a favor."

"Wanna beer, Gum?" Del slurred, the nausea burbling up. "You might can check the fridge. Or maybe you just prefer suckin donkey dick—"

Del Ray squealed in agony as Gumby drew back a fleshy peel from his chest.

"That's it, boy! Go out in style! Old Devil Ray don't change his tune for no cat!"

"You fucking fuck!" Del Ray cried, squirming, his neck cords engaged. "Do it, motherfucker! Do it!"

Gumby yanked Del forward by the hair. "Aint none of this personal. I always thought of us as equals, reckon-wise, but it seems you lack even the commonest of sense. When the bossman asks you to play ball, you always say yes, even when you mean no. That's basic math."

"You think you're safe?" seethed Del Ray, shying from the insistent blade. "You got the stink on you too."

"What you yappin 'bout, stink?" Gumby twittered, fascinated yet again by how people facing the certainty of death succumb to wholesale bartering and gallows charm. It was a tactic used against rapists, forcing upon the attacker one's most human qualities as a way to stir up empathy. Problem was, Gumby wasn't human. Gumby was a vampire.

"Nothing comes between a junkie and his junk," said Del Ray. "Someday you'll do something—"

"Don't go preaching loyalty to me, Ray. Them brothers outright said they was coming for us, and you chose to protect them. A clean case of either/or, and you chose or."

"I'm trying to protect everyone!" barked Del. "He's burying us one by one!"

"You sound like Buffalo did at the end."

The mention of Corey stopped Del Ray from squirming.

"Oh yeah, I was there," said Gumby. "Jesse called it in. Warehouse, couple rough types. I's just a casual observer, but your cowboy was giving it up left, right, and center. Spilled the beans on Seizer asking him and Barns to take out Cueball. Promised Buffalo an Enforcer job—*my job*—if he could get it done quietly."

"You *tortured* him," spit Del Ray. "What the fuck else would he say?"

"Maybe you even helped out, eh, old buddy?" said Gumby, tapping the knife tip along Del's ribs. "Disgraced bounty hunter, plucked off some farm working sixty hours in the heat, with that cripple boy back home. Got him a real sweet job at the camps, knowing he'd owe you a few favors. And when the time came, mentioned him to Seizer for a certain nasty inside job, all hush-hush. Knock off the son, lure the father into gang territory, and off him too. Maybe figured Bird got too big for his britches, and this was your shot at a top spot."

Del Ray stared up at him, recognizing the lies he'd helped Bird concoct had come full circle. "Gum, that's the dumbest fucking thing I ever heard. First Barns, then Corey, now me? Who's Bird gonna accuse next? He's fucking delusional!"

"Well dang, maybe I've been led astray!" Gumby hawed, leaning back. "But honestly, that shit don't matter to me. Buffalo made it crystal clear he was after my job."

Del Ray couldn't believe what he was hearing, the whole tragedy unfolding in his mind. All the deceitfulness, mayhem, and death—just because Bird felt patronized, and Gumby slighted. The most trivial discourtesies and the walls came tumbling down. Even after Seizer allowed Cueball back into the club with no more than a slap on the wrist, Bird couldn't get his ego out from under it, feeding Gumby and who knows who else bullshit stories they swallowed whole like catfish.

But none of that mattered now. Even if Gumby didn't believe Bird's conspiracies, Del Ray understood there'd be no disabusing his killer of fulfilling his orders—not now, with the honeyed scent of death in his nostrils.

"After tonight we'll have Miami outright," continued Gumby, "and the Law will have its shank kingpin. Exploded superlabs, dead kids. That's right, big fella . . . you're the big bow on the box top. And to think, you coulda been the one doing the wrapping."

Del Ray smiled; then spit in Gumby's face.

Gumby responded by pinching and severing off the top of his left nipple.

Del Ray screamed through his teeth.

"That's right, let it out! Let go of that old pepperoni! You don't need it! You a man! You a man!" Gumby howled with Del Ray, a mocking cry. "Louder, Ray! God can't hear you!"

The blade moved swiftly under Del Ray's testicles as Gumby locked him to the cushions with an arm to his throat and the promise of castration. "You a pussy, boy? I'll give you a pussy."

The sudden creak of floorboards quieted them.

Gumby paused . . . then leapt away, scrambling for the taser on the steamer chest, his blade aimed in Del Ray's general direction. But this only made him a bigger target.

The shotgun blast transformed his upper half to mist and fleshy shrapnel and flung his body back over the chest and onto the dog.

Colt hugged the shotgun to her chest, trembling, then dropped it to the floor. "Baby?"

Del Ray raised himself with a hand over his wound as Colt fell to his side, afraid to touch him.

"Oh god oh god! What do you need? Should I call the cops? An ambulance or or or—"

"Calm down, it's okay, I'm okay," Del said, lifting his bloody hand to see if it was true. "I'm okay-ish. Zippo. Ah, fuck. Get me a towel, and some alcohol from the cabinet."

Covering twelve states in three days with the help of an assortment of night riders, Colt had descended upon Del Ray's swamp estate with a gleeful Zippo by her side in the early hours of dawn, much to the biker's delight. Among other gifts she carried was a handbag of discount glow-in-the-dark Halloween paints purchased from a truck stop, which accounted for her naked skin glowing with the colors of a neon rooster.

"We need to get you out of here," Colt said, returning with everything he'd asked for plus some bandages she'd found in a first-aid kit. "I know people who can hide us."

"First let's calm down," said Del Ray. "Bird needs to think the job's done. Please, sweetheart, let's just take a minute. Bless you, thank you."

Del Ray held her chin in his hand, blood mixing with paint.

"You lying son of a bitch," she said. "What the hell are you doing with a shotgun in your house? Don't you know it's three strikes you're out?"

The belly laugh forced the tears from Del Ray's eyes. He didn't know whether to get up or stay put. The pain was intense. He wanted to send Colt over to look for his missing nipple part, but that's just not something you asked someone else to do.

The laughter of the night guards filtered into the safehouse, where Eddy sat alone anxiously refreshing his Twitter feed. Not finding any posts reporting a major drug bust or police action in the area, he began to wonder if he'd misread the situation.

Bird had disappeared into a back room for a spell only to reappear reinvigorated, high off a cocktail of his own make. Fingers pushed deep into his biceps, lost in his mind's perturbations, he begged from Eddy an understanding of the hardships that plagued a man of his position, for which Eddy had no context or understanding.

When Bird finally broke the news of Lisbon's execution and Duke's kidnapping, Eddy nearly missed it among the more trifling grievances.

Responding to an outburst of shrieks, the guards busted in to find Eddy frenzied and distraught as a robber bee in a burning apiary. The alarms in his head rang out for evacuation as an inner storm notched its Category 5 and threatened to drag him howling into some boundless gulf of misery.

Bird pushed the guards back outside with a glare, catching Eddy in an awkward embrace. "Look at me! Right here! Calm down! We're okay, we're gonna make it."

Bird walked Eddy to the couch, then began offering up a nostrum of convoluted evidence toward a positive outlook. The hijackers were Los Toros, most likely, in league with some rogue coalition of enemies. His cop friend said in addition to Lisbon, they'd found the body of a puerto rican kid on-scene. The moving van was parked, lights on, but Duke was missing. To keep from making the situation worse, they needed to stay put and let the facts roll in. He expected a ransom demand for Duke anytime now.

Yet his effort to bring Eddy to his side derailed itself when arguing that though the Twins were dedicated workers, smart and reliable, they were still essentially outsiders, doomed by their blood ties to a notorious crook with countless rivals.

"Count yourself lucky, Eddy. We got you off that job just in time."

Bird's coldness made Eddy queasy as he gripped the cushions for support.

"It's time you knew my mind," Bird said, rubbing his hands together. "I think Del Ray pulled together a crew to undercut me. Hear me out—I have evidence. Duke was likely his point man."

"That can't be true," muttered Eddy, fingers moving to tent his eyes.

"There's things you don't know about, Ed—bad, terrible things. What if I told you Seizer hired someone to murder Heath? Oh yeah! After that Kaos brat hit his cousin's warehouse and blamed it on my son, Seizer extorted money from me! And we recovered some of that shipment, so he got paid twice! All this after I handed the thieving sonofabitch the East Coast on a platter! And know this, Eddy . . . I've had my bug antennas out there, taking in the vibrations . . . and just yesterday we got word Del Ray gave up Seizer's real name to some county clerk, who turned it over to the government! And all that land Seizer owned where the old camps were, that he tried to pawn off, well now there's a paper trail leading right back to him and, you bet your ass, them nephews! And if those boys talk . . . guess who's ass is in the crosshairs? Seems bad right now, but saying it out loud . . . hell, this might just be a blessing in disguise."

"But why would Del do that?" begged Eddy, stupefied.

Bird shrugged. "Maybe he wants to rule the coop. And Duke, rest his soul, was convinced I murdered his uncle. A little nugget no doubt planted in his head by Del Ray. Know what else? Ray didn't think you were man enough for your job. He said, 'Eddy don't have it in him.' Well I looked him square in the eye and said, 'That boy's like a son to me, and smart as anyone. I have every faith.' Yup. And where is he now? Where's Del, when we need him most?"

Bird snapped his fingers, a disappearing act.

Eddy had too many questions—about Del Ray, about Seizer's murder, about why Bird spoke as if Duke were already dead and not just missing. It occurred to him his boss might be lying, or at least withholding the whole truth. He wondered what Cueball might know.

Bird read his thoughts. "Has Heath called you?"

Eddy checked his phone. No messages or voicemail.

"Probably off drunk somewhere," said Bird. "If he calls, *you* don't talk to him. *I* talk to him."

The next hour proved near insufferable. Eddy kept the TV on for noise, checking tweets. When the tears finally came, he hid his face under his shirt.

Then Bird exploded through the front door, phone in hand, waving for the remote. "What station?"

He flipped to the news. Scenes straight out of Hollywood—tear gas, squad cars, helicopters, a SWAT team rappelling down the face of a residential building overlooking Biscayne Bay.

"Ho-ly shit!" Bird exclaimed. "I'll call you back." As Eddy waited for an explanation, Bird said, "It's done, over. They nailed that sorry sack of shit. Miami Toros are history. The fuzz busted up Alex's crew an hour ago. Doesn't look real, does it? Bloodbath. Fucking amateurs. We dodged a bullet today, Eddy. A real massacre. One anonymous call and the world changes."

Bird stopped bothering to hide the baggie, snorting powder straight off his fist. "You hit me, I hit back harder! We got the south, the ports. All it cost was two shipments—one for the Feds, one for the cubans. Rebuilding their Corporation. Alex won't make it out of County alive. Mm-mm. We got Chicago set to go. Michigan. New York. I move mountains. The Feds were this close," he said, pinching the air.

"Are they coming for us?" Eddy asked.

"What? No. Yeah, no." Bird stopped himself, the lies becoming mixed up with the truth in his own mind as unforeseeable adversaries threatened his tenure. "Don't worry. Let me worry."

Bird's phone went off. "Talk to me," he said. Eddy gauged his reactions for clues. "Fuck, Charlie! What do you mean ran off? Your boys are like wolves in a shark tank—out of their fucking depths! When. Who's looking for him. Where. No, listen . . . LISTEN! Bring him to me. What? Get rid of it, dump it where they'll find it." Glancing back at Eddy, as if only then remembering he was there, his tone shifted. "Really? Oh no. That's terrible news."

Hanging up, Bird cinched his nasal ridge between thumb and forefinger. "They found Duke's body."

Eddy warped with pain, but Bird hardly noticed, concocting lies he'd later repeat. "Those goddamn Toros must have kidnapped Duke for ransom. Or no no no . . . to try and find out where the new camps are located! I bet that's it! I bet Duke fought 'em off too! You know he would have! I'll get Gumby after them, we'll make this right."

Eddy was left envisioning wolves writhing within a bottomless ocean.

"We got situation on top of situation here," said Bird, crouching down to stare at the TV. Seconds later, his head ducked abruptly as he forced himself into boxed breathing. "Eddy, go home. Oh, man. Go home, I've poisoned myself. I can't think straight. I'll call you later."

Rising, Eddy's movements felt lethargic, robotic.

At the door, Bird called out to him wearily: "If my son calls, you tell him to call me. Don't answer for anyone else. And if Del Ray calls, you call me *immediately*. Don't speak to him. That's an order. I bet he'd say just about anything to tear us apart."

Eddy stepped into a night terrorized by bug sounds. Before him, a cigarette cherry illuminated a ghoulish face. The bodyguard lingering an extra few seconds before stepping aside.

To keep from fainting, Eddy dug his car keys into his thigh. Nothing made sense. The mushy lawn beneath his shoes felt like the slimy back of some gigantic organism, old as time itself, he imagined, a greenish interstellar blob that hopped between planets, and when the conditions were right, sprouted sensual creatures, dreamers, to act as agents of its consciousness. Thus arose humankind: a generative, desperate, violent race. This seemed plausible. The blob, Eddy understood, was dying and afraid. The beings it created to act as stewards, caring for it and for each other, were too self-determined, and from this nature sprouted an unintended barbarism: unbalanced, prideful inventors of murderous technologies that led to rapid deforestation and warfare. The interstellar beast was now too weak to make its next jump, and so remained saddled with its autogenetic infestation, crippled and defenseless.

Eddy sensed the creature's hot breath in the muggy air, sketching the comic book panels in his mind. Away from the safehouse, though, a few reality-based thoughts skittered up, causing the beast to stir—which sent Eddy crashing into the side of his Mustang. He quickly slid himself upside the car, cracked the door, and fell into the front seat, hoping the guards hadn't noticed.

The lawn lit up red as he backed away.

He couldn't go home. There was no home, not with a war on. Problem was, he didn't know whose side he was on. Bird was guilty of something, for sure. To bring Gumby back meant a plan had been enacted. But Del Ray's exit meant the plan was a bad one.

He needed to find somewhere to hole up and wait.

olt situated herself between Cueball and Del Ray, who sat in his underwear on the couch. She was dressed and crouching, eyes bugged out. But Del Ray, sensing an unjust end to her bravery, tugged her elbow back: "Sit down, baby, it's okay."

Holding a bloody towel to his chest, he motioned Cueball indoors. Weapon raised, Cueball stepped in and leaned against the doorframe, saying nothing.

"There's a shotgun by my feet, so you don't think I'm hiding anything," said Del Ray.

"Grab it if you want," Cueball replied. He scrunched his face: "The fuck's that smell?"

"End of an era," Del Ray answered, glancing to his right.

Cueball cautiously approached a mound of blankets. Jutting out from beneath was a man's arm and a dog's tail.

"Who's in there?"

"The beast," Del replied.

Out of sheer sport or something heroically darker, Del Ray ignored Cueball to pluck from the chest a shot glass of whiskey, downing it.

"Here comes the hard part, good buddy," Del said, gritting against the abrasiveness of the towel on his wound. "I believe you're capable of near-anything right now, but information has come to light, and we both got stories to tell, so I'm asking you, as a friend and colleague, to hear me out. Can you do that for me?"

Cueball considered it. "There's this boy I knew," he said. "What happened to him, and Lisbon and Duke, it can't ever happen again." He cocked the gun. "I won't let it."

Eddy arrived at Gin's place after midnight, wrapping his fingers through the metal loops of her security door and ringing the bell in haunting intervals until she showed up, her skin pale blue in the moonlight. She couldn't smell booze, but that didn't mean he was sober. Without breaking her stare, Eddy rang the doorbell again, and the apartment shrank behind her. She was fairly confident she could reach the phone before he busted his way inside.

Instead, Gin gripped the frame and held her ground, choosing to believe it was an accident.

"You know I should call the cops."

"I thought we could talk," said Eddy.

"Maybe check with the working girls down the block, they'll listen to whatever."

Eddy nodded, knowing he deserved this. "I'm in trouble."

"Sounds about right."

Eddy's head dropped, obscured by darkness. "I know you probably don't want to hear this, but I'm sorry. I almost called lots of times, but thought it was better not to. In any case . . ."

He turned and left. Halfway across the yard, he paused to scan the street both ways. After a few more steps, he did it again, seemingly overly cautious.

What happened next was inexplicable. A desire to confront or comfort him welled up, a tether loose for so long suddenly snapped back like a measuring tape. Gin reeled with its mechanism and swooshed the door open, stepping barefoot into the grass.

"I'm not a person you can just do this to!" she said, immediately lowering her voice.

"I'm sorry. I got nowhere else to go."

"Then go home."

"It's not safe," he said. "This is what I'm telling you."

She searched for lights in an upstairs neighbor's window. Then crossed her arms, quiet in the dark.

"If I let you in, it doesn't mean anything."

He avoided touching her as he slumped past. The hominess of the apartment stoked in him a warm sensation as he glanced down the hall toward the bedroom before finding a seat on the couch.

Gin turned on a small lamp and reclined in a nearby chair, curling her feet up under her. She wore blue jeans and a halter top from the day before, black hair fanning her shoulders. Like so many other nights, except it wasn't. He asked how she was. She asked what he wanted. He asked what she'd been up to and she peered at the microwave clock and wiggled a finger between each of her toes. The familiarity of the gesture broke his heart, but it also cleared the air and made it safe for him to speak in the way they used to, for all hours of the night.

He began his story unafraid, neither lying nor withholding any aspects he felt might distress her. The honesty was refreshing. It felt good to come clean.

Gin managed to keep her expression untroubled, despite being reminded several times of a strong reaction she'd recently had to a movie, an aversion to a popular theme suggesting a woman's most vital role was playing caretaker to broken men.

She actually thought Eddy was too immature to be broken; but he could be wounded, even traumatized, and that's what she believed she was hearing—a person in shock.

"You need to leave town, right now," Gin said when he finished. "Don't go home, just drive. Go to Texas, Idaho, somewhere they can't find you."

"I think Bird's involved somehow," said Eddy, half-dazed. "He kept saying how lucky we were that this happened. Like, are you kidding me?"

Gin was wide-awake now, leg bouncing to dispel the tension. She understood how desperation sometimes masked itself as vulnerability, and wondered what Eddy might be capable of in this mindset. He did not sound well. His furtive glances were unsettling. Even when describing horrific moments—the disturbing imagery plucked from some mental archive as of yet untouched by introspection—his voice remained troublingly calm. Spooky. She wondered if he'd considered his own role in this fiasco, or if that notion would short-circuit his brain. She knew she should keep quiet, or risk entanglement—she had, after all, her own conscience to look after— but she couldn't hold back.

"What did you expect?" Gin suddenly blurted out. "Really though, Eddy, what the hell did you expect? You're all drug dealers! This is what happens to drug dealers!"

"Jesus f-f-fucking Christ, Gin," he stuttered, tears in his eyes. "Duke and Lisbon are dead."

"Don't make me sound cold," she said. "If you were there you'd be dead too! I'm sorry, but this isn't even the worst thing that could have happened."

She got up and went to the bathroom for Kleenex.

Eddy wasn't a bad guy, exactly, but he managed decisions poorly. Toward the end there, he'd been cranky and morose, shuffling along like an irritated beachgoer to upend parts of her like seashells, squashing whatever jellied life lay beneath. The hardships she'd suffered because of him, she told herself, were not irrelevant. He'd cut her deeply in ways she'd never forget. But neither could she disavow that whatever love had passed between them had formed an indelible bond, and she still cared for him. There were things needing to be said, but she shelved those words as she watched him deposit crumpled Kleenex balls into a glass, sorrowful and irresolute. This felt akin to closure, but with caveats. When he reached for her neck, she leaned away, taking his hand in hers.

"Thanks," he said. "I appreciate you listening. I can go if you want."

She yawned. "It's okay. I haven't been able to sleep lately."

"No?"

She wavered on telling him about Kathy. "Weird breakup. Discovered we were better off as friends."

He cinched his lips. "Men are a handful."

Women too, she thought. Instead, she said: "Men never seem to know what they want. Only that they want *something*. And want other people to get it for them."

"You psychic?" he chuckled.

"They say I'm an old soul."

"True, true. But hey, it wasn't all bad with us, was it?"

In the ensuing hours, their talk turned to their former life together, focusing on the better aspects. Gin boiled Sleepytime tea and heated up wheat scones. They spoke of vacation spots and restaurant closures and situations where they'd helped each other out, bolstered by memories the other had misplaced. They even found reason for laughter. And when sex came, it passed quickly, their bodies falling together like rogue waves at sea, smashing and mixing and dividing, not an act of concession on either's part, nor reconciliation, exactly, but a peace achieved individually and for separate reasons.

Afterwards Eddy slipped the covers from his naked thighs and sat up, lost and spirit-thin with afterglow. From his lips a whispered concession—*I don't know if this repairs anything*—offering with raw accountability, some hope of mending.

Gin waited to speak. "Don't take this the wrong way . . . but this doesn't change anything."

"Of course. No, I understand."

Whatever he'd once shared with Gin had lost its purity, making him feel older. It was like finding among a box of heirlooms an envelope containing your first haircut—and the hair is fine and soft and beautiful, but it is no longer yours, but more you and yours than anyone else's.

"Gin, after you . . . I lost the shape of myself. I know that sounds stupid," he said in the dark. "But I just didn't *fit inside me* anymore."

It wasn't exactly what she had imagined, when she'd imagined him ever apologizing. It still centered his perspective, his hurt and his needs—but it came from a sincere place of remorse, and touched her unexpectedly. "What do you actually want?"

"Besides you?"

Gin tilted a damaged grin his way. "You made choices. They asked for loyalty and you went all in. With terrifying people. I mean, god, when Gumby busted in here—"

"What?" asked Eddy, glancing back. "Gumby?"

"I thought Cueball would have told you this."

"Told me what?"

"Cueball broke into my house. Slept in my bed. *Yeah*."

"Why? Wait, when was this? What'd he say?"

"All sorts of things," said Gin. "He wanted to know if I'd seen you. He talked about being in Fort Lauderdale, about some little kid getting shot. Then Gumby barged in and dragged him off. Scared the crap out of me."

Eddy rushed to get dressed. It *was* Cueball the Toros had seen at the Mission that day. And Bird had covered it up. Lied about it just a few hours ago. The various implications winnowed the networks of his brain like scalding water poured down an anthill.

"Did Cueball say why he was in Lauderdale?"

"Okay, I don't know anything, and I really don't want to talk about this stuff. This stuff is exactly what I don't wanna talk about. You should leave town. Seriously, people are wrong, sometimes it's just best to run away."

At the bedroom door, Eddy paused, tapping his fingers on the frame. "Where am I even going?" he muttered aloud. Then, turning: "Would you go with me to the beach? Just for a bit? I know it's asking a lot. I feel like I'm gonna have a panic attack."

Gin gazed at the slender security bars the landlord installed over the window after Cueball had knifed his way through. The beach was only ten minutes away. "Sure," she said. "Okay."

She drove. The Tracking Station was local-famous for the white structure built atop the dunes, which rumor had it housed a NASA telescope used for tracking shuttles. The spot was less than a mile away from where they'd spent their first night together.

They found a hilly slope and nestled in. Offshore, cruise ship lights drummed the dark waters. They watched the crashing waves slide over each other like the lips of a rambling oracle as Eddy envisioned a new life for them together, reconfiguring the details for Gin until they took on the plausible aspect of reality. Yet more nebulous thoughts kept interrupting: what had been his last conversation with Duke? Cueball's raid on the warehouse: had he actually shot anyone himself?

Gin let the sand sift through her fingers, loving the texture. "You still drawing?"

"No," said Eddy absentmindedly.

"That's too bad," she said. "God, you created whole worlds! I was always like, where do these things come from? Don't you miss that?"

"My ambition's been zero lately," he said. "I used to be so contemplative. Testing myself against moral quandaries and shit. Now I just want to keep everyone safe. And I've failed at that."

Gin collapsed her shoulders. "You should move on."

"Like you?"

"Exactly," said Gin. "And now I have new friends. And I'm happy with who I am. I'm even working at getting my AA at BCC."

"You're back in school? That's great," Eddy said, though his voice carried some hurt. "I'm happy for you."

"Just part-time, but it's like, a real effort to be the person I want to be."

"I took my own curiosity for granted," said Eddy, "and now it's gone. Put my head down, chased the money. Turns out *better off* didn't make me any better off. But can I ask you something—was I ever good for you in any way? I know I hurt you. That's not really a question. I'm just trying to pinpoint where I started fucking things up. I mean, did it always feel like I was treating you like some random chick?"

"It wasn't just you," said Gin, "it was all of you. And it wasn't that you treated me like some random woman, it was that *all of you* treated *all of us* like the *same* woman."

Eddy held up a finger. "I get that, absolutely. And I'm sorry for that. I just wanted to say I'm sorry for that." He breathed in deeply. "So are we gonna take off together, or what? *C'mon*, purely as friends. Bam, here we go, blazing across the hemispheres. Alaska, Tahiti . . . Galápagos. I've got a little cash, enough to float us for a while."

Gin dug her toes into the crisp sand. "You can go anywhere you want. Imagine that. What a privilege."

She was right, he could disappear. Eddy saw himself in a movie, his Mustang ripping by the world's largest thermometer in Death Valley. On your right you'll find the haunted misty mountains of New Hampshire; on your left, the crumbling banded peaks of the Badlands; but today we're headed for the craggy, creeping rivers of Oregon, where a body could disappear.

But even as he gave himself over to the fantasy, a fear rose up. Would someone recognize him in these places? Would that be an issue from now on? The beach was vacant in both directions. Nobody on the dunes, either, so far as he could tell.

"Maybe I'll just disappear into the woods. Some small town."

He thanked her for staying up all night with him. Gin glanced up at the fading stars. "The last space shuttle will launch next summer, they say. You know I come out here to watch them now." She smiled. "I have you to thank for that."

A convoluted nostalgia passed through Eddy, here at the end of another history, where they take everything you know and love and put it in a book, and you're left forever trying to explain how they got it all wrong.

"I wonder what those laid-off folks will do for work," he said.

"Who knows?" Gin said. "Something else."

"But not something better."

"No, probably not better. Just else."

A new day advanced on the horizon, the sky like ripening mulberries. The gambling ships maneuvered back to port like satellites in slow apogee. Eddy imagined being in orbit, gazing back upon that big, textured, blue-green bubble teeming with people hacking their way through forests of symbols. *What did you find out there, Major? Was it a better world?*

The faces of Duke and Lisbon swam to the fore, and Eddy balled his fists into his eyes until they frizzled with light.

"I'm so tired," he said. "I'm daydreaming."

Eddy's phone buzzed and Bird's number leapt to the screen. "I shouldn't answer this," he said, partly to himself. "Hello?"

"Hey," grumbled Bird. "You alone?"

"Yeah," said Eddy, holding up a finger to Gin and rising to walk toward the shoreline. "Any news?"

"You sound awake," said Bird. "You slept? You haven't been home."

"I've just been driving around," said Eddy, disturbed that Bird knew this.

"Anyone call you?"

"No. Was someone supposed to?"

Bird left him wallowing in the mystery. "I need you at Ma Kettle's in an hour," he said.

"Of course, sure."

Eddy hung up and glanced about to find Gin marching over the dunes. As he went to follow, a sudden cold filled his socks. He'd wandered too close to the ocean, and found himself stuck in the sand.

Leaning against the Mustang, Eddy found there was no way to say goodbye that felt right. They held hands briefly, Eddy pinching the crease of her knuckle, fingernails no longer chewed to the pink. A truck full of construction workers pulled over for a sleepy neighbor carrying a coffee thermos. The workmen gawked at the pair's morning-after posturing, and for a moment Eddy enjoyed being seen as a couple again.

"If I decide to take off, I'll call you first," he said.

"No need," Gin said, leaning to kiss his cheek. "Be safe. Be careful." Then gave a small wave as she stepped into her apartment, leaving him alone in the yard.

The Mustang seat felt cold. Before he could feel sorry for himself, his phone buzzed.

It was Del Ray, which was no good. Bird's warning bonged its kettle-drum, but in the end, his hunger for information won out.

"Eddy?"

"Del, I can't talk to you. What the fuck's going on?"

"Where are you? Is Bird around?"

"I can't talk to you!" he said. "Shit. I'm going to meet him now at Ma Kettle's."

"You don't wanna do that," said Del Ray. "We need to meet up, right now."

"I can't. I shouldn't even be—"

"Listen here, do not—"

Eddy hung up and started the car. Fuck, he was terrified now. Dammit. Every remaining straw was the short straw. Why'd he pick up the stupid phone?

Instinctively he checked under his seat—no Glock. He'd put off replacing the gun Colt stole, and now this.

The phone buzzed again but he ignored it.

The traffic lights along the Dixie Highway remained obstinately green, unwilling to hinder his passage. He took comfort in folks yawning on their way to work, characterizing any normal day.

Turning right at Malabar Road, he found the driveway of Ma Kettle's barricaded by twin carpentry horses. A motorcycle helmet rested atop a nearby pike. As he approached, a leathered biker appeared and spoke into a handheld transceiver, squatting before the window.

"We're closed for a private event."

"I'm the First Contact, here to see Seizer."

The handheld spurted out a confirmation and the man waved him past.

The lawn collected early shadows as Eddy waited in his car, working up his courage. Insects swarmed the crushed remains of an armadillo near the trash. Fly and midge, aphid and mosquito—disregarded populations that would one day inherit the earth. If Eddy were to act like a bug, a weak little nothing, cooperative, unquestioning, maybe he could go unnoticed long enough to figure out who murdered his friends. Then he'd do something heroic—something merciless and vindictive. Then he'd leave town.

The daydream trembled there a moment longer before collapsing.

The back lot was filled with bikers, thirty or so men huddling picnic tables. The first thing Eddy noticed was that their uniform leather vests lacked any sort of club affiliation or colors—no top- or bottom-rockers—and only the rare embroidered patch: *1%, DFFL.* He'd never seen anything like it. This must be Bird's—check that, *Seizer's*—anonymous personal guard. Some roaming caravan of Enforcers. The sonorous nasal whine of McGraw bleating "Indian Outlaw" emanated from outdoor speakers in back, where bikers milled about a breakfast spread of eggs and pork. Beyond them, men took turns lobbing grapefruits into the air and splitting the fruits with a power bow.

Whoo-hoo! Didn't I say my great-great-uncle shot nickels with Jesse James?

Eddy played it cool, even when he caught two guards peering inside his Mustang.

The bar's screen door flung open and Bird pushed a coffee mug into his chest, saying, "Thanks for showing up," and marched Eddy toward the picnic tables. He was bare-chested under his vest, tattoos somehow darker in daylight. Bird looked confident and in charge, bringing a cold beer to his neck. "Already got the jungle heat out here today. You hungry? Go dig into that scrapple, you'll need your energy. We've razed the old homestead, now we pour the new foundation. We're all heading down to Miami, but first I got a little private matter to take care of."

Before Eddy could ask what that meant, or inquire about Cueball's whereabouts, he caught sight of Django standing among a group of leather-backs. The Head responsible for the club's westward expansion was dressed in khakis and a biker's vest over a polo shirt. Django raised a hand and smiled when he saw Eddy.

Bird noticed. "We're taking Django down to meet some cubans. I'll fill you in along the way. They wanted to meet a couple Heads, and I figured bringing another latin would be best—even if he is a mexican. This transition away from Alex needs to be clean and quick."

Mid-stride, Bird was accosted by a husky man in pilot glasses and a red neckerchief who took him aside and whispered in his ear. Bird waved Eddy toward the breakfast line. "I'll catch up."

Nobody seemed much interested in Eddy, so he loaded up his plate and found a table away from folks, sipping coffee and keeping his cool by noting the bikers' peculiarities: bandana knotted at the forearm, long curls shaved into a mohawk mullet. These were his people, he told himself. His tribe. He strained to believe it. Bird might've already explained to them how important he was, an original member, the First Contact. And with Django backing him up, maybe Eddy was secretly popular, respected as a kind of outside insider, a Tom Hagen type to Seizer's Vito Corleone.

Bird's hand was on his shoulder. "How's the grub?"

"I just had a sausage."

"Was it good?"

"It was a pretty good sausage."

"Let's take a walk, Eddy," he said gruffly, tugging him slightly but assuredly by the neck.

Eddy wiped his mouth and left his plate behind. As they headed for the woods, he watched several bikers turn to follow. Django didn't seem to notice.

"Is there a problem?" Eddy asked.

"Just need to hash out some irregularities," said Bird. "Not for everyone's ears."

They entered the woods. A dreamy, intangible light broke through the pine canopy as a sad sort of mood crept over him.

"Eddy, I've built something of an empire here. People respect me. I'd be a liar if I said I don't believe I earned it."

Eddy rubbed his oily arms, his stomach grumbling from lack of sleep. A clearing soon appeared alongside a grassy backroad, and resting there was Cueball's orange Nova, warming in the sun.

"You found him!" Eddy piped up eagerly.

"Heath called about an hour ago," Bird said. "You and me are gonna take a ride, go pick him up. But first, you've got some explaining to do."

"I was at Gin's," Eddy blurted out. "I didn't want to be alone. And I didn't think my house was safe."

Bird regarded him funny. "Okay. Did you talk to anyone?"

"It was just me and her."

Bird held up Eddy's phone, which he'd forgotten on the car seat. He watched as Bird opened the call list, showing Del Ray's name several times. Around them the trailing bikers filed in. Eddy realized they'd been summoned as witnesses.

"I'm giving you a chance to come clean here," said Bird. "Now I remember telling you not to answer your phone for anyone but me. But you didn't listen. I bet you're listening now." He smiled in a way that looked like frowning. "Now, this doesn't have to get heavy. I just need to know where Del Ray is."

Eddy had viewed Bird as many things during his life: a caretaker, a father to Cueball and Charlotte's husband, a partner in the tattoo business—but this here was a more inscrutable figure, a man worn sharp by duplicitous natures. Looking into Bird's eyes, he found a Seizer.

"He called me," Eddy began, unsure of his footing. "But I didn't talk to him."

Bird grunted. He raised the phone again, his black eyes unwavering—no dance to them, nerveless, the bags underneath puffed as if he were smiling, which he was not. "This says he called, and this says you answered. Which means you probably got all kinds of new info to sort through."

"I hit the talk button by accident," Eddy tried explaining, "but then hung up."

Someone laughed and Bird shook his head. "This isn't the time to lie, Eddy. I could have you torn apart right now. Christ, you don't just sneak up on a lion, kid. Now, we've been through a lot together. I just want to know where he is, then you can go. No harm, no foul."

Eddy trembled softly over his own voice. "I've been at the beach all night—"

A sudden, blinding flash of light erupted as Bird's open hand slammed into his cheekbone.

Sugar sand clogged his mouth. Blood was in there too, along with pine needles prickling his ear amid the astonished hoots of men. Raised by his collar and guided to a vertical position like a bowling pin wobbled by the nick, he awaited gravity's orders to stand or collapse. And was surprised to learn he was to stand, hugged close to Bird's sweaty chest and rotting mouth.

"You continue to lie to me. Why? It's over."

"I swear to God I don't know! I swear to God!"

"No! You swore to *me*! You swore your allegiance to *me*."

Eddy was flung into a tree. The onlookers mocked his effort to raise up to his knees. Clawing bark, Eddy caught a punch in the gut, landing him face-first on the ground again.

Fists of fucking fury! someone howled as the cajolers gathered close.

Specks of sand cluttered his eyes. The left side of his face vacillated between intense heat and a cool numbness that jumped with his heartbeat. His tongue found all his teeth in place, and some part of Eddy giggled internally at this final vanity.

Bird knelt beside him. "Are we talking now?"

Eddy shook his head, meaning no more, but Bird took it differently, snapping him sideways with a boot to the chest.

Eddy was done. Wouldn't even try hiding his stomach anymore, lying flat and exposed.

"Get him in the trunk."

"Ten-four, chief," said one sunglassed Enforcer.

"The rest of you, get them boys ready to ride."

Eddy felt himself being helped up as he blinked the dirt from his eyes. The Enforcer walked him hipbone-to-hipbone to the Nova, popping the trunk. Then ordered Eddy to get in his damn self.

"Bird!" Eddy wailed.

The Enforcer smacked his face. "It's Seizer, you fucking moron," he said, loud enough for his boss to hear. Then leaned in to whisper: "Kid, do yourself a favor . . . whatever you're hiding, you best fess up."

The bikers' jeers offered no additional humiliation to Eddy's crushed spirit. Nothing made sense and his body demanded rest, so he lowered his head to the warm carpet and relaxed.

Bird's voice hovered overhead: "Breaks my heart." He called for an army blanket, which was tossed over Eddy. "If you start banging or try to get out, I'll pull over and end this."

The trunk slammed shut.

Eddy dreamt of Duke and Lisbon lying face down in a patch of mud and bileswell under the charge of an unrelenting rain. Every so often one brother lifted his head to gargle some bloody incrimination before returning to the muck. Like this they rehashed their story in tatters as Eddy listened intently for the name of their undoer. No matter how gut-wrenching it was to watch, he would not turn away, for this was no longer a land for cowards.

Coming to, Eddy found his gummy eyes seared shut. The army blanket lay shrugged off by his feet, the trunk cracked to reveal a strip of blue sky. Cramped neck and stomach boiled in sickness. All he knew for sure was he was alive and close to the river, the stench of marine funk unmistakable.

"You coming?"

Eddy ducked reflexively away from Bird's voice.

"Finishing my smoke," said Cueball, standing out of sight.

"You need to see this. It's partly your responsibility."

Cueball didn't answer. Bird's large Iron Horse Saloon belt buckle came into view. "You should've called me the second you got loose. Making me worry like that. Now come here."

"H-hold up a minute," said Cueball.

The trunk squeaked open, subjecting Eddy to a prison of light.

Bird hunched over, hands on his knees, in the posture of a crab. He leaned in and grabbed Eddy's elbows and nimbly scooted him forward. The anger in his face was gone, which told Eddy this was the end of the line.

"How you feeling?"

Eddy blinked, his throat numb.

"We've all done terrible things, Eddy. Hurt those we care most about. I don't give a shit what Ray told you, now's the time to save yourself. You listening? I just need to know where he is. This here's your last chance."

Beyond Bird stretched a sandy white path and palmettos . . . and strangely enough, Del Ray.

Del Ray approached in black socks and no boots. In his hands he carried a baseball bat, low and at an angle.

Bird regarded Eddy's inability to focus as insolence, and swung a backhand across his face. As Eddy tipped back, unconsciousness lunged to embrace him.

"Are you thick?" Bird asked, then snapped his fingers in Cueball's direction. "Hand me that gun."

Watching his own death unfold, Eddy found he was not afraid, and what a thing to realize.

At that moment, he heard Cueball's sneakers take off at a sprint. Bird straightened up, clearly surprised.

Del Ray approached Bird in a crouch from behind. Eddy watched him plant his feet, tighten his grip, and with all his might, swing the bat down quickly.

The wood connecting with Bird's head crackled through the air with disgusting vibration as Eddy watched his boss quiver like a water tower in an earthquake before collapsing.

"Greedy pongo motherfucker!" Del Ray roared, reveling in gravitas, every color of the rainbow sparking from his body. Raising the bat he swung down over and over again, pulping Bird's skull.

Eddy rolled toward the trunk's rear, the oily carpet smell intensifying his sudden nausea. Emotions fought for domination and random thoughts exploded like flak over an embattled fortress. Clarity required a deliberate parsing of information, and his brain simply could not command its troops under this pernicious onslaught—they ran for their lives.

Del Ray fished the Nova keys from Bird's pocket, going about his business with sickening efficiency. Tucking the wrapped army blanket under Bird's arms, he hoisted the body up and dragged it away.

Green fronds swayed in a warm breeze. Then came the sound of shells crunching underfoot. Eddy dipped his head just as the trunk slammed down overhead.

• • •

When the trunk popped open sometime later, Eddy waited a full minute before crawling out. A drop in pressure had chilled the air. Pulling himself over the edge, he flopped onto the ground.

Just beyond, Del Ray chatted on his phone without urgency, a gun in his hand. Apparently the bat was used for personal reasons. Del's shirt was off and two bloody pieces of duct tape over gauze formed an X over his heart.

"We've got a massive cleanup coming our way, so make sure nobody goes anywhere—we don't want a whisper campaign on our hands. And this Django fella, use kid gloves, let him know Seizer's been pulled onto another job but that the Maven's on his way. Say we'll have him in Miami later today or tomorrow, for sure. Just get him away from the others and wait for me, we'll weed out the malcontents together. Alright, brother, see you in a few. Out."

Spying Eddy, Ray put a hand up and grinned, a retiree who'd caught sight of a neighbor over the fence. "How you feeling, bud?" he called out, walking over.

At first Eddy kept to his knees. His stomach was impatient to heave and his muscles proved uncooperative. It felt like heatstroke. Del Ray shut the trunk and helped him stand. Eddy wobbled back to lean against the Nova.

"God almighty, I can't worry to think," said Del Ray, overtaken by a brief fit, turning away to wipe his eyes with his shirt. Eddy was having an altogether different experience, suspended in an emotional vacuum. Who knew purgatory had a sun?

"You grow up and find life don't compute with what you'd envisioned. Brother was a bad, bad man," said Del Ray, pressing one nostril and blowing snot out the other. "A monstrous warlord on a campaign of terror. All power and no principles. Sitting on his heap like a fat fucking walrus, gulping down scraps."

Eddy crossed his arms. "Who was that you were talking to?"

Del shrugged a shoulder. "Just another professional nobody."

"So what now?" asked Eddy.

Del Ray tapped his bottom lip. "Promise not to tell anyone?" he asked, grin widening. "Off the top of my head, hell, I'm thinking maybe three Seizers. Triumvirate of old—get me a Pompey and Crassus. Fix the tat, make it a Foxtail—three fronds. If I assign duties by natural talent, I can maximize efficiency, minimize complacency. Thinking I can manage transport and funds, get Jesse to unite the front and huddle the Heads, and settle on a Fixer to fix the leaks. Grab the whole mess by the shorthairs."

Eddy waited for his name's mention. "What about Cueball?"

"Heath, Heath. Heathen Heath. No longer a nonbeliever. Not even a name no more."

"Please," said Eddy.

"Cueball's off the radar. When he comes back around, there'll be a place for him. That boy may not have chosen this, but it sure as hell chose him. But he's not running anymore. Young man just inherited a fortune, needs a guiding hand to help manage it."

"How long you been planning this?" asked Eddy.

Del spit. "Does any of this feel planned?"

"They'll come after us," said Eddy.

"They who? Shit, son, we are the *They*. We got the camps, the connections, the bounty . . . Render unto Seizer what is *mine*, motherfucker! That's what I'm talkin 'bout! I may not have sought this out, but having it foisted upon me now, I will abide by the knowing nature of the universe."

"Sounds like you got it all figured out."

"We'll see how the sands shift. Things can't get much worse. We need to get back to making our money work for us, market-wise. *Futures.* Bird's passions were fleeting and lustful. What this outfit needs is a few good leaders with enough foresight to refurbish the machine, grease the cogs, recode the whole goddamn apparatus, and get things working properly again," Del Ray said, then reached into the Nova. "Lend me the keys to your Mustang."

Eddy didn't understand what for, but unclipped the car key from his house keys and passed them over. Del Ray handed him the keys to the Nova, along with a manila envelope bound by rubber bands.

"What's this?"

"Severance."

"What? Del—"

"Can't do it, Ed. Part of the deal."

"With who?"

"Interested parties. With trust comes responsibility, and with responsibility, sacrifice," said Del Ray, echoing Colt's words. "Someone's gotta bear the burden, Wildeboar. Ditch the Nova somewhere. Send me a postcard."

"But I live here. Everything, my house . . . I didn't do anything wrong!"

"No?" asked Del, fixing Eddy with a knowing stare. It was then that Eddy noticed the gun in Del Ray's hand was his own—a Glock—the very one Colt had stolen from him at Snake Lake.

"Aw, come on," Del continued, "you never wanted any of this. All this drama bullshit, the anxiety. Be honest: wouldn't you be happier doing something weary, stale, flat, and unprofitable? The world's your sandbox, Eddy, positively bursting with low-key, shits-and-giggles, humdrum opportunity—and minor mayhem, whenever you get the itch. No more guns or goombahs, just a regular ol' life."

"Where would I go?"

"Don't matter. Just don't ever come back." Del Ray watched him understand. "Don't you get it, son? You just murdered a Seizer."

Eddy backed up slowly as Del Ray shook his head. "It's over. This world will pass into meaninglessness and brotherhood will fail, but in the meantime it exists in me and I will do right by it. You need to find someone to cover up that palm tree, I'm thinking it just might be a curse for you now." Del Ray's attention shifted to the sky. "Time to go. Rain's coming."

"Wait, just wait! Please. Let me talk to him."

"It won't help, but be my guest. He's down by the river. I suggest you hurry, though, there's gonna be folks out looking for you real soon."

Del Ray stepped away to ford a cluster of palmettos and returned wheeling out his motorcycle. Climbed on and kick-started the engine, shouting: "I hear people live longer doing the things they love best! See you in another life, brother!"

Then raised a hand, walked the bike in a circle, and peeled off.

Eddy frisbeed the envelope through the Nova's window and hustled his wobbly legs awkwardly down the trail of shells.

Dark storm clouds glowered over the tops of now-swaying fronds and soon the trail gave way to the Indian River, where Eddy spotted Underwear Island, that old party spot, rising between mainland and coastal strand. Something caught his eye about halfway there—a jon boat, bobbing in the harshening wavelets.

Cueball tugged the oars through dappled waters with an inspired, focused strength. Whatever this voyage meant, it was meant to be done alone.

Along the shell and pebbled bank Eddy struggled with his footing, arms flapping to get his friend's attention, yet Cueball continued spooning hindward, coasting, not looking up. Cupping his hands, Eddy called out over the water, but either Cueball couldn't hear or chose to ignore him. The opaque rain clouds webbing the coastline advanced, and would soon drown out his voice.

With the last bellow he could muster, a plea of no discernible words, Eddy let his voice plow high and hearty through the din.

Cueball stopped rowing.

Eddy couldn't tell, but his friend's eyes may have raised toward shore. There were no sailboats along the river, no speedboats or trash barges, no gulls swinging overhead, no one else on earth but them. It was then that Eddy noticed the army blanket spread before Cueball's knees, covering a large misshapen lump. This was a new world, with new leaders in it. Perhaps he'd brought some cinder blocks with him, or a shovel.

As if pausing merely to catch his second wind, Cueball re-dipped the oars in the water and renewed his passage, leaving Eddy to watch the easterly storm approach as they so often do in Florida—casually, methodically. The sliver of coast vanished as the wide gray scrim approached the jon boat, with great sweeping tendrils of rain having lagged, but catching up.

Eddy felt the mist at his face, the salt vapor on his lips. And in a moment he would forever recall as the greatest example of beauty restored to a fallen world, watched his friend lean forward to gather strength, dip the oars, and, heaving back in one fierce stride, vanish through the great gray empty veil.

Eddy focused on that spot. Some transformation was occurring within himself. A fist's grip cut loose of his heart and lungs, and he was suddenly able to breathe, sinuses draining, as the tension he'd been holding sloughed away, leaving behind a drained, blubbery coil.

Beyond him the storm advanced, roughing the waters and crisping the wave edges white. Aware of the keys in his hand, Eddy stumbled back, hustling through the palmetto corridor.

He reached the Nova quickly and locked himself inside, where he sat motionless, breath fogging up the glass. He placed the key in the key lock. Moisture began beading the windows, each droplet aglow, as if conscious. All he had to do was drive away. No one would stop him. The world was big. It was massive. A person could leave and never be heard from again. He pinched the ignition. All he had to do was turn the key and the club and the whole line of Seizers would be out of his life forever. Gin was already gone. As soon as he thought it, he knew it was true.

Or he could wait. When Cueball returned, he could sit his friend down and try to hash it out. Cueball would realize he'd acted rashly, and persuade Del Ray to reinstate him—or even demote him, whatever, it didn't matter. But Eddy needed to decide what to do, and quick—the storm was approaching and it brought questions he couldn't answer. Would they really try to pin Seizer's death on him? Was Cueball trying to help him by forcing him out? Was this a test? Was he being asked to prove his loyalty? If he stayed, would they actually kill him? He needed to go. He needed to stay or go. He had to decide. Now.

"Make a fucking decision!" Eddy shouted, banging his fists against the steering wheel. "For once in your fucking life!"

But the storm had arrived.

About him the palm fronds danced and sizzled. The last bit of sky disappeared as the sweeping blades of a gray combine descended upon the mainland, popping up seashells like flipped quarters. The trail disappeared into abstraction as a pounding music erupted, raindrops leaping off the hood, belly-flopping the windshield. Eddy wept loudly and without shame, feeling for all the world abandoned and hopeless and alone.

Before long, though, the rain let up a little. Eddy lowered the window to let a coolness sweep into the car. His body felt worn, but it was good. With perverse satisfaction he imagined the jon boat capsizing in the storm, father and son sucked into the umbral depths, shifting in the swells and currents and dragged through an inlet and out to sea.

To be gnawed on by bull sharks, the fuckers.

He turned the engine key.

The drive home felt mechanized, his surroundings grown vague and unfamiliar, as if in reprocessing the land in exile, Eddy discovered it altered beyond reckoning.

He passed a café, a pedicure palace, a tax refund station—civilization, of a kind. Instead of heading straight home, he parked at the end of the Black Road a final time. A good portion of his youth had been spent along this narrow stretch of asphalt. Skateboard ramps and parties, a tender scene of boys around a campfire, imagining their futures. Should he call Jesse? No need—his old friend would comply with the club's ruling, which was now Del Ray's to fashion.

He yanked Cueball's fuzzy dice from the rearview and dropped them in the cul-de-sac. Sensing again the bulge of Del Ray's envelope under his thigh, he stuffed it in the glove box. It didn't matter the amount—hush money just confirmed this was betrayal.

After loading the cash from his closet safe into a pillowcase, he halted before the telephone on his way to the garage, thinking of calling Gin. In the end, he cut the circuit breaker and locked all the doors and windows, burying the house key beside a fence pole out back. He would call his mother later and inform her of his absence. Or he wouldn't. It really didn't matter.

Traffic was light on I-95, but Eddy kept to the slow lane, reminded of that first time he'd set out on the road with Cueball as a Runner, a couple of apprehensive tenderfoots on a journey to stake their claims. Glancing up and to the right, he wanted more than anything to spy the white trail of a rocket or a shuttle blasting up from the Cape, parting the heavy purple clouds on a mission to Elsewhere, providing his departure with a sense of significance or closure. But there was nothing—no rocket, no excuses, no sense of having escaped of his own free will. He'd been ousted, disgraced, and left to wander without discernible purpose or guide.

Crossing the border into Georgia, eyes raw and windshield wipers tearing at the rain, Eddy searched again for a greater sense of relief, but found only exhaustion. He'd lived as a wild, free thing—bounding through the woods, indifferent to the peculiar ambitions of other species—only to be trapped and gutted by poachers and cooked for his insides. It crossed his mind to escalate the situation, head for a police station in Atlanta or retaliate with some other stinging breach of loyalty, but every outcome he considered eventually played into a nightmare scenario that returned him to this very point in time, wishing he'd made a safer decision.

The winding country road was barren of light for twenty miles beyond the highway junction leading into the appalachian foothills, woods of impending doom or well-enveloped privacy, depending on one's frame of mind.

He arrived at Duke's cabin near midnight. Fearing Enforcers on his trail, he parked behind the house, amid the grapefruit grove.

The back door was unlocked, as they'd left it. A quick check with a flashlight proved the cabin deserted, hunting rifles resting in a closet. He unpacked his things and tossed the pillowcase of cash behind the fridge, which called to mind Suzie Fuentes and her bag of cash. For a while he sat in the buzzing silence, giving his worries time to assume their new shapes, then took up his keys and went back out.

He found a greasy spoon across from the football stadium of a community college, wolfing down a burger and fries. He even made room for pie. From now on, he'd always sit facing the door.

Outside, he was greeted unexpectedly by the ruckus of horns and chanting. There was a game in progress—lively, cheery.

He hit the local CVS for toiletries and stopped by a liquor store, where he convinced a local to buy him a bottle of Jack in exchange for a six-pack. He considered driving the four-plus hours to Greensboro to greet Dag with the bottle come morning, but reconsidered once he realized he'd have to break the terrible news of the murders of Duke and Lisbon. Instead, he'd lay low and pay his respects the best way he knew how, by getting drunk and pretending he didn't understand how any of this could have happened.

Back at the cabin, resting on the couch, Eddy cracked the seal of the Jack. He opened the envelope. Fifty thousand dollars. More than he'd expected, but it was impossible to care.

Tossing the envelope to the coffee table, he noticed something written on the back: a single patronizing word penned in Cueball's handwriting.

A lifetime ago, Cueball said if he could ever scrounge up fifty grand, he'd retire on the beach. Eddy glanced around the cabin, thinking of Duke's promise. Had he earned this? Then took another large, eye-watering swig of whiskey. Hell yeah, he'd earned everything coming his way. Even the bad things. Tomorrow he'd buy a large aromatic candle, heat a spoon over the flame, and burn the tattoo off. It was a stupid plan—and because he was now fairly buzzed and everything felt symbolic, this too, this failure to progress a mere spark of courage into something quasi-heroic, was symbolic.

The living room gave a pretty good impersonation of a jail cell, so Eddy stumbled back out into a night smelling of squelched yard fires. He stood smoking on the porch, hoping to spy that old skunk again, listening to the cheering sounds carrying up the hills. Someone had scored a touchdown, or perhaps the game was ending. His body tensed when he heard a motorcycle grunting in the distance.

Eddy ambled over and ducked back in the Nova, relaxing in the glow of the overhead light, letting his drunk take over. He considered visiting the lake for a night swim—a dangerous idea, and yet it called to him.

Instead, he set the booze bottle on the seat next to him and pulled the empty money envelope from his pants pocket.

They'd used him for his youthfulness and naivety; he used them to feel loved, which everyone knew should be given freely only, and never as reward. It felt like no matter whose side you were on, there were always people rooting against you. To survive, you had to catch a break. By making the right play. Growing up in the right neighborhood. Sliding out the right womb. Having the right skin color. The right gender. Going to the right school. Turning left. Turning right. One of a thousand freak instances of chance that led you anywhere but here, drunk and disparaged in a parked car, the recognition of which could get you killed. He wanted to discuss it all, but there was nobody left to listen.

Maybe we're all just one bad decision away from total collapse and failure. But that could also mean, if one were given to grandiose notions of hope, that each of us was just one good break away from being cheered from the sidelines.

He squeezed the envelope's inner lining of bubble wrap. Turning it over, he found the single word Cueball had scribbled on the backside in blue ballpoint pen:

Parlor.

It needled him, because the intention was unclear. Was it a fire under his ass? A final jab to the gut? Or was it simply a shrewd business decision, a cartel tying up loose ends? Eddy figured it didn't really matter. He was pretty sure Del wasn't going to come after him, or why bother handing over this much cash? And why this shitty note? No, it was a gift—his life was a gift—and a generous one at that. Opening the car door, the crisp country air welcomed him.

Instead of heading back inside, Eddy lay flat on the warm hood of the Nova. He took his time popping the individual bubbles of the bubble wrap as constellations unknown to him stirred blindly overhead, grinding out their unheard celestial music amid great spans of emptiness. He wanted to be small again, and small among them. He closed his eyes and imagined himself floating upward.

Within moments he was surrounded.

Acknowledgments

My grandmother, Rosalie Rhoden, was the matriarch of our family, her small house in West Melbourne, Florida, a space for storytelling, caregiving, laughter, and struggle. A transplant from West Virginia, daughter of a coal miner, she introduced to us the harsh, exciting mythology of her youth, where real-world antagonisms met supernatural forces. According to Grandma Rhoden, she kept a hybridized bear-dog as a pet, could foretell pregnancies with a hand to a belly, and was once chased home from school by a ball of fire. This magical brand of storytelling was passed along to my mother, Ava Millar, who on many a muggy Florida night kept us kids fascinated by tales of her own creation, like Junior Fly, a young buzzer who learned everything the hard way—by constantly disobeying his mother—and Gitchy Goomie, an oak tree that twisted the heads off kissing lovers who snuck out to meet at night. Stories told for fun but also in preparation for life, for facing hard truths—the innocent and weak are often preyed upon by the powerful; love is sometimes not enough; strong people don't win every fight, but there's strength in their persistence. They showed us the world isn't how any one person sees it—there are collective views, cultural truths, hidden agendas, and persuasive storytellers, and I wouldn't be who I am without the teachings and guidance of these two women who persevered through so much and taught us to have faith in ourselves, accept people as they come, and fight for what's right. Sharing these values was my father, who before heading off to his graveyard shift as a jail guard would sometimes spook us with Bible stories—morality plays dressed up as horror stories, and vice versa. Nightly he walked the corridors of Sharpes Correctional Facility listening to the lost accounts of prisoners and dishing out what comfort he could, which was his way. It was my father who came to my aid in third grade, when a teacher threatened to send me off to the school psychologist for writing a story where a panther disembowels a child—no doubt an imitation of a certain Stephen King tale. Instead of trying to diagnose my behavior as somehow bad, my father argued that perhaps this teacher should be praising my creativity, and it was this occasion, in my mind, which provided a sturdy base for my own attempts at storytelling—knowing I had people in my corner.

Whatever spirit of place I've successfully invoked here I share with the friends of my youth, especially those who skated and partied along the Black Road, a street in Palm Bay known only to a few. Though this is a work of fiction, I tried to capture a little of what it was like growing up in my time, and married that to a different time, when the Great Recession forced a lot of people I knew into terrible situations they worked to claw themselves out from, in terms of money, menace, and, sadly, addiction. As long as people take advantage of the poor and underprivileged, those folks trying to make ends meet will use whatever options they have at their disposal to survive.

This book would not have happened without the care and guidance of Stephanie Cabot, agent extraordinaire—brilliant, savvy, strategic—whose deep love of character and place helped push me to better my manuscript, and Tim O'Connell, my editor, who encouraged me to elevate characters in ways that created the right amount of tension and urgency—those twin wings keeping stories aloft—to carry this book forward, and who I failed perhaps in word count but not, I hope, in craft and energy.

Thank you to my wife, Wendy, who read every sentence of this book rewritten many times over, and whose faith in my ability sustains me, even when my own falters. Thanks to my brother Jason, who was with me in childhood poverty and good times, and who pulled himself out of dangers I can only imagine to become a fireman of some renown. To my brother Jon, a senior intelligence analyst, for offering some interesting ideas for the novel, and my brother Tony, who continues to give me a better understanding of life from inside prison, and the battles that still need to be won there.

I want to thank my readers of this novel and its excerpts over the years: JC Hallman, Elizabeth Wetmore, Johnny Schmidt, Dawn Poirier, Devin McIntyre; Kate Angus, Joe Fletcher, Sheila Maldonado, Nader Serafy, Mat & Becky Willows, John Leitera, Heather Morgan, Matt Shears, Joyce Li, Jim Sidel, Peyton Marshall, Martin Ott, Reed Smith, Joshua Corey, Seth Harwood, Jon Wheeler Rappe, Bill Rasmovicz, Jorge Sanchez, Stephanie Soileau, Jason Jackson, Gregory Crosby, Jack Smyth, Marcus Gray, Maria Dahvana Headley, and Stephanie Rivera. Thanks to Alexander Boldizar, Colette Sartor, Megan Levad Beisner, Laurel Snyder, and Julianna Baggot for their advice. Apologies in advance to those readers whose names my brain has buried or released.

Special thanks to Francesca Orsi, Clint LaVigne, Stacy Shirk, Samantha Byrnes-Mandelbaum, Gabe Fisher, Josh Stern, John Patton Ford, and Tom Bissell for sharing their wonderful thoughts on the book and its potential.

I'd also like to thank the fiction editor who told me he vacationed in Tampa and never once ran into characters like those I described—that really put a fire under my ass. I'd like to thank the professor who shook my hand while telling me I couldn't write but that my ideas were interesting. I'd like to thank the small press that sent me a rejection while accidentally including me in their chain email that said nobody really wanted to read a father-son story again. All this toughened my skin, and made me dig down further, and realize all I can do is make art according to my own ear, heart, and principles.

Which brings me to the many, many people who supported me over the years, far too numerous to note here. So I will just refer to a few teachers who pushed me: Jim Clark of UNCG, in loving memory; Fred Chappell of UNCG, in loving memory; Lee Zacharias of UNCG; and Stuart Dischell of UNCG. I wasn't planning to go to college, thinking I'd just be a writer somehow, and so applied to only one school, and it was the right one. Thanks also to those fiction and poetry writers at the Iowa Writers' Workshop who kept me alive and culturally nourished. Thanks to the modern dancers, who taught me to see gesture as movement. Special thanks to the four pillars: Cormac McCarthy, Toni Morrison, Don DeLillo, and Denis Johnson. Thanks Camus, Spinoza, and Marcus Aurelius. "Men must begin to challenge notions of masculinity that equate manhood with ability to exert power over others, especially through the use of coercive force."—bell hooks. "Write in the magisterial voice—what a character might say, if they had the language to say it, feeling the thing intensely. Be a present, sensitive storyteller."—from a friend paraphrasing advice from James Alan McPherson. Thanks to all the Grey Dog cafés in New York, Kellogg's and El Beit in Williamsburg, and the many, many diners in which lines from this novel were first scribbled or tapped out.

To those who might be a bit hesitant to visit the Space Coast after reading this book—fear not, it's a lovely place. Much of my family still lives there and they love it. You likely have just as many problems in your own neck of the woods. Search out those suffering. Help if you can.

And finally, a prayer from a former Baptist: may Florida never sink completely underwater. It contains multitudes.

About the Author

JOE PAN is the author of five poetry books; founder of Brooklyn Arts Press, one of the smallest independent houses ever honored with a National Book Award in Poetry; and publisher of Augury Books, honored with a Lambda Literary Award in Lesbian Poetry. His writing has appeared in *Boston Review*, *Hyperallergic*, *The New York Times*, and *Poets & Writers*, and he's been profiled by *Publishers Weekly*, *The Rumpus*, and *The Wall Street Journal*. He grew up along the Space Coast of Florida and now lives in Los Angeles. With his wife he cofounded Brooklyn Artists Helping (BAH), an activist group that serves unhoused populations with sleeping bags and goods. *Florida Palms* is his debut novel.